THE MYSTERIOUS ISLAND

The Mysterious Island

Jules Verne

NEW ENGLISH LIBRARY
TIMES MIRROR

NEL Books are published by
New English Library Limited from Barnard's Inn, Holborn, London E.C.1.
Made and printed in Great Britain by Hunt Barnard Printing Ltd., Aylesbury, Bucks.

45001348 0

CHAPTER 1

'ARE we rising again?' 'No. On the contrary.' 'Are we descending?'
'Worse than that, captain! we are falling!' 'For Heaven's sake
heave out the ballast!' 'There! the last sack is empty!' 'Does the
balloon rise?' 'No!' 'I hear a noise like the dashing of waves!'
'The sea is below the car! It cannot be more than 500 feet from
us!' 'Overboard with every weight! . . . everything!'

Such were the loud and startling words which resounded
through the air, above the vast watery desert of the Pacific,
about four o'clock in the evening of the 23rd of March, 1865.

In fact, a balloon, as a ball might be carried on the summit of
a waterspout, had been taken into the circling movement of a
column of air and had traversed space at the rate of ninety miles
an hour, turning round and round as if seized by some aerial
maëlstrom.

Beneath the lower point of the baloon swung a car, containing
five passengers, scarcely visible in the midst of the thick vapour
mingled with spray which hung over the surface of the ocean.

Whence, it may be asked, had come that plaything of the
tempest? From what part of the world did it rise? It surely
could not have started during the storm. But the storm has
raged five days already, and the first symptoms were manifested
on the 18th. It cannot be doubted that the balloon came from a
great distance, for it could not have travelled less than two
thousand miles in twenty-four hours.

At any rate the passengers, destitute of all marks for their
guidance, could not have possessed the means of reckoning the
route traversed since their departure. It was a remarkable fact
that, although in the very midst of the furious tempest, they did
not suffer from it. They were thrown about and whirled round
and round without feeling the rotation in the slightest degree,
or being sensible that they were removed from a horizontal
position.

By the following morning the storm appeared to have exhausted itself. But at the same time, it was also evident that the
balloon was again slowly descending with a regular movement.
It appeared as if it were, little by little, collapsing, and that its
case was lengthening and extending, passing from a spherical to
an oval form. Towards mid-day the balloon was hovering
above the sea at a height of only 2000 feet. It contained 50,000
cubic feet of gas, and, thanks to its capacity, it could maintain

itself a long time in the air, although it should reach a great altitude or might be thrown into a horizontal position.

Perceiving their danger, the passengers cast away the last articles which still weighted down the car, the few provisions they had kept, everything, even to their pocket-knives, and one of them, having hoisted himself on to the circles which united the cords of the net, tried to secure more firmly the lower point of the balloon.

It was, however, evident to the voyagers that the gas was failing, and that the balloon could no longer be sustained in the higher regions. They must infallibly perish!

There was not a continent, nor even an island, visible beneath them. The watery expanse did not present a single speck of land, not a solid surface upon which their anchor could hold.

It was the open sea, whose waves were still dashing with tremendous violence! It was the ocean, without any visible limits, even for those whose gaze, from their commanding position, extended over a radius of forty miles. The vast liquid plain, lashed without mercy by the storm, appeared as if covered with herds of furious chargers, whose white and dishevelled crests were streaming in the wind. No land was in sight, not a solitary ship could be seen. It was necessary at any cost to arrest their downward course, and to prevent the balloon from being engulfed in the waves. The voyagers directed all their energies to this urgent work. But not withstanding their efforts, the balloon still fell, it was also suddenly overthrown, following the direction of the wind, that is to say, from the north-east to the south-west.

Frightful indeed was the situation of these unfortunate men. They were evidently no longer masters of the machine. All their attempts were useless. The case of the balloon collapsed more and more. The gas escaped without any possibility of retaining it. Their descent was visibly accelerated, and soon after mid-day the car hung within 600 feet of the ocean.

It was impossible to prevent the escape of gas, which rushed through a large rent in the silk. By lightening the car of all the articles which it contained, the passengers had been able to prolong their suspension in the air for a few hours. But the inevitable catastrophe could only be retarded, and if land did not appear before night, voyagers, car, and balloon must to a certainty vanish beneath the waves.

They now resorted to the only remaining expedient. They were truly dauntless men, who knew how to look death in the face. Not a single murmur escaped from their lips. They were determined to struggle to the last minute, to do anything to retard their fall. The car was only a sort of willow basket unable to float, and there was not the slightest possibility of maintaining it on the surface of the sea.

Two more hours passed and the balloon was scarcely 400 feet above the water.

At that moment a loud voice, the voice of a man whose heart was inaccessible to fear, was heard. To this voice responded others not less determined. 'Is everything thrown out?' 'No, here are still 2000 dollars in gold.' A heavy bag immediately plunged into the sea. 'Does the balloon rise?' 'A little, but it will not be long before it falls again.' 'What still remains to be thrown out?' 'Nothing.' 'Yes! the car!' 'Let us catch hold of the net, and into the sea with the car.'

This was, in fact, the last and only mode of lightening the balloon. The ropes which held the car were cut, and the balloon, after its fall, mounted 2000 feet.

The five voyagers had hoisted themselves into the net, and clung to the meshes, gazing at the abyss.

The delicate sensibility of balloons is well known. It is sufficient to throw out the lightest article to produce a difference in its vertical position. The apparatus in the air is like a balance of mathematical precision. It can be thus easily understood that when it is lightened of any considerable weight its movement will be impetuous and sudden. So it happened on this occasion. But after being suspended for an instant aloft, the balloon began to redescend, the gas escaping by the rent which it was impossible to repair.

The men had done all that men could do. No human efforts could save them now. They must trust to the mercy of Him who rules the elements.

At four o'clock the balloon was only 500 feet above the surface of the water.

A loud barking was heard. A dog accompanied the voyagers, and was held pressed close to his master in the meshes of the net.

'Top has seen something,' cried one of the men. Then immediately a loud voice shouted, –

'Land! land!' The balloon, which the wind still drove towards the south-west, had since daybreak gone a considerable distance, which might be reckoned by hundreds of miles, and a tolerably high land had, in fact, appeared in that direction. But this land was still thirty miles off. It would not take less than an hour to get to it, and then there was a chance of falling to leeward.

An hour! Might not the balloon before that be emptied of all the fluid it yet retained?

Such was the terrible question! The voyagers could distinctly see that solid spot which they must reach at any cost. They were ignorant of what it was, whether an island or a continent, for they did not know to what part of the world the hurricane had driven them. But they must reach this land, whether inhabited or desolate, whether hospitable or not.

7

It was evident that the balloon could no longer support itself! Several times already had the crests of the enormous billows licked the bottom of the net, making it still heavier, and the balloon only half rose, like a bird with a wounded wing. Half an hour later the land was not more than a mile off, but the balloon, exhausted, flabby, hanging in great folds, had gas in its upper part alone. The voyagers, clinging to the net, were still too heavy for it, and soon, half plunged in the sea, they were beaten by the furious waves. The balloon case bulged out again, and the wind, taking it, drove it along like a vessel. Might it not possibly thus reach the land?

But, when only two fathoms off, terrible cries resounded from four pairs of lungs at once. The balloon, which had appeared as if it would never again rise, suddenly made an unexpected bound, after having been struck by a tremendous sea. As if it had been at that instant relieved of a new part of its weight, it mounted to a height of 1500 feet, and there it met a current of wind, which instead of taking it directly to the coast, carried it in a nearly parallel direction.

At last, two minutes later, it reapproached obliquely, and finally fell on a sandy beach, out of the reach of the waves.

The voyagers, aiding each other, managed to disengage themselves from the meshes of the net. The balloon, relieved from their weight, was taken by the wind, and like a wounded bird which revives for an instant, disappeared into space.

But the car had contained five passengers, with a dog, and the balloon only left four on the shore.

The missing person had evidently been swept off by the sea, which had just struck the net, and it was owing to this circumstance that the lightened balloon rose the last time, and then soon after reached the land. Scarcely had the four castaways set foot on firm ground, than they all, thinking of the absent one, simultaneously exclaimed, 'Perhaps he will try to swim to land! Let us save him! let us save him!'

CHAPTER 2

THOSE whom the hurricane had just thrown on this coast were neither aeronauts by profession nor amateurs. They were prisoners of war whose boldness had induced them to escape in this extraordinary manner.

A hundred times they had almost perished! A hundred times had they almost fallen from their torn balloon into the depths of the ocean. But heaven had reserved them for a strange destiny, and after having, on the 20th of March, escaped from Richmond, besieged by the troops of General Ulysses Grant, they found themselves seven thousand miles from the capital of Virginia, which was the principal stronghold of the South, during the terrible war of Secession. Their aerial voyage had lasted five days.

The curious circumstances which led to the escape of the prisoners were as follows:

That same year, in the month of February, 1865, in one of the coups-de-main by which General Grant attempted, though in vain, to possess himself of Richmond, several of his officers fell into the power of the enemy and were detained in the town. One of the most distinguished was Captain Cyrus Harding. He was a native of Massachusetts, a first-class engineer, to whom the government had confided, during the war, the direction of the railways, which were so important at that time. A true Northerner, thin, bony, lean, about forty-five years of age; his close-cut hair and his beard, of whch he only kept a thick moustache, were already getting grey. He had one of those finely-developed heads which appear made to be struck on a medal, piercing eyes, a serious mouth, the physiognomy of a clever man of the military school. He was one of those engineers who began by handling the hammer and pickaxe, like generals who first act as common soldiers. A man of action as well as a man of thought, all he did was without effort to one of his vigorous and sanguine temperament. Learned, clear-headed, and practical, he fulfilled in all emergencies those three conditions which united ought to insure human success, – activity of mind and body, impetuous wishes, and powerful will. He never spared himself, fortune favoured him till the moment when he was wounded and taken prisoner on the field of battle near Richmond. At the same time and on the same day another important personage fell into the hands of the Southerners. This was no other than Gideon Spilett, a reporter for the *New York Herald*, who had been ordered to follow the changes of the war in the midst of the Northern armies.

Gideon Spilett was one of that race of indomitable English or American chroniclers, like Stanley and others, who stop at nothing to obtain exact information, and transmit it to their journal in the shortest possible time.

He also had been in all the battles, in the first rank, revolver in one hand, note-book in the other; grape-shot never made his pencil tremble. He did not fatigue the wires with incessant telegrams, like those who speak when they have nothing to say, but each of his notes, short, decisive, and clear, threw light on some important point. Besides, he was not wanting in humour. It was he who, after the affair of the Black River, determined at any cost to keep his place at the wicket of the telegraph office, and after having announced to his journal the result of the battle, telegraphed for two hours the first chapters of the Bible. It cost the *New York Herald* two thousand dollars, but the *New York Herald* published the first intelligence.

Gideon Spilett was tall. He was rather more than forty years of age. Light whiskers bordering on red surrounded his face. His eye was steady, lively, rapid in its changes. It was the eye of a man accustomed to take in at a glance all the details of a scene. Well built, he was inured to all climates, like a bar of steel hardened in cold water.

For ten years Gideon Spilett had been the reporter of the *New York Herald*, which he enriched by his letters and drawings, for he was as skilful in the use of the pencil as of the pen. When he was captured, he was in the act of making a description and sketch of the battle. The last words in his note-book were these: 'A Southern rifleman has just taken aim at me, but –' The Southerner notwithstanding missed Gideon Spilett, who, with his usual fortune, came out of this affair without a scratch.

Cyrus Harding and Gideon Spilett, who did not know each other except by reputation, had both been carried to Richmond. The engineer's wounds rapidly healed, and it was during his convalescence that he made acquaintance with the reporter. The two men then learned to appreciate each other. Soon their common aim had but one object, that of escaping, rejoining Grant's army, and fighting together in the ranks of the Federals.

The two Americans had from the first determined to seize every chance; but although they were allowed to wander at liberty in the town, Richmond was so strictly guarded, that escape appeared impossible. In the meanwhile Captain Harding was rejoined by a servant who was devoted to him in life and death. This intrepid fellow was a negro born on the engineer's estate, of a slave father and mother, but to whom Cyrus, who was an Abolitionist from conviction and heart, had long since given his freedom. The once slave, though free, would not leave his master. He would have died for him. He was a man of about thirty, vigorous, active, clever, intelligent, gentle and calm, sometimes naïve, always merry, obliging and honest. His name was Nebuchadnezzar, but he only answered to the familiar abbreviation of Neb.

Meanwhile Grant continued his energetic operations. The victory of Petersburg had been very dearly bought. His forces, united to those of Butler, had as yet been unsuccessful before Richmond, and nothing gave the prisoners any hope of a speedy deliverance.

The reporter, to whom his tedious captivity did not offer a single incident worthy of note, could stand it no longer. His usually active mind was occupied with one sole thought – how he might get out of Richmond at any cost. Several times had he even made the attempt, but was stopped by some insurmountable obstacle. However, the siege continued; and if the prisoners were anxious to escape and join Grant's army, certain of the besieged were no less anxious to join the Southern forces. Amongst them was one Jonathan Forster, a determined Southerner. The truth was, that if the prisoners of the Secessionists could not leave the town, neither could the Secessionists themselves while the Northern army invested it. The Governor of Richmond for a long time had been unable to communicate with General Lee, and he very much wished to make known to him the situation of the town, so as to hasten the march of the army to their relief. This Jonathan Forster accordingly conceived the idea of rising in a balloon, so as to pass over the besieging lines, and in that way reach the Secessionist camp.

The Governor authorised the attempt. A balloon was manufactured and placed at the disposal of Forster, who was to be accompanied by five other persons. They were furnished with arms in case they might have to defend themselves when they alighted, and provisions in the event of their aerial voyage being prolonged.

The departure of the balloon was fixed for the 18th of March. It should be effected during the night, with a north-west wind of moderate force, and the aeronauts calculated that they would reach General Lee's camp in a few hours.

But his north-west wind was not a simple breeze. From the 18th it was evident that it was changing to a hurricane The tempest soon became such that Forster's departure was deferred, for it was impossible to risk the balloon and those whom it carried in the midst of the furious elements.

The balloon, inflated on the great square of Richmond, was ready to depart on the first abatement of the wind, and, as may be supposed, the impatience among the besieged to see the storm moderate was very great.

The night of the 19th passed, but the next morning the storm blew with redoubled force. The departure of the balloon was impossible.

On that day the engineer, Cyrus Harding, was accosted in one of the streets of Richmond by a person whom he did not in the least know. This was a sailor name Pencroft, a man of about thirty-five or forty years of age, strongly built, very sunburnt, and possessed of a pair of bright sparkling eyes and a remarkably good physiognomy. Pencroft was an American from the North, who had sailed all the ocean over, and who had gone through every possible and almost impossible adventure that a being with two feet and no wings could encounter. It is needless to say that he was a bold, dashing fellow, ready to dare anything, and was astonished at nothing. Pencroft at the beginning of the year had gone to Richmond on business, with a young boy of fifteen from New Jersey, son of a former captain, an orphan whom he loved as if he had been his own child. Not having been able to leave the town before the first operations of the siege, he found himself shut up, to his great disgust; but, not accustomed to succumb to difficulties, he resolved to escape by some means or other. He knew the engineer-officer by reputation; he knew with what impatience that determined man chafed under his restraint. On this day he did not, therefore, hesitate to accost him, saying, without circumlocution, 'Have you had enough of Richmond, captain?'

The engineer looked fixedly at the man who spoke, and who added, in a low voice, –

'Captain Harding, will you try to escape?'

'When?' asked the engineer quickly, and it was evident that this question was uttered without consideration, for he had not yet examined the stranger who addressed him. But after having with a penetrating eye observed the open face of the sailor, he was convinced that he had before him an honest man.

'Who are you?' he asked briefly.

Pencroft made himself known.

'Well', replied Harding, 'and in what way do you propose to escape?'

'By that lazy balloon which is left there doing nothing, and which looks to me as if it was waiting on purpose for us –'

There was no necessity for the sailor to finish his sentence. The engineer understood him at once. He seized Pencroft by the arm, and dragged him to his house. There the sailor developed his project, which was indeed extremely simple. They risked nothing but their lives in its execution. The hurricane was in all its violence, it is true, but so clever and daring an engineer as Cyrus Harding knew perfectly well how to manage a balloon. Had he himself been as well acquainted with the art of sailing in the air as he was with the navigation of a ship, Pencroft would not have hesitated to set out, of course taking his young friend Herbert with him; for, accustomed to brave the fiercest tempests of the ocean, he was not to be hindered on account of the hurricane.

Captain Harding had listened to the sailor without saying a word, but his eyes shone with satisfaction. Here was the long-sought-for opportunity, – he was not a man to let it pass. The plan was feasible, though, it must be confessed, dangerous in the extreme. In the night, in spite of their guards, they might approach the balloon, slip into the car, and then cut the cords which held it. There was no doubt that they might be killed, but on the other hand they might succeed, and without this storm! – Without this storm the balloon would have started already, and the looked-for opportunity would not have then presented itself.

'I am not alone!' said Harding at last.

'How many people do you wish to bring with you?' asked the the sailor.

'Two; my friend Spilett, and my servant Neb.'

'That will be three,' replied Pencroft; 'and with Herbert and me five. But the baloon will hold six – '

'That will be enough, we will go,' answered Harding in a firm voice.

This 'we' included Spilett, for the reporter, as his friend well knew, was not a man to draw back, and when the project was communicated to him he aproved of it unreservedly. What astonished him was, that so simple an idea had not occurred to him before.

'This evening, then,' said Pencroft, 'we will all meet out there.'

'This evening, at ten o'clock,' replied Captain Harding; 'and Heaven grant that the storm does not abate before our departure.'

Pencroft took leave of the two friends, and returned to his lodging, where young Herbert Brown had remained. The courageous boy knew of the sailor's plan, and it was not without anxiety that he awaited the result of the proposal being made to the engineer. Thus five determined persons were about to abandon themselves to the mercy of the tempestuous elements!

No! the storm did not abate, and neither Jonathan Forster nor his companions dreamt of confronting it in that frail car. It would be a terrible journey. The engineer only feared one thing, it was that the balloon, held to the ground and dashed about by the wind, would be torn into shreds. For several hours he roamed round the nearly-deserted square, surveying the apparatus. Pencroft did the same on his side, his hands in his pockets, yawning now and then like a man who did not know how to kill the time, but really dreading, like his friend, either the escape or destruction of the balloon. Evening arrived. The night was dark in the extreme. Thick mists passed like clouds close to the ground. Rain fell mingled with snow. It was very cold. A mist hung over Richmond. It seemed as if the violent storm had produced a truce between the besiegers and the besieged, and that the cannon were silenced by the louder detonations of the storm. The streets of the town were deserted. It had not even appeared necessary in that horrible weather to place a guard in the square, in the midst of which plunged the balloon. Everything favoured the departure of the prisoners, but what might possibly be the termination of the hazardous voyage they contemplated in the midst of the furious elements? –

'Dirty weather!' exclaimed Pencroft, fixing his hat firmly on his head with a blow of his fist; 'but pshaw, we shall succed all the same!'

At half-past nine, Harding and his companions glided from different directions into the square, which the gas-lamps, extinguished by the wind, had left in total obscurity. Even the enormous balloon, almost beaten to the ground, could not be seen. Independently of the sacks of ballast, to which the cords of the net were fastened, the car was held by a strong cable passed through a ring in the pavement. The five prisoners met by the car. They had not been perceived, and such was the darkness that they could not even see each other.

Without speaking a word, Harding, Spilett, Neb, and Herbert, took their places in the car, whilst Pencroft by the engineer's order detached successively the bags of ballast. It was the work of a few minutes only, and the sailor rejoined his companions.

The balloon was then only held by the cable, and the engineer had nothing to do but to give the word.

At that moment a dog sprang with a bound into the car. It was Top, a favourite of the engineer. The faithful creature, having broken his chain, had followed his master. He, however, fearing that its additional weight might impede their ascent, wished to send away the animal.

'One more will make but little difference, poor beast!' exclaimed Pencroft, heaving out two bags of sand, and as he spoke letting go the cable; the balloon ascending in an oblique direction, disappeared, after having dashed the car against two chimneys, which it threw down as it swept by them.

Then, indeed, the full rage of the hurricane was exhibited to the voyagers. During the night the engineer could not dream of descending, and when day broke, even a glimpse of the earth below was intercepted by fog.

Five days had passed when a partial clearing allowed them to see the wide extending ocean beneath their feet, now lashed into the maddest fury by the gale.

Our readers will recollect what befell these five daring individuals who set out on their hazardous expedition in the balloon on the 20th of March. Five days afterwards four of them were thrown on a desert coast, seven thousand miles from their country! But one of their number was missing, the man who was to be their guide, their leading spirit, the engineer, Captain Harding! The instant they had recovered their feet they all hurried to the beach in the hopes of rendering him assistance.[1]

[1]On the 5th of April Richmond fell into the hands of Grant; the revolt of the Secessionists was suppressed, Lee retreated to the West, and the cause of the Federals triumphed.

CHAPTER 3

THE engineer, the meshes of the net having given way, had been carried off by a wave. His dog also had disappeared. The faithful animal had voluntarily leaped out to help his master. 'Forward,' cried the reporter; and all four, Spilett, Herbert, Pencroft, and Neb, forgetting their fatigue, began their search.

Only two minutes had passed from the time when Cyrus Harding disappeared to the moment when his companions set foot on the ground. They had hopes therefore of arriving in time to save him. 'Let us look for him! let us look for him!' cried Neb.

'Yes, Neb,' replied Gideon Spilett, 'and we will find him too!'

'Living, I trust!'

'Still living!'

'Can he swim?' asked Pencroft.

'Yes,' replied Neb, 'and besides, Top is there.'

The sailor, observing the heavy surf on the shore, shook his head.

The engineer had disappeared to the north of the shore, and nearly half a mile from the place where the castaways had landed. The nearest point of the beach he could reach was thus fully that distance off.

It was then nearly six o'clock. A thick fog made the night very dark. The castaways proceeded towards the north of the land on which chance had thrown them, an unknown region, the geographical situation of which they could not even guess. They were walking upon a sandy soil, mingled with stones, which appeared destitute of any sort of vegetation. The ground, very unequal and rough, was in some places perfectly riddled with holes, making walking extremely painful. From these holes escaped every minute great birds of clumsy flight, which flew in all directions. Others, more active, rose in flocks, and passed in clouds over their heads. The sailor thought he recognised gulls and cormorants, whose shrill cries rose above the roaring of the sea.

From time to time the castaways stopped and shouted, then listened for some response from the ocean for they thought that if the engineer had landed, and they had been near to the place, they would have heard the barking of the dog Top, even should Harding himself have been unable to give any sign of existence. They stopped to listen, but no sound arose above the roaring of the waves and the dashing of the surf. The little band then continued their march forward, searching into every hollow of the shore.

After walking for twenty minutes, the four castaways were suddenly brought to a standstill by the sight of foaming billows close to their feet. The solid ground ended here. They found themselves at the extremity of a sharp point on which the sea broke furiously.

It was too evident that they were powerless to help him. They must wait with what patience they could for daylight. Either the engineer had been able to save himself, and had already found a refuge on some point of the coast, or he was lost for ever! The long and painful hours passed by. The cold was intense. The castaways suffered cruelly, but they scarcely perceived it. They did not even think of taking a minute's rest. Forgetting everything but their chief, hoping or wishing to hope on, they continued to walk up and down on this sterile spot where they calculated Harding would have been washed up, always returning to its northern point where they could approach nearest to the scene of the catastrophe. They listened, they called, and then uniting their voices, they endeavoured to raise even a louder shout than before, whch would be transmitted to a great distance. The wind had now fallen almost to a calm, and the noise of the sea began also to subside.

Meanwhile, the sky was clearing little by little. Towards midnight the stars shone out, and if the engineer had been there with his companions he would have remarked that these stars did not belong to the northern hemisphere. The polar star was not visible, the constellations were not those which they had been accustomed to see in the United States; the Southern Cross glittered brightly in the sky.

The night passed away. Towards five o'clock in the morning of the 25th of March, the sky began to lighten; the horizon still remained dark, but with daybreak a thick mist rose from the sea, so that the eye could scarcely penetrate beyond twenty feet or so from where they stood. At length the fog gradually unrolled itself in great heavily moving waves.

It was only a fine weather mist. A hot sun soon penetrated to the surface of the island. About half-past six, three-quarters of an hour after sunrise, the mist became more transparent.

The beach consisted first of sand, covered with black stones, which were now appearing little by little above the retreating tide. The second level was separated by a perpendicular granite cliff, terminated at the top by an unequal edge at a height of at least 300 feet. It continued thus for a length of three miles, ending suddenly on the right with a precipice which looked as if cut by the hand of man. On the left, above the promontory, this irregular and jagged cliff descended by a long slope of conglomerate rocks till it mingled with the ground of the southern point. On the upper plateau of the coast not a tree appeared. It was a flat table-land like that above Cape Town at the Cape of Good Hope, but of reduced proportions: However, verdure was not wanting to the right beyond the precipice. They could easily distinguish a confused mass of great trees, which extended beyond the limits of their view. This verdure relieved the eye, so long wearied by the continued ranges of granite. Lastly, beyond and above the plateau, in a north-westerly direction and at a distance of at least seven miles, glittered a white summit which reflected the sun's rays. It was that of a lofty mountain, capped with snow.

The question could not at present be decided whether this land formed an island, or whether it belonged to a continent. But on beholding the convulsed masses heaped up on the left, no geologist would have hesitated to give them a volcanic origin, for they were unquestionably the work of subterranean convulsions.

Gideon Spilett, Pencroft, and Herbert attentively examined this land, on which they might perhaps have to live many long years; on which indeed they might even die, should it be out of the usual track of vessels, as was too likely to be the case.

CHAPTER 4

ALL at once the reporter sprang up, and telling the sailor that he would rejoin them at that same place, he set off to look for his friend. Neb got up immediately and went with him, eager to find the man he respected so much. Herbert wished to accompany them.

'Stop here, my boy,' said the sailor; 'we have to prepare an encampment, and to try and find rather better grub than these shell-fish. Our friends will want something when they come back. There is work for everybody.'

'I am ready,' replied Herbert.

'All right,' said the sailor; 'that will do. We must set about it regularly. We are tired, cold, and hungry; therefore we must have shelter, and food. There is food in the forest; we have only to find a house.'

'Very well,' returned Herbert, 'I will look for a cave amongst the rocks, and I shall be sure to discover some hole into which we can creep.'

'All right,' said Pencroft; 'go on, my boy.'

They both walked to the foot of the enormous wall over the beach, far from which the tide had now retreated; but instead of going towards the north, they went southwards. Pencroft had remarked, several hundred feet from the place at which they landed, a narrow cutting, out of which he thought a river or stream might issue. Now, on the one hand it was important to settle themselves in the neighbourhood of a good stream of water and on the other it was possible that the current had washed Cyrus Harding on the shore there.

On reaching this cutting they did indeed find a river. The water of the river was limpid. The sailor ascertained that at this time – that is to say, at low tide, when the rising floods did not reach it – it was sweet. This important point established, Herbert looked for some cavity which would serve them as a retreat, but in vain; everywhere the wall appeared smooth, plain, and perpendicular.

However, at the mouth of the watercourse and above the reach of the high tide, the convulsions of nature had formed, not a grotto, but a pile of enormous rocks, such as are often met with in granite countries and which bear the name of 'chimneys'.

Pencroft and Herbert penetrated quite far in amongst the rocks, by sandy passages in which light was not wanting, for it entered through the openings which were left between the blocks, of which some were only sustained by a miracle of equilibrium; but with the light came also air – a regular corridor-gale – and with the wind the sharp cold from the exterior. However the sailor thought that by stopping-up some of the openings with a mixture of stones and sand, the chimneys could be rendered habitable.

It was five in the evening when he and Herbert finished their work. But at least the cave would now provide an adequate shelter for the four companions. Towards six o'clock, when the sun was disappearing behind the high lands of the west, Herbert, who was walking up and down on the strand, signalised the return of Neb and Spilett.

They were returning alone! . . . The boy's heart sank; the sailor had not been deceived in his forebodings; the engineer, Cyrus Harding, had not been found!

They sat down on a rock, without saying anything. Exhausted with fatigue, dying of hunger, they had not strength to utter a word.

The reporter recounted all that they had done in their attempt to recover Cyrus Harding. He and Neb had surveyed the coast for a distance of eight miles, and consequently much beyond the place where the balloon had fallen the last time but one, a fall which was followed by the disappearance of the engineer and the dog Top. The shore was solitary; not a vestige of a mark. Not even a pebble recently displaced; not a trace on the sand; not a human footstep on all that part of the beach. It was clear that that portion of the shore had never been visited by a human being. The sea was as deserted as the land, and it was there, a few hundred feet from the coast that the engineer must have found a tomb.

The reporter got up, and, guided by the boy, went towards the cave. On the way, Pencroft asked him in the most natural tone, if by chance he happened to have a match or two.

The reporter stopped, felt in his pockets, but finding nothing, said, 'I had some, but I must have thrown them away.'

The seaman then put the same question to Neb and received the same answer.

'Confound it!' exclaimed the sailor.

The reporter heard him, and seizing his arm, 'Have you no matches?' he asked.

'Not one, and no fire in consequence.'

The problem of having no fire greatly troubled the castaways: It meant that there was no way of keeping warm at night, but more important, that there was no way of cooking food. The problem was not resolved that evening though they all tried various methods of producing fire. They ate shell food that Pencroft and Herbert had collected during the day and then slowly they went to sleep, worn out by the day's worries.

Meanwhile the night advanced with the storm ever increasing it's fury, and it was perhaps two hours from morning, when Pencroft, then sound asleep, was vigorously shaken.

'What's the matter?' he cried, rousing himself, and collecting his ideas with the promptitude usual to seamen.

The reporter was leaning over him, and saying, –

'Listen, Pencroft, listen!'

The sailor strained his ears, but could hear no noise beyond that caused by the storm.

'It is the wind,' said he.

'No,' replied Gideon Spilett, listening again, 'I thought I heard – '

'What?'

'The barking of a dog!'

'A dog!' cried Pencroft, springing up.

'Yes – barking – it's a dog barking,' cried Neb.

'It's not possible!' replied the sailor. 'And besides, how, in the roaring of the storm – '

'Stop – listen – ' said the reporter.

Pencroft listened more attentively, and really thought he heard, during a lull, distant barking.

'Well!' said the reporter, pressing the sailor's hand.

'Yes – yes!' replied Pencroft.

'It is Top! It is Top!' cried Herbert, who had just awoke; and all four rushed towards the opening of the chimneys. They had great difficulty in getting out. The wind drove them back. But at last they succeeded, and could only remain standing by leaning against the rocks. They looked about, but could not speak. The darkness was intense. The sea, the sky, the land were all mingled in one black mass. Not a speck of light was visible.

The reporter and his companions remained thus for a few minutes, overwhelmed by the wind, drenched by the rains blinded by the sand.

Pencroft whistled shrilly. It appeared as if this signal had been waited for; the barking immediately came nearer, and soon a dog bounded up to them.

'It is Top!' cried Herbert.

It was indeed Top, a magnificent Anglo-Norman, who derived from these two races crossed the swiftness of foot and the acuteness of smell, which are the pre-eminent qualities of coursing dogs. It was the dog of the engineer Cyrus Harding. But he was alone!

How was it that his instinct had guided him straight to the chimneys, which he did not know? It appeared inexplicable, above all, in the midst of this black night and in such a tempest! But what was still more inexplicable was, that Top was neither tired, nor exhausted, nor even soiled with mud or sand! – Herbert had drawn him towards him, and was patting his head, the dog rubbing his neck against the lad's hands.

'If the dog is found, the master will be found also?' said the reporter.

'God grant it!' responded Herbert. 'Let us set off! Top will guide us!' So preceeded by Top they set off.

The storm was then at all its violence, and perhaps at its height. Not a single ray of light from the moon pierced through the clouds. To follow a straight course was difficult. It was best to rely on Top's instinct. They did so. The reporter and Herbert walked behind the dog, and the sailor and Neb brought up the rear. It was impossible to exchange a word. The rain was not very heavy, but the wind was terrific.

However, one circumstance favoured the seaman and his three companions. The wind being south-east, consequently blew on their backs. The clouds of sand, which otherwise would have been insupportable, from being received behind did not in consequence impede their progress. In short, they sometimes went faster than they liked, and had some difficulty in keeping their feet; but hope gave them strength, for it was not at random that they made their way along the shore. They had no doubt that Neb had found his master, and that he had sent them the faithful dog. But was the engineer living?

They ascended towards the north, having on their left an interminable extent of billows, which broke with a deafening noise, and on their right a dark country, the aspect of which it was impossible to guess. But they felt that it was comparatively flat, for the wind passed completely over them, without being driven back as it was when it came in contact with the cliff.

At four o'clock in the morning, they reckoned that they had cleared about five miles. The clouds were slightly raised, and the wind, though less damp, was very sharp and cold. Insufficiently protected by their clothing, Pencroft, Herbert, Neb and Spilett suffered cruelly but not a complaint escaped their lips. They were determined to follow Top, wherever the intelligent animal wished to lead them.

Towards five o'clock day began to break. At the zenith, where the fog was less thick, grey shades bordered the clouds; under an opaque belt, a luminous line clearly traced the horizon. The crests of the billows were tipped with a wild light, and the foam regained its whiteness. At the same time on the left the hilly parts of the coast could be seen, though very indistinctly.

At six o'clock day had broken. The clouds rapidly lifted. The seaman and his companions were then about six miles from the chimneys. They were following a very flat shore bounded by a reef of rocks, whose heads scarcely emerged from the sea, for they were in deep water. On the left, the country appeared to be one vast extent of sandy downs, bristling with thistles. There was no cliff, and the shore offered no resistance to the ocean but a chain of irregular hillocks. Here and there grew two or three trees, inclined towards the west, their branches projecting in that direction. Quite behind, in the south-west extended the border of the forest.

At this moment, Top became very excited. He ran forward, then returned, and seemed to entreat them to hasten their steps. The dog then left the beach, and guided by his wonderful instinct, without showing the least hesitation, went straight in amongst the downs. They followed him. The country appeared an absolute desert. Not a living creature was to be seen.

The downs, the extent of which was large, were composed of hillocks and even of hills, very irregularly distributed. They resembled a Switzerland modelled in sand, and only an amazing instinct could have possibly recognised the way.

Five minutes after having left the beach, the reporter and his three companions arrived at a sort of excavation, hollowed out at the back of a high mound. There Top stopped, and gave a loud, clear bark. They dashed into the cave.

The body lying there was that of the engineer, Cyrus Harding.

CHAPTER 5

THE reporter knelt down beside the motionless body, and placed his ear to the engineer's chest, having first torn open his clothes.

A minute – an age! – passed, during which he endeavoured to catch the faintest throb of the heart.

Gideon Spilett at last rose, after a long and attentive examination. 'He lives!' said he.

Pencroft knelt in his turn beside the engineer, he also heard a throbbing, and even felt a slight breath on his cheek.

Herbert at a word from the reporter ran out to look for water. He found, a hundred feet off, a limpid stream, which seemed to have been greatly increased by the rains, and which filtered through the sand; but nothing in which to put the water, not even a shell amongst the downs. The lad was obliged to content himself with dipping his handerkerchief in the stream, and with it hastened back to the grotto.

Happily the wet handkerchief was enough for Gideon Spilett, who only wished to wet the engineer's lips. The cold water produced an almost immediate effect. His chest heaved and he seemed to try to speak.

'We will save him!' exclaimed the reporter.

First of all, Cyrus Harding was carried to the chimneys. There they managed to arrange for him a couch of seaweed which still remained almost dry.

Night had closed in, and the temperature, which had modified when the wind shifted to the north-west, again became extremely cold. Also, the sea having destroyed the partitions which Pencroft had put up in certain places in the passages, the chimneys, on account of the draughts, had become scarcely habitable. The engineer's condition would, therefore, have been bad enough, if his companions had not carefully covered him with their coats and waistcoats.

They ate a meal of the inevitable lithodomes, of which Herbert and Pencroft picked up a plentiful supply on the beach. However, to these molluscs the lad added some edible sea-weed, which he gathered on high rocks, whose sides were only washed by the sea at the time of high tides. This sea-weed, which belongs to the order of Sucacae, of the genus Sargussum, produces, when dry, a gelatinous matter, rich and nutritious. The reporter and his companions, after having eaten a quantity of lithodomes, sucked the sargussum, of which the taste was very tolerable. It is used in parts of the East very considerably by the natives. 'Never mind!' said the sailor, 'the captain will help us soon.' Meanwhile the cold became very severe, and unhappily they had no means of defending themselves from it.

The sailor, extremely vexed, tried in all sorts of ways to procure fire. Neb helped him in this work. He found some dry moss, and by striking together two pebbles he obtained some sparks, but the moss, not being inflammable enough, did not take fire, for the sparks were really only incandescent, and not at all of the same consistency as those which are emitted from flint when struck in the same manner. The experiment, therefore, did not succeed.

Pencroft, although he had no confidence in the proceeding, then tried rubbing two pieces of dry wood together as savages do. Certainly, the movement which he and Neb gave themselves, if they had been transformed into heat, according to the new theory, would have been enough to heat the boiler of a steamer! It came to nothing. The bits of wood became hot, to be sure, but much less so than the operators themselves.

After working an hour, Pencroft, who was in a complete state of perspiration, threw down the pieces of wood in disgust.

'I can never be made to believe that savages light their fires in this way, let them say what they will,' he exclaimed. 'I could sooner light my arms by rubbing them against each other!'

The sailor was wrong to despise the proceeding. Savages often kindle wood by means of rapid rubbing. But every sort of wood does not answer for the purpose, and besides, there is 'the knack', following the usual expression, and it is probable that Pencroft had not 'the knack'.

Pencroft's ill humour did not last long. Herbert had taken the bits of wood which he had thrown down, and was exerting himself to rub them. The hardy sailor could not restrain a burst of laughter on seeing the efforts of the lad to succeed where he had failed.

'Rub, my boy, rub!' said he.

'I am rubbing,' replied Herbert, laughing, 'but I don't pretend to do anything else but warm myself instead of shivering, and soon I shall be as hot as you are, my good Pencroft!'

This soon happened. However, they were obliged to give up, for this night at least, the attempt to procure fire. Gideon Spilett repeated, for the twentieth time, that Cyrus Harding would not have been troubled for so small a difficulty. And, in the meantime, he stretched himself in one of the passages on his bed of sand. Herbert, Neb, and Pencroft did the same, whilst Top slept at his master's feet.

Next day, the 28th of March, the engineer awoke about eight in the morning, he saw his companions around him watching his sleep, his first words were: 'Island or continent?'

This was his uppermost thought.

'Well!' replied Pencroft, 'we don't know anything about it, captain!'

'You don't know yet?'

'But we shall know,' rejoined Pencroft, 'when you have guided us into the country.'

'I think I am able to try it,' replied the engineer, who, without much effort, rose and stood upright.

'That's capital!' cried the sailor.

'I feel dreadfully weak,' replied Harding. 'Give me something to eat, my friends, and it will soon go off. You have fire, haven't you?'

This question was not immediately replied to. But in a few seconds –

'Alas! we have no fire,' said Pencroft.

'We shall consider,' replied the engineer, 'and if we do not find some substance similar to tinder – '

'Well?' asked the sailor.

'Well, we will make matches.'

'Chemicals?'

'Chemicals!'

'It is not more difficult than that,' cried the reporter, striking the sailor on the shoulder.

The latter did not think it so simple, but he did not protest. All went out. The weather had become very fine. The sun was rising from the sea's horizon, and touched with golden spangles the prismatic rugosities of the huge precipice.

Having thrown a rapid glance around him, the engineer seated himself on a block of stone. Herbert offered him a few handfuls of shell-fish and sargussum, saying, –

'It is all that we have, Captain Harding.'

'Thanks, my boy,' replied Harding; 'it will do – for this morning at least.'

He ate the wretched food with appetite, and washed it down with a little fresh water, drawn from the river in an immense shell.

His companions looked at him without speaking. Then, feeling somewhat refreshed Cyrus Harding crossed his arms and said, –

'So, my friends, you do not know yet, whether fate has thrown us on an island, or on a continent?'

'No, captain,' replied the boy.

'We shall know tomorrow,' said the engineer; 'till then, there is nothing to be done.'

'Yes,' replied Pencroft.

'What?'

'Fire,' said the sailor, who, also, had a fixed idea.

'We will make it, Pencroft,' replied Harding.

'Whilst you were carrying me yesterday, did I not see in the west a mountain which commands the country?'

'Yes,' replied Spilett, 'a mountain which must be rather high –'

'Well,' replied the engineer, 'we will climb to the summit tomorrow, and then we shall see if this land is an island or a continent Till then, I repeat, there is nothing to be done.'

'Yes, fire!' said the obstinate sailor again.

'But he will make us a fire!' replied Gideon Spilett, 'only have a little patience, Pencroft!'

The seaman looked at Spilett in a way which seemed to say, 'If it depended upon you to do it, we wouldn't taste roast meat very soon;' but he was silent.

Meanwhile Captain Harding had made no reply. He appeared to be very little troubled by the question of fire. For a few minutes he remained absorbed in thought; then again speaking, –

'My friends,' said he, 'our situation is, perhaps, deplorable; but, at any rate, it is very plain. Either we are on a continent, and then, at the expense of greater or less fatigue, we shall reach some inhabited place, or we are on an island. In the latter case, if the island is inhabited, we will try to get out of the scrape by the help of its inhabitants; if it is desert, we will try to get out of the scrape by ourselves.'

'Certainly, nothing could be plainer,' replied Pencroft.

'But, whether it is an island or a continent,' asked Gideon Spilett, 'whereabouts do you think, Cyrus, this storm has thrown us?'

'I cannot say exactly,' replied the engineer, 'but I presume it is some land in the Pacific. In fact, when we left Richmond, the wind was blowing from the north-east, and its very violence greatly proves that it could not have varied. If the direction has been maintained from the north-east to the south-west, we have traversed the States of North Carolina, of South Carolina, of Georgia, the Gulf of Mexico, Mexico itself, in its narrow part then a part of the Pacific Ocean. I cannot estimate the distance traversed by the balloon at less than six to seven thousand miles, and, even supposing that the wind had varied half a quarter, it must have brought us either to the archipelago of Mendava, either on the Pomotous, or even, if it had a greater strength than I suppose, to the land of New Zealand. If the last hypothesis is correct, it will be easy enough to get home again. English or Maoris, we shall always find some one to whom we can speak. If, on the contrary, this is the coast of a desert island in some tiny archipelago, perhaps we shall be able to reconnoitre it from the summit of that peak which overlooks the country, and then we shall see how best to establish ourselves here as if we are never to go away.'

'Never?' cried the reporter. 'You say "Never", my dear Cyrus?'

'Better to put things at the worst at first,' replied the engineer, 'and reserve the best for a surprise.'

'Well said,' remarked Pencroft. 'It is to be hoped, too, that this island, if it be one, is not situated just out of the course of ships; that would be really unlucky!'

'We shall not know what we have to rely on until we have first made the ascent of the mountain,' replied the engineer.

'But tomorrow, captain,' asked Herbert, 'shall you be in a state to bear the fatigue of the ascent?'

'I hope so,' replied the engineer, 'provided you and Pencroft, my boy, show yourselves quick and clever hunters.'

'Captain,' said the sailor, 'since you are speaking of game, if, on my return, I was as certain of being able to roast it as I am of bringing it back –'

'Bring it back all the same, Pencroft,' replied Harding.

It was then agreed that the engineer and the reporter were to pass the day at the chimneys, so as to examine the shore and the upper plateau. Neb, Herbert, and the sailor, were to go to the forest, collect a store of wood, and lay violent hands on every creature, feathered or hairy, which might come within their reach.

They set out accordingly about ten o'clock in the morning, Herbert confident, Neb joyous, Pencroft murmuring aside, –

'If, on my return, I find a fire at the house, I shall believe that the thunder itself came to light it.' All three climbed the bank; and arrived at the angle made by the river, the sailor, stopping said to his two companions, –

'Shall we begin by being hunters or wood-men?'

'Hunters,' replied Herbert. 'There is Top already in quest.'

'We will hunt, then,' said the sailor, 'and afterwards we can come back and collect our wood.'

This agreed to, Herbert, Neb, and Pencroft, after having torn three sticks from the trunk of a young fir, followed Top, who was bounding about amongst the long grass.

The hunters, instead of following the course of the river, plunged straight into the heart of the forest. There were still the same trees, belonging, for the most part, to the pine family. In certain places, less crowded, growing in clumps, these pines exhibited considerable dimensions, and appeared to indicate, by their development, that the country was situated in a higher latitude than the engineer had supposed. Glades, bristling with stumps worn away by time, were covered with dry wood, which formed an inexhaustible store of fuel. Then, the glade passed, the underwood thickened again, and became almost impenetrable.

It was difficult enough to find the way amongst the groups of trees, without any beaten track. So the sailor from time to time broke off branches which might be easily recognised. But, perhaps, he was wrong not to follow the watercourse, as he and Herbert had done on their first excursion, for after walking an hour not a creature had shown itself. Top, running under the branches, only roused birds which could not be approached. Even the couroucous were invisible, and it was probable that the sailor would be obliged to return to the marshy part of the forest, in which he had so happily performed his tétra fishing.

'Well, Pencroft,' said Neb, in a slightly sarcastic tone, 'if this is all the game which you promised to bring back to my master, it won't need a large fire to roast it!'

'Have patience,' replied the sailor, 'it isn't the game which will be wanting on our return.'

'Have you not confidence in Captain Harding?'

'Yes.'

'But you don't believe that he will make fire?'

'I shall believe it when the wood is blazing in the fireplace.'

'It will blaze, since my master has said so.'

'We shall see!'

Meanwhile, the sun had not reached the highest point in its course above the horizon. The exploration, therefore, continued and was usefully marked by a discovery which Herbert made of a tree whose fruit was edible. This was the stone-pine, which produces an excellent almond, very much esteemed in the temperate regions of America and Europe. These almonds were in a perfect state of maturity, and Herbert described them to his companions, who feasted on them.

'Come,' said Pencroft, 'sea-weed by way of bread, raw mussels for meat, and almonds for desert, that's certainly a good dinner for those who have not a single match in their pocket!'

'We mustn't complain,' said Herbert.

'I am not complaining, my boy,' replied Pencroft; 'only I repeat, that meat is a little too much economised in this sort of meal.'

'Top has found something!' cried Neb, who ran towards a thicket, in the midst of which the dog had disappeared, barking. With Top's barking were mingled curious gruntings.

The sailor and Herbert had followed Neb. If there was game there, this was not the time to discuss how it was to be cooked, but rather, how they were to get hold of it.

The hunters had scarcely entered the bushes when they saw Top engaged in a struggle with an animal which he was holding by the ear. This quadruped was a sort of pig nearly two feet and a half long, of a blackish brown colour, lighter below, having hard scanty hair; its toes, then strongly fixed in the ground, seemed to be united by a membrane. Herbert recognised in this animal the capybara, that is to say, one of the largest members of the rodent order.

Meanwhile, the capybara did not struggle against the dog. It stupidly rolled its eyes, deeply buried in a thick bed of fat. Perhaps it saw men for the first time.

However, Neb having tightened his grasp on his stick, was just going to fell the pig, when the latter, tearing itself from Top's teeth, by which it was only held by the tip of its ear, uttered a vigorous grunt, rushed upon Herbert, almost overthrew him, and disappeared in the wood.

'The rascal!' cried Pencroft.

All three directly darted after Top, but at the moment when they joined him the animal had disappeared under the waters of a large pond shaded by venerable pines.

Neb, Herbert, and Pencroft stopped, motionless. Top plunged into the water, but the capybara, hidden at the bottom of the pond, did not appear.

'Let us wait,' said the boy, 'for he will soon come to the surface to breathe.'

'Won't he drown?' asked Neb.

'No,' replied Herbert, 'since he has webbed feet, and is almost an amphibious animal. But watch him.'

Top remained in the water. Pencroft and his two companions went to different parts of the bank, so as to cut off the retreat of the capybara, which the dog was looking for beneath the water.

Herbert was not mistaken. In a few minutes the animal appeared on the surface of the water. Top was upon it in a bound, and kept it from plunging again. An instant later the capybara, dragged to the bank, was killed by a blow from Neb's stick.

'Hurrah!' cried Pencroft, who was always ready with this cry of triumph. 'Give me but a good fire, and this pig shall be gnawed to the bones!'

Pencroft hoisted the capybara on his shoulders, and judging by the height of the sun that it was about two o'clock, he gave the signal to return.

Top's instinct was useful to the hunters, who, thanks to the intelligent animal, were enabled to discover the road by which they had come. Half an hour later they arrived at the river.

Pencroft soon made a raft of wood and following the current, they returned towards the chimneys.

But the sailor had not gone fifty paces when he stopped, and again uttering a tremendous hurrah, pointed towards the angle of the cliff, –

'Herbert! Neb! Look' he shouted.

Smoke was escaping and curling up amongst the rocks.

In a few minutes the three hunters were before a crackling fire. The captain and the reporter were there. Pencroft looked from one to the other, his capybara in his hand, without saying a word.

'Well, yes, my brave fellow,' cried the reporter.

'Fire, real fire, which will roast this splendid pig perfectly, and we will have a feast presently!'

'But who lighted it?' asked Pencroft.

'The sun.'

Gideon Spilett was quite right in his reply. It was the sun which had furnished the heat which so astonished Pencroft. The sailor could scarcely believe his eyes, and he was so amazed that he did not think of questioning the engineer.

'Had you a burning-glass, sir?' asked Herbert of Harding.

'No, my boy,' replied he, 'but I made one.'

And he showed the apparatus which served for a burning-glass. It was simply two glasses which he had taken from his own and the reporter's watches. Having filled them with water and rendered their edges adhesive by means of a little clay, he thus fabricated a regular burning-glass, which, concentrating the solar rays on some very dry moss, soon caused it to blaze.

They supped capitally. The flesh of the capybara was declared excellent. The sargussum and the almonds of the stone-pine completed the repast, during which the engineer spoke little. He was preoccupied with projects for the next day.

Once or twice Pencroft gave forth some ideas upon what it would be best to do; but Cyrus Harding, who was evidently of a methodical mind, only shook his head without uttering a word. 'Tomorrow,' he repeated, 'we shall know what we have to depend upon, and we will act accordingly.'

The meal ended, fresh armfuls of wood were thrown on the fire, and the inhabitants of the chimneys, including the faithful Top, were soon buried in a deep sleep. No incident disturbed this peaceful night, and the next day they awoke fresh and active, ready to undertake the excursion which must determine their fate.

All was ready for the start. The remains of the capybara would be enough to sustain Harding and his companions for at least twenty-four hours. Besides, they hoped to find more food on the way. Following Pencroft's advice, it appeared best to take the road already traversed through the forest, and to return by another route. It was also the most direct way to reach the mountain.

They traversed through the forest all morning and just before twelve o'clock began the ascent of the mountain. Evening came on by degrees, and it was almost night when Cyrus Harding and his companions, much fatigued by an ascent of seven hours, arrived at the plateau of the first cone. It was then necessary to prepare an encampment, and to restore their strength by eating first and sleeping afterwards.

Cyrus Harding, however, was not content to wait until morning to find out if they inhabited an island or continent. So, regardless of fatigue and accompanied by Herbert, he began to follow the edge of the plateau, going towards the north.

It was nearly eight o'clock when Cyrus Harding and Herbert

set foot on the highest ridge of the mountain at the summit of the cone.

It was then perfectly dark, and their gaze could not extend over a radius of two miles. Did the sea surround this unknown land, or was it connected in the west with some continent of the Pacific? It could not yet be made out. Towards the west, a cloudy belt, clearly visible at the horizon, increased the gloom, and the eye could not discover if the sky and water were blended together in the same circular line.

But at one point of the horizon a vague light suddenly appeared, which descended slowly in proportion as the cloud mounted to the zenith.

It was the slender crescent moon, already almost disappearing; but its light was sufficient to show clearly the horizontal line, then detached from the cloud, and the engineer could see its reflection trembling for an instant on a liquid surface. Cyrus Harding seized the lad's hand, and in a grave voice, –

'An island!' said he, at the moment when the lunar crescent disappeared beneath the waves.

CHAPTER 6

HALF an hour later Cyrus Harding and Herbert had returned to the encampment. The engineer merely told his companions that the land upon which fate had thrown them was an island, and that the next day they would consult. Then each settled himself as well as he could to sleep, and in that rocky hole, at a height of two thousand five hundred feet above the level of the sea, through a peaceful night, the islanders enjoyed profound repose.

The next day, the 30th of March, after a hasty breakfast, which consisted solely of the roasted tragopan, the engineer wished to climb again to the summit of the volcano, so as more attentively to survey the island upon which he and his companions were imprisoned for life perhaps, should the island be situated at a great distance from any land, or if it was out of the course of vessels which visited the archipelagos of the Pacific Ocean. This time his companions followed him in the new exploration. They also wished to see the island, on the productions of which they must depend for the supply of all their wants.

The crater was reached. It was what Harding had made it out to be in the dark.

The engineer and his companions, mute and motionless, surveyed for some minutes every point of the ocean, examining it to its most extreme limits. Even Pencroft, who possessed a marvellous power of sight, saw nothing; certainly if there had been land at the horizon, if it appeared only as an indistinct vapour, the sailor would undoubtedly have found it out, for nature had placed regular telescopes under his eyebrows.

From the ocean their gaze returned to the island which they commanded entirely, and the first question was put by Gideon Spilett in these terms:

'About what size is this island?'

Truly, it did not appear large in the midst of the immense ocean.

Cyrus Harding reflected a few minutes; he attentively observed the perimeter of the island, taking into consideration the height at which he was placed; then, –

'My friends,' said he, 'I do not think I am mistaken in giving to the shore of the island a circumference of more than a hundred miles.'

'And consequently an area?'

'That is difficult to estimate,' replied the engineer, 'for it is so uneven.'

If Cyrus Harding was not mistaken in his calculation, the Island had almost the extent of Malta or Zante, in the Mediterranean, but it was at the same time much more irregular and less rich in capes, promontories, points, bays, or creeks. Its strange form caught the eye, and when Gideon Spilett, on the engineer's advice, had drawn the outline, they found that it resembled some fantastic animal, a monstrous leviathan, which lay sleeping on the surface of the Pacific.

As to the interior of the island, its general aspect was this, – very woody throughout the southern part from the mountain to the shore, and arid and sandy in the northern part. Between the volcano and the east coast Cyrus Harding and his companions were surprised to see a lake, bordered with green trees, the existence of which they had not suspected. Seen from this height, the lake appeared to be on the same level as the ocean but, on reflection, the engineer explained to his companions that the altitude of this little sheet of water must be about three hundred feet, because the plateau, which was its basin, was but a prolongation of the coast.

'Is it a freshwater lake?' asked Pencroft.

'Certainly,' replied the engineer, 'for it must be fed by the water which flows from the mountain.'

'I see a little river which runs into it,' said Herbert, pointing out a narrow stream, which evidently took its source somewhere in the west.

'Yes,' said Harding; and since this stream feeds the lake, most probably on the side near the sea there is an outlet by which the surplus water escapes. We shall see that on our return.'

Cyrus Harding and his companions remained an hour at the top of the mountain. The island was displayed under their eyes, like a plan in relief with different tints, green for the forests, yellow for the sand, blue for the water. They viewed it in its *toute-ensemble*, nothing remained concealed but the ground hidden by verdure, the hollows of the valleys, and the interior of the volcanic chasms.

The exploration of the island was finished, its shape determined, its features made out, its extent calculated, the water and mountain systems ascertained. The disposition of the forests and plains had been marked in a general way on the reporter's plan. They had now only to descend the mountain slopes again, and explore the soil, in the triple point of view, of its mineral, vegetable, and animal resources.

But before their departure Pencroft said that there was one thing he would like to say.

'What is that?' said the reporter.

'It is, that we do not consider ourselves castaways, but colonists, who have come here to settle.' Harding could not help smiling, and the sailor's idea was adopted. He then thanked his companions, and added, that he would rely on their energy and on the aid of Heaven.

'Well, now let us set off to the chimneys!' cried Pencroft.

'One minute, my friends,' said the engineer. 'It seems to me it would be a good thing to give a name to this island, as well as to the capes, promonotories, and watercourses, which we can see.'

'Very good,' said the reporter. 'In the future, that will simplify the instructions which we shall have to give and follow.'

'Indeed,' said the sailor, 'already it is something to be able to say where one is going, and where one has come from. At least, it looks like somewhere.'

'The chimneys, for example,' said Herbert.

'Exactly!' replied Pencroft. 'The name was the most convenient, and it came to me quite of myself. Shall we keep the name of the Chimneys for our first encampment captain?'

'Yes, Pencroft, since you have so christened it.'

'Good! as for the others, that will be easy,' returned the sailor, who was in high spirits. 'Let us give them names, as the Robinsons did, whose story Herbert has often read to me: Providence Bay, Whale Point, Cape Disappointment!'

'Or, rather, the names of Captain Harding,' said Herbert, 'of Mr Spilett, of Neb! – '

'My name!' cried Neb, showing his sparkling white teeth.

'Why not?' replied Pencroft. 'Port Neb, that would do very well! And Cape Gideon – '

'I should prefer borrowing names from our country,' said the reporter, 'which would remind us of America.'

So, first of all, they named the vast bay on the east Union Bay, the large hollow on the south, Washington Bay, and the mountain on which they stood they named Mount Franklin.

'Now,' said the reporter, 'to this peninsula at the southwest of the island, I propose to give the name of Serpentine Peninsula, and that of Reptile-end to the bent tail which terminates it, for it is just like a reptile's tail.'

'Adopted,' said the engineer.

'Now,' said Herbert, pointing to the other extremity of the island, 'let us call this gulf which is so singularly like a pair of open Jaws, Shark Gulf.'

'Capital!' cried Pencroft, 'and we can complete the resemblance by naming the two parts of the Jaws Mandible Cape.'

'But there are two capes,' observed the reporter.

'Well,' replied Pencroft, 'we can have North Mandible Cape and South Mandible Cape.'

'They are inscribed,' said Spilett.

'There is only the point at the south-eastern extremity of the island to be named,' said Pencroft.

'That is, the extremity of Union Bay?' asked Herbert.

'Claw Cape,' cried Neb directly, who also wished to be god-father to some part of his domain.

In truth, Neb had found an excellent name, for this cape was very like the powerful claw of the fantastic animal which this singularly-shaped island represented.

Pencroft was delighted at the turn things had taken; and their imaginations soon gave to the river which furnished the settlers with drinking water and near which the balloon had thrown them, the name of the Mercy, in true gratitude to Providence; to the plateau which crowned the high granite precipice above the Chimneys, and from whence the gaze could embrace the whole of the vast bay, the name of Prospect Heights.

Lastly, all the masses of impenetrable wood which covered the Serpentine Peninsula were named the forest of the Far West.

Everything was finished, and the settlers had only to descend Mount Franklin to return to the Chimneys, when Pencroft cried out, –

'Well! we are preciously stupid!'

'Why?' asked Gideon Spilett, who had closed his note-book and risen to depart.

'Why! our island! we have forgotten to christen it!'

Herbert was going to propose to give it the engineer's name and all his companions would have applauded him, when Cyrus Harding said simply, –

'Let us give it the name of a great citizen, my friends; of him who now struggles to defend the unity of the American Republic! Let us call it Lincoln Island!'

The engineer's proposal was replied to by three hurrahs.

And that evening, before sleeping, the new colonists talked of their absent country; they spoke of the terrible war which stained it with blood: they could not doubt that the South would soon be subdued, and that the cause of the North, the cause of justice, would triumph, thanks to Grant, thanks to Lincoln!

Now this happened the 30th of March, 1865. They little knew that sixteen days afterwards a frightful crime would be committed in Washington, and that on Good Friday Abraham Lincoln would fall by the hand of a fanatic.

Their next task was that of finding a permanent residence.

'We must consider the matter thoroughly,' remarked Cyrus Harding, 'before coming to any decision. A natural dwelling would spare us much work and would be a surer retreat, for it would be as well defended against enemies from the interior as those from outside.

It was by chance that the opportunity of discovering this natural dwelling arose. On their return from Mount Franklin, the colonists had travelled via Lake Grant. Particular attention had been drawn to this lake because of a strange event which took place there.

The five companions had been walking besides the lake for some time when Top, after much agitated barking, plunged into the water. All ran towards the bank. The dog was already more than twenty feet off, and Cyrus was calling him back, when an enormous head emerged from the water, which did not appear to be deep in that place.

It was a dugong. The enormous animal rushed on the dog, who tried to escape by returning towards the shore. His master could do nothing to save him and within a minute Top was seized by the dugong and disappeared beneath the water. The struggle continued under the water; it could not but terminate in the death of the dog, judging by the commotion in that part of the lake. But suddenly, in the middle of a foaming circle, Top reappeared. Thrown in the air by some unknown power, he rose ten feet above the surface of the lake, fell again into the midst of the agitated waters, and then soon gained the shore, without any severe wounds, miraculously saved.

Cyrus Harding and his companions could not understand it. What was not less inexplicable was that the struggle still appeared to be going on. Doubtless the dugong, attacked by some powerful animal, after having released the dog, was fighting on its own account. But it did not last long. The water became red with blood, and the body of the dugong, emerging from the sheet of scarlet which spread around, soon stranded on a little beach at the south angle of the lake. The colonists ran towards it. The dugong was dead. It was an enormous animal, fifteen or

34

sixteen feet long, and must have weighed from three to four thousand pounds. At its neck was a wound, which appeared to have been produced by a sharp blade.

What could the amphibious creature have been who, by this terrible blow, had destroyed the formidable dugong? No one could tell.

Harding was much perplexed by this incident. So, a few days later, accompanied by Pencroft, Spilett, Herbert and Neb, he returned to Lake Grant in order to make a thorough search and, if possible, discover the cause of the strange events there.

Though they found nothing which even gave them a clue to the indentification of the thing or person which was responsible for Top's survival, they did discover an ideal dwelling place. It was Harding who first noticed during the search, that the outlet from the lake was an underground river and that there was a possibility that this could be exploited for their own purposes if the means were found. Cyrus Harding, needless to say, found the means. Over a period of ten days he lowered the depth of the lake by three feet thus making the cavity, where the outlet river had previously escaped through the rock of Prospect Heights, accessable. He did this by utilising all his skill as a scientist to manufacture nitro-glycerine and then using this substance to blow a hole in the bank of the lake some way from the cavity in the granite. Thus, a new outlet river was formed and the old one ceased to be used.

The cavity in the rock was then widened with pickaxes to allow them to pass through. Resinous branches were cut and used as torches, then Cyrus Harding leading, the settlers ventured into the dark passage, which the overflow of the lake had formerly filled.

Contrary to what might have been supposed, the diameter of the passage increased as the explorers proceeded, so that they very soon were able to stand upright. The granite, worn by the water for an infinite time, was very slippery, and falls were to be dreaded. But the settlers were all attached to each other by a cord, as is frequently done in ascending mountains. Happily some projections of the granite, forming regular steps, made the descent less perilous. Drops, still hanging from the rocks, shone here and there under the light of the torches, and the explorers guessed that the sides were clothed with innumerable stalactites. The engineer examined this black granite. There was not a stratum, not a break in it. The mass was compact, and of an extremely close grain. The passage dated, then, from the very origin of the island. It was not the water which little by little had hollowed it. Pluto and not Neptune had bored it with his own hand, and on the wall traces of an eruptive work could be distinguished, which all the washing of the water had not been able totally to efface.

The settlers descended very slowly. They could not but feel a certain awe, in thus venturing into these unknown depths, for the first time visited by human beings. They did not speak, but they thought; and the thought came to more than one, that some polypus or other gigantic cephalopod might inhabit the interior cavities, which were in communication with the sea. However, Top kept at the head of the little band, and they could rely on the sagacity of the dog, who would not fail to give the alarm if there was any need for it.

The settlers had gone some fifty feet farther, when their attention was attracted by distant sounds which came up from the depths. They stopped and listened. These sounds, carried through the passage as through an acoustic tube, came clearly to the ear. 'That is Top barking!' cried Herbert.

'Yes,' replied Pencroft, 'and our brave dog is barking furiously!'

'We have our iron-tipped spears,' said Cyrus Harding. 'Keep on your guard, and forward!'

'It is becoming more and more interesting,' murmured Gideon Spilett in the sailor's ear, who nodded. Harding and his companions rushed to the help of their dog. Top's barking became more and more perceptible, and it seemed strangely fierce. Was he engaged in a struggle with some animal whose retreat he had disturbed? Without thinking of the danger to which they might be exposed, the explorers were now impelled by an irresistible curiosity, and in a few minutes, sixteen feet lower they rejoined Top.

There the passage ended in a vast and magnificent cavern. Top was running backwards and forwards, barking furiously. Pencroft and Neb, waving their torches, threw the light into every crevice; and at the same time, Harding, Gideon Spilett, and Herbert, their spears raised, were ready for any emergency which might arise. The enormous cavern was empty. The settlers explored it in every direction. There was nothing there, not an animal, not a human being; and yet Top continued to bark. Neither caresses nor threats could make him be silent.

'There must be a place somewhere, by which the waters of the lake reached the sea,' said the engineer.

'Of course,' replied Pencroft, 'and we must take care not to tumble into a hole.'

'Go, Top, go!' cried Harding.

The dog, excited by his master's words, ran towards the extremity of the cavern, and there redoubled his barking.

They followed him, and by the light of the torches, perceived the mouth of a regular well in the granite. It was by this that the water escaped; and this time it was not an oblique and practicable passage, but a perpendicular well, into which it was impossible to venture.

The torches were held over the opening: nothing could be

seen. Harding took a lighted branch, and threw it into the abyss. The blazing resin, whose illuminating power increased still more by the rapidity of its fall, lighted up the interior of the well, but yet nothing appeared. The flame then went out with a slight hiss, which showed that it had reached the water, that is to say, the level of the sea.

The engineer, calculating the time employed in its fall, was able to calculate the depth of the well, which was found to be about ninety feet. The floor of the cavern must thus be situated ninety feet above the level of the sea.

'Here is our dwelling,' said Cyrus Harding.

'But it was occupied by some creature,' replied Gideon Spilett, whose curiosity was not yet satisfied.

'Well, the creature, amphibious or otherwise, has made off through this opening,' replied the engineer, 'and has left the place for us.'

'Never mind,' added the sailor, 'I should like very much to be Top, just for a quarter of an hour, for he doesn't bark for nothing!'

Cyrus Harding looked at his dog, and those of his companions who were near him, might have heard him murmur these words, –

'Yes, I believe that Top knows more than we do about a great many things.'

However, the wishes of the settlers were for the most part satisfied. Chance, aided by the marvellous sagacity of their leader, had done them great service. They had now at their disposal a vast cavern, the size of which could not be properly calculated by the feeble light of their torches, but it would certainly be easy to divide it into rooms, by means of brick partitions, or to use it, if not as a house, at least as a spacious apartment. The water which had left it could not return The place was free.

And so the colonists settled in to their new home, making it light by knocking six large holes through the rock on the seaward side to serve as windows, one large enough for a door which opened eighty feet above the ground, and dividing the interior into five compartments. A ladder was manufactured and extended from the door to the ground.

Immediately this was done, Harding blocked up the entrance to Granite House as it had been called on the first day, from the lake; he rolled masses of rock over the entrance which were strongly cemented together and hidden beneath grass and shrubs which later made their work complete by growing profusely and hiding all traces. There was a double reason for this. Firstly access was easier for the colonists by the front way up the ladder, and secondly the engineer felt the need for the security offered by their high sanctuary which could be made inaccessable and safe just by pulling up a ladder!

The final touch to this independent seclusion was the diverting of a small stream to run beneath the cemented rocks to Granite House itself, so there would never be any want of water.

CHAPTER 7

THE winter season set in with the month of June, which corresponds with the month of December in the northern hemisphere. It began with showers and squalls, which succeeded each other without intermission. The tenants of Granite House could appreciate the advantages of a dwelling which sheltered them from the inclement weather. The Chimneys would have been quite insufficient to protect them against the rigour of winter, and it was to be feared that the high tides would make another irruption.

During the whole of the month of June the time was employed in different occupations, which excluded neither hunting nor fishing, the larder being therefore abundantly supplied. Pencroft, so soon as he had leisure, proposed to set some traps, from which he expected great results. He soon made some snares with creepers, by the aid of which the warren henceforth every day furnished its quota of rodents. Neb employed nearly all his time in salting or smoking meat, which insured their always having plenty of provisions. The question of clothes was now seriously discussed, the settlers having no other garments than those they wore when the balloon threw them on the island. These clothes were warm and good; they had taken great care of them as well as of their linen, and they were pefectly whole, but they would soon need to be replaced. Moreover if the winter was severe, the settlers would suffer greatly from cold.

During this month there was no want of work. A successful seal hunt was conducted which provided the settlers with enough material to make a winter's supply of candles which was promptly done. Minerals such as tin, iron and coal had been discovered on the island some time ago but now they were mined in greater quantities in order to facilitate the manufacture of more tools and weapons which were needed more than ever now for laying in stores for the winter months. They tried their hands at all things, from pots and kitchen utensils to the construction of two bridges, one on Prospect Heights, one on the shore.

Great excitement was created one day when Herbert found a grain of corn. It had been considered the one privation on Lincoln Island that there was never any hope of producing bread. The one grain in the lining of Herbert's waistcoat accounted for by the fact that he had formally been in the habit of feeding pigeons when at Richmond, and was duly planted with great care and ceremony.

From this time Pencroft did not let a single day pass without going to visit what he gravely called his 'corn – field'. And woe to the insects which dared to venture there. No mercy was shown them.

This intense cold lasted till the 15th August with no let up. When the atmosphere was calm, the low temperature was easily borne, but when the wind blew, the poor settlers, insufficiently clothed, felt it severely. Pencroft regretted that Lincoln Island was not the home of a few families of bears rather than of so many foxes and seals.

'Bears,' said he, 'are generally very well dressed, and I ask no more than to borrow for the winter the warm cloaks which they have on their backs.'

'But,' replied Neb, laughing, 'perhaps the bears would not consent to give you their cloaks, Pencroft. These beasts are not St Martins.'

'We would make them do it, Neb, we would make them,' replied Pencroft, in quite an authoritative tone.

But these formidable carnivora did not exist in the island, or at any rate they had not as yet shown themselves.

In the meanwhile, Herbert, Pencroft, and the reporter, occupied themselves with making traps on Prospect Heights and at the border of the forest.

According to the sailor, any animal, whatever it was, would be a lawful prize, and the rodents or carnivora which might get into the new snares would be well received at Granite House.

The traps were besides extremely simple; being pits dug in the ground, a platform of branches and grass above, which concealed the opening, and at the bottom some bait, the scent of which would attract animals. It must be mentioned also, that they had not been dug at random, but at certain places where numerous footprints showed that quadrupeds frequented the ground. They were visited every day, and at three different times, during the first days, specimens of those Antarctic foxes which they had already seen on the right bank of the Mercy were found in them.

'Why, there are nothing but foxes in this country!' cried Pencroft, when for the third time he drew one of the animals out of the pit. Looking at it in great disgust, he added, 'beasts which are good for nothing!'

'Yes,' said Gideon Spilett, 'they are good for something!'

'And what is that?'

'To make bait to attract other creatures!'

The reporter was right, and the traps were henceforward baited with the foxes' carcasses.

The sailor had also made snares from the long tough fibres of a certain plant, and they were even more successful than the traps. Rarely a day passed without some rabbits from the warren being caught. It was always rabbit, but Ned knew how to vary his sauces, and the settlers did not think of complaining.

However, once or twice in the second week of August the traps supplied the hunters with other animals more useful than foxes, namely, several of those small wild boars which had already been seen to the north of the lake. Pencroft had no need to ask if these beasts were eatable. He could see that by their resemblance to the pig of America and Europe.

'But these are not pigs,' said Herbert to him, 'I warn you of that, Pencroft.'

'My boy,' replied the sailor, bending over the trap and drawing out one of these representatives of the family of *sus* by the little appendage which served it as a tail, 'let me believe that these are pigs!'

'Why?'

'Because that pleases me!'

'Are you very fond of pig, then, Pencroft?'

'Yes, extremely,' replied Pencroft.

The cold continued to the middle of September, and the prisoners in Granite House began to find their captivity rather tedious. Nearly every day they attempted sorties which they could not prolong. They constantly worked at the improvement of their dwelling. They talked whilst working. Harding instructed his companions in many things, principally explaining to them the practical applications of science. The colonists had no library at their disposal; but the engineer was a book which was always at hand, always open at the page which one wanted, a book which answered all their questions, and which they often consulted. The time thus passed away pleasantly, these brave men not appearing to have any fears for the future.

However, all were anxious to see, if not the fine season, at least the cessation of the insupportable cold. If only they had been clothed in a way to meet it, how many excursions they would have attempted, either to the downs or to Tadorn's Fens! Game would have been easily approached, and the chase would certainly have been most productive. But Cyrus Harding considered it of importance that no one should injure his health, for he had need of all his hands, and his advice was followed.

But it must be said, that the one who was most impatient of this imprisonment, after Pencroft perhaps, was Top. The faithful dog found Granite House very narrow. He ran backwards and forwards from one room to another, showing in his way how weary he was of being shut up. Harding often remarked that when he approached the dark well which communicated with the sea, and of which the orifice opened at the back of the store-room, Top uttered singular growlings. He ran round and round this hole, which had been covered with a wooden lid. Some-times even he tried to put his paws under the lid, as if he wished to raise it. He then yelped in a peculiar way, which showed at once anger and uneasiness.

The engineer observed this manoeuvre several times.

What could there be in this abyss to make such an impression on the intelligent animal? The well led to the sea, that was certain. Could narrow passages spread from it through the foundations of the island? Did some marine monster come from time to time, to breathe at the bottom of this well? The engineer did not know what to think, and could not refrain from dreaming of many strange improbabilities. Accustomed to go far into the regions of scientific reality, he would not allow him-self to be drawn into the regions of the strange and almost of the supernatural; but yet how to explain why Top, one of those sensible dogs who never waste their time in barking at the moon, should persist in trying with scent and hearing to fathom this abyss, if there was nothing there to cause his uneasiness? Top's conduct puzzled Cyrus Harding even more than he cared to acknowledge to himself.

At all events, the engineer only communicated his impression to Gideon Spilett, for he thought it useless to explain to his com-panions the suspicions which arose from what perhaps was only Top's fancy.

At last the cold ceased. There had been rain, squalls mingled with snow, hailstorms, gusts of wind, but these inclemencies did not last. The ice melted, the snow disappeared; the shore, the plateau, the banks of the Mercy, the forest, again became practicable. This return of spring delighted the tenants of Granite House, and they soon only passed in it the hours necessary for eating and sleeping.

They hunted much in the second part of September, which led Pencroft to again entreat for the fire-arms, which he asserted had been promised by Cyrus Harding. The latter, knowing well that without special tools it would be nearly impossible for him to manufacture a gun which would be of any use, still drew back, and put off the operation to some future time, observing in his usual dry way, that Herbert and Spilett had become very skilful archers, so that many sorts of excellent animals, agouties, kangaroos, capyboras, pigeons, bustards, wild ducks, snipes, in short, game both with fur and feathers, fell victims to their arrows, and that, consequently, they could wait. But the ob-stinate sailor would listen to nothing of this, and he would give the engineer no peace till he promised to satisfy his desire. Gideon Spilett, however, supported Pencroft.

'If, which may be doubted,' said he, 'the island is inhabited by wild beasts, we must think how to fight with and exterminate them. A time may come when this will be our first duty.'

But at this period, it was not the question of fire-arms which occupied Harding, but that of clothes. Those which the settlers wore had passed this winter, but they would not last until next winter. Skins of carnivora or the wool of ruminants must be procured at any price, and since there were plenty of musmons, it was agreed to consult on the means of forming a flock which might be brought up for the use of the colony. An enclosure for the domestic animals, a poultry-yard for the birds, in a word to establish a sort of farm in the island, such were the two important projects for the fine season.

In consequence and in view of these future establishments, it became of much importance that they should penetrate into all the yet unknown parts of Lincoln Island, that is to say, through that thick forest which extended on the right bank of the Mercy, from its mouth to the extremity of the Serpentine peninsula, as well as on the whole of its western side. But this needed settled weather, and a month must pass before this exploration could be profitably undertaken.

They therefore waited with some impatience, when an incident occured which increased the desire the settlers had to visit the whole of their domain.

It was the 24th of October. On this day, Pencroft had gone to visit his traps, which he always kept properly baited. In one of them he found three animals which would be very welcome for the larder. They were a female peccary and her two young ones.

Pencroft then returned to Granite House, enchanted with his capture, and as usual, he made a great show of his game.

'Come, we shall have a grand feast, captain!' he exclaimed. 'And you too, Mr Spilett, you will eat some!'

'I shall be very happy,' replied the reporter; 'but what is it that I am going to eat?'

'Sucking-pig.'

'Oh, indeed, sucking-pig, Pencroft? To hear you, I thought that you were bringing back a young partridge stuffed with truffles!'

'What?' cried Pencroft. 'Do you, mean to say that you turn up your nose at sucking-pig?'

'No,' replied Gideon Spilett, without showing any enthusiasm; 'provided one doesn't eat too much – '

'That's right, that's right,' returned the sailor, who was not pleased whenever he heard his chase made light of. 'You like to make objections. Seven months ago, when we landed on the island, you would have been only too glad to have met with such game!'

'Well, well,' replied the reporter, 'man is never perfect, nor contented.'

'Now,' said Pencroft, 'I hope that Neb will distinguish himself. Look here! These two little peccaries are not more than three months old! They will be as tender as quails! Come along, Neb, come! I will look after the cooking myself.'

And the sailor, followed by Neb, entered the kitchen, where they were soon absorbed in their culinary labours.

They were allowed to do it in their own way. Neb, therefore, prepared a magnificent repast – the two little peccaries, Kangaroo soup, a smoked ham, stone-pine almonds, Oswego tea; in fact, all the best that they had, but amongst all the dishes figured in the first rank the savoury peccaries.

At five o'clock dinner was served in the dining-room of Granite House. The kangaroo soup was smoking on the table. They found it excellent.

To the soup succeeded the peccaries, which Pencroft insisted on carving himself, and of which he served out monstrous portions to each of the guests.

These sucking-pigs were really delicious, and Pencroft was devouring his share with great gusto, when all at once a cry and an oath escaped him.

'What's the matter?' asked Cyrus Harding.

'The matter? the matter is that I have just broken a tooth!' replied the sailor.

'What, are there pebbles in your peccaries?' said Gideon Spilett.

'I suppose so,' replied Pencroft, drawing from his lips the object which had cost him a grinder! –

It was not a pebble – it was a leaden bullet.

CHAPTER 8

IT was now exactly seven months since the balloon voyagers had been thrown on Lincoln Island. During that time, notwithstanding the researches they had made no human being had been discovered. No smoke even had betrayed the presence of man on the surface of the island. No vestiges of his handiwork showed that either at an early or at a late period had man lived there. Not only did it now appear to be uninhabited by any but themselves, but the colonists were compelled to believe that it never had been inhabited. And now, all this scaffolding of reasonings fell before a simple ball of metal, found in the body of an inoffensive rodent! In fact, this bullet must have issued from a fire-arm, and who but a human being could have used such a weapon?

When Pencroft had placed the bullet on the table, his companions looked at it with intense astonishment. All the consequences likely to result from this incident, notwithstanding its apparent insignificance, immediately took possession of their minds. The sudden apparition of a supernatural being could not have startled them more completely.

Cyrus Harding did not hesitate to give utterance to the suggestions which this fact, at once surprising and unexpected, could not fail to raise in his mind. He took the bullet, turned it over and over, rolled it between his finger and thumb; then, turning to Pencroft, he asked, –

'Are you sure that the peccary wounded by this bullet was not more than three months old?'

'Not more, captain,' replied Pencroft. 'It was still sucking its mother when I found it in the trap.'

'Well,' said the engineer, 'that proves that within three months a gun-shot was fired in Lincoln Island.'

'And that a bullet,' added Gideon Spilett, 'wounded, though not mortally, this little animal.'

'That is unquestionable,' said Cyrus Harding, 'and these are the deductions which must be drawn from this incident that the island was inhabited before our arrival, or that men have landed here within three months. Did these men arrive here voluntarily or involuntarily, by disembarking on the shore or by being wrecked? This point can only be cleared up later. As to what they were, Europeans or Malays, enemies or friends of our race, we cannot possibly guess; and if they still inhabit the island, or if they have left it, we know not. But these questions are of too much importance to be allowed to remain long unsettled.'

'No! a hundred times no! a thousand times no!' cried the sailor, springing up from the table. 'There are no other men than ourselves on Lincoln Island! By my faith! The island isn't large, and if it had been inhabited, we should have seen some of the inhabitants long before this!'

'In fact, the contrary would be very astonishing,' said Herbert.

'But it would be much more astonishing, I should think,' observed the reporter, 'that this peccary should have been born with a bullet in its inside!'

'At least,' said Neb seriously, 'if Pencroft has not had – '

'Look here, Neb,' burst out Pencroft. 'Do you think I could have a bullet in my jaw for five or six months without finding it out? Where could it be hidden?' he asked, opening his mouth to show the two-and-thirty teeth with which it was furnished. 'Look well, Neb, and if you find one hollow tooth in this set, I will let you pull out half a dozen!'

'Neb's supposition is certainly inadmissible,' replied Harding, who, notwithstanding the gravity of his thoughts, could not restrain a smile. 'It is certain that a gun has been fired in the island, within three months at most. But I am inclined to think that the people who landed on this coast were only here a very short time ago, or that they just touched here; for if, when we surveyed the island from the summit of Mount Franklin, it had been inhabited, we should have seen them or we should have been seen ourselves. It is therefore probable that within only a few weeks castaways have been thrown by a storm on some part of the coast. However that may be, it is of consequence to us to have this point settled.'

'I think that we should act with caution,' said the reporter.

'Such is my advice,' replied Cyrus Harding, 'for it is to be feared that Malay pirates have landed on the island!'

'Captain,' asked the sailor, 'would it not be a good plan, before setting out, to build a canoe in which we could either ascend the river, or, if we liked, coast round the island? It will not do to be unprovided.'

'Your idea is good, Pencroft,' replied the engineer, 'but we cannot wait for that. It would take at least a month to build a boat.'

'Yes, a real boat,' replied the sailor; 'but we do not want one for a sea voyage, and in five days at the most, I will undertake to construct a canoe fit to navigate the Mercy.'

'Five days,' cried Neb, 'to build a boat?'

'Yes, Neb; a boat in the Indian fashion.'

'Of wood?' asked the negro, looking still unconvinced.

'Of wood,' replied Pencroft, 'or rather of bark. I repeat, captain, that in five days the work will be finished!'

'In five days, then, be it,' replied the engineer.

'But till that time we must be very watchful,' said Herbert.

'Very watchful indeed, my friends,' replied Harding; 'and I beg you to confine your hunting excursions to the neighbourhood of Granite House.'

The dinner ended less gaily than Pencroft had hoped.

So, then, the island was, or had been, inhabited by others than the settlers. Proved as it was by the incident of the bullet, it was hereafter an unquestionable fact, and such a discovery could not but cause great uneasiness amongst the colonists.

Cyrus Harding and Gideon Spilett, before sleeping, conversed long about the matter. They asked themselves if by chance this incident might not have some connection with the inexplicable way in which the engineer had been saved, and the other peculiar circumstances which had struck them at different times. So great haste was made by the sailor, seconded by the engineer, in building the boat. Gideon Spilett and Herbert, were not idle either. They went out each day, both to hunt and survey the area within a two mile radius of Granite House.

Two days after – the 28th of October – another incident occurred, for which an explanation was again required.

Whilst strolling along the shore about two miles from Granite House, Herbert and Neb were fortunate enough to capture a magnificent specimen of the order of chelonia. It was a turtle of the species Midas, the edible green turtle, so called from the colour of its shell and fat.

Herbert caught sight of this turtle as it was crawling among the rocks to reach the sea.

'Help, Neb, help!' he cried.

Neb ran up.

'What a fine animal!' said Neb, 'but how are we to catch it?'

'Nothing is easier, Neb,' replied Herbert. 'We have only to turn the turtle on its back, and it cannot possibly get away. Take your spear and do as I do.'

The reptile, aware of danger, had retired between its carapace and plastron. They no longer saw its head or feet, and it was motionless as a rock.

Herbert and Neb then drove their sticks underneath the animal, and by their united efforts managed without difficulty to turn it on its back. The turtle, which was three feet in length, would have weighed at least four hundred pounds.

'Capital!' cried Neb; 'this is something which will rejoice friend Pencroft's heart.'

In fact, the heart of friend Pencroft could not fail to be rejoiced, for the flesh of the turtle, which feeds on wrackgrass, is extremely savoury. At this moment the creature's head could be seen, which was small, flat but widened behind by the large temporal fossae hidden under the long roof.

'And now, what shall we do with our prize?' said Neb. 'We can't drag it to Granite House!'

'Leave it here, since it cannot turn over,' replied Herbert, 'and we will come back with the cart to fetch it.'

'That is the best plan.'

However, for greater precaution, Herbert took the trouble, which Neb deemed superfluous, to wedge up the animal with great stones; after which the two hunters returned to Granite House, following the beach, which the tide had left uncovered. Herbert, wishing to surprise Pencroft, said nothing about the 'superb specimen of a chelonian' which they had turned over on the sand; but, two hours later, he and Neb returned with the cart to the place where they had left it. The 'superb specimen of a chelonian' was no longer there!

Neb and Herbert stared at each other first; then they stared about them. It was just at this spot that the turtle had been left. The lad even found the stones which he had used, and therefore he was certain of not being mistaken.

'Well!' said Neb, 'these beasts can turn themselves over, then?'

'It appears so,' replied Herbert, who could not understand it at all, and was gazing at the stones scattered on the sand.

'Well, Pencroft will be disgusted!'

'And Captain Harding will perhaps be very perplexed how to explain this disappearance,' thought Herbert.

'Look here,' said Neb, who wished to hide his ill-luck, 'we won't speak about it.'

'On the contrary, Neb, we must speak about it,' replied Herbert.

And the two, taking the cart, which there was now no use for, returned to Granite House.

Arrived at the dockyard, where the engineer and the sailor were working together, Herbert recounted what had happened.

'Oh! the stupids!' cried the sailor, 'to have let at least fifty meals escape!'

'But, Pencroft,' replied Neb, 'it wasn't our fault that the beast got away; as I tell you, we had turned it over on its back!'

'Then you didn't turn it over enough!' returned the obstinate sailor.

'Not enough!' cried Herbert.

And he told how he had taken care to wedge up the turtle with stones.

'It is a miracle, then!' replied Pencroft.

'I thought, captain,' said Herbert, 'that turtles, once placed on their backs, could not regain their feet, especially when they are of a large size?'

'That is true, my boy,' replied Cyrus Harding.

'Then how did it manage?'

'At what distance from the sea did you leave this turtle?' asked the engineer, who, having suspended his work, was reflecting on this incident.

'Fifteen feet at the most,' replied Herbert.

'And the tide was low at the time?'

'Yes, captain.'

'Well,' replied the engineer, 'what the turtle could not do on the sand it might have been able to do in the water. It turned over when the tide overtook it, and then quietly returned to the deep sea.'

'Oh! what stupids we were!' cried Neb.

'That is precisely what I had the honour of telling you before!' returned the sailor.

Cyrus Harding had given this explanation, which no doubt, was admissible. But was he himself convinced of the accuracy of this explanation? It cannot be said that he was.

CHAPTER 9

On the 9th of October the bark canoe was entirely finished. Pencroft had kept his promise, and a light boat, the shell of which was joined together by the flexible twigs of the crejimba, had been constructed in five days. A seat in the stern, a second seat in the middle to preserve the equilibrium, a third seat in the bows, rowlocks for the two oars, a scull to steer with, completed the little craft, which was twelve feet long, and did not weigh more than 200 pounds.

The operation of launching it was extremely simple. The canoe was carried to the beach and laid on the sand before Granite House, and the rising tide floated it. Pencroft, who leapt in directly, manoeuvred it with the scull and declared it to be just the thing for the purpose to which they wished to put it.

Neb took one of the oars, Herbert the other, and Pencroft remained in the stern in order to use the scull.

The sailor first crossed the channel, and steered close to the southern point of the islet. A light breeze blew from the south. No roughness was found either in the channel or the green sea. A long swell, which the canoe scarcely felt, as it was heavily laden, rolled regularly over the surface of the water. They pulled out about half a mile distant from the shore, that they might have a good view of Mount Franklin.

After a voyage of three quarters of an hour, the canoe reached the extremity of the point, and Pencroft was preparing to return, when Herbert, rising, pointed to a black object saying, –

'What do I see down there, on the beach?'

All eyes turned towards the point indicated.

'Why,' said the reporter, 'there is something. It looks like part of a wreck half buried in the sand.'

'Ah!' cried Pencroft, 'I see what it is!'

'What?' asked Neb.

'Barrels, barrels, which perhaps are full,' replied the sailor.

'Pull to the shore, Pencroft!' said Cyrus.

A few strokes of the oar brought the canoe into a little creek, and its passengers leapt on shore.

Pencroft was not mistaken. Two barrels were there, half buried in the sand, but still firmly attached to a large chest, which, sustained by them, had floated to the moment when it stranded on the beach.

'There has been a wreck, then, in some part of the island,' said Herbert.

'Evidently,' replied Spilett.

'But what's in this chest?' cried Pencroft, with very natural impatience. 'What's in this chest? It is shut up, and nothing to open it with! Well, perhaps a stone – '

And the sailor, raising a heavy block, was about to break in one of the sides of the chest, when the engineer arrested his hand.

'Pencroft,' said he, 'can you restrain your impatience for one hour only?'

'But, captain, just think! Perhaps there is everything we want in there!'

'We shall find that out, Pencroft,' replied the engineer; 'but trust to me, and do not break the chest, which may be useful to us. We must convey it to Granite House, where we can open it easily, and without breaking it. It is quite prepared for a voyage; and, since it has floated here, it may just as well float to the mouth of the river.'

'You are right, captain, and I was wrong, as usual,' replied the sailor.

Having towed the barrels to Granite House, canoe and chest were then hauled up on the sand.

The covering of zinc was torn off and thrown back over the sides of the chest, and by degrees numerous articles of very varied character were produced and strewn about on the sand. At each new object Pencroft uttered fresh hurrahs.

'Even the photographic box!' exclaimed the sailor incredulously.

'As to that apparatus,' replied Harding, 'I do not quite see the use of it; and a more complete supply of clothes or more abundant ammunition would have been more valuable to us as well as to any other castaways!'

'But isn't there any mark or direction on these instruments, tools, or books, which would tell us something about them?' asked Gideon Spilett.

Looking at the entire contents laid out on the sand before them there seemed to be everything that the colonists needed: tools, weapons, instruments, clothes, books, chemicals and paper. Each article was carefully examined, especially the books, instruments, and weapons. Neither the weapons nor the instruments, contrary to the usual custom, bore the name of the maker; they were, besides, in a perfect state, and did not appear to have been used. The same peculiarity marked the tools and utensils; all were new, which proved that the articles had not been taken by chance and thrown into the chest; but, on the contrary, that the choice of the things had been well considered, and arranged with care.

It was considered by the colonists that there had been a shipwreck very recently on the shores of Lincoln Island and it meant that a serious exploration of their domain was more urgent than ever.

Consequently they set off in the canoe the next day. They rowed up the Mercy all morning but by the middle of the afternoon they could go no farther. The boat grated on the stony bottom of the river, which was now not more than twenty feet in breadth. The trees met like a bower overhead and caused a half-darkness. They moored the boat to a tree and agreed to camp just there.

They set off on foot at six o'clock the following morning. Progress was much slower now, they were forced to cut much of their way through when the undergrowth was too thick. At half-past nine the way was suddenly barred by an unknown stream, deep and clear but absolutely unnavigable. It was agreed to follow this river rather than attempt to cross it, as it must eventually come to the sea anyway. They advanced more rapidly and easily along the bank of the river than through the forest and within an hour the sea, and the whole western shore of the island lay before their eyes.

They immediately settled the name of the river as Falls River, owing to a small waterfall that had been created farther up the river which they had greatly admired, and the land before them, Serpentine peninsula. There was, however, nothing to show that a shipwreck had taken place recently.

They then began to prepare a camp for the night. A secluded site was chosen in front of masses of bamboo canes.

'This is a valuable discovery,' exclaimed Herbert.

'But why?' asked Pencroft.

'In India these bamboos are eaten like asparagus.'

'Asparagus thirty feet high!' exclaimed the sailor. 'And are they good?'

'Excellent,' replied Herbert. 'Only it is not the stems of thirty feet high which are eaten, but the young shoots.'

'Perfect, my boy, perfect!' replied Pencroft.

'I will also add that the pith of the young stalks, preserved in vinegar, makes a good pickle.'

'Better and better, Herbert!'

'And lastly, that the bamboos exude a sweet liquor which can be made into a very agreeable drink.'

'Is that all!' asked the sailor.

'That is all.'

'And they don't happen to do for smoking?'

'No, my poor Pencroft.'

Herbert and the sailor had not to look long for a place in which to pass the night. The rocks, which must have been violently beaten by the sea under the influence of the winds of the south-west, presented many cavities in which shelter could be found against the night air. But just as they were about to enter one of these caves a loud roaring arrested them.

'Back!' cried Pencroft. 'Our guns are only loaded with small shot, and beasts which can roar as loud as that would care no more for it than for grains of salt!' And the sailor, seizing Herbert by the arm, dragged him behind a rock, just as a magnificent animal showed itself at the entrance of the cavern.

It was a jaguar of a size at least equal to its Asiatic congeners, that is to say, it measured five feet from the extremity of its head to the beginning of its tail. The yellow colour of its hair was relieved by streaks and regular oblong spots of black, which contrasted with the white of its chest. Herbert recognised it as the ferocious rival of the tiger, as formidable as the puma, which is the rival of the largest wolf.

The jaguar advanced and gazed around him with blazing eyes, his hair bristling as if this was not the first time he had scented men.

At this moment the reporter appeared round a rock, and Herbert, thinking that he had not seen the jaguar, was about to rush towards him, when Gideon Spilett signed to him to remain where he was. This was not his first tiger, and advancing to within ten feet of the animal, he remained motionless, his gun to his shoulder, without moving a muscle. The jaguar collected itself for a spring, but at that moment a shot struck it in the eyes, and it fell dead.

Herbert and Pencroft rushed towards the jaguar. Neb and Harding also ran up, and they remained for some instants contemplating the animal as it lay stretched on the ground, thinking that its magnificent skin would be a great ornament to the hall at Granite House.

'Oh, Mr Spilett, how I admire and envy you!' cried Herbert, in a fit of very natural enthusiasm.

'Well, my boy,' replied the reporter, 'you could have done the same.'

'I! with such coolness! –'

'Imgaine to yourself, Herbert, that the jaguar is only a hare, and you would fire as quietly as possible.'

'That is,' rejoined Pencroft, 'that it is not more dangerous than a hare!'

'And now,' said Gideon Spilett, 'since the jaguar has left its abode, I do not see, my friends, why we should not take possession of it for the night.'

'But others may come,' said Pencroft.

'It will be enough to light a fire at the entrance of the cavern,' said the reporter, 'and no wild beasts will dare to cross the threshold.'

'Into the jaguar's house then!' replied the sailor, dragging after him the body of the animal.

Whilst Neb skinned the jaguar, his companions collected an

abundant supply of dry wood from the forest which they heaped up at the cave.

Cyrus Harding, seeing the clump of bamboos, cut a quantity which he mingled with the other fuel.

This done, they entered the grotto, of which the floor was strewn with bones, the guns were carefully loaded, in case of a sudden attack, they had supper, and then just before they lay down to rest, the heap of wood piled at the entrance was set fire to. Immediately, a regualr explosion, or rather, a series of reports, broke the silence! The noise was caused by the bamboos, which, as the flames reached them, exploded like fireworks. The noise was enough to terrify even the boldest of wild beasts.

It was not the engineer who had invented this way of causing loud explosions, for, according to Marco Polo, the Tartars have employed it for many centuries to drive away from their encampments the formidable wild beasts of Central Asia.

*

The southern coast still remained to be explored and this they did the following day. Pencroft was a little apprehensive about the safety of their boat though.

'The boat has remained by itself for one day at the source of the Mercy,' explained Gideon Spilett, 'it may just as well stay there two days. As yet, we have no reason to think that the island is infested by thieves!'

'Yet,' said the sailor, 'when I remember the history of the turtle, I am far from confident of that.'

Again they found nothing that indicated the presence of a wreck. Top, however, did find something of great use – it was a piece of cloth from the balloon which had transported them to Lincoln Island. Having shown the piece to the explorers he then led them to where the entire balloon case was caught in a glade of trees. This lucky find would furnish them with linen for years. It took them two hours to collect the cloth from the trees and it was five very weary explorers who set off once again in the direction of Granite House.

They had another four miles to go and it was midnight when, after having followed the shore to the mouth of the Mercy, the settlers arrived at the first angle formed by the Mercy. This river was about eighty feet in breadth and had to be crossed, so Pencroft decided that the best plan was to construct a sort of raft on which to make the passage.

*

Cyrus Harding and Spilett, seated on the bank, waited till their companions were ready for their help, whilst Herbert roamed about, though without going to any distance. All at once the lad, who had strolled by the river, came running back, and pointing up the Mercy, exclaimed, –

'What is floating there?'

Pencroft stopped working, and seeing an indistinct object moving through the gloom, – 'A canoe!' cried he.

All approached, and saw, to their extreme surprise, a boat floating down the current.

'Boat ahoy!' shouted the sailor, without thinking that perhaps it would be best to keep silence.

No reply. The boat still drifted onwards, and it was not more than twelve feet off, when the sailor exclaimed, –

'But it is our boat! she has broken her moorings, and floated down the current. I must say she has arrived very opportunely.'

'Our boat?' murmured the engineer.

Pencroft was right. It was indeed the canoe, of which the rope had undoubtedly broken, and which had come alone from the sources of the Mercy. It was very important to seize it before the rapid current should have swept it away out of the mouth of the river, but Neb and Pencroft cleverly managed this by means of a long pole.

The canoe touched the shore. The engineer leapt in first, and found, on examining the rope, that it had been really worn through by rubbing against the rocks.

'Well,' said the reporter to him, in a low voice; 'this is a strange thing.'

'Strange indeed!' returned Cyrus Harding.

Strange or not, it was very fortunate. Herbert, the reporter, Neb, and Pencroft, embarked in turn. There was no doubt about the rope having been worn through, but the astonishing part of the affair was, that the boat should have arrived just at the moment when the settlers were there to seize it on its way, for a quarter of an hour earlier or later it would have been lost in the sea.

If they had been living in the time of genii, this incident would have given them the right to think that the island was haunted by some supernatural being, who used his power in the service of the castaways!

A few strokes of the oar brought the settlers to the mouth of the Mercy. The canoe was hauled up on the beach near the Chimneys, and all proceeded towards the ladder of Granite House.

But at that moment, Top barked angrily, and Neb, who was looking for the first steps, uttered a cry.

There was no longer a ladder!

'I begin to think that very curious things happen in Lincoln Island!' said Pencroft.

'Curious?' replied Gideon Spilett, 'not at all, Pencroft, nothing can be more natural. Some one has come during our absence, and taken possession of our dwelling and drawn up the ladder.'

'Some one!' cried the sailor. 'But who?'

'Who but the hunter who fired the bullet?' replied the reporter.

'Well, if there is any one up there,' replied Pencroft, who began to lose patience, 'I will give them a hail, and they must answer.'

And in a stentorian voice the sailor gave a prolonged 'Halloo!' which was echoed again and again from the cliff and rocks.

The settlers listened, and they thought they heard a sort of chuckling laugh, of which they could not guess the origin. But no voice replied to Pencroft, who in vain repeated his vigorous shouts.

The weary companions wandered around beneath Granite House for several hours, but there was nothing that they could do except wait until morning and so they went to sleep at the Chimneys, leaving Top on guard at Granite House.

The following morning they rose very early, eager to discover who had invaded their home. Herbert thought of fastening a cord to an arrow, and shooting the arrow so that it should pass between the first rounds of the ladder which hung from the threshold. By means of the cord they would then be able to draw the ladder.

The bow was bent, the arrow flew, taking the cord with it and passed between the two last rounds.

The operation had succeeded.

Herbert immediately seized the end of the cord, but, at that moment when he gave it a pull to bring down the ladder, an arm, thrust suddenly out between the wall and the door, grasped it and dragged it inside Granite House.

'Apes, apes!' cried Herbert 'We have been invaded by apes!'

And as if to verify this statement several big apes appeared at the windows of Granite House. Pencroft shot one of them but the others rushed away from the openings at this.

All morning they waited around the entrance to Granite House without any further movement from inside or any further appearances. Finally Harding announced that their only solution was to enter their home by the old opening at the lake, although they had wanted to avoid this as it would ruin the camouflage there. It was agreed they should do this immediately.

It was already past twelve o'clock, when the colonists, well armed and provided with picks and spades, left the Chimneys, passed beneath the windows of the Granite House, after telling Top to remain at his post, and began to ascend the left bank of the Mercy, so as to reach Prospect Heights.

But they had not made fifty steps in this direction, when they heard the dog barking furiously.

And all rushed down the bank again.

Arrived at the turning, they saw that the situation had changed.

In fact, the apes, seized with a sudden panic, from some unknown cause, were trying to escape. Two or three ran and clambered from one window to another with the agility of acrobats. They were not even trying to replace the ladder, by which it would have been easy to descend; perhaps in their terror they had forgotten this way of escape. The colonists, now being able to take aim without difficulty, fired. Some, wounded or killed, fell back into the rooms, uttering piercing cries. The rest, throwing themselves out, were dashed to pieces in their fall, and in a few minutes, so far as they knew, there was not a living quadrumana in Granite House.

At this moment the ladder was seen to slip over the threshold, then unroll and fall to the ground.

'Hullo!' cried the sailor, 'this is queer!'

'Very strange!' murmured the engineer, leaping first up the ladder.

'Take care, captain!' cried Pencroft, 'perhaps there are still some of these rascals. . . .'

'We shall soon see,' replied the engineer, without stopping however.

All his companions followed him, and in a minute they had arrived at the threshold. They searched everywhere. There was no one in the rooms nor in the storehouse, which had been respected by the band of quadrumana.

'Well, now, and the ladder,' cried the sailor; 'who can the gentleman have been who sent us that down?'

But at that moment a cry was heard, and a great orang, who had hidden himself in the passage, rushed into the room, pursued by Neb.

'Ah, the robber!' cried Pencroft.

And hatchet in hand, he was about to cleave the head of the animal, when Cyrus Harding seized his arm, saying, –

'Spare him, Pencroft.'

'Pardon this rascal?'

'Yes! It was he who threw us the ladder!'

And the engineer said this in such a peculiar voice that it was difficult to know whether he spoke seriously or not.

Nevertheless, they threw themselves on the orang, who defended himself gallantly, but was soon overpowered and bound.

'There!' said Pencroft. 'And what shall we make of him, now we've got him?'

'A servant!' replied Herbert.

The lad was not joking in saying this, for he knew how this intelligent race could be turned to account.

Thus the Colony was increased by a new member. He was named Jupiter, and Jup for short.

CHAPTER 10

THE settlers in Lincoln Island had now regained their dwelling, without having been obliged to reach it by the old opening, and were therefore spared the trouble of mason's work. It was certainly lucky, that at the moment they were about to set out to do so, the apes had been seized with that terror, no less sudden than inexplicable, which had driven them out of Granite House. Had the animals discovered that they were about to be attacked from another direction? This was the only explanation of their sudden retreat.

During the day the bodies of the apes were carried into the wood, where they were buried: then the settlers busied themselves in repairing the disorder caused by the intruders, disorder but not damage, for although they had turned everything in the rooms topsy-turvy, yet they had broken nothing. Neb relighted his stove, and the stores in the larder furnished a substantial repast, to which all did ample justice.

Jup was not forgotten, and he ate with relish some stone pine almonds and rhizome roots, with which he was abundantly supplied. Pencroft had unfastened his arms, but judged it best to have his legs tied until they were more sure of his submission.

Then, before retiring to rest, Harding and his companions, seated round their table, discussed those plans, the execution of which was most pressing. The most important and most urgent was the establishment of a bridge over the Mercy, so as to form a communication with the southern part of the island and Granite House; then the making of an enclosure for the musmons or other woolly animals which they wished to capture.

These two projects would help to solve the difficulty as to their clothing, which was now serious. The bridge would render easy the transport of the balloon case, which would furnish them with linen, and the inhabitants of the enclosure would yield wool which would supply them with winter clothes.

As to the enclosure, it was Cyrus Harding's intention to establish it at the sources of the Red Creek, where the ruminants would find fresh and abundant pasture. The road between Prospect Heights and the sources of the stream was already partly beaten, and with a better cart than the first, the material could be easily conveyed to the spot, especially if they could manage to capture some animals to draw it.

But though there might be no inconvenience in the enclosure being so far from Granite House, it would not be the same with the poultry-yard, to which Neb called the attention of the colonists. It was indeed necessary that the birds should be close within reach of the cook, and no place appeared more favourable for the establishment of the said poultry-yard than that portion of the banks of the lake which was close to the old opening.

Water-birds would prosper there as well as others, and the couple of tinamous taken in their last excursion would be the first to be domesticated.

The next day, the 3rd of November, the new works were begun by the construction of the bridge, and all hands were required for this important task. Saws, hatchets, and hammers were shouldered by the settlers, who, now transformed into carpenters, descended to the shore.

There Pencroft observed, –

'Suppose that during our absence, Master Jup takes it into his head to draw up the ladder which he so politely returned to us yesterday?'

'Let us tie its lower end down firmly,' replied Cyrus Harding.

This was done by means of two stakes securely fixed in the sand. Then the settlers, ascending the left bank of the Mercy, soon arrived at the angle formed by the river.

There they halted, in order to ascertain if the bridge could be thrown across. The place appeared suitable.

In fact, from this spot, to Port Balloon, discovered the day before on the southern coast, there was only a distance of three miles and a half, and from the bridge to the Port, it would be easy to make a good cart-road which would render the communication between Granite House and the south of the island extremely easy.

Cyrus Harding now imparted to his companions a scheme for completely isolating Prospect Heights so as to shelter it from the attacks both of apes and other animals. In this way, Granite House, the Chimneys, the poultry-yard, and all the upper part of the plateau which was to be used for cultivation, would be protected against the depredations of animals. Nothing could be easier than to execute this project, and this is how the engineer intended to set to work.

The plateau was already defended on three sides by watercourses, either artificial or natural. On the north-west, by the shores of Lake Grant, from the entrance of the passage to the breach made in the banks of the lake for the escape of the water.

On the north, from this breach to the sea, by the new watercourse which had hollowed out a bed for itself across the plateau and shore, above and below the fall, and it would be enough to dig the bed of this creek a little deeper to make it impracticable for animals, on all the eastern border by the sea itself, from the mouth of the aforesaid creek to the mouth of the Mercy.

Lastly, on the south, from the mouth to the turn of the Mercy where the bridge was to be established.

The western border of the plateau now remained between the turn of the river and the southern angle of the lake, a distance of about a mile, which was open to all comers. But nothing could be easier than to dig a broad deep ditch, which could be filled from the lake, and the overflow of which would throw itself by a rapid fall into the bed of the Mercy. The level of the lake would, no doubt, be somewhat lowered by this fresh discharge of its waters, but Cyrus Harding had ascertained that the volume of water in the Red Creek was considerable enough to allow of the execution of this project.

'So then,' added the engineer, 'Prospect Heights will become a regular island, being surrounded with water on all sides, and only communicating with the rest of our domain by the bridge which we are about to throw across the Mercy, the two little bridges already established above and below the fall; and, lastly, two other little bridges which must be constructed, one over the canal which I propose to dig, the other across to the left bank of the Mercy, Now if these bridges can be raised at will, Prospect Heights will be guarded from any surprise.

Thus the colonists were kept very busy during the weeks to come. Aided by tools and instruments found in the barrels, a moveable bridge was built across the Mercy. The canal was dug to make Prospect Heights into the envisaged island within an island and the colonists were well pleased with the result. A poultry yard was constructed quite near to Granite House and gradually the inhabitants moved in until quite a community existed there. A lift was built, which was powered by water, to replace the ladder so that getting up to Granite House was easier.

Work was continued in other parts of the island too. An animal enclosure was built at the foot of Mount Franklin to house many of the animals that the colonists had caught at one time or another. This included a pair of onagas, animals similar in build to the zebra, which had been trained by Herbert to be ridden and to pull the cart. Near the corral the second 'corn field' was planted – consisting of ten ears of corn from the first seed that had been planted, Pencroft calculated that these ten ears contained eighty grains and therefore, their second harvest would be proportionally larger than the first.

At least one result of the completion of the main building work which was to have lasting consequences for them all, was the idea that Pencroft had of building a boat large enough to sail round the island. Their construction work of late had proved it possible and the momentary pause in the work, due to the winter months advancing stimulated the desire.

When Pencroft had once got a plan into his head, he had no peace till it was executed.

He talked about it a great deal and it was finally decided that a decked boat should be built.

What wood should be employed? Elm or fir, both of which abounded in the island? They decided for the fir, as being easy to work, but which stands water as well as the elm.

These details settled, it was agreed that since the fine season would not return before six months, Cyrus Harding and Pencroft should work alone at the boat. Gideon Spilett and Herbert were to continue to hunt, and neither Neb nor Master Jup his assistant were to leave the domestic duties which had devolved upon them.

Directly the trees were chosen, they were felled, stripped of their branches, and sawn into planks as well as sawyers would have been able to do it. A week after, in the recess between the Chimneys and the cliff, a dockyard was prepared, and a keel five-and-thirty feet long, furnished with a stern-post at the stern and a stem at the bows, lay along the sand.

Cyrus Harding was not working in the dark at this new trade. He knew as much about shipbuilding as about nearly everything else, and he had at first drawn the model of his ship on paper. Besides, he was ably seconded by Pencroft, who, having worked for several years in a dockyard at Brooklyn, knew the practical part of the trade. It was not until after careful calculation and deep thought that the timbers were laid on the keel.

Pencroft, as may be believed, was all eagerness to carry out his new enterprise, and would not leave his work for an instant.

A single thing had the honour of drawing him, but for one day only, from his dockyard. This was the second wheat harvest, which was gathered in on the 15th April. It was as much a success as the first, and yielded the number of grains which had been predicted.

'Five bushels, captain,' said Pencroft, after having scrupulously measured his treasure.

'Five bushels,' replied the engineer; 'and a hundred and thirty thousand grains a bushel will make six hundred and fifty thousand grains.'

'Well, we will sow them all this time,' said the sailor, 'except a little in reserve.'

'Yes, Pencroft, and if the next crop gives a proportionate yield, we shall have four thousand bushels.'

'And shall we eat bread?'

'We shall eat bread.'

'But we must have a mill.'

'We will make one.'

The third corn-field was very much larger than the two first, and the soil, prepared with extreme care, received the precious seed. That done, Pencroft returned to his work.

During this time Spilett and Herbert hunted in the neighbourhood, and they ventured deep into the still unknown parts of the

Far West, their guns loaded with ball, ready for any dangerous emergency. It was a vast thicket of magnificent trees, crowded together as if pressed for room. The exploration of these dense masses of wood was difficult in the extreme, and the reporter never ventured there without the pocket-compass, for the sun scarcely pierced through the thick foliage, and it would have been very difficult for them to retrace their way. It naturally happened that game was more rare in those situations where there was hardly sufficient room to move; two or three large herbivorous animals were however killed during the last fortnight of April. These were koalas, specimens of which the settlers had already seen to the north of the lake, and which stupidly allowed themselves to be killed among the thick branches of the trees in which they took refuge. Their skins were brought back to Granite House, and there, by the help of sulphuric acid, they were subjected to a sort of tanning process which rendered them capable of being used.

On the 30th of April, the two sportsmen were in the depth of the Far West, when the reporter, preceding Herbert a few paces, arrived in a sort of clearing, into which the trees, more sparsely scattered, had permitted a few rays to penetrate. Gideon Spilett was at first surprised at the odour which exhaled from certain plants with straight stalks, round and branchy, bearing grape-like clusters of flowers and very small berries. The reporter broke off one or two of these stalks and returned to the lad, to whom he said, –

'What can this be, Herbert?'

'Well, Mr Spilett,' said Herbert, 'this is a treasure which will secure you Pencroft's gratitude for ever.'

'Is it tobacco?'

'Yes, and though it may not be of the first quality, it is none the less tobacco!'

'Oh, good old Pencroft! Won't he be pleased? But we must not let him smoke it all, he must give us our share.'

'Ah! an idea occurs to me, Mr Spilett,' replied Herbert. 'Don't let us say anything to Pencroft yet; we will prepare these leaves, and one fine day we will present him with a pipe already filled!'

'All right, Herbert, and on that day our worthy companion will have nothing left to wish for in this world.'

The reporter and the lad secured a good store of the precious plant, and then returned to Granite House, where they smuggled it in with as much precaution as if Pencroft had been the most vigilant and severe of custom-house officers.

Cyrus Harding and Neb were taken into confidence, and the sailor suspected nothing during the whole time, necessarily somewhat long, which was required in order to dry the small leaves, chop them up, and subject them to a certain torrefaction on hot stones. This took two months; but all these manipulations were successfully carried on unknown to Pencroft, for, occupied with the construction of his boat, he only rturned to Granite House at the hour of rest.

For some days they had observed an enormous animal two or three miles out in the open sea swimming around Lincoln Island. This was a whale of the largest size, which apparently belonged to the southern species, called the 'Cape Whale.'

'What a lucky chance it would be if we could capture it!' cried the sailor. 'Ah? if we only had a proper boat and a good harpoon, I would say, "After the beast," for he would be well worth the trouble of catching!'

'Well, Pencroft,' observed Harding, 'I should much like to watch you handling a harpoon. It would be very interesting.'

'I am astonished,' said the reporter, 'to see a whale in this comparatively high latitude.'

'Why so, Mr Spilett?' replied Herbert. 'We are exactly in that part of the Pacific which the English and American whalemen call the whale-field, and it is here, between New Zealand and South America, that the whales of the southern hemisphere are met with in the greatest numbers.'

And Pencroft returned to his work, not without uttering a sigh of regret, for every sailor is a born fisherman, and if the pleasure of fishing is in exact proportion to the size of the animal, one can judge how a whaler feels in sight of a whale. And if this had only been for pleasure! But they could not help feeling how valuable such a prize would have been to the colony, for the oil, the fat, and the bones would have been put to many uses.

Now it happened that this whale appeared to have no wish to leave the waters of the island. Therefore, whether from the windows of Granite House, or from Prospect Heights, Herbert and Gideon Spilett, when they were not hunting, or Neb unless presiding over his fires, never left the telescope, but watched all the animal's movements. The cetacean, having entered far into Union Bay, made rapid furrows across it from Mandible Cape to Claw Cape, propelled by its enormously powerful flukes, on which it supported itself, and making its way through the water at the rate little short of twelve knots an hour. Sometimes also it approached so near to the island that it could be clearly distinguished. It was the southern whale, which is completely black, the head being more depressed than that of the northern whale.

They could also see it throwing up from its air-holes to a great height, a cloud of vapour or of water, for, strange as it may appear, naturalists and whalers are not agreed on this subject. Is it air or is it water which is thus driven out? It is generally admitted to be vapour, which, condensing suddenly by contact with the cold air, falls again as rain.

However, the presence of this mammifer preocupied the

colonists. It irritated Pencroft especially, as he could think of nothing else while at work. He ended by longing for it, like a child for a thing which it has been denied At night he talked about it in his sleep, and certainly if he had had the means of attacking it, if the sloop had been in a fit state to put to sea, he would not have hesitated to set out in pursuit.

But what the colonists could not do for themselves, chance did for them, and on the 3rd of May, shouts from Neb, who had stationed himself at the kitchen window, announced that the whale was stranded on the beach of the island.

Herbert and Gideon Spilett, who were just about to set out hunting, left their guns, Pencroft threw down his axe, and Harding and Neb joining their companions, all rushed towards the scene of action.

The stranding had taken place on the beach of Flotsam Point, three miles from Granite House, and at high tide. It was therefore probable that the cetacean would not be able to extricate itself easily; at any rate it was best to hasten, so as to cut off its retreat if necessary. They ran with pickaxes and iron-tipped poles in their hands, passed over the Mercy bridge, descended the right bank of the river, along the beach, and in less than twenty minutes the settlers were close to the enormous animal, above which flocks of birds already hovered.

'What a monster!' cried Neb.

And the exclamation was natural, for it was a southern whale, eighty feet long, a giant of the species, probably not weighing less than a hundred and fifty thousand pounds!

In the meanwhile, the monster thus stranded did not move, nor attempt by struggling to regain the water whilst the tide was still high.

It was dead, and a harpoon was sticking out of its left side.

'There are whalers in these quarters, then?' said Gideon Spilett directly.

'Oh, Mr Spilett, that doesn't prove anything!' replied Pencroft. 'Whales have been known to go thousands of miles with a harpoon in the side, and this one might even have been struck in the north of the Atlantic and come to die in the south of the Pacific, and it would be nothing astonishing.'

Pencroft, having torn the harpoon from the animal's side, read this inscription on it : –

'"MARIA STELLA,"
VINEYARD.'

'A vessel from the Vineyard! A ship from my country!' he cried. 'The "Maria Stella!" A fine whaler, 'pon my word; I know her well! Oh, my friends, a vessel from the Vineyard! – a whaler from the Vineyard!' [1]

And the sailor brandishing the harpoon, repeated, not without

[1] A port in the State of New York.

emotion, the name which he loved so well – the name of his birth-place.

But as it could not be expected that the 'Maria Stella' would come to reclaim the animal harpooned by her, they resolved to begin cutting it up before decomposition should commence. The birds, who had watched this rich prey for several days, had determined to take possession of it without further delay, and it was necessary to drive them off by firing at them repeatedly.

The whale was a female, and a large quantity of milk was taken from it, which, according to the opinion of the naturalist Duffenbach, might pass for cow's milk, and, indeed, it differs from it neither in taste, colour, nor density.

Pencroft had formerly served on board a whaling-ship, and he could methodically direct the operation of cutting up – a sufficiently disagreeable operation lasting three days, but from which the settlers did not flinch, not even Gideon Spilett, who, as the sailor said, would end by making a 'real good cast-away.'

The blubber, cut in parallel slices of two feet and a half in thickness, then divided into pieces which might weigh about a thousand pounds each, was melted down in large earthen pots brought to the spot, for they did not wish to taint the environs of Granite House, and in this fusion it lost nearly a third of its weight.

But there was an immense quantity of it; the tongue alone yielded six thousand pounds of oil, and the lower lip four thousand. Then, besides the fat, which would insure for a long time a store of stearine and glycerine, there were still the bones, for which a use could doubtless be found, although there were neither umbrellas nor stays used at Granite House. The upper part of the mouth of the cetacean was, indeed, provided on both sides with eight hundred horny blades, very elastic, of a fibrous texture, and fringed at the edge like great combs, of which the teeth, six feet long, served to retain the thousands of animalculae, little fish, and molluscs, on which the whale fed.

The operation finished, to the great satisfaction of the operators the remains of the animal were left to the birds, who would soon make every vestige of it disappear, and their usual daily occu-pations were resumed by the inmates of Granite House.

However, before returning to the dockyard, Cyrus Harding conceived the idea of fabricating certain machines, which greatly excited the curiosity of his companions. He took a dozen of the whale's bones, cut them into six equal parts, and sharpened their ends.

'This machine is not my own invention, and it is frequently employed by the Aleutian hunters in Russian America. You see these bones, my friends; well, when it freezes, I will bend them, and then wet them with water till they are entirely covered

63

with ice, which will keep them bent, and I will strew them on the snow, having previously covered them with fat. Now, what will happen if a hungry animal swallows one of these baits? Why, the heat of his stomach will melt the ice, and the bone, springing straight, will pierce him with its sharp points.'

'Well! I do call that ingenious!' said Pencroft.

'And it will spare the powder and shot,' rejoined Cyrus Harding.

'That will be better than traps!' added Neb.

In the meanwhile the boat-building progressed, and towards the end of the month half the planking was completed. It could already be seen that her shape was excellent, and that she would sail well.

Pencroft worked with unparalleled ardour, and only a sturdy frame could have borne such fatigue; but his companions were preparing in secret a reward for his labours, and on the 31st of May he was to meet with one of the greatest joys of his life.

On that day, after dinner, just as he was about to leave the table, Pencroft felt a hand on his shoulder.

It was the hand of Gideon Spilett, who said, –

'One moment, Master Pencroft, you mustn't sneak off like that! You've forgotten your dessert.'

'Thank you, Mr Spilett,' replied the sailor, 'I am going back to my work.'

'Well, a cup of coffee, my friend?'

'Nothing more.'

'A pipe, then?'

Pencroft jumped up, and his great good-natured face grew pale when he saw the reporter presenting him with a ready-filled pipe, and Herbert with a glowing coal.

The sailor endeavoured to speak, but could not get out a word; so seizing the pipe, he carried it to his lips then applying the coal, he drew five or six great whiffs. A fragrant blue cloud soon arose, and from its depths a voice was heard repeating excitedly, –

'Tobacco! Real tobacco!'

'Yes, Pencroft,' returned Cyrus Harding, 'and very good tobacco too!'

'Oh, divine Providence! sacred Author of all things!' cried the sailor. 'Nothing more is now wanting to our island.'

And Pencroft smoked, and smoked, and smoked.

'And who made this discovery?' he asked at length. 'You, Herbert, no doubt?'

'No, Pencroft, it was Mr Spilett.'

'Mr Spilett!' exclaimed the sailor, seizing the reporter, and clasping him to his breast with such a squeeze that he had never felt anything like it before.

'Oh, Pencroft,' said Spilett, recovering his breath at last, 'a truce for one moment. You must share your gratitude with Herbert, who recognised the plant; with Cyrus, who prepared it; and with Neb, who took a great deal of trouble to keep our secret.'

'Well, my friends, I will repay you some day,' replied the sailor. 'Now we are friends for life.'

CHAPTER 11

THE first snow fell towards the end of the month of June. The corral had previously been largely supplied with stores, so that daily visits to it were not requisite; but it was decided that more than a week should never be allowed to pass without some one going to it.

Traps were again set, and the machines manufactured by Harding were tried. The bent whalebones, imprisoned in a case of ice, and covered with a thick outer layer of fat, were placed on the border of the forest at a spot where animals usually passed on their way to the lake.

To the engineer's great satisfaction, this invention, copied from the Aleutian fisherman, succeeded perfectly. A dozen foxes, a few wild boars, and even a jaguar, were taken in this way, the animals being found dead, their stomachs pierced by the unbent bones.

An incident must here be related, not only as interesting in itself, but because it was the first attempt made by the colonists to communicate with the rest of mankind.

Gideon Spilett had already several times pondered whether to throw into the sea a letter enclosed in a bottle, which currents might perhaps carry to an inhabited coast, or to confide it to pigeons. But how could it be seriously hoped that either pigeons or bottles could cross the distance of twelve hundred miles which separated the island from any inhabited land? It would have been pure folly.

But on the 30th of June the capture was effected, not without difficulty, of an albatross, which a shot from Herbert's gun had slightly wounded in the foot. It was a magnificent bird, measuring ten feet from wing to wing, and which could traverse seas as wide as the Pacific.

Herbert would have liked to keep this superb bird, as its wound would soon heal, and he thought he could tame it; but Spilett explained to him that they should not neglect this opportunity of attempting to communicate by this messenger with the lands of the Pacific; for if the Albatross had come from some inhabited region, there was no doubt but that it would return there so soon as it was set free.

Perhaps in his heart Gideon Spilett, in whom the journalist sometimes came to the surface, was not sorry to have the opportunity of sending forth to take its chance an exciting article relating the adventures of the settlers in Lincoln Island. What a success for the authorised reporter of the *New York Herald*, and for the number which should contain the article, if it should ever reach the address of its editor, the Honourable John Benett!

Gideon Spilett then wrote out a concise account, which was placed in a strong waterproof bag, with an earnest request to whoever might find it to foward it to the office of the *New York Herald*. This little bag was fastened to the neck of the albatross, and not to its foot, for these birds are in the habit of resting on the surface of the sea; then liberty was given to that swift courier of the air, and it was not without some emotion that the colonists watched it disappear in the misty west.

'Where is he going to?' asked Pencroft.

'Towards New Zealand,' replied Herbert.

'A good voyage to you!' shouted the sailor, who himself did not expect any great result from this mode of correspondence.

With the winter work had been resumed in the interior of Granite House, mending clothes and different occupations; amongst others, making the sails for their vessel, which were cut from the inexhaustible balloon-case.

During the month of July the cold was intense, but there was no lack of either wood or coal. Cyrus Harding had established a second fire-place in the dining-room, and there the long winter evenings were spent. Talking whilst they worked, reading when the hands remained idle, the time passed with profit to all.

It was real enjoyment to the settlers when in their room, well lighted with candles, well warmed with coal, after a good dinner, elder-berry coffee smoking in the cups, the pipes giving forth an odoriferous smoke, they could hear the storm howling without. Their comfort would have been complete, if complete comfort could ever exist for those who are far from their fellow-creatures, and without any means of communication with them. They often talked of their country, of the friends whom they had left, of the grandeur of the American Republic, whose influence could not but increase; and Cyrus Harding, who had been much mixed up with the affairs of the Union, greatly interested his auditors by his recitals, his views, and his prognostics.

It was on one such evening when they were all sitting in the warm discussing various topics of interest common to them all, when Top suddenly began to bark.

'What can Top be barking in that way for?' asked Pencroft.

'And Jup be growling like that?' added Herbert.

In fact the orang, joining the dog, gave unequivocal signs of agitation, and, singular to say, the two animals appeared more uneasy than angry.

'It is evident,' said Gideon Spilett, 'that this well is in direct communication with the sea, and that some marine animal comes from time to time to breathe at the bottom.'

'That's evident,' replied the sailor, 'and there can be no other explanation to give. Quiet there, Top!' added Pencroft, turning to the dog, 'and you, Jup, be off to your room!'

The ape and the dog were silent. Jup went off to bed, but Top remained in the room, and continued to utter low growls at intervals during the rest of the evening. There was no further talk on the subject, but the incident, however, clouded the brow of the engineer.

During the remainder of the month of July there was alternate rain and frost. The temperature was not so low as during the preceding winter, and its maximum did not exceed eight degrees Fahrenheit. But although this winter was less cold, it was more troubled by storms and squalls; the sea besides often endangered the safety of the Chimneys. At times it almost seemed as if an under-current raised these monstrous billows which thundered against the wall of Granite House.

When the settlers, leaning from their windows, gazed on the huge watery masse beneath their eyes, they could not but admire the magnificent spectacle of the ocean in its impotent fury. The waves rebounded in dazzling foam, the beach entirely disappearing under the raging flood, and the cliff appearing to emerge from the sea itself, the spray rising to a height of more than a hundred feet.

During these storms it was difficult and even dangerous to venture out, owing to the frequently falling trees; however, the colonists never allowed a week to pass without having paid a visit to the corral. Happily this enclosure, sheltered by the south-eastern spur of Mount Franklin, did not greatly suffer from the violence of the hurricanes, which spared its trees, sheds, and palisades; but the poultry-yard on Prospect Heights, being directly exposed to the gusts of wind from the east, suffered considerable damage.

Why did Top so often run round this opening? Why did he utter such strange barks when a sort of uneasiness seemed to draw him towards this well? Why did Jup join Top in a sort of common anxiety? Had this well branches besides the communication with the sea? Did it spread towards other parts of the island? This is what Cyrus Harding wished to know. He had resolved, therefore, to attempt the exploration of the well during the absence of his companions, and an opportunity for doing so had now presented itself – the other four were going on a hunting expedition, taking advantage of a day of moderate weather.

It was easy to descend to the bottom of the well by employing the rope-ladder which had not been used since the establishment of the lift. The engineer drew the ladder to the hole, the diameter of which measured nearly six feet, and allowed it to unroll itself after having securely fastened its upper extremity. Then, having lighted a lantern, taken a revolver, and placed a cutlass in his belt, he began the descent.

The sides were everywhere entire; but points of rock jutted out here and there, and by means of these points it would have been quite possible for an active creature to climb to the mouth of the well.

The engineer remarked this; but although he carefully examined these points by the light of his lantern, he could find no impression, no fracture which could give any reason to suppose that they had either recently or at any former time been used as a staircase. Cyrus Harding descended deeper, throwing the light of his lantern on all sides.

He saw nothing suspicious.

When the engineer had reached the last rounds he came upon the water, which was then perfectly calm. Neither at its level nor in any other part of the well, did any passage open which could lead to the interior of the cliff. The wall which Harding struck with the hilt of his cutlass sounded solid. It was compact granite, through which no living being could force a way. To arrive at the bottom of the well and then climb up to its mouth it was necessary to pass through the channel under the rocky sub-soil of the beach, which placed it in communication with the sea, and this was only possible for marine animals. As to the question of knowing where this channel ended, at what point of the shore, and at what depth beneath the water, it could not be answered.

Then Cyrus Harding, having ended his survey, re-ascended, drew up the ladder, covered the mouth of the well, and returned thoughtfully to the dining-room, saying to himself, –

'I have seen nothing, and yet there *is* something there!'

In the evening the hunters returned, having enjoyed good sport, and being literally loaded with game; indeed, they had as much as four men could possibly carry. Top wore a necklace of teal and Jup wreaths of snipe round his body.

'Here, master,' cried Neb; 'here's something to employ our time! Preserved and made into pies we shall have a welcome store! But I must have some one to help me. I count on you, Pencroft.'

'No, Neb,' replied the sailor; 'I have the rigging of the vessel to finish and to look after, and you will have to do without me.'

'And you, Mr Herbert?'

'I must go to the corral tomorrow, Neb,' replied the lad.

'It will be you then, Mr Spilett, who will help me?'

'To oblige you, Neb, I will,' replied the reporter; 'but I warn you that if you disclose your receipts to me, I shall publish them.'

'Whenever you like, Mr Spilett,' replied Neb; 'whenever you like.'

And so the next day Gideon Spilett became Neb's assistant, and was installed in his culinary laboratory. The engineer had previously made known to him the result of the exploration which he had made the day before, and on this point the reporter shared Harding's opinion, that although he had found nothing, a secret still remained to be discovered!

The frost continued for another week, and the settlers did not leave Granite House unless to look after the poultry-yard. The dwelling was filled with appetising odours, which were emitted from the learned manipulation of Neb and the reporter. But all the results of the chase were not made into preserved provisions; and as the game kept perfectly in the intense cold, wild duck and other fowl were eaten fresh, and declared superior to all other aquatic birds in the known world.

During this week Pencroft, aided by Herbert, who handled the sail-maker's needle with much skill, worked with such energy that the sails of the vessel were finished. There was no want of cordage. Thanks to the rigging which had been recovered with the case of the balloon, the ropes and cables from the net were all of good quality, and the sailor turned them all to account. To the sails were attached strong bolt ropes, and there still remained enough from which to make the halliards, shrouds, and sheets, &c. The blocks were manufactured by Cyrus Harding, under Pencroft's directions, by means of the turning-lathe. It therefore happened that the rigging was entirely prepared before the vessel was finished. Pencroft also manufactured a flag, that flag so dear to every true American, containing the stars and stripes of their glorious Union. The colours for it were supplied from certain plants used in dyeing, and which were very abundant in the island; only to the thirty-seven stars, representing the thirty-seven States of the Union, which shine on the American flag, the sailor added a thirty-eighth, the star of 'the State of Lincoln', for he considered his island as already united to the great republic. 'And,' said he, 'it is so already in heart, if not in deed!'

In the meantime, the flag was hoisted at the central window of Granite House, and the settlers saluted it with three cheers.

The cold season was now almost at an end, and it appeared as if this second winter was to pass without any unusual occurrence, when, on the night of the 11th August, the plateau of Prospect Heights was menaced with complete destruction.

After a busy day the colonists were sleeping soundly, when

towards four o'clock in the morning they were suddenly awakened by Top's barking.

The dog was not this time barking near the mouth of the well, but at the threshold of the door, at which he was scratching as if he wished to burst it open. Jup was also uttering piercing cries.

'Hallo, Top!' cried Neb, who was the first awake. But the dog continued to bark more furiously than ever.

'What's the matter now?' asked Harding.

And all, dressing in haste, rushed to the windows, which they opened.

Beneath their eyes was spread a sheet of snow which looked grey in the dim light. The settlers could see nothing, but they heard a singular yelping noise away in the darkness. It was evident that the beach had been invaded by a number of animals which could not be seen.

'What are they?' cried Pencroft.

'Wolves, jaguars, or apes?' replied Neb.

'They have nearly reached the plateau,' said the reporter.

'And our poultry-yard,' exclaimed Herbert, 'and our garden!'

'Where can they have crossed?' asked Pencroft.

'They must have crossed the bridge on the shore,' replied the engineer, 'which one of us must have forgotten to close.'

'True,' said Spilett, 'I remember to have left it open.'

'A fine job you have made of it, Mr Spilett,' cried the sailor.

'What is done cannot be undone,' replied Cyrus Harding. 'We must consult what it will now be best to do.'

Such were the questions and answers which were rapidly exchanged between Harding and his companions. It was certain that the bridge had been crossed, that the shore had been invaded by animals, and that whatever they might be, they could, by ascending the left bank of the Mercy, reach Prospect Heights. They must therefore be advanced against quickly and fought with if necessary.

'But what are these beasts?' was asked a second time, as the yelpings were again heard more loudly than before. These yelps made Herbert start, and he remembered to have already heard them during his first visit to the sources of the Red Creek.

'They are culpeux foxes!' he exclaimed.

'Forward!' shouted the sailor.

And all arming themselves with hatchets, carbines, and revolvers, threw themselves into the lift and soon set foot on the shore.

Culpeux are dangerous animals when in great numbers and irritated by hunger; nevertheless the colonists did not hesitate to throw themselves into the midst of the troop, and their first shots, vividly lighting up the darkness, made their assailants draw back.

The chief thing was to hinder these plunderers from reaching the plateau, for the garden and the poultry-yard would then have been at their mercy, and immense, perhaps irreparable mischief, would inevitably be the result, especially with regard to the corn-field. But as the invasion of the plateau could only be made by the left bank of the Mercy, it was sufficient to oppose the culpeux on the narrow bank between the river and the cliff of granite.

This plain to all, and by Cyrus Harding's orders they reached the spot indicated by him, while the culpeux rushed fiercely through the gloom. Harding, Gideon Spilett, Herbert, Pencroft and Neb, posted themselves in impregnable line. Top, his formidable jaws open, preceded the colonists, and he was followed by Jup, armed with knotty cudgel, which he brandished like a club.

The night was extremely dark, it was only by the flashes from the revolvers as each person fired that they could see their assailants, who were at least a hundred in number, and whose eyes were glowing like hot coals.

'They must not pass!' shouted Pencroft.

'They shall not pass!' returned the engineer.

But if they did not pass it was not for want of having attempted it. Those in the rear pushed on the foremost assailants, and it was an incessant struggle with revolvers and hatchets. Several culpeux already lay dead on the ground, but their number did not appear to diminish, and it might have been supposed that reinforcements were continually arriving over the bridge.

The colonists were soon obliged to fight at close quarters, not without receiving some wounds, though happily very slight ones. Herbert had, with a shot from his revolver, rescued Neb, on whose back a culpeux had sprung like a tiger cat. Top fought with actual fury, flying at the throats of the foxes and strangling them instantaneously. Jup wielded his weapon valiantly, and it was in vain that they endeavoured to keep him in the rear. Endowed doubtless with sight which enabled him to pierce the obscurity, he was always in the thick of the fight, uttering from time to time a sharp hissing sound, which was with him the sign of great rejoicing.

At one moment he advanced so far, that by the light from revolver he was seen surrounded by five or six large culpeux, with whom he was coping with great coolness.

However the struggle was ended at last, and victory was on the side of the settlers, but not until they had fought for two long hours! The first signs of the approach of day doubtless determined the retreat of their assailants, who scampered away towards the North, passing over the bridge, which Neb ran immediately to raise. When day had sufficiently lighted up the field of battle, the settlers counted as many as fifty dead bodies scattered about on the shore.

'And Jup!' cried Pencroft, 'where is Jup?' Jup had disappeared. His friend Neb called him, and for the first time Jup did not reply to his friend's call.

Every one set out in search of Jup, trembling lest he should be found amongst the slain; they cleared the place of the bodies which stained the snow with their blood, Jup was found in the midst of a heap of culpeux, whose broken jaws and crushed bodies showed that they had to do with the terrible club of the intrepid animal.

Poor Jup still held in his hand the stump of his broken cudgel, but deprived of his weapon he had been overpowered by numbers, and his chest was covered with severe wounds.

'He is living,' cried Neb, who was bending over him.

'And we will save him,' replied the sailor. 'We will nurse him as if he was one of ourselves.'

It appeared as if Jup understood, for he leant his head on Pencroft's shoulder as if to thank him. The sailor was wounded himself, but his wound was insignificant, as were those of his companions; for thanks to their fire-arms they had been almost always able to keep their assailants at a distance. It was therefore only the orang whose condition was serious.

Jup, carried by Neb and Pencroft, was placed in the lift, and only a slight moan now and then escaped his lips. He was gently drawn up to Granite House. There he was laid on a mattress taken from one of the beds, and his wounds were bathed with the greatest care. It did not appear that any vital part had been reached, but Jup was very weak from loss of blood, and a high fever soon set in after his wounds had been dressed. He was laid down, strict diet was imposed, 'just like a real person,' as Neb said, and they made him swallow several cups of a cooling drink, for which the ingredients were supplied from the vegetable medicine chest of Granite House. Jup was at first restless, but his breathing gradually became more regular, and he was left sleeping quietly. From time to time Top, walking on tip-toe, as one might say, came to visit his friend, and seemed to approve of all the care that had been taken of him. One of Jup's hands hung over the side of his bed, and Top licked it with a sympathising air.

They employed the day in interring the dead, who were dragged to the forest of the Far West, and there buried deep.

This attack, which might have had such serious consequences, was a lesson to the settlers, who from this time never went to bed until one of their number had made sure that all the bridges were raised, and that no invasion was possible.

However Jup, after having given them serious anxiety for several days, began to recover. His constitution brought him through, the fever gradually subsided, and Gideon Spilett, who was a bit of a doctor, pronounced him quite out of danger. On the 16th of August, Jup began to eat. Neb made him nice little sweet dishes, which the invalid ate with great relish, for if he had a pet failing it was that of being somewhat of a gourmand, and Neb had never done anything to cure him of this fault.

'What would you have?' said he to Gideon Spilett, who sometimes expostulated with him for spoiling the ape. 'Poor Jup has no other pleasure than that of the palate, and I am only too glad to be able to reward his services in this way!'

Ten days after having taken to his bed, on the 21st of August, Master Jup arose. His wounds were healed, and it was evident that he would not be long in regaining his usual strength and agility. Like all convalescents, he was tremendously hungry, and the reporter allowed him to eat as much as he liked, for he trusted to that instinct, which is too often wanting in reasoning beings, to keep the orang from any excess. Neb was delighted to see his pupil's appetite returning.

'Eat away, my Jup,' said he, 'and don't spare anything; you have shed your blood for us, and it is the least I can do to make you strong again!'

On the 25th of August Neb's voice was heard calling to his companions, –

'Captain, Mr Spilett, Mr Herbert, Pencroft, come! come!'

The colonists, who were together in the dining-room, rose at Neb's call, who was then in Jup's room.

'What's the matter?' asked the reporter.

'Look,' replied Neb with a shout of laughter. And what did they see? Master Jup smoking calmly and seriously, sitting cross-legged like a Turk at the entrance to Granite House!

'My pipe,' cried Pencroft. 'He has taken my pipe! Hallo, my honest Jup, I make you a present of it! Smoke away, old boy, smoke away!'

And Jup gravely puffed out clouds of smoke which seemed to give him great satisfaction. Harding did not appear to be much astonished at this incident, and he cited several examples of tame apes to whom the use of tobacco had become quite familiar.

But from this day Master Jup had a pipe of his own, the sailor's ex-pipe, which was hung in his room near his store of tobacco. He filled it himself, lighted it with a glowing coal, and appeared to be the happiest of quadrumana. It may readily be understood that this similarity of tastes of Jup and Pencroft served to tighten the bonds of friendship which already existed between the honest ape and the worthy sailor.

'Perhaps he is really a man,' said Pencroft sometimes to Neb. 'Should you be surprised to hear him beginning to speak to us some day?'

'My word, no,' replied Neb. 'What astonishes me is that he hasn't spoken to us before, for now he wants nothing but speech!'

'It would amuse me all the same,' resumed the sailor, 'if some fine day he said to me, "Suppose we change pipes, Pencroft".'

'Yes,' replied Neb, 'what a pity he was born dumb!'

With the month of September the winter ended, and the works were again eagerly commenced. The building of the vessel advanced rapidly, she was already completely decked over, and all the inside parts of the hull were firmly united with ribs bent by means of steam, which answered all the purposes of a mould.

As there was no want of wood, Pencroft proposed to the engineer to give a double lining to the hull, so as to completely insure the strength of the vessel.

Harding, not knowing what the future might have in store for them, approved the sailor's idea of making the craft as strong as possible. The interior and the deck of the vessel were entirely finished towards the 15th of September. For calking the seams they made oakum of dry seaweed, which was hammered in between the planks; then these seams were covered with boiling tar, which was obtained in great abundance from the pines in the forest.

The management of the vessel was very simple. She had from the first been ballasted with heavy blocks of granite walled up in a bed of lime, twelve thousand pounds of which they stowed away.

A deck was placed over this ballast, and the interior was divided into two cabins; two benches extended along them and served also as lockers. The foot of the mast supported the partition which separated the two cabins, which were reached by two hatchways let into the deck.

Pencroft had no trouble in finding a tree suitable for the mast. He chose a straight young fir, with no knots, and which he had only to square at the step, and round off at the top. The ironwork of the mast, the rudder, and the hull, had been roughly but strongly forged at the Chimneys. Lastly, yards, masts, boom, spars, oars, etc., were all finished by the first week in October, and it was agreed that a trial trip should be taken round the island, so as to ascertain how the vessel would behave at sea, and how far they might depend upon her.

During all this time the necessary works had not been neglected. The corral was enlarged, for the flock of musmons and goats had been increased by a number of young ones, who had to be housed and fed. The colonists had paid visits also to the oyster bed, the warren, the coal and iron mines, and to the till then unexplored districts of the Far West forest, which abounded in game. Certain indigenous plants were discovered, and those fit for immediate use, contributed to vary the vegetable stores of Granite House.

They were a species of ficoide, some similar to those of the Cape, with eatable fleshy leaves, others bearing seeds containing a sort of flour.

On the 10th of October the vessel was launched. Pencroft was radiant with joy, the operation was perfectly successful; the boat completely rigged, having been pushed on rollers to the water's edge, was floated by the rising tide, amidst the cheers of the colonists, particularly of Pencroft, who showed no modesty on this occasion. Besides, his importance was to last beyond the finishing of the vessel, since, after having built her, he was to command her. The grade of captain was bestowed upon him with the approbation of all. To satisfy Captain Pencroft, it was now necessary to give a name to the vessel, and after many propositions had been discussed, the votes were all in favour of the 'Bonadventure'. As soon as the 'Bonadventure' had been lifted by the rising tide, it was seen that she lay evenly in the water, and would be easily navigated. However, the trial trip was to be made that very day, by an excursion off the coast. The weather was fine, the breeze fresh, and the sea smooth, especially towards the south coast, for the wind was blowing from the north-west.

They set off almost at once. All greatly admired the new boat and also their island which lay before their eyes, while Pencroft took them on a long excursion of the coast.

After standing off the shore the 'Bonadventure' again approached it in the direction of Fort Balloon. It was important to ascertain the channels between the sandbanks and reefs, that buoys might be laid down, since this little creek was to be the harbour.

They were not more than half a mile from the coast, and it was necessary to tack to beat against the wind. The 'Bonadventure' was then going at a very moderate rate, as the breeze, partly intercepted by the high land, scarcely swelled her sails, and the sea, smooth as glass, was only rippled now and then by passing gusts.

Herbert had stationed himself in the bows that he might indicate the course to be followed among the channels, when all at once he shouted, –

'Luff, Pencroft, Luff!'

'What's the matter?' replied the sailor; 'a rock?'

'No – wait,' said Herbert; 'I don't quite see. Luff again – right – now.'

So saying, Herbert, leaning over the side, plunged his arm into the water and pulled it out, exclaiming, –

'A bottle!'

He held in his hand a corked bottle which he had just seized a few cables length from the shore.

Cyrus Harding took the bottle. Without uttering a single

word he drew the cork, and took from it a damp paper, on which were written these words:

'Castaway . . . Tabor Island: 153° W. long., 37° 11′ S. lat.

CHAPTER 12

'A CASTAWAY!' exclaimed Pencroft; 'left on this Tabor Island. Ah, Captain Harding, you won't oppose my going? It cannot be more than two hundred miles from us if the position of Lincoln Island that we calculated with the sextant found in the chest is correct.'

'No, Pencroft,' replied Cyrus Harding; 'and you shall set out as soon as possible.'

'Tomorrow?'

'Tomorrow!'

The engineer still held in his hand the paper which he had taken from the bottle. He contemplated it for some instants, then resumed, –

'From this document, my friends, from the way in which it is worded, we may conclude this: first, that the castaway on Tabor Island is a man possessing a considerable knowledge of navigation, since he gives the latitude and longitude of the island exactly; secondly, that he is either English or American, as the document is written in the English language.'

'That is perfectly logical,' answered Spilett; 'and the presence of this castaway explains the arrival of the case on the shores of our island. There must have been a wreck, since there is a castaway. As to the latter, whoever he may be, it is lucky for him that Pencroft thought of building this boat and of trying her this very day, for a day later and this bottle might have been broken on the rocks.'

'Indeed,' said Herbert, 'it is a fortunate chance that the 'Bonadventure' passed exactly where the bottle was still floating!'

'Does not this appear strange to you?' asked Harding of Pencroft.

'It appears fortunate, that's all,' answered the sailor. 'Do you see anything extraordinary in it, captain? The bottle must go somewhere, and why not here as well as anywhere else?'

'Perhaps you are right, Pencroft,' replied the engineer; 'and yet – '

'But,' observed Herbert, 'there's nothing to prove that his bottle has been floating long in the sea.'

'Nothing,' replied Gideon Spilett; 'and the document appears even to have been recently written. What do you think about it, Cyrus?'

'It is difficult to say, and besides we shall soon know,' replied Harding. During this conversation Pencroft had not remained inactive. He had put the vessel about, and the 'Bonadventure', all sails set, was running rapidly towards Claw Cape.

Every one was thinking of the castaway on Tabor Island. Should they be in time to save him? This was a great event in the life of the colonists! They themselves were but castaways, but it was to be feared that another might not have been so fortunate, and their duty was to go to his succour.

Claw Cape was doubled, and about four o'clock the 'Bonadventure' dropped her anchor at the mouth of the Mercy.

That same evening the arrangements for the new expedition were made. It appeared best that Pencroft and Herbert, who knew how to work the vessel, should undertake the voyage alone. By setting out the next day, the 10th of October, they would arrive on the 13th, for with the present wind it would not take more than forty-eight hours to make this passage of a hundred and fifty miles. One day in the island, three or four to return, they might hope therefore that on the 17th they would again reach Lincoln Island. The weather was fine, the barometer was rising, the wind appeared settled, everything then was in favour of these brave men whom an act of humanity was taking far from their island.

Thus it had been agreed that Cyrus Harding, Neb, and Gideon Spilett, should remain at Granite House, but an objection was raised, and Spilett, who had not forgotten his business as reporter to the *New York Herald*, having declared that he would go by swimming rather than lose such an opportunity, he was admitted to take a part in the voyage.

The evening was occupied in transporting on board the 'Bonadventure' articles of bedding, utensils, arms, ammunition, a compass, provisions for a week, and this business being rapidly accomplished, the colonists ascended to Granite House.

The next day, at five o'clock in the morning, the farewells were said, not without some emotion on both sides, and Pencroft, setting sail, made towards Claw Cape, which had to be doubled in order to proceed to the south west.

The 'Bonadventure' was already a quarter of a mile from the coast, when the passengers perceived on the heights of Granite House two men waving their farewells; they were Cyrus Harding and Neb.

'Our friends,' exclaimed Spilett, 'this is our first separation for fifteen months.'

Pencroft, the reporter, and Herbert, waved in return, and Granite House soon disappeared behind the high rocks of the Cape.

During the first part of the day the 'Bonadventure' was still in sight of the southern coast of Lincoln Island, which soon appeared just like a green basket, with Mount Franklin rising from the centre. The heights, diminished by distance, did not present an appearance likely to tempt vessels to touch there. Reptile End was passed in about an hour, though at a distance of about ten miles.

At this distance it was no longer possible to distinguish anything of the Western Coast, which stretched away to the ridges of Mount Franklin, and three hours after the last of Lincoln Island sank below the horizon.

The 'Bonadventure' behaved capitally. Bounding over the waves, she proceeded rapidly on her course. Pencroft had hoisted the foresail, and steering by the compass, followed a rectilinear direction. From time to time Herbert relieved him at the helm, and the lad's hand was so firm that the sailor had not a point to find fault with.

Gideon Spilett chatted sometimes with one, sometimes with the other; if wanted, he lent a hand with the ropes, and Captain Pencroft was perfectly satisfied with his crew. The night passed without event and the following morning land was sighted.

'Land!' shouted Pencroft at about six o'clock.

And it was impossible that Pencroft should be mistaken, it was evident that land was there. Imagine the joy of the little crew of the 'Bonadventure.' In a few hours they would land on the beach of the island!

The low coast of Tabor Island, scarcely emerging from the sea, was not more than fifteen miles distant.

The head of the 'Bonadventure,' which was a little to the south of the island, was set directly towards it, and as the sun mounted in the east, his rays fell upon one or two headlands.

'This is a much less important isle than Lincoln Island,' observed Herbert 'and is probably due like ours to some submarine convulsion.'

At eleven o'clock the 'Bonadventure' was not more than two miles off, and Pencroft, whilst looking for a suitable place at which to land, proceeded very cautiously through the unknown waters. The whole of the island could now be surveyed, and on it could be seen groups of gum and other large trees of the same species as those growing on Lincoln Island. But the astonishing thing was that no smoke arose to show that the island was inhabited, not a signal appeared on any point of the shore whatever!

And yet the document was clear enough; there was a castaway, and this castaway should have been on the watch.

In the meanwhile the 'Bonadventure' entered the winding channels among the reefs, and Pencroft observed every turn with extreme care. He had put Herbert at the helm, posting himself in the bows, inspecting the water, whilst he held the halliard in his hand, ready to lower the sail at a moment's notice. Gideon Spilett with his glass eagerly scanned the shore, though without perceiving anything.

However, at about twelve o'clock the keel of the 'Bonadventure' grated on the bottom. The anchor was let go, the sails furled, and the crew of the little vessel landed.

And there was no reason to doubt that this was Tabor Island, since according to the most recent charts there was no island in this part of the Pacific between New Zealand and the American coast.

The vessel was securely moored, so that there should be no danger of her being carried away by the receding tide; then Pencroft and his companions, well armed, ascended the shore so as to gain an elevation of about two hundred and fifty or three hundred feet, which rose at a distance of half a mile.

'From the summit of that hill,' said Spilett, 'we can no doubt obtain a complete view of the island, which will greatly facilitate our search.'

'Exactly so,' answered Pencroft; 'and it is the best plan of proceeding.'

Whilst thus talking, the explorers had advanced along a clearing which terminated at the foot of the hill. Flocks of rock-pigeons and sea-swallows, similar to those of Lincoln Island, fluttered around them. Under the woods which skirted the glade on the left they could hear the bushes rustling, and see the grass waving, which indicated the presence of timid animals, but still nothing to show that the island was inhabited.

Arrived at the foot of the hill, Pencroft, Spilett, and Herbert climbed it in a few minutes, and gazed anxiously round the horizon.

They were on an islet which did not measure more than six miles in circumference, its shape not much bordered by capes or promontories, bays or creeks, being a lengthened oval. All around, the lonely sea extended to the limits of the horizon. No land nor even a sail was in sight.

This woody islet did not offer the varied aspects of Lincoln Island, arid and wild in one part, but fertile and rich in the other. On the contrary, this was a uniform mass of verdure, out of which rose two or three hills of no great height. Obliquely to the oval of the island ran a stream through a wide meadow falling into the sea on the west by a narrow mouth.

'The domain is limited,' said Herbert.

'Yes,' rejoined Pencroft. 'It would have been too small for us.'

'And moreover,' said the reporter, 'it appears to be uninhabited.'

'Indeed,' answered Herbert, 'nothing here betrays the presence of man.'

'Let us go down,' said Pencroft, 'and search.'

The sailor and his two companions returned to the shore, to the place where they had left the 'Bonadventure.'

They had decided to make the tour of the island on foot, before exploring the interior, so that not a spot should escape their investigations. The beach was easy to follow, and only in some places was their way barred by large rocks, which, however, they easily passed round. The explorers proceeded towards the south, disturbing numerous flocks of sea-birds and herds of seals, which threw themselves into the sea as soon as they saw the strangers at a distance.

'Those beasts yonder,' observed the reporter, 'do not see men for the first time. They fear them, therefore they must know them.'

An hour after their departure they arrived on the southern point of the islet, terminated by a sharp cape, and proceeded towards the north along the western coast, equally formed by sand and rocks, the background bordered with thick woods.

There was not a trace of an habitation in any part, not the print of a human foot on the shore of the island, which after four hours' walking had been gone completely round.

It was to say the least very extraordinary, and they were compelled to believe that Tabor Island was not or was no longer inhabited. Perhaps, after all, the document was already several months or several years old, and it was possible in this case, either that the castaway had been enabled to return to his country, or that he had died of misery.

Pencroft, Spilett, and Herbert, forming more or less probable conjectures, dined rapidly on board the 'Bonadventure' so as to be able to continue their excursion until nightfall. This was done at five o'clock in the evening, at which hour they entered the wood.

Numerous animals fled at their approach, being principally, one might say, only goats and pigs, which it was easy to see belonged to European species.

Doubtless some whaler had landed them on the island, where they had rapidly increased. Herbert resolved to catch one or two living, and take them back to Lincoln Island.

It was no longer doubtful that men at some period or other had visited this islet, and this became still more evident when paths appeared trodden through the forest, felled trees, and everywhere traces of the hand of man; but the trees were becoming rotten, and had been felled many years ago; the marks of the axe were velveted with moss, and the grass grew long and thick on the paths, so that it was difficult to find them.

'But,' observed Gideon Spilett, 'this not only proves that men have landed on the island, but also that they lived on it for some time. Now, who were these men? How many of them remain?'

'The document,' said Herbert, 'only spoke of one castaway.'

'Well, if he is still on the island,' replied Pencroft, 'it is impossible but that we shall find him.'

The exploration was continued. The sailor and his companion naturally followed the route which cut diagonally across the island, and they were thus obliged to follow the stream which flowed towards the sea.

If the animals of European origin, if works due to a human hand, showed incontestably that men had already visited the island, several specimens of the vegetable kingdom did not prove it less. In some places, in the midst of clearings, it was evident that the soil had been planted with culinary plants, at probably the same distant period.

What, then, was Herbert's joy, when he recognised potatoes, chicory, sorrel, carrots, cabbages, and turnips, of which it was sufficient to collect the seed to enrich the soil of Lincoln Island.

'Capital! Jolly!' exclaimed Pencroft. 'That will suit Neb as well as us. Even if we do not find the castaway, at least our voyage will not have been useless, and God will have rewarded us.'

'Doubtless,' replied Gideon Spilett; 'but to see the state in which we find these plantations, it is to be feared that the island has not been inhabited for some time.'

'Indeed,' answered Herbert, 'an inhabitant, whoever he was, could not have neglected such an important culture!'

'Yes,' said Pencroft, 'the castaway has gone.'

'We must suppose so.'

'It must then be admitted that the document has already a distant date?'

'Evidently.'

'And that the bottle only arrived at Lincoln Island after having floated in the sea a long time.'

'Why not?' returned Pencroft. 'But night is coming on.' added he, 'and I think that it will be best to give up the search for the present.'

'Let us go on board, and tomorrow we will begin again.' said the reporter.

This was the wisest course, and it was about to be followed when Herbert, pointing to a confused mass among the trees, exclaimed, –

'A hut!'

All three immediately ran towards the dwelling. In the twilight it was just possible to see that it was built of planks and covered with a thick tarpaulin.

The half-closed door was pushed open by Pencroft, who entered with a rapid step.

The hut was empty!

CHAPTER 13

PENCROFT, Herbert and Gideon Spilett, remained silent in the midst of the darkness.

Pencroft shouted loudly.

No reply was made.

The sailor then struck a light and set fire to a twig. This lighted for a minute a small room, which appeared perfectly empty. At the back was a rude fireplace, with a few cold cinders, supporting an armful of dry wood. Pencroft threw the blazing twig on it, the wood cracked and gave forth a bright light.

The sailor and his two companions then perceived a disordered bed, of which the damp and yellow coverlets proved that it had not been used for a long time. In the corner of the fireplace were two kettles, covered with rust, and an overthrown pot. A cupboard, with a few mouldy sailor's clothes; on the table a tin plate and a Bible, eaten away by damp; in a corner a few tools, a spade, pickaxe, two fowling-pieces, one of which was broken; on a plank, forming a shelf, stood a barrel of powder, still untouched, a barrel of shot, and several boxes of caps, all thickly covered with dust, accumulated, perhaps, by many long years.

'There is no one here,' said the reporter.

'No one,' replied Pencroft.

'It is a long time since this room has been inhabited,' observed Herbert.

'Yes, a very long time!' answered the reporter.

'Mr Spilett,' then said Pencroft, 'instead of returning on board, I think that it would be well to pass the night in this hut.'

'You are right, Pencroft,' answered Gideon Spilett, 'and if its owner returns, perhaps he will not be sorry to find the place taken possession of.'

'He will not return,' said the sailor, shaking his head.

'You think that he has quitted the island?' asked the reporter.

'If he had quitted the island he would have taken away his weapons and his tools,' replied Pencroft. 'You know the value which castaways set on such articles as these, the last remains of a wreck? No! no!' repeated the sailor, in a tone of conviction, 'no, he has not left the island! If he had escaped in a boat made by himself, he would still less have left these indispensable and necessary articles. No! he is on the island!'

'Living?' asked Herbert.

'Living or dead. But if he is dead, I suppose he has not buried himself, and so we shall at least find his remains!'

It was then agreed that the night should be passed in the deserted dwelling, and a store of wood found in a corner was sufficient to warm it. The door closed, Pencroft, Herbert, and Spilett remained there, seated on a bench, talking little but wondering much. They were in a frame of mind to imagine anything or expect anything. They listened eagerly for sounds outside. The door might have opened suddenly, and a man presented himself to them without their being in the least surprised, notwithstanding all that the hut revealed of abandonment, and they had their hands ready to press the hands of this man, this castaway, this unknown friend, for whom friends were waiting.

But no voice was heard, the door did not open. The hours thus passed away.

Day dawned; Pencroft and his companions immediately proceeded to survey the dwelling. It had certainly been built in a favourable situation, at the back of a little hill, sheltered by branches of magnificent gum-trees. Before its front and through the trees the axe had pepared a wide clearing which allowed the view to extend to the sea. Beyond a lawn, surrounded by a wooden fence falling to pieces, was the shore, on the left of which was the mouth of the stream.

The hut had been built of planks, and it was easy to see that these planks had been obtained from the hull or deck of a ship. It was probable that a disabled vessel had been cast on the coast of the island, that one at least of the crew had been saved, and that by means of the wreck this man, having tools at his disposal, had built the dwelling.

And this became still more evident when Gideon Spilett, after having walked round the hut, saw on a plank, probably one of those which had formed the armour of the wrecked vessel, these letters, already half effaced:

'Br—tan—a.'

'Britannia', exclaimed Pencroft, whom the reporter had called; 'it is a common name for ships, and I could not say if she was English or American!'

'It matters very little, Pencroft!'

'Very little indeed,' answered the sailor; 'and we will save the survivor of her crew if he is still living, to whatever country he may belong. But before beginning our search again let us go on board the "Bonadventure".'

A sort of uneasiness had seized Pencroft upon the subject of his vessel. Should the island be inhabited after all, and should some one have taken possession of her? But he shrugged his shoulders at such an unreasonable supposition. At any rate the sailor was not sorry to go to breakfast on board. The road already trodden was not long, scarcely a mile. They set out on their walk, gazing into the wood and thickets, through which goats and pigs fled in hundreds.

Twenty minutes after leaving the hut Pencroft and his companions reached the western coast of the island, and saw the 'Bonadventure' held fast by her anchor, which was buried deep in the sand.

Pencroft could not restrain a sigh of satisfaction. After all this vessel was his child, and it is the right of fathers to be often uneasy when there is no occasion for it.

They returned on board, breakfasted, so that it should not be necessary to dine until very late; then the repast being ended, the exploration was continued, and conducted with the most minute care. Indeed, it was very probable that the only inhabitant of the island had perished. It was therefore more for the traces of a dead than of a living man that Pencroft and his companions searched But their searches were vain, and during the half of that day they sought to no purpose among the thickets of trees which covered the islet. There was then scarcely any doubt that, if the castaway was dead, no trace of his body now remained, but that some wild beast had probably devoured it to the last bone.

'We will set off tomorrow at daybreak,' said Pencroft to his two companions, as about two o'clock they were resting for a few minutes under the shade of a clump of firs.

'I should think that we might without scruple take the utensils which belonged to the castaway,' added Herbert.

'I think so too,' returned Gideon Spilett; 'and these arms and tools will make up the stores of Granite House. The supply of powder and shot is also most important.'

'Yes,' replied Pencroft; 'but we must not forget to capture a couple or two of those pigs, of which Lincoln Island is destitute –'

'Nor to gather those seeds,' added Herbert, 'which will give us all the vegetables of the Old and the New Worlds.'

'Then perhaps it would be best,' said the reporter, 'to remain a day longer on Tabor Island, so as to collect all that may be useful to us.'

'No, Mr Spilett,' answered Pencroft, 'I will ask you to set off tomorrow at daybreak. The wind seems to me to be likely to shift to the west, and after having had a fair wind for coming we shall have a fair wind for going back.'

'Then do not let us lose time,' said Herbert, rising.

'We won't waste time,' returned Pencroft. 'You, Herbert, go and gather the seeds, which you know better than we do. Whilst you do that, Mr Spilett and I will go and have a pig-hunt, and even without Top I hope we shall manage to catch a few!'

Herbert accordingly took the path which led towards the cultivated part of the islet, whilst the sailor and the reporter entered the forest.

Many specimens of the porcine race fled before them, and these animals, which were singularly active, did not appear to be in a humour to allow themselves to be approached.

However, after an hour's chase, the hunters had just managed to get hold of a couple lying in a thicket, when cries were heard resounding from the north part of the island. With the cries were mingled terrible yells, in which there was nothing human.

Pencroft and Gideon Spilett were at once on their feet and the pigs by this movement began to run away, at the moment when the sailor was getting ready the rope to bind them.

'That's Herbert's voice,' said the reporter.

'Run!' exclaimed Pencroft.

And the sailor and Spilett immediately ran at full speed towards the spot from whence the cries proceeded.

They did well to hasten, for at a turn of the path near a clearing they saw the lad thrown on the ground and in the grasp of a savage being, apparently a gigantic ape who was about to do him some great harm.

To rush on this monster, throw him on the ground in his turn, snatch Herbert from him, then bind him securely, was the work of a minute for Pencroft and Gideon Spilett. The sailor was of Herculean strength, the reporter also very powerful, and in spite of the monster's resistance he was firmly tied so that he could not even move.

'You are not hurt, Herbert,' asked Spilett.

'No, no!'

'Oh, if this ape had wounded him!' exclaimed Pencroft.

'But he is not an ape,' answered Herbert.

At these words Pencroft and Gideon Spilett looked at the singular being who lay on the ground. Indeed it was not an ape, it was a human being, a man. But what a man! A savage in all the horrible acceptation of the word, and so much the more frightful that he seemed fallen to the lowest degree of brutishness!

Shaggy hair, untrimmed beard descending to the chest, the body almost naked except a rag round the waist, wild eyes, enormous hands with immensely long nails, skin the colour of mahogany, feet as hard as if made of horn, – such was the miserable creature who yet had a claim to be called a man. But it might justly be asked if there were yet a soul in this body, or if the brute instinct alone survived in it!

'Are you quite sure that this is a man, or that he has ever been one?' said Pencroft to the reporter.

'Alas! there is no doubt about it,' replied Spilett.

'Then this must be the castaway?' asked Herbert.

'Yes,' replied Gideon Spilett, 'but the unfortunate man has no longer anything human about him!'

The reporter spoke the truth. It was evident that if the castaway had ever been a civilised being, solitude had made him a savage, or worse, perhaps a regular man of the woods. Hoarse sounds issued from his throat between his teeth, which were sharp as the teeth of a wild beast made to tear raw flesh.

Memory must have deserted him long before, and for a long time also he had forgotten how to use his gun and tools, and he no longer knew how to make a fire! It could be seen that he was active and powerful, but the phsyical qualities had been developed in him to the injury of the moral qualities. Gideon Spilett spoke to him. He did not appear to understand or even to hear. And yet on looking into his eyes, the reporter thought he could see that all reason was not extinguished in him. However, the prisoner did not struggle, nor even attempt to break his bonds. Was he overwhelmed by the presence of men whose fellow he had once been? Had he found in some corner of his brain a fleeting remembrance which recalled him to humanity? If free would he attempt to fly, or would he remain? They could not tell, but they did not make the experiment; and after gazing attentively at the miserable creature, – 'Whoever he may be,' remarked Gideon Spilett; 'whoever he may have been, and whatever he may become, it is our duty to take him with us to Lincoln Island.'

'Yes, yes!' replied Herbert; 'and perhaps with care we may arouse in him some gleam of intelligence.'

The cords which shackled the prisoner's feet were cut off, but his arms remained securely fastened. He got up by himself and did not manifest any desire to run away. His hard eyes darted a piercing glance at the three men who walked near him, but nothing denoted that he recollected being their fellow, or at least having been so. A continual hissing sound issued from his lips, his aspect was wild, but he did not attempt to resist.

By the reporter's advice the unfortunate man was taken to the hut. Perhaps the sight of the things that belonged to him would make some impression on him! Perhaps a spark would be sufficient to revive his obscured intellect, to rekindle his dulled soul. The dwelling was not far off. In a few minutes they arrived there, but the prisoner remembered nothing, and it appeared that he had lost consciousness of everything.

Evidently there was nothing to be done, for the time at least, but to take him on board the 'Bonadventure.' This was done, and he remained there in Pencroft's charge.

Herbert and Spilett returned to finish their work; and some hours after they came back to the shore, carrying the utensils and guns, a store of vegetables, of seeds, some game, and two couple of pigs.

All was embarked, and the 'Bonadventure' was ready to weigh anchor and sail with the morning tide.

The prisoner had been placed in the fore cabin, where he remained quiet, silent, apparently deaf and dumb.

Pencroft offered him something to eat, but he pushed away the cooked meat that was presented to him and which doubtless did not suit him. But on the sailor showing him one of the ducks which Herbert had killed, he pounced on it like a wild beast, and devoured it greedily.

'You think that he will recover his senses?' asked Pencroft. 'It is not impossible that our care will have an effect upon him, for it is solitude that has made him what he is, and from this time forward he will be no longer alone.'

The night passed, and whether the prisoner slept or not could not be known; but at any rate, although he had been unbound, he did not move. He was like a wild animal, which appears stunned at first by its capture, and becomes wild again afterwards.

At daybreak the next morning, the 15th of October, the change of weather predicted by Pencroft occured. The wind having shifted to the north-west, favoured the return of the 'Bonadventure,' but at the same time it freshened, which would render navigation more difficult.

At five o'clock in the morning the anchor was weighed. Pencroft took a reef in the mainsail, and steered towards the north-east, so as to sail straight for Lincoln Island.

The first day of the voyage was not marked by any incident. The prisoner remained quiet in the fore-cabin, and as he had been a sailor it appeared that the motion of the vessel might produce on him a salutary reaction. Did some recollection of his former calling return to him? However that might be, he remained tranquil, astonished rather than depressed.

The next day the wind increased, blowing more from the north, consequently in a less favourable direction for the 'Bonadventure'. Pencroft was soon obliged to sail close-hauled, and without saying anything about it, he began to be uneasy at the state of the sea, which frequently broke over the bows. Certainly, if the wind did not moderate, it would take a longer time to reach Lincoln Island than it had taken to make Tabor Island.

Indeed, on the morning of the 17th, the 'Bonadventure' had been forty-eight hours at sea, and nothing showed that she was near the island. It was impossible, besides, to estimate the distance traversed, or to trust to the reckoning for the direction, as the speed had been very irregular.

Twenty-four hours after there was yet no land in sight. The wind was right ahead and the sea very heavy. The sails were close-reefed, and they tacked frequently. On the 18th, a wave swept completely over the 'Bonaventure'; and if the crew had not taken the precaution of lashing themselves to the deck, they would have been carried away.

On this occasion Pencroft and his companions, who were occupied with loosing themselves, received unexpected aid from the prisoner, who emerged from the hatchway as if his sailor's instinct had suddenly returned, broke a piece out of the bulwarks with a spar so as to let the water which filled the deck escape. Then the vessel being clear, he descended to his cabin without having uttered a word. Pencroft, Gideon Spilett, and Herbert, greatly astonished, let him proceed.

Their situation was truly serious, and the sailor had reason to fear that he was lost on the wide sea without any possibility of recovering his course.

The night was dark and cold. However, about eleven o'clock the wind fell, the sea went down, and the speed of the vessel, as she laboured less, greatly increased.

Neither Pencroft, Spilett, nor Herbert thought of taking an hour's sleep. They kept a sharp look-out, for either Lincoln Island could not be far distant and would be sighted at daybreak, or the 'Bonadventure', carried away by currents, had drifted so much that it would be impossible to rectify her course. Pencroft, uneasy to the last degree, yet did not despair, for he had a gallant heart, and grasping the tiller, he anxiously endeavoured to pierce the darkness which surrounded them.

About two o'clock in the morning he started forward, –

'A light! a light!' he shouted.

Indeed, a bright light appeared twenty miles to the north-east. Lincoln Island was there, and this fire, evidently lighted by Cyrus Harding, showed them the course to be followed. Pencroft, who was bearing too much to the north, altered his course and steered towards the fire, which burned brightly above the horizon like a star of the first magnitude.

CHAPTER 14

THE next day, the 20th of October, at seven o'clock in the morning, after a voyage of four days, the 'Bonadventure' gently glided up to the beach at the mouth of the Mercy.

Cyrus Harding and Neb, who had become very uneasy at the bad weather and the prolonged absence of their companions, had climbed at daybreak to the plateau of Prospect Heights, and they had at last caught sight of the vessel which had been so long in returning.

'God be praised! There they are!' exclaimed Cyrus Harding.

The engineer's first idea, on counting the people on the deck of the 'Bonadventure', was that Pencroft had not found the castaway of Tabor Island, or at any rate that the unfortunate man had refused to leave his island and change one prison for another.

Indeed Pencroft, Gideon Spilett, and Herbert were alone on the deck of the 'Bonadventure'.

The moment the vessel touched, the engineer and Neb were waiting on the beach, and before the passengers had time to leap on to the sand, Harding said: 'We have been very uneasy at your delay, my friends! Did you meet with any accident?'

'No,' replied Gideon Spilett; 'on the contrary, everything went wonderfully well. We will tell you all about it.'

'However,' returned the engineer, 'your search has been unsuccessful, since you are only three, just as you went!'

'Excuse me, captain,' replied the sailor, 'we are four.'

'You have found the castaway?'

'Yes.'

'And you have brought him?'

'Yes.'

'Living?'

'Yes.'

'Where is he? Who is he?'

'He is,' replied the reporter, 'or rather he was, a man! There, Cyrus, that is all we can tell you!'

The engineer was then informed of all that had passed during the voyage, and under what conditions the search had been conducted; how the only dwelling in the island had long been abandoned; how at last a castaway had been captured, who appeared no longer to belong to the human species.

'And that's just the point,' added Pencroft. 'I don't know if we have done right to bring him here.'

'Certainly you have, Pencroft,' replied the engineer quickly.

'But the wretched creature has no sense!'

'That is possible at present,' replied Cyrus Harding; 'but only a few months ago the wretched creature was a man like you and me. And who knows what will become of the survivor of us after a long solitude on this island? It is a great misfortune to be alone, my friends; and it must be believed that solitude can quickly destroy reason, since you have found this poor creature in such a state!'

'But, captain,' asked Herbert, 'what leads you to think that the brutishness of the unfortunate man began only a few months back?'

'Because the document we found had been recently written,' answered the engineer, 'and the castaway alone can have written it.'

'Always supposing,' observed Gideon Spilett, 'that it had not been written by a companion of this man, since dead.'

'That is impossible, my dear Spilett.'

'Why so?' asked the reporter.

'Because the document would then have spoken of two castaways,' replied Harding, 'and it mentioned only one.'

Herbert then in a few words related the incidents of the voyage, and dwelt on the curious fact of the sort of passing gleam in the prisoner's mind, when for an instant in the height of the storm he had become a sailor.

'Well, Herbert,' replied the engineer, 'you are right to attach great importance to this fact. The unfortunate man cannot be incurable, and despair has made him what he is; but here he will find his fellow-men, and since there is still a soul in him, this soul we shall save!'

The castaway of Tabor Island, to the great pity of the engineer and the great astonishment of Neb, was then brought from the cabin which he occupied in the fore part of the 'Bonadventure'; when once on land he manifested a wish to run away.

But Cyrus Harding approaching, placed his hand on his shoulder with a gesture full of authority, and looked at him with infinite tenderness. Immediately the unhappy man, submitting to a superior will, gradually became calm, his eyes fell, his head bent, and he made no more resistance.

'Poor fellow!' murmured the engineer.

Cyrus Harding had attentively observed him. To judge by his appearance this miserable being had no longer anything human about him, and yet Harding, as had the reporter already, observed in his look an indefinable trace of intelligence.

It was decided that the castaway, or rather the stranger, as he was thenceforth termed by his companions, should live in one of the rooms of Granite House, from which, however, he could not escape. He was led there without difficulty; and with careful attention, it might, perhaps, be hoped that some day he would be a companion to the settlers in Lincoln Island.

It was decided that the boat should be moored in the safety of Port Balloon and so when the boat was unloaded Herbert and the sailor then re-embarked on board the 'Bonadventure', the anchor was weighed, the sail hoisted, and the wind drove her rapidly towards Claw Cape. Two hours after, she was reposing on the tranquil waters of Port Balloon.

During the first days passed by the stranger in Granite House had he already given them reason to think that his savage nature was becoming tamed? Did a brighter light burn in the depths of that obscured mind? In short, was the soul returning to the body?

Yes, to a certainty, and to such a degree, that Cyrus Harding and the reporter wondered if the reason of the unfortunate man had ever been totally extinguished. At first, accustomed to the open air, to the unrestrained liberty which he had enjoyed on Tabor Island the stranger manifested a sullen fury, and it was feared that he might throw himself on to the beach, out of one of the windows of Granite House. But gradually he became calmer, and more freedom was allowed to his movements.

They had reason to hope, and to hope much. Already, forgetting his carnivorous instincts, the stranger accepted a less bestial nourishment than that on which he fed on the islet, and cooked meat did not produce in him the same sentiment of repulsion which he had showed on board the 'Bonadventure'. Cyrus Harding had profited by a moment when he was sleeping, to cut his hair and matted beard, which formed a sort of mane, and gave him such a savage aspect. He had also been clothed more suitably, after having got rid of the rag which covered him. The result was that, thanks to these attentions, the stranger resumed a more human appearance, and it even seemed as if his eyes had become milder. Certainly when formerly lighted up by intelligence, this man's face must have had a sort of beauty.

Every day, Harding imposed on himself the task of passing some hours in his company. He came and worked near him, and occupied himself in different things, so as to fix his attention.

The calm of the stranger was deep, as has been said, and he even showed a sort of attachment for the engineer, whose influence he evidently felt. Cyrus Harding resolved then to try him, by transporting him to another scene, from that ocean which formerly his eyes had been accustomed to contemplate, to the border of the forest, which might perhaps recall those where so many years of his life had been passed!

'But,' said Gideon Spilett, 'can we hope that he will not escape, if once set at liberty?'

'The experiment must be tried,' replied the engineer.

'Well!' said Pencroft. 'When that fellow is outside, and feels the fresh air, he will be off as fast as his legs can carry him!'

'I do not think so,' returned Harding.

'Let us try,' said Spilett,

'We will try,' replied the engineer.

This was on the 30th of October, and consequently the castaway of Tabor Island had been a prisoner in Granite House for nine days. It was warm, and a bright sun darted his rays on the island, Cyrus Harding and Pencroft went to the room occupied by the stranger, who was found lying near the window and gazing at the sky.

'Come, my friend,' said the engineer to him.

The stranger rose immediately. His eyes were fixed on Cyrus Harding, and he followed him, whilst the sailor marched behind them, little confident as to the result of the experiment.

Arrived at the door, Harding and Pencroft made him take his place in the lift, whilst Neb, Herbert, and Gideon Spilett waited for them before Granite House. The lift descended, and in a few moments all were united on the beach.

The settlers went a short distance from the stranger, so as to leave him at liberty.

He then made a few steps towards the sea, and his look brightened with extreme animation, but he did not make the slightest attempt to escape. He was gazing at the little waves, which broken by the islet rippled on the sand.

'This is only the sea,' observed Gideon Spilett, 'and possibly it does not inspire him with any wish to escape!'

'Yes,' replied Harding, 'we must take him to the plateau, on the border of the forest. There the experiment will be more conclusive.'

'Besides, he could not run away,' said Neb, 'since the bridge is raised.'

'Oh,' said Pencroft, 'that isn't a man to be troubled by a stream like Creek Glycerine! He could cross it directly, at a single bound!'

'We shall soon see,' Harding contented himself with replying, his eyes not quitting those of his patient.

The latter was then led towards the mouth of the Mercy, and all climbing the left bank of the river, reached Prospect Heights.

Arrived at the spot on which grew the first beautiful trees of the forest, their foliage slightly agitated by the breeze, the stranger appeared greedily to drink in the penetrating odour which filled the atmosphere, and a long sigh escaped from his chest.

The settlers kept behind him, ready to seize him if he made any movement to escape!

And, indeed, the poor creature was on the point of springing into the creek which separated him from the forest, and his legs were bent for an instant as if for a spring, but almost immediately he stepped back, half sank down, and a large tear fell from his eyes.

'Ah!' exclaimed Cyrus Harding, 'you have become a man again, for you can weep!'

Yes! the unfortunate man had wept! Some recollection, doubtless had flashed across his brain, and to use Cyrus Harding's expression, by those tears he was once more a man.

The colonists left him for some time on the plateau, and withdrew themselves to a short distance, so that he might feel himself free; but he did not think of profiting by this liberty, and Harding soon brought him back to Granite House. Two days after this occurrence the stranger appeared to wish gradually to mingle with their common life. He evidently heard and understood, but no less evidently was he strangely determined not to speak to the colonists; for one evening, Pencroft, listening at the door of his room, heard these words escape from his lips:—

'No! here! I! never!'

The sailor reported these words to his companions.

'There is some painful mystery there!' said Harding.

The stranger had begun to use the labouring tools, and he worked in the garden. When he stopped in his work, as was often the case, he remained retired within himself; but on the engineer's recommendation, they respected the reserve which he apparently wished to keep. If one of the settlers approached him, he drew back, and his chest heaved with sobs, as if over-burthened!

Was it remorse that overwhelmed him thus? They were compelled to believe so, and Gideon Spilett could not help one day making this observation, –

'If he does not speak it is because he has, I fear, things too serious to be told!'

They must be patient and wait.

A few days later, on the 3rd of November, the stranger, working on the plateau, had stopped, letting his spade drop to the ground, and Harding, who was observing him from a little distance, saw that tears were again flowing from his eyes. A sort of irresistible pity led him towards the unfortunate man, and he touched his arm lightly. 'My friend!' said he.

The stranger tried to avoid his look, and Cyrus Harding having endeavoured to take his hand, he drew back quickly.

'My friend,' said Harding in a firmer voice, 'look at me, I wish it!'

The stranger looked at the engineer, and seemed to be under his power, as a subject under the influence of a mesmerist. He wished to run away. But then his countenance suddenly underwent a transformation. His eyes flashed. Words struggled to escape from his lips. He could no longer contain himself! . . . At last he folded his arms; then, in a hollow voice, –

'Who are you?' he asked Cyrus Harding.

'Castaways, like you,' replied the engineer, whose emotion was deep. 'We have brought you here, among your fellow-men.'

'My fellow-men! . . . I have none!'

'You are in the midst of friends.'

'Friends! – for me! friends!' exclaimed the stranger, hiding his face in his hands. 'No – never – leave me! leave me!'

Then he rushed to the side of the plateau which overlooked the sea, and remained there a long time motionless.

Harding rejoined his companions and related to them what had just happened.

'Yes! there is some mystery in that man's life,' said Gideon

Spilett, 'and it appears as if he had only re-entered society by the path of remorse.'

'I don't know what sort of a man we have brought here,' said the sailor. 'He has secrets – '

'Which we will respect,' interrupted Cyrus Harding quickly. 'If he has committed any crime, he has most fearfully expiated it, and in our eyes he is absolved.'

For two hours the stranger remained alone on the shore, evidently under the influence of recollections which recalled all his past life – a melancholy life doubtless – and the colonists, without losing sight of him, did not attempt to disturb his solitude. However, after two hours, appearing to have formed a resolution, he came to find Cyrus Harding. His eyes were red with the tears he had shed, but he wept no longer. His countenance expressed deep humility. He appeared anxious, timorous, ashamed, and his eyes were constantly fixed on the ground.

'Sir,' said he to Harding, 'your companions and you, are you English?'

'No,' answered the engineer, 'we are Americans.'

'Ah!' said the stranger, and he murmured, – 'I prefer that!'

'And you, my friend?' asked the engineer.

'English,' replied he hastily.

And as if these few words had been difficult to say, he retreated to the beach, where he walked up and down between the cascade and the mouth of the Mercy, in a state of extreme agitation.

Then, passing one moment close to Herbert, he stopped, and in a stifled voice, –

'What month?' he asked.

'December,' replied Herbert.

'What year?'

'1866.'

'Twelve years! twelve years!' he exclaimed.

'One word only – am I free?'

'You are free' answered the engineer.

'Farewell, then!' he cried, and fled like a madman.

Neb, Pencroft, and Herbert ran also towards the edge of the wood – but they returned alone.

'He will never come back!' exclaimed Pencroft.

But Harding persisted over the following days that it was the last revolt of his wild nature and that he would return eventually.

The event justified Cyrus Harding's predictions. On the 3rd of December, Herbert had left the plateau to go and fish on the southern bank of the lake. He was unarmed, and till then had never taken any precautions for defence, as dangerous animals had not shown themselves on that part of the island.

Meanwhile, Pencroft and Neb were working in the poultry-yard, whilst Harding and the reporter were occupied at the Chimneys in making soda, the store of soap being exhausted.

Suddenly cries resounded, – 'Help! Help!'

Cyrus Harding and the reporter, being at too great a distance had not been able to hear the shouts. Pencroft and Neb, leaving the poultry-yard in all haste, rushed towards the lake.

But before them, the stranger, whose presence at this place, no one had suspected, crossed Creek Glycerine, which separated the plateau from the forest, and bounded up the opposite bank.

Herbert was there face to face with a fierce jaguar, similar to the one which had been killed on Reptile End. Suddenly surprised, he was standing with his back against a tree, whilst the animal gathering itself together was about to spring.

But the stranger, with no other weapon than a knife, rushed on the formidable animal, who turned to meet this new adversary.

The struggle was short. The stranger possessed immense strength and activity. He seized the jaguar's throat with one powerful hand, holding it as in a vice, without heeding the beast's claws which tore his flesh, and with the other he plunged his knife into its heart.

The jaguar fell. The stranger kicked away the body, and was about to fly at the moment when the settlers arrived on the field of battle; but Herbert, clinging to him, cried, –

'No, no! you shall not go!'

Harding advanced towards the stranger, who frowned when he saw him approaching. The blood flowed from his shoulder under his torn shirt, but he took no notice of it.

'My friend,' said Cyrus Harding, 'we have just contracted a debt of gratitude to you. To save our boy you have risked your life!'

'My life!' murmured the stranger. 'What is that worth? Less than nothing!'

'You are wounded?'

'It is no matter.'

'Will you give me your hand?'

And as Herbert endeavoured to seize the hand which had just saved him, the stranger folded his arms, his chest heaved, his look darkened, and he appeared to wish to escape; but making a violent effort over himself, and in an abrupt tone, –

'Who are you?' he asked; 'and what do you claim to be to me?'

It was the colonists' history which he thus demanded, and for the first time. Perhaps this history recounted, he would tell his own.

In a few words Harding related all that had happened since their departure from Richmond; how they had managed, and what resources they now had at their disposal.

The stranger listened with extreme attention.

Then the engineer told who they all were, Gideon Spilett, Herbert, Pencroft, Neb, himself; and he added, that the greatest happiness they had felt since their arrival in Lincoln Island was on the return of the vessel from Tabor Island, when they had been able to include amongst them a new companion.

At these words the stranger's face flushed, his head sank on his breast, and confusion was depicted on his countenance.

'And now that you know us,' added Cyrus Harding, 'will you give us your hand?'

'No,' replied the stranger in a hoarse voice; 'No! You are honest men, you! And I – '

'Gentlemen,' said he, after a long pause, 'it is right that you should know my history. I will tell it you.'

'We ask you nothing, my friend,' said the engineer; 'it is your right to be silent.'

'It is my duty to speak.'

'We are ready to hear you.' replied Harding.

He spoke in a hoarse voice like someone who forces himself to speak, and his auditors did not once interrupt.

'On the 20th of December, 1854, a steam yacht, belonging to a Scots nobleman, Lord Glenarvan, anchored off Cape Bermouilli, on the western coast of Australia, in the thirty-seventh parallel. On board this yacht were Lord Glenarvan a major in the British Army, and his wife, a French geographer, a young girl and a young boy. These two last were the children of Captain Grant, whose ship, the "Britannia", had been lost, crew and cargo, a year before. The "Duncan" was commanded by Captain John Mangles, and manned by a crew of fifteen men.

'Six months before, a bottle, enclosing a document written in English, German and French, had been found in the Irish Sea and picked up by the "Duncan". This document stated in substance that there still existed three survivors from the wreck of the "Britannia", that these survivors were Captain Grant and two of his men, and that they had found refuge on some land, of which the document gave the latitude, but of which the longitude, effaced by the sea, was no longer legible.

'This latitude was 37° 11' south; therefore, the longitude being unknown, if they followed the thirty-seventh parallel over continents and seas, they would be certain to reach the spot inhabited by Captain Grant and his two companions. The Admiralty having hesitated to undertake this search, Lord Glenarvan resolved to attempt everything to find the captain. He communicated with Mary and Robert Grant, who joined him. The "Duncan" was equipped for the distant voyage, in which the nobleman's family and the captain's children wished to take part; and the "Duncan" leaving Glasgow, proceeded toward the Atlantic, passed through the Straits of Magellan, and ascended the Pacific as far as Patagonia, where, according to a previous interpretation of the document, they supposed that Captain Grant was a prisoner among the Indians.

'The "Duncan" disembarked her passengers on the western

coast of Patagonia, and sailed to pick them up again on the eastern coast of Cape Corrientes. Lord Glenarvan traversed Patagonia, following the thirty-seventh parallel, and having found no trace of the captain, he re-embarked on the 13th of November, so as to pursue his search through the ocean.

'After having unsuccessfully visited the islands of Tristan d'Acunha and Amsterdam, situated in her course, the "Duncan" as I have said, arrived at Cape Bermouilli on the Australian coast, on the 20th of December, 1854.

'It was Lord Glenarvan's intention to traverse Australia as he had traversed America, and he disembarked. A few miles from the coast was established a farm belonging to an Irishman, who offered hospitality to the travellers. Lord Glenarvan made known to the Irishman the cause which had brought him to these parts, and asked if he knew whether a three-masted English vessel, the "Britannia", has been lost less than two years before on the west coast of Australia.

'The Irishman had never heard of this wreck; but, to the great surprise of the bystanders, one of his servants came forward and said:

' "My lord, praise and thank God! If Captain Grant is still living, he is living on the Australian shores."

' "Who are you?" asked Lord Glenarvan.

' "A Scotsman like yourself, my lord," replied the man; "I am one of Captain Grant's crew – one of the castaways of the "Britannia".'

'This man was called Ayrton. He was, in fact, the boatswain's mate of the "Britannia", as his papers showed. But separated from Captain Grant at a moment when the ship struck upon the rocks, he had till then believed that the captain with all his crew had perished, and that he, Ayrton, was the sole survivor of the "Britannia".

' "Only," he added, "it was not on the west coast, but on the east coast of Australia that the vessel was lost; and if Captain Grant is still living, as his document indicates, he is a prisoner among the natives, and it is on the other coast that he must be looked for."

'This man spoke in a frank voice and with a confident look; his words could not be doubted. The Irishman, in whose service he had been for more than a year, answered for his trustworthiness. Lord Glenarvan, therefore, believed in the fidelity of this man, and, by his advice, resolved to cross Australia, following the thirty-seventh parallel. He, his wife, the two children, the major, the Frenchman, Captain Mangles, and a few sailors, composed the little band under the command of Ayrton, while the "Duncan", under charge of the mate, Tom Austin, proceeded to Melbourne, there to await Lord Glenarvan's instructions.

'They set out on the 23rd of December, 1854.

'It is time to say that Ayrton was a traitor. He was, indeed the boatswain's mate of the "Britannia"; but after some dispute with his captain he had endeavoured to incite the crew to mutiny and seize the ship, and Captain Grant had landed him on the 8th of April, 1852, on the west coast of Australia, and then sailed, leaving him there, as was only just.

'Therefore this wretched man knew nothing of the wreck of the "Britannia"; he had just heard of it from Glenarvan's account. Since his abandonment he had become, under the name of Ben Joyce, the leader of the escaped convicts; and if he boldly maintained that the wreck had taken place on the east coast, and led Lord Glenarvan to proceed in that direction, it was that he hoped to separate him from his ship, seize the "Duncan", and make the yacht a pirate in the Pacific.'

Here the stranger stopped for a moment. His voice trembled, but he continued:

'The expedition set out and proceeded across Australia. It was inevitably unfortunate, since Ayrton, or Ben Joyce, as he may be called, guided it, sometimes preceded, sometimes followed, by his band of convicts, who had been told what they had to do.

'Meanwhile the "Duncan" had been sent to Melbourne for repairs. It was necessary, then, to get Lord Glenarvan to order her to leave Melbourne and go to the east coast of Australia, where it would be easy to seize her. After having led the expedition near enough to the coast, in the midst of vast forests, with no resources, Ayrton obtained a letter which he was charged to carry to the mate of the "Duncan" – a letter which ordered the yacht to repair immediately to the east coast, to Twofold Bay, a few days' journey from the place where the expedition had stopped. It was there that Ayrton agreed to meet his accomplices, and two days after gaining possession of the letter he arrived at Melbourne.

'So far the villain had succeeded in his wicked design. He would be able to take the "Duncan" into Twofold Bay, where it would be easy for the convicts to seize her, and with her crew massacred, Ben Joyce would become master of the seas. But it pleased God to prevent the accomplishment of this terrible project.

'Ayrton arrived at Melbourne, delivered the letter to the mate, Tom Austin, who read it, and immediately set sail; but judge of Ayrton's rage and disappointment when the next day he found that the mate was taking the vessel, not to the east coast of Australia, to Twofold Bay, but to the east coast of New Zealand. He wished to stop him, but Austin showed him the letter! And indeed, by a providential error of the French geographer, who had written the letter, the east coast of New Zealand was mentioned as the place of destination.

'All Ayrton's plans were frustrated! He became outrageous. They put him in irons. He was then taken to the coast of New Zealand, not knowing what would become of his accomplices, or what would become of Lord Glenarvan.

'The "Duncan" cruised about on this coast until the 3rd of March. On that day Ayrton heard the report of guns. The guns of the "Duncan" were being fired, and soon Lord Glenarvan and his companions came on board.

'This is what had happened:

'After many hardships and dangers, Lord Glenarvan accomplished his journey and arrived on the east coast of Australia, at Twofold Bay. Much to his dismay the "Duncan" was not there. He telegraphed to Melbourne. They answered. "'Duncan' sailed on the 18th. Destination unknown."

'Lord Glenarvan could only arrive at one conclusion, that his honest yacht had fallen into the hands of Ben Joyce, and had become a pirate vessel!

'However, Lord Glenarvan would not give up. He was a bold and generous man. He embarked in a merchant vessel, sailed to the west coast of New Zealand, traversed it along the thirty-seventh parallel, without finding any trace of Captain Grant; but on the other side, to his great surprise, and by the will of Heaven, he found the "Duncan" under command of the mate, who had been waiting for him for five weeks!

'This was on the 3rd of March, 1855. Lord Glenarvan was now on board the "Duncan", but Ayrton was there also. He appeared before the nobleman, who wished to extract from him all the villain knew about Captain Grant. Ayrton refused to speak. Lord Glenarvan then told him that at the first port they put into he would be delivered up to the English authorities. Ayrton remained mute.

'Ayrton then proposed that in exchange for what he could tell, Lord Glenarvan should leave him on some island in the Pacific, instead of giving him up to the English authorities. Lord Glenarvan, resolving to do anything to obtain information about Captain Grant, consented.

'Ayrton then related all his life, and it was certain that he knew nothing from the day on which Captain Grant had landed him on the Australian coast.

'Nevertheless, Lord Glenarvan kept the promise which he had given. The Duncan continued her voyage and arrived at Tabor Island. It was there that Ayrton was to be landed, and it was there also that, by a veritable miracle, they found Captain Grant and two men, exactly in the thirty-seventh parallel.

'The convict, then, went to take their place on this desert islet, and at the moment he left the yacht these words were pronounced by Lord Glenarvan:

' "Here, Ayrton, you will be far away from any land, and

without any possible communication with your fellow-creatures. You cannot escape from this islet on which the "Duncan" leaves you. You will be alone, under the eye of a God who reads the depths of the heart; but you will be neither lost nor forgotten, as was Captain Grant. Unworthy as you are to be remembered by men, men will remember you. I know where you are, Ayrton, and I know where to find you. I will never forget it!'

'And the "Duncan", making sail, soon disappeared. This was on the 18th of March, 1855.

'Ayrton was alone, but he had no want of either ammunition, weapons, tools or seeds.

'At his, the convict's, disposal, was the house built by honest Captain Grant. He had only to live and expiate in solitude the crimes which he had committed.

'Gentlemen, he repented, he was ashamed of his crimes, and was very miserable! He said to himself that, if men came some day to take him from that islet, he must be worthy to return among them! How he suffered, that wretched man! How he laboured to recover himself by work! How he prayed to be reformed by prayer! For two years, three years, this went on; but Ayrton, humbled by solitude, always looking for some ship to appear on the horizon, asking himself if the time of expiation would soon be complete, suffered as none other ever suffered! Oh! how dreadful is solitude to a heart tormented by remorse!

'But doubtless Heaven had not sufficiently punished this unhappy man, for he felt that he was gradually becoming a savage! He felt that brutishness was gradually gaining on him!

'He could not say if it was after two or three years of solitude; but at last he became the miserable creature you found! I have no need to tell you, gentlemen, that Ayrton, Ben Joyce, and I, are the same.'

Cyrus Harding and his companions rose at the end of this account. It is impossible to say how much they were moved! What misery, grief, and despair lay revealed before them!

'Ayrton,' said Harding, rising, 'you have been a great criminal, but Heaven must certainly think that you have expiated your crimes! That has been proved by your having been brought again among your fellow-creatures. Ayrton, you are forgiven! And now you will be our companion?'

Ayrton drew back. 'Here is my hand!' said the engineer.

Ayrton grasped the hand which Harding extended to him, and great tears fell from his eyes.

'Will you live with us?' asked Cyrus Harding.

'Captain Harding, leave me some time longer,' replied Ayrton, 'you have four or five miles from here, a corral for your domesticated animals. These animals need to be taken care of. Will you allow me to live with them?'

'As you like, Ayrton,' answered Cyrus Harding with a feeling of deep commiseration. Ayrton was going to withdraw, when the engineer addressed one more question to him: – 'One word more, my friend. Since it was your intention to live alone, why did you throw into the sea the document which put us on your track?'

'A document?' repeated Ayrton, who did not appear to know what he meant.

'Yes, the document which we found enclosed in a bottle, giving us the exact position of Tabor Island!'

Ayrton passed his hand over his brow, then after having thought, 'I never threw any document into the sea!' he answered.

'Never?' exclaimed Pencroft.

'Never!'

And Ayrton, bowing, reached the door and departed.

CHAPTER 15

The month of January arrived. The year 1867 commenced. The summer occupations were assiduously continued. During the days which followed, Herbert and Spilett having gone in the direction of the corral, ascertained that Ayrton had taken possession of the habitation which had been prepared for him. He busied himself with the numerous flock confided to his care, and spared his companions the trouble of coming every two or three days to visit the corral. Nevertheless, in order not to leave Ayrton in solitude for too long a time, the settlers often paid him a visit.

It was not unimportant either, in consequence of some suspicions entertained by the engineer and Gideon Spilett, that this part of the island should be subject to a surveillance of some sort, and that Ayrton, if any incident occurred unexpectedly, should not neglect to inform the inhabitants of Granite House of it.

Nevertheless it might happen that something would occur which it would be necessary to bring rapidly to the engineer's knowledge. Independently of facts bearing on the mystery of Lincoln Island, many others might happen, which would call for the prompt interference of the colonists, – such as the sighting of a vessel, a wreck on the western coast, the possible arrival of pirates, &c.

Therefore Cyrus Harding resolved to put the corral in instantaneous communication with Granite House.

It was on the 10th of January that he made known his project to his companions.

'Why! how are you going to manage that, captain?' asked Pencroft. 'Do you by chance happen to think of establishing a telegraph?'

'Exactly so,' answered the engineer.

'Electric?' cried Herbert.

'Electric,' replied Cyrus Harding. 'We have all the necessary materials for making a battery, and the most difficult thing will be to stretch the wires, but by means of a draw-plate I think we shall manage it.'

'Well, after that,' returned the sailor, 'I shall never despair of seeing ourselves some day rolling along on a railway!'

They then set to work, beginning with the most difficult thing, for, if they failed in that, it would be useless to manufacture the battery and other accessories. After a great deal of time, and having made full use of the excellent resources on Lincoln Island such as iron, zinc and copper, two batteries were manufactured with a connecting wire extended between Granite House and the corral.

All was completely arranged by the 12th of February. On this day, Harding, having sent the current through the wire, asked if all was going on well at the corral, and received in a few moments a satisfactory reply from Ayrton. Pencroft was wild with joy, and every morning and evening he sent a telegram to the corral, which always received an answer.

This mode of communication presented two very real advantages; firstly, because it enabled them to ascertain that Ayrton was at the corral; and secondly, that he was thus not left completely isolated. Besides, Cyrus Harding never allowed a week to pass without going to see him, and Ayrton came from time to time to Granite House, where he always found a cordial welcome.

The fine season passed away in the midst of the usual work. The resources of the colony, particularly in vegetables and corn, increased from day to day, and the plants brought from Tabor Island had succeeded perfectly.

The plateau of Prospect Heights presented an encouraging aspect. The fourth harvest had been admirable, and it may be supposed that no one thought of counting whether the four hundred thousand millions of grains duly appeared in the crop. However, Pencroft had thought of doing so, but Cyrus Harding having told him that even if he managed to count three hundred grains a minute, or nine thousand an hour, it would take him nearly five thousand five hundred years to finish his task, the honest sailor considered it best to give up the idea.

The weather was splendid, the temperature very warm in the day time; but in the evening the sea-breezes tempered the heat of the atmosphere and procured cool nights for the inhabitants of Granite House. There were, however, a few storms, which, although they were not of long duration, swept over Lincoln

Island with extraordinary fury. The lightning blazed and the thunder continued to roll for some hours.

At this period the little colony was extremely prosperous.

The tenants of the poultry-yard swarmed, and they lived on the surplus, but it became necessary to reduce the population to a more moderate number. The pigs had already produced young, and it may be understood that their care for these animals absorbed a great part of Neb and Pencroft's time. The onagas, who had two pretty colts, were most often mounted by Gideon Spilett and Herbert, who had become an excellent rider under the reporter's instruction, and they also harnessed them to the cart either for carrying wood and coal to Granite House, or different mineral productions required by the engineer.

Several expeditions were made about this time into the depths of the Far West Forests. The explorers could venture there without having anything to fear from the heat, for the sun's rays scarcely penetrated through the thick foliage spreading above their heads. They visited all the left bank of the Mercy, along which ran the road from the corral to the mouth of Falls River.

But in these excursions the settlers took care to be well armed, for they frequently met with savage wild boars, with which they often had a tussle. They also, during this season. made fierce war against the jaguars. Gideon Spilett had vowed a special hatred against them, and his pupil Herbert seconded him well. Armed as they were, they no longer feared to meet one of those beasts. Herbert's courage was superb, and the reporter's *sang-froid* astonishing. Already twenty magnificent skins ornamented the dining-room of Granite House, and if this continued, the jaguar race would soon be extinct in the island, the object aimed at by the hunters.

The engineer sometimes took part in the expeditions made to the unknown parts of the island, which he surveyed with great attention. It was for other traces than those of animals that he searched the thickest of the vast forrest, but nothing suspicious ever appeared. Neither Top Nor Jup, who accompanied him, ever betrayed by their behaviour that there was anything strange there, and yet more than once again the dog barked at the mouth of the well, which the engineer had before explored without result.

It was during this time that the colonists found another incident which baffled them. Pencroft had been praising the beauties of their island and saying how sorry he would be to leave it if the opportunity ever arose.

'It wasn't just fear of the sea,' he continued, 'that made us so grateful to you captain Harding for lighting that guiding fire when we returned from Tabor Island, it was love of our colony.'

'A fire,' cried Harding in amazement.

'Yes, we should have passed to windward if it had not been

for the precaution you took of lighting a fire in the night of the 19th of October, on Prospect Heights.'

'If there is one thing certain,' replied Harding 'It is that I never lighted a fire that night either on Prospect Heights or on any other part of the island!'

CHAPTER 16

Two years already! and for two years the colonists had had no communication with their fellow-creatures! They were without news from the civilised world, lost on this island, as completely as if they had been on the most minute star of the celestial hemisphere!

What was now happening in their country? The picture of their native land was always before their eyes, the land torn by civil war at the time they left it, and which the southern rebellion was perhaps still staining with blood! It was a great sorrow to them, and they often talked together of these things, without ever doubting however that the cause of the North must triumph for the honour of the American Confederation.

During these two years not a vessel had passed in sight of the island; or, at least, not a sail had been seen. It was evident that Lincoln Island was out of the usual track, and also that it was unknown, – as was besides proved by the maps, – for though there was no port, vessels might have visited it for the purpose of renewing their store of water.

In the meanwhile, the bad weather came with the month of May, the November of the northern zones. It appeared that the winter would be severe and forward. The preparations for the winter season were therefore commenced without delay.

Nevertheless the colonists were well prepared to meet the winter, however hard it might be. They had plenty of felt clothing, and the musmons, very numerous by this time, had furnished an abundance of the wool necessary for the manufacture of this warm material.

It is unnecessary to say that Ayrton had been provided with this comfortable clothing. Cyrus Harding proposed that he should come to spend the bad season with them in Granite House, where he would be better lodged than at the corral, and Ayrton promised to do so, as soon as the last work at the corral was finished. He did this towards the middle of April. From that time Ayrton shared the common life, and made himself useful on all occasions; but still humble and sad, he never took part in the pleasures of his companions.

For the greater part of this, the third winter which the settlers passed in Lincoln Island, they were confined to Granite House. There were many violent storms and frightful tempests, which appeared to shake the rocks to their very foundations. Immense waves threatened to overwhelm the island, and certainly any vessel anchored near the shore would have been dashed to pieces. Twice, during one of these hurricanes, the Mercy swelled to such a degree as to give reason to fear that the bridges would be swept away, and it was necessary to strengthen those on the shore, which disappeared under the foaming waters, when the sea beat against the beach.

It may well be supposed that such storms, comparable to water-spouts, in which were mingled rain and snow, would cause great havoc on the plateau of Prospect Heights. The mill and the poultry-yard particularly suffered. The colonists were often obliged to make immediate repairs, without which the safety of the birds would have been seriously threatened.

During the worst weather, several jaguars and troops of quadrumana ventured to the edge of the plateau, and it was always to be feared that the most active and audacious would, urged by hunger, manage to cross the stream, which besides, when frozen offered them an easy passage. Plantations and domestic animals would then have been infallibly destroyed, without a constant watch, and it was often necessary to make use of the guns to keep those dangerous visitors at a respectful distance. Occupation was not wanting to the colonists, for without reckoning their out-door cares, they had always a thousand plans for the fitting up of Granite House.

They had also some fine sporting excursions, which were made during the frost in the vast Tadorn marsh. Gideon Spilett and Herbert, aided by Jup and Top, did not miss a shot in the midst of the myriads of wild duck, snipe, teal, and others. The access to these hunting-grounds was easy; besides, whether they reached them by the road to Port Balloon, after having passed the Mercy Bridge, or by turning the rocks from Flotsam Point, the hunters were never distant from Granite House more than two or three miles.

Thus passed the four winter months which were really rigorous, that is to say, June, July, August, and September. But, in short, Granite House did not suffer much from the inclemency of the weather, and it was the same with corral, which, less exposed than the plateau, and sheltered partly by Mount Franklin, only received the remains of the hurricanes, already broken by the forests and the high rocks of the shore. The damages there were consequently of small importance, and the activity and skill of Ayrton promptly repaired them, when some time in October he returned to pass a few days in the corral. During this winter, no fresh inexplicable incident occurred. Nothing strange happened, although Pencroft and Neb were on the watch for the most insignificant facts to which they attached any mysterious cause. Top and Jup themselves no longer growled round the well or gave any signs of uneasiness. It appeared, therefore, as if the series of supernatural incidents was interrupted, although they often talked of them during the evenings in Granite House, and they remained thoroughly resolved that the island should be searched, even in those parts the most difficult to explore. But an event of the highest importance, and of which the consequences might be terrible, momentarily diverted from their projects Cyrus Harding and his companions.

It was the month of October. The fine season was swiftly returning. Nature was reviving; and among the evergreen foliage of the coniferae which formed the border of the wood, already appeared the young leaves of the banksias, deodars, and other trees.

It may be remembered that Gideon Spilett and Herbert had, at different times, taken photographic views of Lincoln Island.

Now, on the 17th of this month of October, towards three o'clock in the afternoon, Herbert, enticed by the charms of the sky, thought of reproducing Union Bay, which was opposite to Prospect Heights, from Cape Mandible to Claw Cape.

The horizon was beautifully clear and the sea, undulating under a soft beeze, was as calm as the waters of a lake, sparkling here and there under the sun's rays.

The apparatus had been placed at one of the windows of the dining-room at Granite House, and consequently overlooked the shore and the bay. Herbert proceeded as he was accustomed to do, and the negative obtained, he went away to fix it by means of the chemicals deposited in a dark nook of Granite House.

Returning to the bright light, and examining it well, Herbert perceived on his negative an almost imperceptible little spot on the sea horizon. He endeavoured to make it disappear by reiterated washing, but could not accomplish it.

'It is a flaw in the glass,' he thought.

And then he had the curiosity to examine this flaw with a strong magnifier which he unscrewed from one of the telescopes.

But he had scarcely looked at it, when he uttered a cry, and the glass almost fell from his hands.

Immediately running to the room in which Cyrus Harding then was, he extended the negative and magnifier towards the engineer, pointing out the little spot.

Harding examined it; then seizing his telescope he rushed to the window.

The telescope, after having slowly swept the horizon, at last stopped on the looked-for spot, and Cyrus Harding lowering it, pronounced one word only, –

'A vessel!'

And in fact a vessel was in sight, off Lincoln Island!

CHAPTER 17

It was now two years and a half since the castaways from the balloon had been thrown on Lincoln Island, and during that period there had been no communication between them and their fellow-creatures. Once the reporter had attempted to communicate with the inhabited world by confiding to a bird a letter which contained the secret of their situation, but that was a chance on which it was impossible to reckon seriously. Ayrton, alone, under the circumstances which have been related, had come to join the little colony. Now, suddenly, on this day, the 17th of October, other men had unexpectedly appeared in sight of the island, on that deserted sea!

There could be no doubt about it! A vessel was there! But would she pass on, or would she put into port? In a few hours the colonists would definitely know what to expect.

Cyrus Harding and Herbert having immediately called Gideon Spilett, Pencroft, and Neb into the dining-room of Granite House, told them what had happened. Pencroft, seizing the telescope, rapidly swept the horizon, and stopping on the indicated point, that is to say, on that which had made the almost imperceptible spot on the photographic negative, –

'I'm blessed but it is really a vessel!' he exclaimed, in a voice which did not express any great amount of satisfaction.

'Is she coming here?' asked Gideon Spilett.

'Impossible to say anything yet,' answered Pencroft, 'for her rigging alone is above the horizon, and not a bit of her hull can be seen.'

'What is to be done?' asked the lad.

'We must tell Ayrton,' said Gideon Spilett, 'and send for him immediately. He alone can say if it is the "Duncan".'

This was the opinion of all, and the reporter, going to the telegraphic apparatus which placed the corral in communication with Granite House, sent this telegram: –

'Come with all possible speed.'

'In a few minutes the bell sounded.

'I am coming,' replied Ayrton.

Then the settlers continued to watch the vessel.

'If it is the "Duncan",' said Herbert, 'Ayrton will recognise her without difficulty, since he sailed on board her for some time.'

'And if he recognises her,' added Pencroft, 'it will agitate him exceedingly!'

'Yes,' answered Cyrus Harding; 'but now Ayrton is worthy to return on board the "Duncan", and pray Heaven that it is indeed Lord Glenarvon's yacht, for I should be suspicious of any other vessel. These are ill-famed seas, and I have always feared a visit from Malay pirates to our island.'

'We could defend it,' cried Herbert.

'No doubt, my boy,' answered the engineer smiling, 'but it would be better not to have to defend it.'

'A useless observation,' said Spilett. 'Lincoln Island is unknown to navigators, since it is not marked even on the most recent maps. Do you not think, Cyrus, that that is a sufficient motive for a ship, finding herself unexpectedly in sight of new land, to try and visit rather avoid it?'

'Certainly,' replied Pencroft.

'I think so too,' added the engineer. 'It may even be said that it is the duty of a captain to come and survey any land or island not yet known, and Lincoln Island is in this position.'

'Well,' said Pencroft, 'suppose this vessel comes and anchors there a few cables-lenghs from our island, what shall we do?'

This sudden question remained at first without any reply. But Cyrus Harding, after some moments' thought, replied in the calm tone which was usual to him, –

'What we shall do, my friends? What we ought to do, is this: – we will communicate with the ship, we will take our passage on board her, and we will leave our island, after having taken possession of it in the name of the United States. Then we will return with any who may wish to follow us to colonise it definitely, and endow the American Republic with a useful station in this part of the Pacific Ocean.'

'Hurrah!' exclaimed Pencroft, 'and that will be no small present which we shall make to our country! The colonisation is already almost finished; names are given to every part of the island; there is a natural port, fresh water, roads, a telegraph, a dockyard, and manufactories; and there will be nothing to be done but inscribe Lincoln Island on the maps!'

'But if any one seizes it in our absence?' observed Gideon Spilett.

'Hang it!' cried the sailor. 'I would rather remain all alone to guard it; and trust to Pencroft, they shouldn't steal it from him, like a watch from the pocket of a swell!'

For an hour it was impossible to say with any certainty whether the vessel was or was not standing towards Lincoln Island. She was nearer, but in what direction was she sailing? This Pencroft could not determine. However, as the wind was blowing from the north-east, in all probability the vessel was sailing on the starboard tack. Besides, the wind was favourable for bringing her towards the island, and, the sea being calm, she would not be afraid to approach, although the shallows were not marked on the chart.

Towards four o'clock – an hour after he had been sent for – Ayrton arrived at Granite House. He entered the dining-room, saying, – 'At your service, gentlemen.'

Cyrus Harding gave him his hand, as was his custom to do, and, leading him to the window, –

'Ayrton,' said he, 'we have begged you to come here for an important reason. A ship is in sight of the island.'

Ayrton at first paled slightly, and for a moment his eyes became dim; then, leaning out of the window, he surveyed the horizon, but could see nothing.

'Take this telescope,' said Spilett, 'and look carefully, Ayrton, for it is possible that this ship may be the "Duncan" come to these seas for the purpose of taking you home again.'

'The "Duncan"! ' murmured Ayrton. 'Already?' This last word escaped Ayrton's lips as if involuntarily, and his head dropped upon his hands.

Did not twelve years' solitude on a desert island appear to him a sufficient expiation? Did not the penitent yet feel himself pardoned, either in his own eyes or in the eyes of others?

'No,' said he, 'no; it cannot be the "Duncan"! '

'Look, Ayrton,' then said the engineer, 'for it is necessary that we should know beforehand what to expect.'

Ayrton took the glass and pointed it in the direction indicated. During some minutes he examined the horizon without moving, without uttering a word. Then: –

'It is indeed a vessel,' said he, 'but I do not think she is the "Duncan".'

'Why do you not think so?' asked Gideon Spilett.

'Because the "Duncan" is a steam-yacht, and I cannot perceive any trace of smoke either above or near that vessel.'

'Perhaps she is simply sailing,' observed Pencroft. 'The wind is favourable for the direction which she appears to be taking, and she may be anxious to economise her coal, being so far from land.'

'It is possible that you may be right, Mr Pencroft,' answered Ayrton, 'and that the vessel has extinguished her fires. We must wait until she is nearer, and then we shall soon know what to expect.'

Pencroft, after a minute examination, was later able positively to affirm that the vessel was rigged as a brig, and that she was standing obliquely towards the coast, on the starboard tack, under her topsails and topgallant-sails. This was confirmed by Ayrton. But by continuing in this direction she must soon disappear behind Claw Cape, as the wind was from the south-west, and to watch her it would be then necessary to ascend the heights of Washington Bay, near Port Balloon – a provoking circumstance, for it was already five o'clock in the evening, and the twilight would soon make any observation extremely difficult.

'What shall we do when night comes on?' asked Gideon Spilett. 'Shall we light a fire, so as to signal our presence, on the coast?'

This was a serious question, and yet, although the engineer still retained some of his presentiments, it was answered in the affirmative. During the night the ship might disappear and leave for ever, and, this ship gone, would another ever return to the waters of Lincoln Island? Who could foresee what the future would then have in store for the colonists?

'Yes,' said the reporter, 'we ought to make known to that vessel, whoever she may be, that the island is inhabited. To neglect the opportunity which is offered to us might be to create everlasting regrets.'

It was, therefore, decided that Neb and Pencroft should go to Port Balloon, and that there, at nightfall, they should light an immense fire, the blaze of which would necessarily attract the attention of the brig.

But at the moment when Neb and the sailor were preparing to leave Granite House, the vessel suddenly altered her course, and stood directly for Union Bay. The brig was a good sailer, for she approached rapidly. Neb and Pencroft put off their departure, therefore, and the glass was put into Ayrton's hands, that he might ascertain for certain whether the ship was or was not the "Duncan". The Scotch yacht was also rigged as a brig. The question was, whether a chimney could be discerned between the two masts of the vessel, which was now at a distance of only five miles.

The horizon was still very clear. The examination was easy, and Ayrton soon let the glass fall again, saying, –

'It is not the "Duncan"! It could not be her!'

Pencroft again brought the brig within the range of the telescope, and could see that she was of between three and four hundred tons burden, wonderfully narrow, well-masted, admirably built, and must be a very rapid sailer. But to what nation did she belong? That was difficult to say.

'And yet,' added the sailor, 'a flag is floating from her peak, but I cannot distinguish the colours of it.'

'In half an hour we shall be certain about that,' answered the reporter. 'Besides, it is very evident that the intention of the captain of this ship is to land, and consequently, if not today, tomorrow at the latest, we shall make his acquaintance.

'Never mind!' said Pencroft. 'It is best to know whom we have to deal with, and I shall not be sorry to recognise that fellow's colours!'

And, while thus speaking, the sailor never left the glass. The day began to fade, and with the day the breeze fell also. The brig's ensign hung in folds, and it became more and more difficult to observe it.

'It is not the American flag,' said Pencroft from time to time, 'nor the English, the red of which could be easily seen, nor the French or German colours, nor the white flag of Russia, nor the yellow of Spain. One would say it was all one colour. Let's see: in these seas, what do we generally meet with? The Chilian flag? – but that is tri-colour. Brazilian? – it is green. Japanese? – it is yellow and black, whilst this – '

At that moment the breeze blew out the unknown flag. Ayrton, seizing the telescope which the sailor had put down, put it to his eye, and in a hoarse voice, –

'The black flag!' he exclaimed.

And indeed the sombre bunting was floating from the mast of the brig, and they had now good reason for considering her to be a suspicious vessel!

Had the engineer, then, been right in his presentiments? Was this a pirate vessel? Did she scour the Pacific, competing with the Malay proas which still infest it? For what had she come to look at the shores of Lincoln Island? Was it to them an unknown island, ready to become a magazine for stolen cargoes? Had she come to find on the coast a sheltered port for the winter months? Was the settlers' honest domain destined to be transformed into an infamous refuge – the headquarters of the piracy of the Pacific?

All these ideas instinctively presented themselves to the colonists' imaginations. There was no doubt, besides, of the signification which must be attached to the colour of the hoisted flag. It was that of pirates! It was that which the 'Duncan' would have carried, had the convicts succeeded in their criminal design! No time was lost before discussing it.

'My friends,' said Cyrus Harding, 'perhaps this vessel only wishes to survey the coast of the island. Perhaps her crew will not land. There is a chance of it. However that may be, we ought to do everything we can to hide our presence here. The windmill on Prospect Heights is too easily seen. Let Ayrton and Neb go and take down the sails. We must also conceal the windows of Granite House with thick branches. All the fires must be extinguished, so that nothing may betray the presence of men on the island.'

'And our vessel?' said Herbert.

'Oh,' answered Pencroft, 'she is sheltered in Port Balloon, and I defy any of those rascals there to find her!'

The engineer's orders were immediately executed. Neb and Ayrton ascended the plateau, and took the necessary precautions to conceal any indication of a settlement. Whilst they were thus occupied, their companions went to the border of Jacamar Wood, and brought back a large quantity of branches and creepers, which would at some distance appear as natural foliage, and thus disguise the windows in the granite cliff. At the same time, the ammunition and guns were placed ready so as to be at hand in case of an unexpected attack.

When all these precautions had been taken, —

'My friends,' said Harding, and his voice betrayed some emotion, 'if these wretches endeavour to seize Lincoln Island, we shall defend it — shall we not?'

'Yes, Cyrus,' replied the reporter, 'and if necessary we will die to defend it!'

The engineer extended his hand to his companions, who pressed it warmly.

Ayrton alone remained in his corner, not joining the colonists. Perhaps he, the former convict, still felt himself unworthy to do so! Cyrus Harding understood what was passing in Ayrton's mind, and going to him —

'And you, Ayrton,' he asked, 'what will you do?'

'My duty,' answered Ayrton.

He then took up his station near the window and gazed through the foliage.

It was now half-past seven. The sun had disappeared twenty minutes ago behind Granite House. Consequently the Eastern horizon was becoming gradually obscured. In the meanwhile the brig continued to advance towards Union Bay. She was now not more than two miles off, and exactly opposite the plateau of Prospect Heights, for after having tacked off Claw Cape, she had drifted towards the north in the current of the rising tide. One might have said that at this distance she had already entered the vast bay, for a straight line drawn from Claw Cape to Cape Mandible would have rested on her starboard quarter.

Was the brig about to penetrate far into the bay? That was the first question. When once in the bay, would she anchor there? That was the second. Would she not content herself with only surveying the coast, and stand out to sea again without landing her crew? They would know this in an hour. The colonists could do nothing but wait.

Cyrus Harding had not seen the suspected vessel hoist the black flag without deep anxiety. Was it not a direct menace against the work which he and his companions had till now conducted so successfully? Had these pirates — for the sailors of the brig could be nothing else — already visited the island, since on approaching it they had hoisted their colours. Had they formerly invaded it, so that certain unaccountable peculiarities might be explained in this way? Did there exist in the as yet unexplored parts some accomplice ready to enter into communication with them?

To all these questions which he mentally asked himself, Harding knew not what to reply; but he felt that the safety of the colony could not but be seriously threatened by the arrival of the brig.

However, he and his companions were determined to fight to the last gasp. It would have been very important to know if the pirates were numerous and better armed than the colonists. But how was this information to be obtained?

Night fell. The new moon had disappeared. Profound darkness enveloped the island and the sea. No light could pierce through the heavy piles of clouds on the horizon. The wind had died away completely with the twilight. Not a leaf rustled on the trees, not a ripple murmured on the shore. Nothing could be seen of the ship, all her lights being extinguished; and if she was still in sight of the island, her whereabouts could not be discovered.

'Well! who knows?' said Pencroft. 'Perhaps that cursed craft will stand off during the night, and we shall see nothing of her at daybreak.'

As if in reply to the sailor's observation, a bright light flashed in the darkness, and a cannon-shot was heard.

The vessel was still there, and had guns on board.

Six seconds elapsed between the flash and the report.

Therefore the brig was about a mile and a quarter from the coast.

At the same time, the chains were heard rattling through the hawse-holes.

The vessel had just anchored in sight of Granite House!

CHAPTER 18

THERE was no longer any doubt as to the pirates' intentions. They had dropped anchor at a short distance from the island, and it was evident that the next day by means of their boats they purposed to land on the beach!

Cyrus Harding and his companions were ready to act, but, determined though they were, they must not forget to be prudent. Perhaps their presence might still be concealed in the event of the pirates contenting themselves with landing on the shore without examining the interior of the island. It might be, indeed, that their only intention was to obtain fresh water from the Mercy, and it was not impossible that the bridge, thrown across a mile and a half from the mouth, and the manufactory at the Chimneys, might escape their notice.

But why was that flag hoisted at the brig's peak? What was that shot fired for? Pure bravado doubtless, unless it was a sign of the act of taking possession. Harding knew now that the vessel was well-armed. And what had the colonists of Lincoln Island to reply to the pirates' guns? A few muskets only.

'However,' observed Cyrus Harding, 'here we are in an impregnable position. The enemy cannot discover the mouth of the outlet, now that it is hidden under reeds and grass, and consequently it would be impossible for them to penetrate into Granite House.'

'But our plantations, our poultry-yard, our corral, all, everything!' exclaimed Pencroft, stamping his foot. 'They may spoil everything, destroy everything in a few hours!'

'Everything, Pencroft,' answered Harding, 'and we have no means of preventing them.'

'Are they numerous? that is the question,' said the reporter. 'If they are not more than a dozen, we shall be able to stop them; but forty, fifty, more perhaps!'

'Captain Harding,' then said Ayrton, advancing towards the engineer, 'will you give me leave.'

'For what, my friend?'

'To go to that vessel to find out the strength of her crew.'

'But Ayrton – ' answered the engineer, hesitating, 'you will risk your life – '

'Why not, sir?'

'That is more than your duty.'

'I have more than my duty to do,' replied Ayrton.

'Will you go to the ship in the boat?' asked Gideon Spilett.

'No, sir, but I will swim. A boat would be seen where a man may glide between wind and water.'

'Do you know that the brig is a mile and a quarter from the shore?' said Herbert.

'I am a good swimmer, Mr Herbert.'

'I tell you it is risking your life,' said the engineer.

'That is no matter,' answered Ayrton. 'Captain Harding, I ask this as a favour. Perhaps it will be a means of raising me in my own eyes!'

'Go, Ayrton,' replied the engineer, who felt sure that a refusal would have deeply wounded the former convict, now become an honest man.

'I will accompany you,' said Pencroft.

'You mistrust me!' said Ayrton quickly.

Then more humbly, –

'Alas!'

'No! no!' exclaimed Harding with animation; 'no, Ayrton, Pencroft does not mistrust you. You interpret his words wrongly.'

'Indeed,' returned the sailor, 'I only propose to accompany Ayrton as far as the islet. It may be, although it is scarcely possible, that one of these villains has landed, and in that case two men will not be too many to hinder him from giving the alarm. I will wait for Ayrton on the islet, and he shall go alone to the vessel, since he has proposed to do so.' These things agreed to, Ayrton made preparations for his departure. His plan was bold, but it might succeed, thanks to the darkness of the night. Once arrived at the vessel's side, Ayrton, holding on to the main chains, might reconnoitre the number and perhaps overhear the intentions of the pirates.

Ayrton and Pencroft, followed by their companions, descended to the beach. Ayrton undressed and rubbed himself with grease, so as to suffer less from the temperature of the water, which was still cold. He might, indeed, be obliged to remain in it for several hours.

Pencroft and Neb, during this time, had gone to fetch the boat, moored a few hundred feet higher up, on the bank of the Mercy, and by the time they returned, Ayrton was ready to start. A coat was thrown over his shoulders, and the settlers all came round him to press his hand.

Ayrton then shoved off with Pencroft in the boat.

It was half-past ten in the evening when the two adventurers disappeared in the darkness. Their companions returned to wait at the Chimneys.

The channel was easily traversed, and the boat touched the opposite shore of an islet. This was not done without precaution, for fear lest the pirates might be roaming about there. But after a careful survey, it was evident that the islet was deserted. Ayrton then, followed by Pencroft, crossed it with a rapid step, scaring the birds nestled in the holes of the rocks; then, without hesitating, he plunged into the sea, and swam noiselessly in the direction of the ship, in which a few lights had recently appeared, showing her exact situation. As to Pencroft, he crouched down in a cleft of the rock, and awaited the return of his companion. In the meanwhile, Ayrton, swimming with a vigorous stroke, glided through the sheet of water without producing the slightest ripple. His head just emerged above it and his eyes were fixed on the dark hull of the brig, from which the lights were reflected in the water. He thought only of the duty which he had promised to accomplish, and nothing of the danger which he ran, not only on board the ship, but in the sea, often frequented by sharks. The current bore him along and he rapidly receded from the shore.

Half an hour afterward, Ayrton, without having been either

seen or heard, arrived at the ship and caught hold of the mainchains. He took breath, then hoisting himself up, he managed to reach the extremity of the cutwater. There were drying several pairs of sailor's trousers. He put on a pair. Then settling himself firmly, he listened. They were not sleeping on board the brig. On the contrary, they were talking, singing, laughing. And these were the sentences, accompanied with oaths, which principally struck Ayrton: –

'Our brig is a famous acquisition.'

'She sails well, and merits her name of the "Speedy".'

'She would show all the navy of Norfolk a clean pair of heels.'

'Hurrah for her captain!'

'Hurrah for Bob Harvey!'

What Ayrton felt when he overheard this fragment of conversation may be understood when it is known that in this Bob Harvey he recognised one of his old Australian companions, a daring sailor, who had continued his criminal career. Bob Harvey had seized, on the shores of Norfolk Island, this brig, which was loaded with arms, ammunition, utensils, and tools of all sorts, destined for one of the Sandwich Islands. All his gang had gone on board, and pirates after having been convicts, these wretches, more ferocious than the Malays themselves, scoured the Pacific, destroying vessels, and massacring their crews.

The convicts spoke loudly, they recounted their deeds, drinking deeply at the same time, and this is what Ayrton gathered. The actual crew of the 'Speedy' was composed solely of English prisoners, escaped from Norfolk Island.

Here it may be well to explain what this island was. In 29° 2′ south latitude, and 165° 42′ east longitude, to the east of Australia, is found a little island, six miles in circumference, overlooked by Mount Pitt, which rises to a height of 1100 feet above the level of the sea. This is Norfolk Island, once the seat of an establishment in which were lodged the most intractable convicts from the English penitentiaries. They numbered 500, under an iron discipline, threatened with terrible punishments, and were guarded by 150 soldiers, and 150 employed under the orders of the governor. It would be difficult to imagine a collection of greater ruffians. Sometimes, – although very rarely, – notwithstanding the extreme surveillance of which they were the object, many managed to escape, and seizing vessels which they surprised, they infested the Polynesian Archipelagos.[1]

Thus had Bob Harvey and his companions done. Thus had Ayrton formerly wished to do. Bob Harvey had seized the brig 'Speedy', anchored in sight of Norfolk Island; the crew had been massacred; and for a year this ship had scoured the Pacific, under the command of Harvey, now a pirate, and well known to Ayrton!

[1] Norfolk Island has long since been abondoned as a penal settlement.

The convicts were, for the most part, assembled under the poop; but a few, stretched on the deck, were talking loudly.

The conversation still continued amidst shouts and libations. Ayrton learned that chance alone had brought the 'Speedy' in sight of Lincoln Island: Bob Harvey had never yet set foot on it; but, as Cyrus Harding had conjectured, finding this unknown land in his course, its position being marked on no chart, he had formed the project of visiting it, and, if he found it suitable, of making it the brig's headquarters.

As to the black flag hoisted at the 'Speedy's' peak, and the gun which had been fired, in imitation of men-of-war when they lower their colours, it was pure piratical bravado. It was in no way a signal, and no communication yet existed between the convicts and Lincoln Island.

The settlers' domain was now menaced with terrible danger. Evidently the island, with its water, its harbour, its resources of all kinds so increased in value by the colonists, and the concealment afforded by Granite House, could not but be convenient for the convicts; in their hands it would become an excellent place of refuge, and, being unknown, it would assure them, for a long time perhaps, impunity and security. Evidently, also, the lives of the settlers would not be respected, and Bob Harvey and his accomplices' first care would be to massacre them without mercy. Harding and his companions had, therefore, not even the choice of flying and hiding themselves in the island, since the convicts intended to reside there, and since, in the event of the 'Speedy' departing on an expedition, it was probable that some of the crew would remain on shore, so as to settle themselves there. Therefore, it would be necessary to fight, to destroy every one of these scoundrels, unworthy of pity, and against whom any means would be right. So thought Ayrton, and he well knew that Cyrus Harding would be of his way of thinking.

But was resistance and, in the last place, victory possible? That would depend on the equipment of the brig, and the number of men which she carried.

This Ayrton resolved to learn at any cost, and as an hour after his arrival the vociferations had begun to die away, and as a large number of the convicts were already buried in a drunken sleep, Ayrton did not hesitate to venture on to the 'Speedy's' deck, which the extinguished lanterns now left in total darkness. He hoisted himself on to the cutwater, and by the bowsprit arrived at the forecastle. Then, gliding among the convicts stretched here and there, he made the round of the ship and found that the 'Speedy' carried four guns. which would throw shot of from eight to ten pounds in weight. He found also, on touching them, that these guns were breech-loaders. They were, therefore, of modern make, easily used, and of terrible effect.

As to the men lying on the deck, they were about ten in number, but it was to be supposed that more were sleeping down below. Besides, by listening to them, Ayrton had understood that there were fifty on board. That was a large number for the six settlers of Lincoln Island to contend with! But now, thanks to Ayrton's devotion, Cyrus Harding would not be surprised, he would know the strength of his adversaries, and would make his arrangements accordingly.

There was nothing more for Ayrton to do but to return, and render to his companions an account of the mission with which he had charged himself, and he prepared to regain the bows of the brig, so that he might let himself down into the water.

But to this man, whose wish was, as he had said, to do more than his duty, there came an heroic thought. This was to sacrifice his own life, but save the island and the colonists. Cyrus Harding evidently could not resist fifty ruffians, all well armed, who, either by penetrating by main force into Granite House, or by starving out the besieged, could obtain from them what they wanted. And then he thought of his preservers – those who had made him again a man, and an honest man, those to whom he owed all – murdered without pity, their works destroyed, their island turned into a pirates' den. He said to himself that he, Ayrton, was the principal cause of so many disasters, since his old companion, Bob Harvey, had but realised his own plans, and a feeling of horror took possession of him. Then he was seized with an irresistible desire to blow up the brig, and with her all whom she had on board. He would perish in the explosion, but he would have done his duty.

Ayrton did not hesitate. To reach the powder-room, which is always situated in the after-part of the vessel, was easy. There would be no want of powder in a vessel which followed such a trade, and a spark would be enough to destory it in an instant.

Ayrton stole carefully along the between-decks, strewn with numerous sleepers, overcome more by drunkenness than sleep. A lantern was lighted at the foot of the mainmast, round which was hung a gun-rack, furnished with weapons of all sorts.

Ayrton took a revolver from the rack, and assured himself that it was loaded and primed. Nothing more was needed to accomplish the work of destruction. He then glided towards the stern, so as to arrive under the brig's poop at the powder-magazine.

It was difficult to proceed along the dimly-lighted deck without stumbling over some half-sleeping convicts, who retorted by oaths and kicks. Ayrton was, therefore, more than once obliged to halt. But at last he arrived at the partition dividing the after-cabin, and found the door opening into the magazine itself.

Ayrton, compelled to force it open, set to work. It was a difficult operation to perform without noise, for he had to break a padlock. But under his vigorous hand the padlock broke, and the door was open.

At that moment a hand was laid on Ayrton's shoulder.

'What are you doing here?' asked a tall man, in a harsh voice, who, standing in the shadow, quickly threw the light of a lantern on Ayrton's face.

Ayrton drew back. In the rapid flash of the lantern, he had recognised his former accomplice, Bob Harvey, who could not have known him, as he must have thought Ayrton long since dead.

'What are you doing here?' again said Bob Harvey, seizing Ayrton by the waistband.

But Ayrton, without replying, wrenched himself from his grasp and attempted to rush into the magazine. A shot fired into the midst of the powder-casks, and all would be over!

'Help, lads!' shouted Bob Harvey.

At his shout two or three pirates awoke, jumped up, and, rushing on Ayrton, endeavoured to throw him down. He soon extricated himself from their grasp. He fired his revolver, and two convicts fell; but a blow from a knife, which he could not ward off, made a gash in his shoulder.

Ayrton perceived that he could no longer hope to carry out his project. Bob Harvey had reclosed the door of the powder-magazine, and a movement on the deck indicated a general awakening of the pirates. Ayrton must reserve himself to fight at the side of Cyrus Harding. There was nothing for him but flight!

But was flight still possible? It was doubtful, yet Ayrton resolved to dare everything in order to rejoin his companions.

Four barrels of the revolver were still undischarged. Two were fired – one, aimed at Bob Harvey, did not wound him, or at any rate only slightly; and Ayrton, profiting by the momentary retreat of his adversaries rushed towards the companion-ladder to gain the deck. Passing before the lantern, he smashed it with a blow from the butt of his revolver. A profound darkness ensured, which favoured his flight. Two or three pirates, awakened by the noise, were descending the ladder at the same moment. A fifth shot from Ayrton laid one low, and the others drew back not understanding what was going on. Ayrton was on deck in two bounds, and three seconds later, having discharged his last barrel in the face of a pirate who was about to seize him by the throat, he leapt over the bulwarks into the sea.

Ayrton had not made six strokes before shots were splashing around him like hail.

What were Pencroft's feelings, sheltered under a rock on the islet! what were those of Harding, the reporter, Herbert, and Neb, crouched in the Chimneys, when they heard the reports on board the brig! They rushed out on to the beach, and, their guns shouldered, they stood ready to repel any attack.

They had no doubt about it themselves! Ayrton, surprised by the pirates, had been murdered, and, perhaps, the wretches would profit by the night to make a descent on the island!

Half an hour was passed in terrible anxiety. The firing had ceased, and yet neither Ayrton nor Pencroft had reappeared. Was the islet invaded? Ought they not to fly to the help of Ayrton and Pencroft? But how? The tide being high at that time, rendered the channel impassable. The boat was not there! We may imagine the horrible anxiety which took posession of Harding and his companions!

At last, towards half-past twelve, a boat, carrying two men, touched the beach. It was Ayrton, slightly wounded in the shoulder, and Pencroft, safe and sound, whom their friends received with open arms.

All immediately took refuge in the Chimneys. There Ayrton recounted all that had passed, even to his plan for blowing up the brig, which he had attempted to put into execution.

All hands were extended to Ayrton, who did not conceal from them that their situation was serious. The pirates had been alarmed. They knew that Lincoln Island was inhabited. They would land upon it in numbers and well armed. They would respect nothing. Should the settlers fall into their hands, they must expect no mercy!

'Well, we shall know how to die!' said the reporter.

'Let us go in and watch,' answered the engineer.

'Have we any chance of escape, captain?' asked the sailor.

'Yes, Pencroft.'

'Hum! six against fifty!'

'Yes! six! without counting –'

'Who?' asked Pencroft.

Cyrus did not reply, but pointed upwards.

CHAPTER 19

The night passed without incident. The colonists were on the *qui vive*, and did not leave their post at the Chimneys. The pirates, on their side, did not appear to have made any attempt to land. Since the last shots fired at Ayrton not a report, not even a sound, had betrayed the presence of the brig in the neighbourhood of the island. It might have been fancied that she had weighed anchor, thinking that she had to deal with her match, and had left the coast.

But it was no such thing, and when day began to dawn the settlers could see a confused mass through the morning mist. It was the 'Speedy'.

'These, my friends,' said the engineer, 'are the arrangements which appear to me best to make before the fog completely clears away. It hides us from the eyes of the pirates, and we can act without attracting their attention. The most important thing is, that the convicts should believe that the inhabitants of the island are numerous, and consequently capable of resisting them. I therefore propose that we divide into three parties, the first of which shall be posted at the Chimneys, the second at the mouth of the Mercy. As to the third, I think it would be best to place it on the islet, so as to prevent, or at all events delay, any attempt at landing. We have the use of two rifles and four muskets. Each of us will be armed, and, as we are amply provided with powder and shot, we need not spare our fire. We have nothing to fear from the muskets, nor even from the guns of the brig. What can they do against these rocks? And, as we shall not fire from the windows of Granite House, the pirates will not think of causing irreparable damage by throwing shell against it. What is to be feared is, the necessity of meeting hand-to-hand, since the convcts have numbers on their side. We must, therefore, try to prevent them from landing, but without discovering ourselves. Therefore, do not economise the ammunition. Fire often, but with a sure aim. We have each eight or ten enemies to kill, and they must be killed!'

The posts were arranged in the following manner:-

Cyrus Harding and Herbert remained in ambush at the Chimneys, thus commanding the shore to the foot of Granite House.

Gideon Spilett and Neb crouched among the rocks at the mouth of the Mercy, from which the drawbridges had been raised, so as to prevent any one from crossing in a boat or landing on the opposite shore.

As to Ayrton and Pencroft, they shoved off in the boat, and prepared to cross the channel and to take up two separate stations on the islet. In this way, shots being fired from four different points at once, the convicts would be led to believe that the island was both largely peopled and strongly defended.

In the event of a landing being effected without their having been able to prevent it, and also if they saw that they were on the point of being cut off by the brig's boat, Ayrton and Pencroft were to return in their boat to the shore and proceed toward the threatened spot.

Before starting to occupy their posts, the colonists for the last time wrung each other's hands.

Pencroft succeeded in controlling himself sufficiently to suppress his emotion when he embraced Herbert, his boy! and then they separated.

In a few moments Harding and Herbert on one side, the reporter and Neb on the other, had disappeared behind the rocks, and five minutes later Ayrton and Pencroft, having without difficulty crossed the channel, disembarked on the islet and concealed themselves in the clefts of its eastern shore.

None of them could have been seen, for they themselves could scarcely distinguish the brig in the fog.

It was half past six in the morning.

Soon the fog began to clear away, and the topmasts of the brig issued from the vapour. For some minutes great masses rolled over the surface of the sea, then a breeze sprang up, which rapidly dispelled the mist.

The 'Speedy' now appeared in full view, with a spring on her cable, her head to the north, presenting her larboard side to the island. Just as Harding had calculated, she was not more than a mile and a quarter from the coast.

The sinister black flag floated from the peak.

The engineer, with his telescope, could see that the four guns on board were pointed at the island. They were evidently ready to fire at a moment's notice.

In the meanwhile the 'Speedy' remained silent. About thirty pirates could be seen moving on the deck. A few were on the poop; two others posted in the shrouds, and armed with spy-glasses, were attentively surveying the island.

Certainly, Bob Harvey and his crew would not be able easily to give an account of what had happened during the night on board the brig. Had this half-naked man, who had forced the door of the powder-magazine, and with whom they had struggled, who had six times discharged his revolver at them, who had killed one and wounded two others, escaped their shot? Had he been able to swim ashore? Whence did he come? What had been his object? Had his design really been to blow up the brig, as Bob Harvey had thought? All this must be confused enough in the convicts' minds. But what they could no longer doubt was that the unknown island before which the 'Speedy' had cast anchor was inhabited, and that there was, perhaps, a numerous colony ready to defend it. And yet no one was to be seen, neither on the shore nor on the heights. The beach appeared to be absolutely deserted. At any rate, there was no trace of dwellings. Had the inhabitants fled into the interior? Thus probably the pirate captain reasoned, and doubtless, like a prudent man, he wished to reconnoitre the locality before he allowed his men to venture there.

During an hour and a half, no indication of attack or landing could be observed on board the brig. Evidently Bob Harvey was hesitating. Even with his strongest telescopes he could not have perceived one of the settlers crouched among the rocks. It was not even probable that his attention had been awakened by the screen of green branches and creepers hiding the windows of Granite House, and showing rather conspiciously on the bare rock. Indeed, how could he imagine that a dwelling was hollowed out, at that height, in the solid granite. From Claw Cape to the Mandible Capes, in all the extent of Union Bay, there was nothing to lead him to suppose that the island was or could be inhabited.

At eight o'clock, however, the colonists observed a movement on board the 'Speedy'. A boat was lowered, and seven men jumped into her. They were armed with muskets: one took the yoke-lines, four others the oars, and the two others, kneeling in the bows, ready to fire, reconnoitred the island. Their object was no doubt to make an examination but not to land, for in the latter case they would have come in larger numbers. The pirates from their look-out could have seen that the coast was sheltered by an islet, separated from it by a channel half a mile in width. However, it was soon evident to Cyrus Harding, on observing the direction followed by the boat, that they would not attempt to penetrate into the channel, but would land on the islet.

Pencroft and Ayrton, each hidden in a narrow cleft of the rock, saw them coming directly towards them, and waited till they were within range.

The boat advanced with extreme caution. The oars only dipped into the water at long intervals. It could now be seen that one of the convicts held a lead-line in his hand, and that he wished to fathom the depth of the channel hollowed out by the current of the Mercy. This showed that it was Bob Harvey's intention to bring his brig as near as possible to the coast. About thirty pirates, scattered in the rigging, followed every movement of the boat, and took the bearings of certain landmarks which would allow them to approach without danger. The boat was not more than two cables-lengths off the islet when she stopped. The man at the tiller stood up and looked for the best place at which to land.

At that moment two shots were heard. Smoke curled up from among the rocks of the islet. The man at the helm and the man with the lead-line fell backwards into the boat. Ayrton and Pencroft's balls had struck them both at the same moment.

Almost immediately a louder report was heard, a cloud of smoke issued from the brig's side, and a ball, striking the summit of the rock which sheltered Ayrton and Pencroft, made it fly in splinters, but the two marksmen remained unhurt.

Horrible imprecations burst from the boat, which immediately continued its way. The man who had been at the tiller was replaced by one of his comrades, and the oars were rapidly plunged into the water. However, instead of returning on board as might have been expected, the boat coasted along the islet, so as to round its southern point. The pirates pulled vigorously at their oars, that they might get out of range of the bullets.

They advanced to within five cables-lengths of that part of the shore terminated by Flotsam Point, and after having rounded it in a semicircular line, still protected by the brig's guns, they proceeded towards the mouth of the Mercy.

Their evident intention was to penetrate into the channel, and cut off the colonists posted on the islet, in such a way, that whatever their number might be, being placed between the fire from the boat and the fire from the brig, they would find themselves in a very disadvantageous position.

A quarter of an hour passed whilst the boat advanced in this direction. Absolute silence, perfect calm, reigned in the air and on the water.

Pencroft and Ayrton, although they knew they ran the risk of being cut off, had not left their post, both that they did not wish to show themselves as yet to their assailants, and expose themselves to the 'Speedy's' guns, and that they relied on Neb and Gideon Spilett, watching at the mouth of the river, and on Cyrus Harding and Herbert, in ambush among the rocks at the Chimneys.

Twenty minutes after the first shots were fired, the boat was less than two cables-lengths off the Mercy. As the tide was beginning to rise with its accustomed violence, caused by the narrowness of the straights, the pirates were drawn towards the river, and it was only by dint of hard rowing that they were able to keep in the middle of the channel. But as they were passing within good range of the mouth of the Mercy, two balls saluted them, and two more of their number were laid in the bottom of the boat. Neb and Spilett had not missed their aim.

The brig immediately sent a second ball on the post betrayed by the smoke, but without any other result than that of splintering the rock.

The boat now contained only three able men. Carried on by the current, it shot through the channel with the rapidity of an arrow, passed before Harding and Herbert, who, not thinking it within range, withheld their fire, then, rounding the northern point of the islet with the two remaining oars, they pulled towards the brig.

Hitherto the settlers had nothing to complain of. Their adversaries had certainly had the worst of it. The latter already counted four men seriously wounded if not dead; they, on the contrary, unwounded, had not missed a shot. If the pirates continued to attack them in this way, if they renewed their attempt to land by means of a boat, they could be destroyed one by one.

It was now seen how advantageous the engineer's arrangements had been. The pirates would think that they had to deal with numerous and well-armed adversaries, whom they could not easily get the better of.

Half an hour passed before the boat, having to pull against the current, could get alongside the 'Speedy'. Frightful cries were heard when they returned on board with the wounded, and two or three guns were fired with no result.

But now about a dozen convicts, maddened with rage, and possibly by the effect of the evening's potations, threw themselves into the boat. A second boat was also lowered, in which eight men took their places, and whilst the first pulled straight for the islet, to dislodge the colonists from thence, the second manoeuvred so as to force the entrance of the Mercy.

The situation was evidently becoming very dangerous for Pencroft and Ayrton, and they saw that they must regain the mainland.

However, they waited till the first boat was within range, when two well-directed balls threw its crew into disorder. Then Pencroft and Ayrton, abandoning their posts, under fire from the dozen muskets, ran across the islet at full speed, jumped into their boat, crossed the channel at the moment the second boat reached the southern end, and ran to hide themselves in the Chimneys.

They had scarcely rejoined Cyrus Harding and Herbert, before the islet was overrun with pirates in every direction. Almost at the same moment, fresh reports resounded from the Mercy station, to which the second boat was rapidly approaching. Two, out of the eight men who manned her, were mortally wounded by Gideon Spilett and Neb, and the boat herself, carried irresistibly on to the reefs, was stove in at the mouth of the Mercy. But the six survivors, holding their muskets above their heads to preserve them from contact with the water, managed to land on the right bank of the river. Then, finding they were exposed to the fire of the ambush there, they fled in the direction of Flotsam Point, out of range of the balls.

The actual situation was this: on the islet were a dozen convicts, of whom some were no doubt wounded, but who had still a boat at their disposal; on the island were six, but who could not by any possibility reach Granite House, as they could not cross the river, all the bridges being raised.

'Hallo,' exclaimed Pencroft as he rushed into the Chimneys, 'hallo, captain! What do you think of it, now?'

'I think,' answered the engineer, 'that the combat will now take a new form, for it cannot be supposed that the convicts will be so foolish as to remain in a position so unfavourable for them!'

'They won't cross the channel,' said the sailor. 'Ayrton and Mr Spilett's rifles are there to prevent them. You know that they carry more than a mile!'

'No doubt,' replied Herbert, 'but what can two rifles do against the brig's guns?'

'Well, the brig isn't in the channel yet, I fancy!' said Pencroft.

'But suppose she does come there?' said Harding.

'That's impossible, for she would risk running aground and being lost!'

'It is possible,' said Ayrton. 'The convicts might profit by the high tide to enter the channel, with the risk of grounding at low tide, it is true; but then, under the fire from her guns, our posts would be no longer tenable.'

'Confound them!' exclaimed Pencroft. 'It really seems as if the blackguards were preparing to weigh anchor.'

'Perhaps we shall be obliged to take refuge in Granite House!' observed Herbert.

'We must wait!' answered Cyrus Harding.

'But Mr Spilett and Neb?' said Pencroft.

'They will know when it is best to rejoin us. Be ready, Ayrton. It is yours and Spilett's rifles which must speak now.'

It was only too true. The 'Speedy' was beginning to weigh her anchor, and her intention was evidently to approach the islet. The tide would be rising for an hour and a half, and the ebb current being already weakened, it would be easy for the brig to advance. But as to entering the channel, Pencroft, contrary to Ayrton's opinion, could not believe that she would dare to attempt it.

In the meanwhile, the pirates who occupied the islet had gradually advanced to the opposite shore, and were now only separated from the mainland by the channel.

Being armed with muskets alone, they could do no harm to the settlers, in ambush at the chimneys and the mouth of the Mercy; but, not knowing the latter to be supplied with long range rifles, they on their side did not believe themselves to be exposed. Quite uncovered, therefore, they surveyed the islet, and examined the shore.

Their illusion was of short duration. Ayrton's and Gideon Spilett's rifles then spoke, and no doubt imparted some very disagreeable intelligence to two of the convicts, for they fell backwards.

Then there was a general helter-skelter. The ten others, not even stopping to pick up their dead or wounded companions, fled to the other side of the islet, tumbled into the boat which had brought them, and pulled away with all their strength.

'Eight less!' exclaimed Pencroft. 'Really, one would have thought that Mr Spilett and Ayrton had given the word to fire together!'

'Gentlemen,' said Ayrton, as he reloaded his gun, 'this is becoming more serious. The brig is making sail!'

'The anchor is weighed!' exclaimed Pencroft.

'Yes; and she is already moving.'

In fact, they could distinctly hear the creaking of the windlass. The 'Speedy' was at first held by her anchor; then, when that had been raised, she began to drift towards the shore. The wind was blowing from the sea; the jib and the fore-topsail were hoisted, and the vessel gradually approached the island.

From the two posts of the Mercy and the Chimneys they watched her without giving a sign of life; but not without some emotion. What could be more terrible for the colonists than to be exposed, at a short distance, to the brig's guns, without being able to reply with any effect? How could they then prevent the pirates from landing.

Cyrus Harding felt this strongly, and he asked himself what it would be possible to do. Before long, he would be called upon for his determination. But what was it to be? To shut themselves up in Granite House, to be beseiged there, to remain there for weeks, for months even, since they had an abundance of provisions? So far good! But after that? The pirates would not the less be masters of the island, which they would ravage at their pleasure, and in time they would end by having their revenge on the prisoners in Granite House.

However, one chance yet remained; it was that Bob Harvey, after all, would not venture his ship into the channel, and that he would keep outside the islet. He would be still separated from the coast by half a mile, and at that distance his shot could not be very destructive.

'Never!' repeated Pencroft, 'Bob Harvey will never, if he is a good seaman, enter that channel! He knows well that it would risk the brig, if the sea got up ever so little! And what would become of him without his vessel?'

In the meanwhile the brig approached the islet, and it could be seen that she was endeavouring to make the lower end. The breeze was light, and as the current had then lost much of its force, Bob Harvey had absolute command over his vessel.

The route previously followed by the boats had allowed her to reconnoitre the channel, and she boldly entered it.

The pirate's design was now only too evident; he wished to bring her broadside to bear on the Chimneys and from there to reply with shell and ball to the shot which had till then decimated her crew.

Soon the 'Speedy' reached the point of the islet; she rounded it with ease; then the mainsail was braced up, and the brig hugging the wind, stood across the mouth of the Mercy.

'The scoundrels! they are coming!' said Pencroft.

At that moment, Cyrus Harding, Ayrton, the sailor, and Herbert, were rejoined by Neb and Gideon Spilett.

The reporter and his companion had judged it best to abandon the post at the Mercy, from which they could do nothing against the ship, and they had acted wisely. It was better that the colonists should be together at the moment when they were about to engage in a decisive action. Gideon Spilett and Neb had arrived by dodging behind the rocks, though not without attracting a shower of bullets, which had not, however, reached them.

'Spilett! Neb!' cried the engineer, 'you are not wounded!'

'No,' answered the reporter; 'a few bruises only from the ricochet! But that cursed brig has entered the channel!'

'Yes,' replied Pencroft, 'and in ten minutes she will have anchored before Granite House!'

'Have you formed any plan, Cyrus?' asked the reporter.

'We must take refuge in Granite House whilst there is still time, and the convicts cannot see us.'

'That is my opinion, too,' replied Gideon Spilett; but once shut up – '

'We must be guided by circumstances,' said the engineer.

'Let us be off, then, and make haste!' said the reporter.

'Would you not wish, captain, that Ayrton and I should remain here?' asked the sailor.

'What would be the use of that, Pencroft?' replied Harding. 'No. We will not separate!'

There was not a moment to be lost. The colonists left the Chimneys. A bend of the cliff prevented them from being seen by those in the brig; but two or three reports, and the crash of bullets on the rock, told them that the 'Speedy' was at no great distance.

To spring into the lift, hoist themselves up to the door of Granite House, where Top and Jup had been shut up since the evening before, to rush into the large room, was the work of a minute only.

It was quite time, for the settlers, through the branches, could see the 'Speedy', surrounded with smoke, gliding up the channel. The firing was incessant, and shot from the four guns struck blindly, both on the Mercy post, although it was not occupied, and on the Chimneys. The rocks were splintered, and cheers accompanied each discharge. However, they were hoping that Granite House would be spared, thanks to Harding's precaution of concealing the windows, when a shot piercing the door, penetrated into the passage.

'We are discovered!' exclaimed Pencroft.

The colonists had not, perhaps been seen; but it was certain that Bob Harvey had thought proper to send a ball through the suspected foliage which concealed that part of the cliff. Soon he redoubled his attack, when another ball having torn away the leafy screen, disclosed a gaping aperture in the granite.

The colonists' situation was desperate. Their retreat was discovered. They could not oppose any obstacle to these missiles, nor protect the stone, which flew in splinters around them. There was nothing to be done but to take refuge in the upper regions of Granite House, and leave their dwelling to be attacked, when a deep roar was heard, followed by frightful roars!

Cyrus Harding and his companions rushed to one of the windows –

The brig, irresistibly raised on a sort of water-spout, had just split in two, and in less than ten seconds she was swallowed up with all her criminal crew!

CHAPTER 20

'SHE has blown up!' cried Herbert.

'Yes! blown up, just as if Ayrton had set fire to the powder!' returned Pencroft, throwing himself into the lift together with Neb and the lad.

'But what has happened?' asked Gideon Spilett, quite stunned by this unexpected catastrophe.

'Oh! this time, we shall know – ' answered the engineer quickly.

'What shall we know? – '

'Later! later! Come, Spilett. The main point is that these pirates have been exterminated!'

And Cyrus Harding, hurrying away the reporter and Ayrton, joined Pencroft, Neb, and Herbert on the beach.

Nothing could be seen of the brig, not even her masts. After having been raised by the water-spout, she had fallen on her side, and had sunk in that position, doubtless in consequence of some enormous leak. But as in that place the channel was not more than twenty feet in depth, it was certain that the sides of the submerged brig would reappear at low water.

A few things from the wreck floated on the surface of the water. A raft could be seen consisting of spare spars, coops of poultry with their occupants still living, boxes and barrels, which gradually came to the surface, after having escaped through the hatchways, but no pieces of the wreck appeared, neither planks from the deck, nor timber from the hull, – which rendered the sudden disappearance of the 'Speedy' perfectly inexplicable.

However, the two masts, which had been broken and escaped from the shrouds and stays, came up, with their sails, some furled and the others spread. But it was not necessary to wait for the tide to bring up these riches, and Ayrton and Pencroft jumped into the boat with the intention of towing the pieces of wreck either to the beach or to the islet. But just as they were shoving off, an observation from Gideon Spilett arrested them. 'What about those six convicts who disembarked on the right bank of the Mercy?' said he.

In fact, it would not do to forget that the six men whose boat had gone to pieces on the rocks, had landed at Flotsam Point.

They looked in that direction. None of the fugitives were visible. It was probable that, having seen their vessel engulfed in the channel, they had fled into the interior of the island.

'We will deal with them later,' said Harding. 'As they are armed, they will still be dangerous; but as it is six against six, the chances are equal. To the most pressing business first.'

Ayrton and Pencroft pulled vigorously towards the wreck.

The sea was calm and the tide very high, as there had been a new moon but two days before. A whole hour at least would elapse before the hull of the brig could emerge from the water of the channel.

Ayrton and Pencroft were able to fasten the masts and spars by means of ropes, the ends of which were carried to the beach. There, by the united efforts of the settlers, the pieces of wreck were hauled up. Then the boat picked up all that was floating, coops, barrels, and boxes, which were immediately carried to the Chimneys.

Several bodies floated also. Amongst them, Ayrton recognised that of Bob Harvey, which he pointed out to his companion, saying with some emotion, –

'That is what I have been, Pencroft.'

'But what you are no longer, brave Ayrton!' returned the sailor warmly.

It was singular enough that so few bodies floated. Only five or six were counted, which were already being carried by the current towards the open sea. Very probably the convicts had not had time to escape, and the ship lying over on her side, the greater number of them had remained below. Now the current, by carrying the bodies of these miserable men out to sea, would spare the colonists the sad task of burying them in some corner of their island.

For two hours, Cyrus Harding and his companions were solely occupied in hauling up the spars on to the sand, and then in spreading the sails, which were perfectly uninjured, to dry. They spoke little, for they were absorbed in their work, but what thoughts occupied their minds!

Towards half-past one, the colonists embarked in the boat to visit the wreck. It was to be regretted that the brig's two boats had not been saved; but one, as has been said, had gone to pieces at the mouth of the Mercy, and was absolutely useless; the other had disappeared when the brig went down, and had not again been seen, having doubtless been crushed.

The hull of the 'Speedy' was just beginning to issue from the water. The brig was lying right over on her side, for her masts being broken, pressed down by the weight of the ballast displaced by the shock, the keel was visible along her whole length. She had been regularly turned over by the inexplicable but frightful submarine action, which had been at the same time manifested by an enormous water-spout.

The settlers rowed round the hull, and, in proportion as the tide went down, they could ascertain, if not the cause which had occasioned the catastrophe, at least the effect produced.

Towards the bows, on both sides of the keel, seven or eight feet from the beginning of the stem, the sides of the brig were frightfully torn. Over a length of at least twenty feet there opened two large leaks, which it would be impossible to stop up. Not only had the copper sheathing and the planks disappeared, reduced, no doubt, to powder, but also the ribs, the iron bolts and treenails which united them. From the entire length of the hull to the stern the false keel had been separated with unaccountable violence, and the keel itself, torn from the carline in several places, was split in all its length.

'I've a notion!' exclaimed Pencroft, 'that this vessel will be difficult to get afloat again.'

'It will be impossible,' said Ayrton.

'At any rate,' observed Gideon Spilett to the sailor, 'the explosion, if there has been one, has produced singular effects! It has split the lower part of the hull, instead of blowing up the deck and topsides! These great rents appear rather to have been made by a rock than by the explosion of a powder-magazine.'

'There is not a rock in the channel!' answered the sailor. 'I will admit anything you like, except the rock.'

'Let us try to penetrate into the interior of the brig,' said the engineer; 'perhaps we shall then know what to think of the cause of her destruction.' This was the best thing to be done, and it was agreed, besides, to take an inventory of all the treasures on board, and to arrange for their preservation.

Access to the interior of the brig was now easy. The tide was still going down, and the deck was practicable. The hull, composed of heavy masses of iron, had broken through in several places. The noise of the sea could be heard as it gushed out at the holes in the hull.

Cyrus Harding and his companions, hatchets in hand, advanced along the shattered deck. Cases of all sorts encumbered it, and, as they had been but a very short time in the water, their contents were perhaps uninjured.

They then busied themselves in placing all this cargo in safety. The water would not return for several hours, and these hours must be employed in the most profitable way. Ayrton and Pencroft had, at the entrance made in the hull, discovered tackle, which would serve to hoist up the barrels and chests. The boat received them and transported them to the shore. They took the articles as they came, intending to sort them afterwards.

At any rate, the settlers saw at once, with extreme satisfaction, that the brig possessed a very varied cargo – an assortment of all sorts of articles, utensils, manufactured goods, and tools – such as the ships which make the great coasting-trade of Polynesia are usually laden with. It was probable that they would find a little of everything, and they agreed that it was exactly what was necessary for the colony of Lincoln Island.

However – and Cyrus Harding observed it in silent astonishment – not only, as has been said, had the hull of the brig enormously suffered from the shock, whatever it was, that had occasioned the catastrophe, but the interior arrangements had been destroyed, especially towards the bows. Partitions and staunchions were smashed, as if some tremendous shell had burst in the interior of the brig. The colonists could easily go fore and aft, after having removed the cases as they were extricated. They were not heavy bales, which would have been difficult to remove, but simple packages, of which the stowage, besides, was no longer recognisable.

The colonists then reached the stern of the brig – the part formerly surmounted by the poop. It was there that, following Ayrton's directions, they must look for the powder-magazine. Cyrus Harding thought that it had not exploded; that it was possible some barrels might be saved, and that the powder, which is usually enclosed in metal coverings, might not have suffered from contact with the water.

This, in fact, was just what had happened. They extricated from amongst a large number of shot twenty barrels, the insides of which were lined with copper. Pencroft was convinced by the evidence of his own eyes that the destruction of the 'Speedy' could not be attributed to an explosion. That part of the hull in which the magazine was situated was, moreover, that which had suffered least.

'It may be so,' said the obstinate sailor; 'but as to a rock, there is not one in the channel!'

'Then, how did it happen?' asked Herbert.

'I don't know,' answered Pencroft, 'Captain Harding doesn't know, and nobody knows or ever will know!'

Several hours had passed during these researches, and the tide began to flow. Work must be suspended for the present. There was no fear of the brig being carried away by the sea, for she was already fixed as firmly as if moored by her anchors.

They could therefore, without inconvenience, wait until the next day to resume operations; but, as to the vessel herself, she was doomed, and it would be best to hasten to save the remains of her hull, as she would not be long in disappearing in the quick-sands of the channel.

It was now five o'clock in the evening. It had been a hard day's work for the men. They ate with good appetite, and, not-withstanding their fatigue, they could not resist, after dinner, their desire of inspecting the cases which composed the cargo of the 'Speedy'.

Most of them contained clothes, which, as may be believed, were well received. There were enough to clothe a whole colony – linen for every one's use, shoes for every one's feet.

'We are too rich!' exclaimed Pencroft. 'But what are we going to do with all this?'

And every moment burst forth the hurrahs of the delighted sailor when he caught sight of the barrels of gunpowder, fire-arms and side-arms, balls of cotton, implements of husbandry, carpenter's, joiner's, and blacksmith's tools, and boxes of all kinds of seeds, not in the least injured by their short sojourn in the water. Ah, two years before, how these things would have been prized! And now, even although the industrious colonists had provided themselves with tools, these treasures would find their use.

There was no want of space in the store-rooms of Granite House, but that daytime would not allow them to stow away the whole. It would not do also to forget that the six survivors of the 'Speedy's' crew had landed on the island, for they were in all probability scoundrels of the deepest dye, and it was necessary that the colonists should be on their guard against them. Although the bridges over the Mercy were raised, the convicts would not be stopped by a river or a stream, and, rendered desperate, these wretches would be capable of anything.

They would see later what plan it would be best to follow; but in the meantime it was necessary to mount guard over cases and packages heaped up near the Chimneys, and thus the settlers employed themselves in turn during the night.

The morning came, however, without the convicts having attempted any attack. Master Jup and Top, on guard at the foot of Granite House, would have quickly given the alarm. The three following days – the 19th, 20th, and 21st of October – were employed in saving everything of value, or of any use whatever, either from the cargo or rigging of the brig. At low tide they overhauled the hold – at high tide they stowed away the rescued articles. A great part of the copper sheathing had been torn from the hull, which every day sank lower. But before the sand had swallowed the heavy things which had fallen through the bottom, Ayrton and Pencroft, diving to the bed of the channel, recovered the chains and anchors of the brig, the iron of her ballast, and even four guns, which, floated by means of empty casks, were brought to shore.

It may be seen that the arsenal of the colony had gained by the wreck, as well as the store-rooms of Granite House. Pencroft, always enthusiastic in his projects, already spoke of constructing a battery to command the channel and the mouth of the river. With four guns, he engaged to prevent any fleet, 'however powerful it might be,' from venturing into the waters of Lincoln Island!

In the meantime, when nothing remained of the brig but a useless hulk, bad weather came on, which soon finished her. Cyrus Harding had intended to blow her up, so as to collect the remains on the shore, but a strong gale from the north-east and a heavy sea compelled him to economise his powder.

In fact, on the night of the 23rd, the hull entirely broke up, and some of the wreck was cast up on the beach.

As to the papers on board, it is useless to say that, although he carefully searched the lockers of the poop, Harding did not discover any trace of them. The pirates had evidently destroyed everything that concerned either the captain or the owners of the 'Speedy', and, as the name of her port was not painted on her counter, there was nothing which would tell them her nationality. However, by the shape of her boats Ayrton and Pencroft believed that the brig was of English build.

A week after the catastrophe – or, rather, after the fortunate, though inexplicable, event to which the colony owed its preservation – nothing more could be seen of the vessel, even at low tide. The wreck had disappeared, and Granite House was enriched by nearly all it had contained.

However, the mystery which enveloped its strange destruction would doubtless never have been cleared away if, on the 30th of November, Neb, strolling on the beach, had not found a piece of a thick iron cylinder, bearing traces of explosion. The edges of this cylinder were twisted and broken, as if they had been subjected to the action of some explosive substance.

Neb brought this piece of metal to his master, who was then occupied with his companions in the workshop of the Chimneys.

Cyrus Harding examined the cylinder attentively, then, turning to Pencroft, –

'You persist, my friend,' said he, 'in maintaining that the "Speedy" was not lost in consequence of a collision?'

'Yes, captain,' answered the sailor. 'You know as well as I do that there are no rocks in the channel.'

'But suppose she had run against this piece of iron?' said the engineer, showing the broken cylinder.

'What, that bit of pipe!' exclaimed Pencroft in a tone of perfect incredulity.

'My friends,' resumed Harding, 'you remember that before she founderd the brig rose on the summit of a regular water-spout?'

'Yes, captain,' replied Herbert.

'Well, would you like to know what occasioned that water-spout? It was this,' said the engineer, holding up the broken tube.

'That?' returned Pencroft.

'Yes! This cylinder is all that remains of a torpedo!'

'A torpedo!' exclaimed the engineer's companions.

'And who put the torpedo there?' demanded Pencroft, who did not like to yield.

'All that I can tell you is, that it was not I,' answered Cyrus Harding; 'but it was there, and you have been able to judge of its incomparable power!'

CHAPTER 21

So, then, all was explained by the submarine explosion of this torpedo. Cyrus Harding could not be mistaken, as, during the war of the Union, he had had occasion to try these terrible engines of destruction.

Yes! all was explained, everything – except the presence of the torpedo in the waters of the channel!

'My friends, then,' said Cyrus Harding, 'we can no longer be in doubt as to the presence of a mysterious being, a castaway like us, perhaps, abandoned on our island, and I say this in order that Ayrton may be acquainted with all the strange events which have occurred during these two years. Who this beneficent stranger is, whose intervention has, so fortunately for us, been manifested on many occasions, I cannot imagine. What his object can be in acting thus, in concealing himself after rendering us so many services, I cannot understand. But his services are not the less real, and are of such a nature that only a man possessed of prodigious power could render them. Ayrton is indebted to him as much as we are, for, if it was the stranger who saved me from the waves after the fall from the balloon, evidently it was he who wrote the document, who placed the bottle in the channel, and who has made known to us the situation of our companion. I will add that it was he who guided that chest, provided with everything we wanted, and stranded it on Flotsam Point; that it was he who lighted that fire on the heights of the island, which permitted you to land; that it was he who fired that bullet found in the body of the peccary; that it was he who immersed that torpedo in the channel, which destroyed the brig; in a word, that all those inexplicable events, for which we could not assign a reason, are due to this mysterious being. Therefore, whoever he may be, whether shipwrecked, or exiled on our island, we shall be ungrateful, if we think ourselves freed from gratitude towards him. We have contracted a debt, and I hope that we shall one day pay it.'

'You are right in speaking thus, my dear Cyrus,' replied Gideon Spilett. 'Yes, there is an almost all-powerful being, hidden in some part of the island, and whose influence has been singularly useful to our colony. I will add that the unknown appears to possess means of action, which border on the supernatural, if, in the events of practical life, the supernatural were recognisable. Is it he who is in secret communication with us by the well in Granite House, and has he thus a knowledge of all our plans? Was it he who threw us that bottle, when the vessel made her first cruise? Was it he who threw Top out of the lake, and killed the dugong? Was it he, who as everything leads us to believe, saved you from the waves, and that under circumstances in which any one else would not have been able to act? If it was he, he possesses a power which renders him master of the elements.'

The reporter's reasoning was just, and every one felt it to be so.

However, a more pressing matter had not yet been resolved. Six pirates still roamed the island and this was a cause of great concern for all at Granite House: Pencroft was adamant in his views and anxious to act on them. 'Are we to leave them to overrun our forests, our fields, our plantations? These pirates are regular jaguars, and it seems to me we ought not to hesitate to treat them as such. What do you think, Ayrton?' added Pencroft, turning to his companion.

Ayrton hesitated at first to reply, and Cyrus Harding regretted that Pencroft had so thoughtlessly put this question. And he was much moved when Ayrton replied, in a humble tone, –

'I have been one of those jaguars, Mr Pencroft. I have no right to speak.'

And with a slow step he walked away.

Pencroft understood.

'What a brute I am!' he exclaimed. 'Poor Ayrton! He has as much right to speak here as any one!'

'Yes,' said Gideon Spilett, 'but his reserve does him honour, and it is right to respect the feeling which he has about his sad past.'

'Certainly, Mr Spilett,' answered the sailor, 'and there is no fear of my doing so again. I would rather bite my tongue off than cause Ayrton any pain! But to return to the question. It seems to me that these ruffians have no right to any pity, and that we ought to rid the island of them as soon as possible.'

'Is that your opinion, Pencroft?' asked the engineer.

'Quite my opinion.'

'And before hunting them mercilessly, you would not wait

until they had committed some fresh act of hostility against us!'

'Isn't what they have done already enough?' asked Pencroft, who did not understand these scruples.

'They may adopt other sentiments!' said Harding, 'and perhaps repent.'

'They repent!' exclaimed the sailor, shrugging his shoulders.

'Pencroft, think of Ayrton!' said Herbert, taking the sailor's hand. 'He became an honest man again!'

Pencroft looked at his companions one after the other. He had never thought of his proposal being met with any objection. His rough nature could not allow that they ought to come to terms with the rascals who had landed on the island with Bob Harvey's accomplices, the murderers of the crew of the 'Speedy'; and he looked upon them as wild beasts which ought to be destroyed without delay and without remorse.

'Come!' said he. 'Everybody is against me! You wish to be generous to those villains! Very well; I hope we mayn't repent it!'

'What danger shall we run,' said Herbert, 'if we take care to be always on our guard?'

'Hum!' observed the reporter, who had not given any decided opinion. 'They are six, and well armed. If they each lay hid in a corner, and each fired at one of us, they would soon be masters of the colony.'

'Why have they not done so?' said Herbert. 'No doubt because it was not their interest to do it. Besides, we are six also.'

'Well, well!' replied Pencroft, whom no reasoning could have convinced. 'Let us leave these good people to do what they like, and don't think anything more about them.'

'Come, Pencroft,' said Neb, 'don't make yourself out so bad as all that. Suppose one of these unfortunate men were here before you within good range of your gun, you would not fire?'

'I would fire on him as I would on a mad dog, Neb,' replied Pencroft, coldly.

'Pencroft,' said the engineer, 'you have always shown much deference to my advice; will you in this matter yield to me?'

'I will do as you please, Captain Harding,' answered the sailor, who was not all convinced.

'Very well, wait, and we will not attack them unless we are attacked first.'

Thus their behaviour towards the pirates was agreed upon, although Pencroft augured nothing good from it. They were not to attack them, but were to be on their guard. After all, the island was large and fertile. If any sentiment of honesty yet remained in the bottom of their hearts, these wretches might perhaps be reclaimed. Was it not their interest, in the situation in which they found themselves, to begin a new life? At any rate, for humanity's sake alone, it would be right to wait. The colonists would no longer, as before, be able to go and come without fear.

Hitherto they had only wild beasts to guard against, and now six convicts of the worst description, perhaps, were roaming over their island. It was serious, certainly, and to less brave men it would have been security lost! No matter! At present, the colonists had reason on their side against Pencroft. Would they be right in the future? That remained to be seen.

So, the chief business of the colonists was to make a complete exploration of the island which would have two objects: to discover the mysterious being whose existence was now indisputable, and at the same time to find out what had become of the pirates, what retreat they had chosen, what sort of life they were leading, and what was to be feared from them. Cyrus Harding wished to set out without delay; but as the expedition would be of some days' duration, it appeared best to load the cart with different materials and tools in order to facilitate the organisation of the encampments. One of the onagers, however, having hurt its leg, could not be harnessed at present, and a few days rest was necessary. The departure was, therefore, put off for a week, until the 20th of November. The month of November in this latitude corresponds to the month of May in the northern zones. It was, therefore, the fine season. The sun was entering the tropic of Capricorn, and gave the longest days in the year. The time was, therefore, very favourable for the projected expedition, which, if it did not accomplish its principal object, would at any rate be fruitful in discoveries, especially of natural productions, since Harding proposed to explore those dense forests of the Far West which stretched to the extremity of the Serpentine Peninsula.

During the nine days which preceded their departure, it was agreed that the work on Prospect Heights should be finished off.

Moreover, it was necessary for Ayrton to return to the corral, where the domesticated animals required his care. It was decided that he should spend two days there, and return to Granite House after having liberally supplied the stables.

As he was about to start, Harding asked him if he would not like one of them to accompany him, observing that the island was less safe than formerly. Ayrton replied that this was unnecessary, as he was enough for the work, and that besides he apprehended no danger. If anything occurred at the corral or in the neighbourhood, he could instantly warn the colonists by sending a telegram to Granite House.

Ayrton departed at dawn on the 9th, taking the cart drawn by one onager, and two hours after the electric wire announced that he had found all in order at the corral.

During these two days Harding busied himself in executing a project which would completely guard Granite House against any surprise. It was necessary to completely conceal the opening of the old outlet, which was already walled up and partly hidden under grass and plants at the southern angle of Lake

Grant. Nothing was easier, since if the level of the lake was raised two or three feet, the opening would be quite beneath it. Now, to raise this level they had only to establish a dam at the two openings made by the lake, and by which were fed Creek Glycerine and Falls River.

The colonists worked with a will, and the two dams, which besides did not exceed eight feet in width by three in height, were rapidly erected by means of well-cemented blocks of stone.

This work finished, it would have been impossible to guess that at that part of the lake there existed a subterranean passage through which the overflow of the lake formerly escaped.

Of course the little stream which fed the reservoir of Granite House and worked the lift, had been carefully preserved, and the water could not fail. The lift once raised, this sure and comfortable retreat would be safe from any surprise.

This work had been so quickly done, that Pencroft, Gideon Spilett, and Herbert, found time to make an expedition to Port Balloon. The sailor was very anxious to know if the little creek in which the 'Bonadventure' was moored had been visited by the convicts.

'These gentlemen,' he observed, 'landed on the south coast, and if they followed the shore, it is to be feared that they may have discovered the little harbour, and in that case, I wouldn't give half-a-dollar for our "Bonadventure".'

Pencroft's apprehensions were not without foundation, and a visit to Port Balloon appeared to be very desirable. The sailor and his companions set off on the 10th of November, after dinner, well armed. Pencroft, ostentatiously slipping two bullets into each barrel of his rifle, shook his head in a way which betokened nothing good to any one who approached too near to him, whether 'man or beast', as he said. Gideon Spilett and Herbert also took their guns, and about three o'clock all three left Granite House.

Neb accompanied them to the turn of the Mercy, and after they had crossed, he raised the bridge. It was agreed that a gunshot should announce the colonists' return, and that at the signal Neb should return and re-establish the communication between the two banks of the river.

The little band advanced directly along the road which led to the southern coast of the island. This was only a distance of three miles and a half, but Gideon Spilett and his companions took two hours to traverse it. They examined all the border of the road, the thick forest, as well as Tabor Marsh. They found no trace of the fugitives, who, no doubt, not having yet discovered the number of the colonists, or the means of defence which they had at their disposal, had gained the less accessible parts of the island.

Arrived at Port Balloon, Pencroft saw with extreme satisfaction that the 'Bonadventure' was tranquilly floating in the narrow creek. However, Port Balloon was so well hidden amongst high rocks, that it could scarcely be discovered either from the land or the sea.

'Come,' said Pencroft, 'the blackguards have not been there yet. Long grass suits reptiles best, and evidently we shall find them in the Far West.'

'And it's very lucky, for if they had found the "Bonadventure",' added Herbert, 'they would have gone off in her, and we should have been prevented from returning to Tabor Island.'

'Indeed,' remarked the reporter, 'it will be important to take a document there which will make known the situation of Lincoln Island, and Ayrton's new residence, in case the Scotch yacht returns to fetch him.'

'Well, the "Bonadventure" is always there, Mr Spilett,' answered the sailor. 'She and her crew are ready to start at a moment's notice!'

'I think, Pencroft, that that is a thing to be done after our exploration of the island is finished. It is possible after all that the stranger, if we manage to find him, may know as much about Tabor Island as about Lincoln Island. Do not forget that he is certainly the author of the document, and he may, perhaps, know how far we may count on the return of the yacht!'

'But,' exclaimed Pencroft, 'who in the world can he be? The fellow knows us and we know nothing about him! If he is a simple castaway, why should he conceal himself? We are honest men, I suppose, and the society of honest men isn't unpleasant to anyone. Did he come here voluntarily? Can he leave the island if he likes? Is he here still? Will he remain any longer?'

Chatting thus, Pencroft, Gideon Spilett, and Herbert, got on board and looked about the deck of the 'Bonadventure'. All at once, the sailor having examined the bitts to which the cable of the anchor was secured, —

'Hallo,' he cried, 'this is queer!'

'What is the matter, Pencroft?' asked the reporter.

'The matter is, that it was not I who made this knot!'

And Pencroft showed a rope which fastened the cable to the bitt itself. 'What, it was not you?' asked Gideon Spilett.

'No! I can swear to it. This is a reef knot, and I always make a running bowline.'

'You must be mistaken, Pencroft.'

'I am not mistaken!' declared the sailor. 'My hand does it so naturally, and one's hand is never mistaken!'

'Then can the convicts have been on board?' asked Herbert.

'I know nothing about that,' answered Pencroft, 'but what is certain is, that some one has weighed the "Bonadventure's" anchor and dropped it again! And look here, here is another proof! The cable of the anchor has been run out, and its service is no longer at the hawse-hole. I repeat that some one has been using our vessel!'

'But if the convicts had used her, they would have pillaged her, or rather gone off with her.'

'Gone off! where to – to Tabor Island?' replied Pencroft. 'Do you think they would risk themselves in a boat of such small tonnage?'

'We must, besides, be sure that they know of the islet,' rejoined the reporter.

'However that may be,' said the sailor, 'as sure as my name is Bonadventure Pencroft, of the Vineyard, our "Bonadventure" has sailed without us!'

The sailor was so positive that neither Gideon Spilett nor Herbert could dispute his statement. It was evident that the vessel had been moved, more or less, since Pencroft had brought her to Port Balloon. As to the sailor, he had not the slightest doubt that the anchor had been raised and then dropped again. Now, what was the use of these two manoeuvres, unless the vessel had been employed in some expedition?

'But how was it we did not see the "Bonadventure" pass in sight of the island?' observed the reporter, who was anxious to bring forward every possible objection.

'Why, Mr Spilett,' replied the sailor, 'they would only have to start in the night with a good breeze, and they would be out of sight of the island in two hours.'

'Well,' resumed Gideon Spilett, 'I ask again, what object could the convicts have had in using the "Bonadventure", and why, after they had made use of her, should they have brought her back to port?'

'Why, Mr Spilett,' replied the sailor, 'we must put that among the unaccountable things, and not think anything more about it. The chief thing is that the "Bonadventure" was there, and she is there now. Only, unfortunately, if the convicts take her a second time, we shall very likely not find her again in her place!'

'Then, Pencroft,' said Herbert, 'would it not be wisest to bring the "Bonadventure" off to Granite House?'

'Yes, and no,' answered Pencroft, 'or rather no. The mouth of the Mercy is a bad place for a vessel, and the sea is heavy there.'

'But by hauling her up on the sand, to the foot of the Chimneys?'

'Perhaps yes,' replied Pencroft. 'At any rate, since we must leave Granite House for a long expedition, I think the "Bonadventure" will be safer here during our absence, and we shall do best to leave her here until the island is rid of these blackguards.'

'That is exactly my opinion,' said the reporter. 'At any rate, in the event of bad weather, she will not be exposed here as she would be at the mouth of the Mercy.'

'But suppose the convicts pay her another visit?' said Herbert.

'Well, my boy,' replied Pencroft, 'not finding her here they would not be long in finding her on the sands of Granite House, and, during our absence, nothing could hinder them from seizing her! I agree, therefore, with Mr Spilett, that she must be left in Port Balloon. But if on our return we have not rid the island of those rascals, it will be prudent to bring our boat to Granite House, until the time when we need not fear any unpleasant visits.'

'That's settled. Let us be off,' said the reporter.

Pencroft, Herbert and Gideon Spilett, on their return to Granite House, told the engineer all that had passed, and the latter approved of their arrangements both for the present and the future. He also promised the sailor that he would study that part of the channel situated between the islet and the coast, so as to ascertain if it would not be possible to make an artificial harbour there by means of damns. In this way the 'Bonadventure' would be always within reach, under the eyes of the colonists, and if necessary, under lock and key.

That evening a telegram was sent to Ayrton, requesting him to bring from the corral a couple of goats, which Neb wished to acclimatise to the plateau. Singularly enough, Aryton did not acknowledge the receipt of the despatch, as he was accustomed to do. This could not but astonish the engineer. But it might be that Ayrton was not at that moment in the corral, or even that he was on his way back to Granite House. In fact, two days had already passed since his departure, and it had been decided that on the evening of the 10th, or at the latest the morning of the 11th, he should return. The colonists waited, therefore, for Ayrton to appear on Prospect Heights. Neb and Herbert even watched at the bridge so as to be ready to lower it the moment their companion presented himself.

But up to ten in the evening there were no signs of Ayrton. It was, therefore, judged best to send a fresh despatch, requiring an immediate reply.

The bell of the telegraph at Granite House remained mute.

The colonists' uneasiness was great. What had happened? Was Ayrton no longer at the corral, or if he was still there, had he no longer control over his movements? Could they go to the corral in this dark night?

They consulted. Some wished to go, the others to remain.

'But,' said Herbert, 'perhaps some accident had happened to the telegraphic apparatus, so that it works no longer?'

'That may be,' said the reporter.

'Wait till tomorrow,' replied Cyrus Harding. 'It is possible, indeed, that Ayrton has not received our despatch, or even that we have not received his.'

They waited, of course not without some anxiety.

At dawn of day, the 11th of November, Harding again sent the electric current along the wire and received no reply.

He tried again: the same result.

'Off to the corral,' said he.

'And well armed!' added Pencroft.

It was immediately decided that Granite House should not be left alone, and that Neb should remain there. After having accompanied his friends to Creek Glycerine, he raised the bridge; and waiting behind a tree he watched for the return of either his companions or Ayrton.

In the event of the pirates presenting themselves and attempting to force the passage, he was to endeavour to stop them by firing on them, and as a last resource he was to take refuge in Granite House, where, the lift once raised, he would be in safety.

Cyrus Harding, Gideon Spilett, Herbert, and Pencroft were to repair the corral, and if they did not find Ayrton, search the neighbouring woods.

At six o'clock in the morning, the engineer and his three companions had passed Creek Glycerine, and Neb posted himself behind a small mound crowned by several dragoniners, on the left bank of the stream.

The colonists, after leaving the plateau of Prospect Heights, immediately took the road to the corral. They shouldered their guns, ready to fire on the smallest hostile demonstration. The two rifles and the two guns had been loaded with ball.

The wood was thick on each side of the road and might easily have concealed the convicts, who owing to their weapons would have been really formidable.

The colonists walked rapidly and in silence. Top preceded them, sometimes running on the road, sometimes taking a ramble into the wood, but always quiet, and not appearing to fear anything unusual. And they could be sure that the faithful dog would not allow them to be surprised, but would bark at the least appearance of danger.

Cyrus Harding and his companions followed beside the road the wire which connected the corral with Granite House. After walking for nearly two miles, they had not as yet discovered any explanation of the difficulty. The posts were in good order, the wire regularly extended. However, at that moment the engineer observed that the wire appeared to be slack, and on arriving at post No. 74, Herbert, who was in advance, stopped, exclaiming, –

'The wire is broken!'

His companions hurried forward and arrived at the spot where the lad was standing. The post was rooted up and lying across the path. The unexpected explanation of the difficulty was here, and it was evident that the despatches from Granite

House had not been received at the corral, nor those from the corral at Granite House.

'It wasn't the wind that blew down this post,' observed Pencroft.

'No,' replied Gideon Spilett. The earth has been dug up round its foot, and it has been torn up by the hand of man.'

'Besides, the wire is broken,' added Herbert, showing that the wire had been snapped.

'Is the fracture recent?' asked Harding.

'Yes,' answered Herbert, 'it has certainly been done quite lately.'

'To the corral! to the corral!' exclaimed the sailor.

The colonists were now half way between Granite House and the corral, having still two miles and a half to go. They pressed forward with redoubled speed.

Indeed, it was to be feared that some serious accident had occurred in the corral. No doubt Ayrton might have sent a telegram, which had not arrived, but this was not the reason why his companions were so uneasy, for – a more unaccountable circumstance – Ayrton, who had promised to return the evening before, had not reappeared. In short, it was not without a motive that all communication had been stopped between the corral and Granite House, and who but the convicts could have any interest in interrupting this communication?

The settlers hastened on, their hearts oppressed with anxiety. They were sincerely attached to their new companion. Were they to find him struck down by the hands of those of whom he was formerly the leader?

Soon they arrived at the place where the road led along the side of the little stream which flowed from the Red Creek and watered the meadows of the corral. They then moderated their pace, so that they should not be out of breath at the moment when a struggle might be necessary. Their guns were in their hands ready cocked. The forest was watched on every side. Top uttered sullen growls which were rather ominous.

At last the palisade appeared through the trees. No trace of any damage could be seen. The gate was shut as usual. Deep silence reigned in the corral. Neither the accustomed bleating of sheep nor Ayrton's voice could be heard.

'Let us enter,' said Cyrus Harding.

And the engineer advanced, whilst his companions, keeping watch about twenty paces behind him, were ready to fire at a moment's notice.

Harding raised the inner latch of the gate and was about to push it back, when Top barked loudly. A report sounded, and was responded to by a cry of pain.

Herbert, struck by a bullet, lay stretched on the ground.

CHAPTER 22

AT Herbert's cry, Pencroft, letting his gun fall, rushed towards him.

'They have killed him!' he cried. 'My boy! They have killed him!'

Cyrus Harding and Gideon Spilett ran to Herbert.

The reporter listened to ascertain if the poor lad's heart was still beating. 'He lives,' said he; 'but he must be carried –

'To Granite House? that is impossible!' replied the engineer.

'Into the corral, then!' said Pencroft.

'In a moment,' said Harding.

And he ran round the left corner of the palisade. There he found a convict, who, aiming at him, sent a ball through his hat. In a few seconds, before he had even time to fire his second barrel, he fell, struck to the heart by Harding's dagger, more sure even than his gun.

During this time, Gideon Spilett and the sailor hoisted themselves over the palisade, leapt into the enclosure, threw down the props which supported the inner door, ran into the empty house, and soon poor Herbert was lying on Ayrton's bed. In a few moments, Harding was by his side.

On seeing Herbert senseless, the sailor's grief was terrible. He sobbed, he cried, he tried to beat his head against the wall. Neither the engineer nor the reporter could calm him. They themselves were choked with emotion. They could not speak.

However, they knew that it depended on them to rescue from death the poor boy who was suffering beneath their eyes. Gideon Spilett had not passed through the many incidents by which his life had been chequered without acquiring some slight knowledge of medicine. He knew a little of everything, and several times he had been obliged to attend to wounds produced either by a sword-bayonet or shot. Assisted by Cyrus Harding, he proceeded to render the aid Herbert required.

The reporter was immediately struck by the complete stupor in which Herbert lay, a stupor owing either to the haemorrhage, or to the shock, the ball having struck a bone with sufficient force to produce a violent concussion.

Herbert was deadly pale, and his pulse so feeble that Spilett only felt it beat at long intervals, as if it was on the point of stopping.

These symptoms were very serious.

Herbert's chest was laid bare, and the blood having been staunched with handkerchiefs, it was bathed with cold water.

The contusion, or rather the contused wound, appeared, – an oval below the chest between the third and fourth ribs. It was there that Herbert had been hit by the bullet.

Cyrus Harding and Gideon Spilett then turned the poor boy over; as they did so, he uttered a moan so feeble that they almost thought it was his last sigh.

Herbert's back was covered with blood from another contused wound, by which the ball had immediately escaped.

'God be praised!' said the reporter, 'the ball is not in the body, and we shall not have to extract it.'

'But the heart?' asked Harding.

'The heart has not been touched; if it had been, Herbert would be dead!'

'Dead!' exclaimed Pencroft, with a groan.

The sailor had only heard the last words uttered by the reporter.

'No, Pencroft,' replied Cyrus Harding, 'no! He is not dead. His pulse still beats. He has even uttered a moan. But for your boy's sake, calm yourself. We have need of all our self-possession. Do not make us lose it, my friend.'

Pencroft was silent, but a reaction set in, and great tears rolled down his cheeks.

In the meanwhile, Gideon Spilett endeavoured to collect his ideas, and proceed methodically. After his examination he had no doubt that the ball, entering in front, between the seventh and eighth ribs, had issued behind between the third and fourth But what mischief had the ball committed in its passage? What important organs had been reached? A professional surgeon would have had difficulty in determining this at once, and still more so the reporter.

Spilett then explained to Cyrus Harding that he thought he ought first of all to stop the haemorrhage, but not close the two wounds, or cause their immediate cicatrisation, for there had been internal perforation, and the suppuration must not be allowed to accumulate in the chest.

Harding approved entirely, and it was decided that the two wounds should be dressed without attempting to close them by immediate coaptation.

And now did the colonists possess an efficacious agent to act against the inflammation which might occur?

'Yes. They had one, for nature had generously lavished it. They had cold water, that is to say, the most powerful sedative that can be employed against inflammation of wounds, the most efficacious therapeutic agent in grave cases, and the one which is now adopted by all physicians. Cold water has, moreover, the advantage of leaving the wound in absolute rest, and preserving it from all premature dressing, a considerable advantage, since it has been found by experience that contact with the air is dangerous during the first days.

Gideon Spilett and Cyrus Harding reasoned thus with their simple good sense, and they acted as the best surgeon would have done. Compresses of linen were applied to poor Herbert's two wounds, and were kept constantly wet with cold water.

The sailor had at first lighted a fire in the hut, which was not wanting in things necessary for life. Maple sugar, medicinal plants, the same which the lad had gathered on the banks of Lake Grant, enabled them to make some refreshing drinks, which they gave him without his taking any notice of it. His fever was extremely high, and all that day and night passed without his becoming conscious.

Herbert's life hung on a thread, and this thread might break at any moment. The next day, the 12th of November, the hopes of Harding and his companions slightly revived. Herbert had come out of his long stupor. He opened his eyes, he recognised Cyrus Harding, the reporter, and Pencroft. He uttered two or three words. He did not know what had happened. They told him, and Spilett begged him to remain perfectly still, telling him that his life was not in danger, and that his wounds would heal in a few days. However, Herbert scarcely suffered at all, and the cold water with which they were constantly bathed, prevented any inflammation of the wounds. The suppuration was established in a regular way, the fever did not increase, and it might now be hoped that this terrible wound would not involve any catastrophe. Pencroft felt the swelling of his heart gradually subside. He was like a sister of mercy, like a mother by the bed of her child.

Herbert dozed again, but his sleep appeared more natural.

'Tell me again that you hope, Mr Spilett,' said Pencroft. 'Tell me again that you will save Herbert!'

'Yes, we will save him!' replied the reporter. 'The wound is serious, and, perhaps, even the ball has traversed the lungs, but the perforation of this organ is not fatal.'

'God bless you!' answered Pencroft.

As may be believed, during the four-and-twenty hours they had been in the corral, the colonists had no other thought than that of nursing Herbert. They did not think either of the danger which threatened them should the convicts return, or of the precautions to be taken for the future.

But on this day, whilst Pencroft watched by the sick-bed, Cyrus Harding and the reporter consulted as to what it would be best to do.

First of all they examined the corral. There was not a trace of Ayrton. Had the unhappy man been dragged away by his former accomplices? Had he resisted, and been overcome in the struggle? Spilett, at the moment he scaled the palisade, had clearly seen some one of the convicts running along the southern spur of Mount Franklin, towards whom Top had sprung. It was one of those whose object had been so completely defeated by the rocks at the mouth of the Mercy. Besides, the one killed by Harding, and whose body was found outside the enclosure, of course belonged to Bob Harvey's crew.

As to the corral, it had not suffered any damage. The gates were closed, and the animals had not been able to disperse in the forest. Nor could they see traces of any struggle, any devastation, either in the hut, or in the palisade. The ammunition only, with which Ayrton had been supplied, had disappeared with him.

'The unhappy man has been surprised,' said Harding, 'and as he was a man to defend himself, he must have been over-powered.'

'Yes, that is to be feared!' said the reporter. 'Then, doubtless, the convicts installed themselves in the corral, where they found plenty of everything, and only fled when they saw us coming. It is very evident, too, that at this moment Ayrton, whether living or dead, is not here!'

'We shall have to beat the forest,' said the engineer, 'and rid the island of these wretches. Pencroft's presentiments were not mistaken, when he wished to hunt them as wild beasts. That would have spared us all these misfortunes!'

'Yes,' answered the reporter, 'but now we have the right to be merciless!'

'At any rate,' said the engineer, 'we are obliged to wait some time, and to remain at the corral until we can carry Herbert without danger to Granite House.'

'But Neb?' asked the reporter.

'Neb is in safety.'

'But if, uneasy at our absence, he would venture to come?'

'He must not come!' returned Cyrus Harding quickly. 'He would be murdered on the road!'

'It is very probable, however, that he will attempt to rejoin us!'

'Ah, if the telegraph still acted, he might be warned! But that is impossible now! As to leaving Pencroft and Herbert here alone, we could not do it! Well, I will go alone to Granite House.'

'No, no! Cyrus,' answered the reporter, 'you must not expose yourself! Your courage would be of no avail. The villains are evidently watching the corral, they are hidden in the thick woods which surround it, and if you go we shall soon have to regret two misfortunes instead of one!'

'But Neb?' repeated the engineer. 'It is now four-and-twenty hours since he has had any news of us! He will be sure to come!'

'And as he will be less on his guard than we should be ourselves,' added Spillett, 'he will be killed!'

'Is there really no way of warning him?'

Whilst the engineer thought, his eyes fell on Top, who, going backwards and forwards, seemed to say, –

'Am not I here?'

'Top!' exclaimed Cyrus Harding.

The animal sprang at his master's call.

'Yes, Top will go,' said the reporter, who had understood the engineer.

'Top can go where we cannot! He will carry to Granite House the news of the corral, and he will bring back to us that from Granite House!'

'Quick!' said Harding. 'Quick!'

Spilett rapidly tore a leaf from his note-book, and wrote these words:- 'Herbert wounded. We are at the corral. Be on your guard. Do not leave Granite House. Have the convicts appeared in the neighbourhood? Reply by Top.'

This laconic note contained all that Neb ought to know, but at the same time asked all that the colonists wished to know. It was folded and fastened to Top's collar in a conspicuous position.

'Top, my dog,' said the engineer, caressing the animal. 'Neb! Top! Neb! Go, go!'

Top bounded at these words. He understood, he knew what was expected of him. The road to the corral was familiar to him. In less than an hour he could clear it, and it might be hoped that where neither Cyrus Harding nor the reporter could have ventured without danger, Top, running amongst the grass or in the wood, would pass unperceived.

The engineer went to the gate of the corral and opened it.

'Neb, Top! Neb!' repeated the engineer, again pointing in the direction of Granite House.

Top sprang forwards, and almost immediately disappeared.

'He will get there!' said the reporter.

'Yes, and he will come back, the faithful animal!'

'What o'clock is it?' asked Gideon Spilett.

'Ten.'

'In an hour he may be here. We will watch for his return.'

The gate of the corral was closed. The engineer and the reporter re-entered the house. Herbert was still in a sleep. Pencroft kept the compresser always wet. Spilett, seeing there was nothing he could do at that moment, busied himself in preparing some nourishment, whilst attentively watching that part of the enclosure against the hill at which an attack might be expected.

The settlers awaited Top's return with much anxiety. A little before eleven o'clock, Cyrus Harding and the reporter, rifle in hand, were behind the gate, ready to open it at the first bark of their dog. They did not doubt that if Top had arrived safely at Granite House, Neb would have sent him back immediately.

They had both been there for about ten minutes, when a report was heard, followed by repeated barks.

The engineer opened the gate, and seeing smoke a hundred

149

feet off in the wood, he fired in that direction.

Almost immediately Top bounded into the corral, and the gate was quickly shut.

'Top, Top!' exclaimed the engineer, taking the dog's great honest head between his hands.

A note was fastened to his neck, and Cyrus Harding read these words, traced in Neb's large writing: – 'No pirates in the neighbourhood of Granite House. I will not stir. Poor Mr. Herbert!'

So the convicts were still there, watching the corral – reduced to five it is true – but well armed and determined to kill the settlers one after the other.

In ten days, on the 22nd of November, Herbert was considerably better. He had begun to take some nourishment. The colour was returning to his cheeks, and his bright eyes smiled at his nurses. He talked a little, notwithstanding Pencroft's efforts, who talked incessantly to prevent him from beginning to speak, and told him the most improbable stories. Herbert had questioned him on the subject of Ayrton, whom he was astonished not to see near him, thinking that he was at the corral. But the sailor, not wishing to distress Herbert, contented himself by replying that Ayrton had rejoined Neb, so as to defend Granite House.

'Humph!' said Pencroft, 'these pirates! they are gentlemen who have no right to any consideration. And the captain wanted to win them by kindness! I'll send them some kindness, but in the shape of a good bullet!'

'And have they not been seen again?' asked Herbert.

'No, my boy,' answered the sailor, 'but we shall find them, and when you are cured we shall see if the cowards, who strike us from behind, will dare to meet us face to face!'

'I am still very weak, my poor Pencroft!'

'Well! your strength will return gradually! What's a ball through the chest? Nothing but a joke! I've seen many, and I don't think much of them!'

At last things appeared to be going on well, and if no complication occurred, Herbert's recovery might be regarded as certain. But what would have been the condition of the colonists if his state had been aggravated, – if, for example, the ball had remained in his body, if his arm or his leg had had to be amputated?

'No,' said Spilett more than once, 'I have never thought of such a contingency without shuddering!'

'And yet, if it had been necessary to operate,' said Harding one day to him, 'you would not have hesitated?'

'No, Cyrus!' said Gideon Spilett, 'but thank God that we have been spared this complication!'

As in so many conjectures, the colonists had appealed to the logic of that simple good sense of which they had made use so often, and once more, thanks to their general knowledge, it had succeeded! But might not a time come when all their science would be at fault? They were alone on the island. Now, men in all states of society are necessary to each other. Cyrus Harding knew this well, and sometimes he asked himself if some circumstance might not occur which they would be powerless to surmount. It appeared to him besides, that he and his companions, till then so fortunate, had entered into an unlucky period. During the three years and a half which had elapsed since their escape from Richmond, it might be said that they had had everything their own way. The island had abundantly supplied them with minerals, vegetables, animals, and as Nature had constantly loaded them, their science had known how to take advantage of what she offered them.

The wellbeing of the colony was therefore complete. Moreover, in certain occurrences an inexplicable influence had come to their aid! . . . But all that could only be for a time.

In short, Cyrus Harding believed that fortune had turned against them.

In fact, the convicts' ship had appeared in the waters of the island, and if the pirates had been, so to speak, miraculously destroyed, six of them, at least, had escaped the catastrophe. They had disembarked on the island, and it was almost impossible to get at the five who survived. Ayrton had no doubt been murdered by these wretches, who possessed fire-arms, and at the first use that they had made of them, Herbert had fallen, wounded almost mortally. Were these the first blows aimed by adverse fortune at the colonists? This was often asked by Harding. This was often repeated by the reporter; and it appeared to him also that the intervention, so strange, yet so efficacious, which till then had served them so well, had now failed them. Had this mysterious being, whatever he was, whose existence could not be denied, abandoned the island? Had he in his turn succumbed?

No reply was possible to these questions. But it must not be imagined that because Harding and his companions spoke of these things, they were men to despair. Far from that. They looked their situation in the face, they analysed the chances, they prepared themselves for any event, they stood firm and straight before the future, and if adversity was at last to strike them, it would find in them men prepared to struggle against it.

CHAPTER 23

THE convalescence of the young invalid was regularly progressing. One thing only was now to be desired, that his state would allow him to be brought to Granite House. However well built and supplied the corral house was, it could not be so comfortable as the healthy granite dwelling. Besides, it did not offer the same security, and its tenants, notwithstanding their watchfulness, were here always in fear of some shot from the convicts. There, on the contrary, in the middle of that impregnable and inaccessible cliff, they would have nothing to fear, and any attack on their persons would certainly fail. They therefore waited impatiently for the moment when Herbert might be moved without danger from his wound, and they were determined to make this move, although the communication through Jacamar Wood was very difficult.

They had no news from Neb, but were not uneasy on that account. The courageous negro, well intrenched in the depths of Granite House, would not allow himself to be surprised. Top had not been sent again to him, as it appeared useless to expose the faithful dog to some shot which might deprive the settlers of their most useful auxiliary.

They waited, therefore, although they were anxious to be reunited at Granite House. It pained the engineer to see his forces divided, for it gave great advantage to the pirates. Since Ayrton's disappearance they were only four against five, for Herbert could not yet be counted, and this was not the least care of the brave boy, who well understood the trouble of which he was the cause.

The question of knowing how, in their condition, they were to act against the pirates, was thoroughly discussed on the 29th of November by Cyrus Harding, Gideon Spilett, and Pencroft, at a moment when Herbert was asleep and could not hear them.

'My friends,' said the reporter, after they had talked of Neb and of the impossibility of communicating with him, 'I think, like you, that to venture on the road to the corral would be to risk receiving a gun-shot without being able to return it, but do you not think that the best thing to be done now is to openly give chase to these wretches?'

'That is just what I was thinking,' answered Pencroft. 'I believe we're not fellows to be afraid of a bullet; and as for me, if Captain Harding approves, I'm ready to dash into the forest! Why, hang it, one man is equal to another!'

'But is he equal to five?' asked the engineer.

'I will join Pencroft,' said the reporter, 'and both of us, well-armed and accompanied by Top – '

'My dear Spilett, and you, Pencroft,' answered Harding, 'let us reason coolly, If the convicts were hid in one spot of the island, if we knew that spot, and had only to dislodge them, I would undertake a direct attack; but is there not occasion to fear, on the contrary, that they are sure to fire the first shot?'

'Well, captain,' cried Pencroft, 'a bullet does not always reach its mark.'

'That which struck Herbert did not miss, Pencroft,' replied the engineer. 'Besides, observe that if both of you left the corral I should remain here alone to defend it. Do you imagine that the convicts will not see you leave it, that they will not allow you to enter the forest, and that they will not attack it during your absence, knowing that there is no one here but a wounded boy and a man?'

'You are right, captain,' replied Pencroft, his chest swelling with sullen anger. 'You are right; they will do all they can to retake the corral, which they know to be well stored; and alone you could not hold it against them.'

'Oh, if we were only at Granite House!'

'If we were at Granite House,' answered the engineer, 'the case would be very different. There I should not be afraid to leave Herbert with one, whilst the other three went to search the forests of the island. But we are at the corral, and it is best to stay here until we can leave it together.'

Cyrus Harding's reasoning was unanswerable, and his companions understood it well.

'If only Ayrton was still one of us!' said Gideon Spilett. 'Poor fellow! his return to social life will have been but of short duration.'

'If he is dead,' added Pencroft, in a peculiar tone.

'Do you hope, then, Pencroft, that the villains have spared him?' asked Gideon Spilett.

'Yes, if they had any interest in doing so.'

'What! you suppose that Ayrton, finding his old companions, forgetting all that he owes us – '

Who knows?' answered the sailor, who did not hazard this shameful supposition without hesitating.

'Pencroft,' said Harding, taking the sailor's arm, 'that is a wicked idea of yours, and you will distress me much if you persist in speaking thus. I will answer for Ayrton's fidelity.'

'And I also,' added the reporter quickly.

'Yes, yes, captain, I was wrong,' replied Pencroft; 'It was a wicked idea indeed that I had, and nothing justifies it. But what can I do? I'm not in my senses. This imprisonment in the corral wearies me horribly, and I have never felt so excited as I do now.'

'Be patient, Pencroft,' replied the engineer. 'How long will it be, my dear Spilett, before you think Herbert may be carried to Granite House?'

'That is difficult to say, Cyrus,' answered the reporter, 'for any imprudence might involve terrible consequences. But his convalescence is progressing, and if he continues to gain strength, in eight days from now – well, we shall see.'

Eight days! That would put off the return to Granite House until the first days of December. At this time two months of spring had already passed. The weather was fine, and the heat began to be great. The forests of the island were in full leaf, and the time was approaching when the usual crops ought to be gathered. The return to the plateau of Prospect Heights would, therefore, be followed by extensive agricultural labours, interrupted only by the projected expedition through the island.

It can, therefore, be well understood how injurious this seclusion in the corral must be to the colonists.

But if they were compelled to bow before necessity, they did not do so without impatience.

Once or twice the reporter ventured out into the road and made the tour of the palisade. Top accompanied him, and Gideon Spilett, his gun cocked, was ready for any emergency.

He met with no misadventure and found no suspicious traces. His dog would have warned him of any danger, and, as Top did not bark, it might be concluded that there was nothing to fear at that moment at least, and that the convicts were occupied in another part of the island.

However, on his second sortie, on the 27th November, Gideon Spilett, who had ventured a quarter of a mile into the wood, towards the south of the mountain, remarked that Top scented something. The dog had no longer his unconcerned manner; he went backwards and forwards ferreting amongst the grass and bushes as if his smell had revealed some suspicious object to him

Gideon Spilett followed Top, encouraged him, exited him by his voice, whilst keeping a sharp look-out, his gun ready to fire and sheltering himself behind the trees. It was not probable that Top scented the presence of man, for in that case he would have announced it by half-uttered, sullen, angry barks. Now, as he did not growl, it was because danger was neither near nor approaching.

Nearly five minutes passed thus, Top rummaging, the reporter following him prudently, when, all at once, the dog rushed towards a thick bush, and drew out a rag.

It was a piece of cloth, stained and torn, which Spilett immediately brought back to the corral. There it was examined by the colonists, who found that it was a fragment of Ayrton's waistcoat, a piece of that felt manufactured solely by the Granite House factory

'You see, Pencroft,' observed Harding, 'there has been resistance on the part of the unfortunate Ayrton. The convicts have dragged him away in spite of himself! Do you still doubt his honesty?'

'No, captain,' answered the sailor, 'and I repented of my suspicion a long time ago! But it seems to me that something may be learned from the incident.'

'What is that?' asked the reporter.

'It is that Ayrton was not killed at the corral! That they dragged him away living, since he has resisted Therefore, perhaps he is still living!'

'Perhaps, indeed,' replied the engineer, who remained thoughtful.

This was a hope, to which Ayrton's companions could still hold. Indeed, they had before believed that, surprised in the corral, Ayrton had fallen by a bullet, as Herbert had fallen. But if the convicts had not killed him at first, if they had brought him living to another part of the island, might it not be admitted that he was still their prisoner? Perhaps even, one of them had found in Ayrton his old Australian companion Ben Joyce, the chief of the escaped convicts. And who knows but that they had conceived the impossible hope of bringing back Ayrton to themselves? He would have been very useful to them, if they had been able to make him turn traitor!

This incident was, therefore, favourably interpreted at the corral, and it no longer appeared impossible that they should find Ayrton again. On his side, if he was only a prisoner, Ayrton would no doubt do all he could to escape from the hands of the villains, and this would be a powerful aid to the settlers!

'At any rate,' observed Gideon Spilett, 'if happily Ayrton did manage to escape, he would go directly to Granite House, for he could not know of the attempt of assassination of which Herbert has been a victim, and consequently would never think of our being imprisoned in the corral.'

'Oh! I wish that he was there, at Granite House!' cried Pencroft, 'and that we were there, too! For, although the rascals can do nothing to our house, they may plunder the plateau, our plantations, our poultry-yard!'

Pencroft had become a thorough farmer, heartily attached to his crops. But it must be said that Herbert was more anxious than any to return to Granite House, for he knew how much the presence of the settlers was needed there. And it was he who was keeping them at the corral! Therefore, one idea occupied his mind – to leave the corral, and when! He believed he could bear removal to Granite House. He was sure his strength would return more quickly in his room, with the air and sight of the sea!

Several times he pressed Gideon Spilett, but the latter, fearing, with good reason, that Herbert's wounds, half healed, might reopen on the way, did not give the order to start.

However, something occurred which compelled Cyrus Harding

and his two friends to yield to the lad's wish, and God alone knew that this determination might cause them grief and remorse.

It was the 29th of November, seven o'clock in the evening. The three settlers were talking in Herbert's room, when they heard Top utter quick barks.

Harding, Pencroft, and Spilett seized their guns and ran out of the house. Top, at the foot of the palisade, was jumping, barking, but it was with pleasure, not anger.

'Someone is coming.'

'Yes.'

'It is not an enemy!'

'Neb, perhaps?'

'Or Ayrton?'

These words had hardly been exchanged between the engineer and his two companions when a body leapt over the palisade and fell on the ground inside the corral.

It was Jup, Master Jup in person, to whom Top immediately gave a most cordial reception.

'Jup!' exclaimed Pencroft.

'Neb has sent him to us,' said the reporter.

'Then,' replied the engineer, 'he must have some note on him.'

Pencroft rushed up to the orang. Certainly if Neb had any important matter to communicate to his master he could not employ a more sure or more rapid messenger, who could pass where neither the colonists could, nor even Top himself

Cyrus Harding was not mistaken. At Jup's neck hung a small bag, and in this bag was found a little note traced by Neb's hand.

The despair of Harding and his companions may be imagined when they read these words:-

'Friday, six o'clock in the morning

'Plateau invaded by convicts.'

'NEB.'

They gazed at each other without uttering a word, then they re-entered the house. What were they to do? The convicts on Prospect Heights! that was disaster, devastation, ruin.

Herbert, on seeing the engineer, the reporter, and Pencroft re-enter, guessed that their situation was aggravated, and when he saw Jup, he no longer doubted that some misfortune menaced Granite House.

'Captain Harding,' said he, 'I must go; I can bear the journey. I must go.'

Gideon Spilett approached Herbert; then, having looked at him –

'Let us go, then!' said he.

The question was quickly decided whether Herbert should be carried on a litter or in the cart which had brought Ayrton to the corral The motion of the litter would have been more easy for the wounded lad, but it would have necessitated two bearers, that is to say, there would have been two guns less for defence if an attack was made on the road Would they not, on the contrary, by employing the cart, leave every arm free? Was it impossible to place the mattress on which Herbert was lying in it, and to advance with so much care that any jolt should be avoided? It could be done.

The cart was brought. Pencroft harnessed the onager. Cyrus Harding and the reporter raised Herbert's mattress and placed it on the bottom of the cart. The weather was fine. The sun's bright rays glanced through the trees.

'Are the guns ready?' asked Cyrus Harding.

They were The engineer and Pencroft, each armed with a double-barrelled gun, and Gideon Spilett carrying his rifle, had nothing to do but start.

'Are you comfortable, Herbert?' asked the engineer.

'Ah, captain,' replied the lad, 'don't be uneasy, I shall not die on the road!'

Whilst speaking thus, it could be seen that the poor boy had called up all his energy, and by the exercise of a powerful will had collected his failing strength.

The engineer felt his heart sink painfully. He still hesitated to give the signal for departure; but that would have driven Herbert to despair – killed him perhaps.

'Forward!' said Harding.

The gate of the corral was opened. Jup and Top, who knew when to be silent, ran in advance. The cart came out, the gate was reclosed, and the onager, led by Pencroft, advanced at a slow pace.

Certainly, it would have been safer to have taken a different road than that which led straight from the corral to Granite House, but the cart would have met with great difficulties in moving under the trees. It was necessary, therefore, to follow this road, although it was well known to the convicts.

Cyrus Harding and Gideon Spilett walked one on each side of the cart, ready to answer to any attack. However, it was not probable that the convicts would have yet left the plateau of Prospect Heights.

Neb's note had evidently been written and sent as soon as the convicts had shown themselves there. Now, this note was dated six o'clock in the morning, and the active orang, accustomed to come frequently to the corral, had taken scarcely three-quarters of an hour to cross the five miles which separated it from Granite House. They would, therefore, be safe at that time, and if there was any occasion for firing, it would probably not be until they were in the neighbourhood of Granite House.

However, the colonists kept a strict watch. Top and Jup, the latter armed with his club, sometimes in front, sometimes beating the wood at the sides of the road, signalised no danger.

The cart advanced slowly under Pencroft's guidance. It had left the corral at half-past seven, An hour after, four out of the five miles had been cleared, without any incident having occurred. The road was as deserted as all that part of the Jacamar Wood which lay between the Mercy and the lake. There was no occasion for any warning. The wood appeared as deserted as on the day when the colonists first landed on the island.

They approached the plateau. Another mile and they would see the bridge over Creek Glycerine. Cyrus Harding expected to find it in its place; supposing that the convicts would have crossed it, and that, after having passed one of the streams which enclosed the plateau, they would have taken the precaution to lower it again, so as to keep open a retreat.

At length an opening in the trees allowed the sea-horizon to be seen. But the cart continued its progress, for not one of its defenders thought of abandoning it.

At that moment Pencroft stopped the onager; and in a hoarse voice –

'Oh! the villains!' he exclaimed.

And he pointed to a thick smoke rising from the mill, the sheds, and the buildings at the poultry-yard.

A man was moving about in the midst of the smoke. It was Neb.

His companions uttered a shout. He heard, and ran to meet them.

The convicts had left the Plateau nearly half-an-hour before, having devasted it!

'And Mr Herbert?' asked Neb.

Gideon Spilett returned to the cart.

Herbert had lost consciousness!

CHAPTER 24

OF the convicts, the dangers which menaced Granite House, the ruins with which the plateau was covered, the colonists thought no longer. Herbert's critical state outweighed all other considerations. Would the removal prove fatal to him by causing some internal injury? The reporter could not affirm it, but he and his companions almost despaired of the result. The cart was brought to the bend of the river. There some branches, disposed as a litter, received the mattress on which lay the unconscious Herbert. Ten minutes after, Cyrus Harding, Spilett and Pencroft were at the foot of the Cliff, leaving Neb to take the cart on to the plateau of Prospect Heights. The lift was put in motion, and Herbert was soon stretched on his bed in Granite House.

What cares were lavished on him to bring him back to life! He smiled for a moment on finding himself in his room, but could scarcely even murmur a few words, so great was his weakness. Gideon Spilett examined his wounds. He feared to find them reopened, having been imperfectly healed. There was nothing of the sort. From whence, then, came this prostration? Why was Herbert so much worse? The lad then fell into a kind of feverish sleep, and the reporter and Pencroft remained near the bed. During this time, Harding told Neb all that had happened at the corral, and Neb recounted to his master the events of which the plateau had just been the theatre.

It was only during the preceding night that the convicts had appeared on the edge of the forest, at the approaches to Creek Glycerine. Neb, who was watching near the poultry-yard had not hesitated to fire at one of the pirates, who was about to cross the stream; but in the darkness he could not tell whether the man had been hit or not. At any rate, it was not enough to frighten away the band, and Neb had only just time to get up to Granite House, where at least he was in safety.

Neb then thought of employing Jup, and confiding a note to him. He knew the orang's great intelligence, which had been often put to the proof. Jup understood the word corral, which had been frequently pronounced before him, and it may be remembered, too, that he had been often driven thither in company with Pencroft. Day had not yet dawned. The active orang would know how to pass unperceived through the woods, of which the convicts, besides, would think he was a native.

Neb did not hesitate. He wrote the note, he tied it to Jup's neck, he brought the ape to the door of Granite House, from which he let down a long cord to the ground; then, several times, he repeated these words, –

'Jup, Jup! corral, corral!'

The creature understood, seized the cord, glided rapidly down to the beach, and disappeared in the darkness without the convicts' attention having been in the least excited.

'You did well, Neb,' said Harding; 'but perhaps in not warning us you would have done still better!'

And, in speaking thus, Cyrus Harding thought of Herbert, whose recovery the removal had so seriously checked.

Neb ended his account. The convicts had not appeared at all on the beach. Not knowing the number of the island's inhabitants, they might suppose that Granite House was defended by a large party. They must have remembered that during the attack by the brig numerous shots had been fired both from the lower and upper rocks, and no doubt they did not wish to expose themselves. But the plateau of Prospect Heights was open to them, and not covered by the fire of Granite House. They gave themselves up, therefore, to their instinct of destruction, – plundering, burning, devastating everything, – and only retiring half an hour before the arrival of the colonists, whom they believed still confined in the corral.

On their retreat, Neb hurried out. He climbed the plateau at the risk of being perceived and fired at, tried to extinguish the fire which was consuming the buildings of the poultry-yard, and had struggled, though in vain, against it until the cart appeared at the edge of the wood.

Such had been these serious events. The presence of the convicts constituted a permanent source of danger to the settlers in Lincoln Island, until then so happy, and who might now expect still greater misfortunes.

The following days were the saddest of any that the colonists had passed on the island! Herbert's weakness visibly increased. It appeared that a more serious malady, the consequence of the profound physiological disturbance he had gone through, threatened to declare itself, and Gideon Spilett feared such an aggravation of his condition that he would be powerless to fight against it!

In fact, Herbert remained in an almost continuous state of drowsiness, and symptoms of delirium began to manifest themselves. Refreshing drinks were the only remedies at the colonists' disposal. The fever was not as yet very high, but it soon appeared that it would probably recur at regular intervals. Gideon Spilett first recognised this on the 6th of December.

The poor boy, whose fingers, nose, and ears had become extremely pale, was at first seized with slight shiverings, horripilations, and tremblings. His pulse was weak and irregular, his skin dry, his thirst intense. To this soon succeeded a hot fit; his face became flushed; his skin reddened; his pulse quick; then a profuse perspiration broke out, after which the fever seemed to diminish. The attack had lasted nearly five hours.

Gideon Spilett had not left Herbert, who, it was only too certain, was now seized by an intermittent fever, and this fever must be cured at any cost before it should assume a more serious aspect.

'And in order to cure it,' said Spilett to Cyrus Harding, 'we need a febrifuge.'

'A febrifuge!' asnwered the engineer. 'We have neither Peruvian bark nor sulphate of quinine.'

'No,' said Gideon Spilett, 'but there are willows on the border of the lake, and the bark of the willow might, perhaps, prove to be a substitute for quinine.'

'Let us try it without losing a moment,' replied Cyrus Harding.

The bark of the willow has, indeed, been justly considered as a succedaneum for Peruvian bark, as has also that of the horse-chestnut-tree, the leaf of the holly, the snake-root etc. It was evidently necessary to make trial of this substance, although not so valuable as Peruvian bark, and to employ it in its natural state, since they had no means for extracting its essence.

Cyrus Harding went himself to cut from the trunk of a species of black willow a few pieces of bark; he brought them back to Granite House, and reduced them to a powder, which was administered that same evening to Herbert.

The night passed without any important change. Herbert was somewhat delirious, but the fever did not reappear in the night, and did not return either during the following day.

Pencroft again began to hope. Gideon Spilett said nothing. It might be that the fever was not quotidian, but tertian, and that it would return next day. Therefore, he awaited the next day with the greatest anxiety.

It might have been remarked besides that during this period Herbert remained utterly prostrate, his head weak and giddy. Another symptom alarmed the reporter to the highest degree. Herbert's liver became congested, and soon a more intense delirium showed that his brain was also affected.

Gideon Spilett was overwhelmed by this new complication. He took the engineer aside.

'It is a malignant fever,' said he.

'A malignant fever!' cried Harding. 'You are mistaken, Spilett. A malignant fever does not delcare itself spontaneously ; its germ must previously have existed.'

'I am not mistaken,' replied the reporter. 'Herbert no doubt contracted the germ of this fever in the marshes of the island. He has already had one attack; should a second come on and should we not be able to prevent a third, he is lost.'

'But the willow bark?'

'That is insufficient,' answered the reporter; 'and the third attack of a malignant fever, which is not arrested by means of quinine, is always fatal.'

Fortunately Pencroft heard nothing of this conversation, or he would have gone mad.

It may be imagined what anxiety the engineer and the reporter suffered during the day of the 7th of December and the following night.

Towards the middle of the day the second attack came on. The crisis was terrible. Herbert felt himself sinking. He stretched his arms towards Cyrus Harding, towards Spilett, towards Pencroft. He was so young to die! The scene was heartrending. They were obliged to send Pencroft away.

The fit lasted five hours. It was evident that Herbert could not survive a third.

The night was frightful. In his delirium Herbert uttered words which went to the hearts of his companions. He struggled with the convicts, he called to Ayrton, he poured forth entreaties to that mysterious being, – that powerful unknown protector, – whose image was stamped upon his mind; then he again fell into a deep exhaustion which completely prostrated him. Several times Gideon Spilett thought that the poor boy was dead.

The next day, the 8th of December, was but a succession of the fainting fits. Herbert's thin hands clutched the sheets. They had administered further doses of pounded bark, but the reporter expected no result from it.

'If before tomorrow morning we have not given him a more energetic febrifuge,' said the reporter, 'Herbert will be dead.'

Night arrived – the last night, it was too much to be feared, of the good, brave, intelligent boy, so far in advance of his years, and who was loved by all as their own child. The only remedy which existed against this terrible malignant fever, the only specific which could overcome it, was not to be found in Lincoln Island.

During the night of the 8th of December, Herbert was seized by a more violent delirium. His liver was fearfully congested, his brain affected, and already it was impossible for him to recognise anyone.

Would he live until the next day, until that third attack which must infallibly carry him off? It was not probable. His strength was exhausted, and in the intervals of fever he lay as one dead.

Towards three o'clock in the morning Herbert uttered a piercing cry. He seemed to be torn by a supreme convulsion. Neb, who was near him, terrified, ran into the next room where his companions were watching.

Top, at that moment, barked in a strange manner.

All rushed in immediately and managed to restrain the dying boy, who was endeavouring to throw himself out of his bed, whilst Spilett, taking his arm, felt his pulse gradually quicken.

It was five in the morning. The rays of the rising sun began to shine in at the windows of Granite House. It promised to be a fine day, and this day was to be poor Herbert's last!

A ray glanced on the table placed near the bed.

Suddenly Pencroft, uttering a cry, pointed to the table.

On it lay a little oblong box, of which the cover bore these words:-

'Suphate of Quinine.'

CHAPTER 25

GIDEON SPILETT took the box and opened it. It contained nearly two hundred grains of a white powder, a few particles of which he carried to his lips. The extreme bitterness of the substance precluded all doubt; it was certainly the precious extract of quinine that pre-eminent antifebrile.

This powder must be administered to Herbert without delay. How it came there might be discussed later.

'Some coffee!' said Spilett.

In a few moments Neb brought a cup of the warm infusion. Gideon Spilett threw into it about eighteen grains of quinine, and they succeeded in making Herbert drink the mixture.

There was still time, for the third attack of the malignant fever had not yet shown itself. How they longed to be able to add that it would not return!

Besides, it must be remarked, the hopes of all had now revived. The mysterious influence had been again exerted, and in a critical moment, when they had despaired of it.

In a few hours Herbert was much calmer. The colonists could now discuss this incident. The intervention of the stranger was more evident than ever. But how had he been able to penetrate during the night into Granite House? It was inexplicable, and, in truth, the proceedings of the genius of the island were not less mysterious than was that genius himself. During this day the sulphate of quinine was administered to Herbert every three hours.

The next day some improvement in Herbert's condition was apparent. Certainly, he was not out of danger, intermittent fevers being subject to frequent and dangerous relapses, but the most assiduous care was bestowed on him. And besides, the specific was at hand; nor, doubtless, was he who had brought it far distant! and the hearts of all were animated by returning hope.

This hope was not disappointed. Ten days after, on the 20th of December, Herbert's convalescence commenced.

He was still weak, and strict diet had been imposed upon him, but no access of fever supervened. And then, the poor boy submitted with such docility to all the prescriptions ordered him! He longed so to get well!

Pencroft was as a man who has been drawn up from the bottom of an abyss. Fits of joy approaching to delirium seized him. When the time for the third attack had passed by, he nearly suffocated the reporter in his embrace. Since then, he always called him Dr Spilett.

The real doctor, however, remained undiscovered.

'We will find him!' repeated the sailor.

Certainly, this man, whoever he was, might expect a somewhat too energetic embrace from the worthy Pencroft!

The month of December ended, and with it the year 1867, during which the colonists of Lincoln Island had of late been so severely tried. They commenced the year 1868 with magnificent weather, great heat, and a tropical temperature, delightfully cooled by the sea-breeze. Herbert's recovery progressed, and from his bed, placed near one of the windows of Granite House, he could inhale the fresh air, charged with ozone, which could not fail to restore his health. His appetite returned, and what numberless delicate, savoury little dishes Neb prepared for him!

'It is enough to make one wish to have a fever oneself!' said Pencroft.

During all this time, the convicts did not once appear in the vicinity of Granite House. There was no news of Ayrton, and though the engineer and Herbert still had some hopes of finding him again, their companions did not doubt but that the unfortunate man had perished. However, this uncertainty could not last, and when once the lad should have recovered, the expedition, the result of which must be so important, would be undertaken. But they would have to wait a month, perhaps, for all the strength of the colony must be put into requisition to obtain satisfaction from the convicts.

However, Herbert's convalescence progressed rapidly. The congestion of the liver had disappeared, and his wounds might be considered completely healed.

During the month of January, important work was done on the plateau of Prospect Heights; but it consisted solely in saving as much as was possible from the devastated crops, either of corn or vegetables. The grain and the plants were gathered, so as to provide a new harvest for the approaching half-season. With regard to rebuilding the poultry-yard, wall, or stables, Cyrus Harding preferred to wait. Whilst he and his companions were in pursuit of the convicts, the latter might very probably pay another visit to the plateau, and it would be useless to give them an opportunity of recommencing their work of destruction. When the island should be cleared of these miscreants, they would set about rebuilding. The young convalescent began to get up in the second week of January, at first for one hour a day, then two, then three. His strength visibly returned, so vigorous was his constitution. He was now eighteen years of age. He was tall, and promised to become a man of noble and commanding presence. From this time his recovery, while still requiring care, – and Dr Spilett was very strict, – made rapid progress. Towards the end of the month, Herbert was already walking about on Prospect Heights, and the beach.

He derived, from several sea-baths, which he took in company with Pencroft and Neb, the greatest possible benefit. Cyrus Harding thought he might now settle the day for their departure, for which the 15th of February was fixed. The nights, very clear at this time of year, would be favourable to the researches they intended to make all over the island.

The necessary preparations for this exploration were now commenced, and were important, for the colonists had sworn not to return to Granite House until their twofold object had been achieved; on the one hand, to exterminate the convicts, and rescue Ayrton, if he was still living; on the other, to discover who it was that presided so effectually over the fortunes of the colony.

The cart was in good condition. The onagers, well rested, could go a long journey. Provisions, camp effects, a portable stove, and various utensils, were packed in the cart, as also weapons and ammunition, carefully chosen from the now complete arsenal of Granite House. But it was necessary to remember that the convicts were, perhaps, roaming about the woods, and that in the midst of these thick forests a shot might quickly be fired and received. It was therefore resolved that the little band of settlers should remain together, and not separate under any pretext whatever.

It was also decided that no one should remain at Granite House. Top and Jup themselves were to accompany the expedition; the inaccessible dwelling needed no guard. The 14th of February, eve of the departure, was Sunday. It was consecrated entirely to repose, and thanksgivings addressed by the colonists to the Creator. A place in the cart was reserved for Herbert, who, though thoroughly convalescent, was still a little weak. The next morning, at daybreak, Cyrus Harding took the necessary measures to protect Granite House from any invasion. The ladders, which were formerly used for the ascent, were brought to the Chimneys and buried deep in the sand, so that they might be available on the return of the colonists, for the machinery of the lift had been taken to pieces, and nothing of the apparatus remained. Pencroft stayed the last in Granite House in order to finish this work, and he then lowered himself down by means of a double rope held below, and which, when once hauled down, left no communication between the upper landing and the beach.

The weather was magnificent.

'We shall have a warm day of it,' said the reporter, laughing.

'Pooh! Dr Spilett,' answered Pencroft; 'we shall walk under the shade of the trees, and shan't even see the sun!'

'Forward!' said the engineer.

The cart was waiting on the beach before the Chimneys. The reporter made Herbert take his place in it during the first hours at least of the journey, and the lad was obliged to submit to his doctor's orders.

Neb placed himself at the onagers' heads. Cyrus Harding, the reporter, and the sailor, walked in front. Top bounded joyfully along. Herbert offered a seat in his vehicle to Jup, who accepted it without ceremony. The moment for departure had arrived, and the little band set out.

The cart first turned the angle of the mouth of the Mercy, then, having ascended the left bank for a mile, crossed the bridge, at the other side of which commenced the road to Port Balloon; and there the explorers, leaving this road on their left, entered the cover of the immense woods which formed the region of the Far West.

On the evening of the first day the colonists encamped about nine miles from Granite House, on the border of a little stream falling into the Mercy, and of the existence of which they had till then been ignorant.

The next day was devoted to the exploration of all that wooded region forming the shore from Reptile End to Falls River. The colonists were able to search this forest thoroughly, for, as it was comprised between the two shores of the Serpentine Peninsula, it was only from three to four miles in breadth. The trees, both by their height and their thick foliage, bore witness to the vegetative power of the soil, more astonishing here than in any other part of the island. One might have said that a corner from the virgin forests of Americaa or Africa had been transported into this temperate zone. This led them to conclude that the superb vegetation found a heat in this soil, damp in its uper layer, but warmed in the interior by volcanic fires, which could not belong to a temperate climate. The most frequently-occurring trees were kauries and eucalypti of gigantic dimensions.

But the colonists' object was not simply to admire the magnificent vegetation. No traces were found on the western coast and after much though it was deduced that the convicts had found this part of the coast unsuitable for a retreat and had made their way to Mount Franklin, though the general opinion was that they would revisit the corral before finding a lair in order to collect stores.

The next day the colonists, leaving the shore, where, beyond the mouth, basalts of every shape were so picturesquely piled up, ascended Falls River by its left bank. The road had been already partially cleared in their former excursions made from the corral to the west coast. The settlers were now about six miles from Mount Franklin.

The engineer's plan was this: – To minutely survey the valley forming the bed of the river, and to cautiously approach the neighbourhood of the corral; if the corral was occupied, to seize it by force; if it was not, to intrench themselves there and make it the center of the operations which had for their object the exploration of Mount Franklin.

This plan was unanimously approved by the colonists, for they were impatient to regain entire possession of their island.

They made their way then along the narrow valley separating two of the largest spurs of Mount Franklin. The trees, crowded on the river's bank, became rare on the upper slopes of the mountain. The ground was hilly and rough, very suitable for ambushes, and over which they did not venture without extreme precaution. Top and Jup skirmished on the flanks, springing right and left through the thick brushwood, and emulating each other in intelligence and activity. But nothing showed that the banks of the stream had been recently frequented – nothing announced either the presence or the proximity of the convicts. Towards five in the evening the cart stopped nearly 600 feet from the palisade. A semicircular screen of trees still hid it.

It was necessary to reconnoitre the corral, in order to ascertain if it was occupied. To go there openly, in broad daylight, when the convicts were probably in ambush, would be to expose themselves, as poor Herbert had done, to the fire-arms of the ruffians. It was better then, to wait until night came on.

However, Gideon Spilett wished without further delay to reconnoitre the approaches to the corral, and Pencroft, who was quite out of patience, volunteered to accompany him.

'No, my friends,' said the engineer, 'wait till night. I will not allow one of you to expose himself in open day.'

'But, captain – ' answered the sailor, little disposed to obey.

'I beg you, Pencroft,' said the engineer.

'Very well!' replied the sailor, who vented his anger in another way, by bestowing on the convicts the worst names in his maritime vocabulary.

The colonists remained, therefore, near the cart, and carefully watched the neighbouring parts of the forest.

Three hours passed thus. The wind had fallen, and absolute silence reigned under the great trees. The snapping of the smallest twig, a footstep on the dry leaves, the gliding of a body amongst the grass, would have been heard without difficulty. All was quiet. Besides, Top, lying on the grass, his head stretched out on his paws, gave no sign of uneasiness. At eight o'clock the day appeared far enough advanced for the reconnaissance to be made under favourable conditions. Gideon Spilett declared himself ready to set out accompanied by Pencroft. Cyrus Harding consented. Top and Jup were to remain with the engineer, Herbert, and Neb, for a bark or a cry at a wrong moment would give the alarm.

'Do not be imprudent,' said Harding to the reporter and Pencroft, 'you have not to gain possession of the corral, but only to find out whether it is occupied or not.'

'All right,' answered Pencroft.

And the two departed.

Under the trees, thanks to the thickness of their foliage, the obscurity rendered any object invisible beyond a radius of from thirty to forty feet. The reporter and Pencroft, halting at any suspicious sound, advanced with great caution.

They walked a little distance apart from each other, so as to offer a less mark for a shot. And, to tell the truth, they expected every moment to hear a report. Five minutes after leaving the cart, Gideon Spilett and Pencroft arrived at the edge of the wood before the clearing beyond which rose the palisade.

They stopped. A few straggling beams still fell on the field clear of trees. Thirty feet distant was the gate of the corral, which appeared to be closed. This thirty feet, which it was necessary to cross from the border of the wood to the palisade, constituted the dangerous zone, to coin a term: in fact, one or more bullets fired from behind the palisade might knock over any one who ventured on to this zone. Gideon Spilett and the sailor were not men to draw back, but they knew that any imprudence on their part, of which they would be the first victims, would fall afterwards on their companions. If they themselves were killed, what would become of Harding, Neb, and Herbert?

But Pencroft, excited at feeling himself so near the corral where he supposed the convicts had taken refuge, was about to press forward, when the reporter held him back with a grasp of iron.

'In a few minutes it will be quite dark,' whispered Spilett in the sailor's ear; 'then will be the time to act.'

Pencroft, convulsively clasping the butt-end of his gun, restrained his eagerness, and waited, swearing to himself.

Soon the last of the twilight faded away. Darkness, which seemed as if it issued from the dense forest, covered the clearing. Mount Franklin rose like an enormous screen before the western horizon, and night spread rapidly over all, as it does in regions of low latitudes. Now was the time.

The reporter and Pencroft, since posting themselves on the edge of the wood, had not once lost sight of the palisade. The corral appeared to be absolutely deserted. The top of the palisade formed a line, a little darker than the surrounding shadow, and disturbed its distinctness. Nevertheless, if the convicts were there, they must have posted one of their number to guard against any surprise.

Spilett grasped his companion's hand, and both crept towards the corral, their guns ready to fire.

They reached the gate without the darkness being illuminated by a single ray of light.

Pencroft tried to push open the gate, which, as the reporter and he had supposed, was closed. However, the sailor was able to ascertain that the outer bars had not been put up. It might, then, be concluded that the convicts were there in the corral, and that very probably they had fastened the gate in such a way that it could not be forced open.

Gideon Spilett and Pencroft listened.

Not a sound could be heard inside the palisade. The musmons and the goats, sleeping no doubt in their huts, in no way disturbed the calm of night.

The reporter and the sailor hearing nothing, asked themselves whether they had not better scale the palisades and penetrate into the corral. This would have been contrary to Cyrus Harding's instructions.

It is true that the enterprise might succeed, but it might also fail. Now, if the convicts were suspecting nothing, if they knew nothing of the expedition against them, if, lastly, there now existed a chance of surprising them, ought this chance to be lost by inconsiderately attempting to cross the palisade?

This was not the reporter's opinion. He thought it better to wait until all the settlers were collected together before attempting to penetrate into the corral. One thing was certain, that it was possible to reach the palisade without being seen, and also that it did not appear to be guarded. This point settled, there was nothing to be done but to return to the cart, where they would consult.

Pencroft probably agreed with this decision, for he followed the reporter without making any objection when the latter turned back to the wood.

In a few minutes the engineer was made acquainted with the state of affairs.

'Well,' said he, after a little thought, 'I now have reason to believe that the convicts are not in the corral.'

'We shall soon know,' said Pencroft, 'when we have scaled the palisade.'

'To the corral, my friends!' said Cyrus Harding.

'Shall we leave the cart in the wood?' asked Neb.

'No,' replied the engineer; 'it is our waggon of ammunition and provisions, and, if necessary, it would serve as an intrench-ment.'

'Forward, then!' said Gideon Spilett.

The cart emerged from the wood and began to roll noiselessly towards the palisade. The darkness was now profound, the silence as complete as when Pencroft and the reporter crept over the ground. The thick grass completely muffled their footsteps.

The colonists held themselves ready to fire. Jup, at Pencroft's orders, kept behind. Neb led Top in a leash, to prevent him from bounding forward.

The clearing soon came in sight. It was deserted. Without hesitating, the little band moved towards the palisade. In a short space of time the dangerous zone was passed. Not a shot had been fired. When the cart reached the palisade, it stopped. Neb remained at the onagers' heads to hold them. The engineer, the reporter, Herbert, and Pencroft, proceeded to the door, in order to ascertain if it was barricaded inside.

It was open!

'What do you say now?' asked the engineer, turning to the sailor and Spilett.

Both were stupefied.

'I can swear,' said Pencroft, 'that this gate was shut just now!'

The colonists now hesitated. Were the convicts in the corral when Pencroft and the reporter made their reconnaissance? it could not be doubted, as the gate then closed could only have been opened by them. Were they still there, or had one of their number just gone out?

All these questions presented themselves simultaneously to the minds of the colonists, but how could they be answered?

At that moment, Herbert, who had advanced a few steps into the enclosure, drew back hurriedly, and seized Harding's hand.

'What's the matter?' asked the engineer.

'A light!'

'In the house?'

'Yes!'

All five advanced, and indeed, through the window fronting them, they saw glimmering a feeble light. Cyrus Harding made up his mind rapidly. 'It is our only chance,' said he to his companions, 'of finding the convicts collected in this house suspecting nothing! They are in our power! Forward!' The colonists crossed through the enclosure, holding their guns ready in their hands. The cart had been left outside under the charge of Jup and Top, who had been prudently tied to it.

Cyrus Harding, Pencroft, and Gideon Spilett on one side, Herbert and Neb on the other, going along by the palisade, surveyed the absolutely dark and deserted corral.

In a few moments they were near the closed door of the house.

Harding signed to his companions not to stir, and approached the window, then feebly lighted by the inner light.

He gazed into the apartment.

On the table burned a lantern. Near the table was the bed formerly used by Ayrton.

On the bed lay the body of a man.

Suddenly Cyrus Harding drew back, and in a hoarse voice, – 'Ayrton!' he exclaimed.

Immediately the door was forced rather than opened, and the colonists rushed into the room.

Ayrton appeared to be asleep. His countenance showed that he had long and cruelly suffered. On his wrists and ankles could be seen great bruises.

Harding bent over him.

'Ayrton!' cried the engineer, seizing the arm of the man whom he had just found again under such unexpected circumstances.

At this exclamation Ayrton opened his eyes, and, gazing at Harding, then at the others, –

'You!' he cried, 'You?'

'Ayrton! Ayrton!' repeated Harding.

'Where am I?'

'In the house in the corral!'

'Alone?'

'Yes!'

'But they will come back!' cried Ayrton. 'Defend yourselves! defend yourselves!'

And he fell back exhausted.

'Spilett,' exclaimed the engineer, 'we may be attacked at any moment. Bring the cart into the corral. Then barricade the door, and all come back here.'

Pencroft, Neb, and the reporter hastened to execute the engineer's orders. There was not a moment to be lost. Perhaps even now the cart was in the hands of the convicts!

In a moment the reporter and his two companions had crossed the corral and reached the gate of the palisade behind which Top was heard growling sullenly.

The engineer, leaving Ayrton for an instant, came out ready to fire. Herbert was at his side. Both surveyed the crest of the spur overlooking the corral. If the convicts were lying in ambush there, they might knock the settlers over one after the other.

At that moment the moon appeared in the east, above the black curtain of the forest, and a white sheet of light spread over the interior of the enclosure. The corral, with its clumps of trees, the little stream which watered it, and its wide carpet of grass, was suddenly illuminated. From the side of the mountain, the house and a part of the palisade stood out white in the moonlight. On the opposite side towards the door, the enclosure remained dark.

A black mass soon appeared. This was the cart entering the circle of light, and Cyrus Harding could hear the noise made by the door, as his companions shut it and fastened the interior bars.

But, at that moment, Top, breaking loose, began to bark furiously and rush to the back of the corral, to the right of the house.

'Be ready to fire, my friends!' cried Harding.

The colonists raised their pieces and awaited the moment to fire.

Top still barked, and Jup, running towards the dog, uttered shrill cries.

The colonists followed him, and reached the borders of the little stream, shaded by large trees. And there, in the bright moonlight, what did they see? Five corpses, stretched on the bank!

They were those of the convicts who, four months previously, had landed on Lincoln Island!

How had it happened? Who had killed the convicts? Was it Ayrton? No, for a moment before he was dreading their return. But Ayrton was now in a profound stupor, from which it was no longer possible to rouse him. After uttering those few words he had again become unconscious, and had fallen back motionless on the bed.

The colonists, a prey to a thousand confused thoughts, under the influence of violent excitement, waited all night, without leaving Ayrton's house, or returning to the spot where lay the bodies of the convicts. It was very probable that Ayrton would not be able to throw any light on the circumstances under which the bodies had been found, since he himself was not aware that he was in the corral. But at any rate he would be in a position to give an account of what had taken place before this terrible execution. The next day Ayrton awoke from his stupor, and his companions cordially manifested all the joy they felt, on seeing him again, almost safe and sound, after a hundred and four days' separation.

Ayrton then in a few words recounted what had happened, or at least, as much as he knew.

The day after his arrival at the corral, on the 10th of last November, at nightfall, he was surprised by the convicts, who had scaled the palisade. They bound and gagged him; then he was led to a dark cavern, at the foot of Mount Franklin, where the convicts had taken refuge.

His death had been decided upon, and the next day the convicts were about to kill him, when one of them recognised him, and called him by the name which he bore in Australia. The wretches had no scruples as to murder Ayrton! They spared Ben Joyce!

But from that moment Ayrton was exposed to the importunities of his former accomplices. They wished him to join them again, and relied upon his aid to enable them to gain possession of Granite House, to penetrate into that hitherto inaccessible dwelling and to become masters of the island, after murdering the colonists!

Ayrton remained firm. The once convict, now repentant and pardoned, would rather die than betray his companions. Ayrton – bound, gagged, and closely watched – lived in this cave for four months.

Nevertheless the convicts had discovered the corral a short time after their arrival in the island, and since then they had subsisted on Ayrton's stores, but did not live at the corral.

On the 11th of November, two of the villains, surprised by the colonists' arrival, fired at Herbert, and one of them returned, boasting of having killed one of the inhabitants of the island;

but he returned alone. His companion, as is known, fell by Cyrus Harding's dagger.

Ayrton's anxiety and despair may be imagined when he learnt the news of Herbert's death. The settlers were now only four, and, as it seemed, at the mercy of the convicts. After this event, and during all the time that the colonists, detained by Herbert's illness, remained in the coral, the pirates did not leave the cavern, and even after they had pillaged the pleaeau of Prospect Heights, they did not think it prudent to abandon it.

The ill-treatment inflicted on Ayrton was now redoubled. His hands and feet still bore the bloody marks of the cords which bound him day and night. Every moment he expected to be put to death, nor did it appear possible that he could escape.

Matters remained thus until the third week of February. The convicts, still watching for a favourable opportunity, rarely quitted their retreat, and only made a few hunting excursions, either to the interior of the island, or the south coast.

Ayrton had no further news of his friends, and relinquished all hope of ever seeing them again. At last, the unfortunate man, weakened by ill-treatment, fell into a prostration so profound that sight and hearing failed him. From that moment, that is to say, since the last two days, he could give no information whatever of what had occurred.

'But Captain Harding' he added, 'since I was imprisoned in that cavern, how is it that I find myself in the corral?'

'How is it that the convicts are lying yonder dead, in the middle of the enclosure?' answered the engineer.

'Dead!' cried Ayrton, half rising from his bed, notwithstanding his weakness.

His companions supported him, He wished to get up, and with their assistance he did so. They then proceeded together towards the little stream. It was now broad daylight.

There, on the bank, in the position in which they had been stricken by death in its most instantaneous form, lay the corpses of the five convicts!

Ayrton was astounded. Harding and his companions looked at him without uttering a word. On a sign from the engineer, Neb and Pencroft examined the bodies, already stiffened by the cold. They bore no apparent traces of any wound.

Only, after carefully examining them, Pencroft found on the forehead of one, on the chest of another, on the back of this one, on the shoulder of that, a little red spot, a sort of scarcely visible bruise, the cause of which it was impossible to conjecture.

'It is there that they have been struck!' said Cyrus Harding.

'But with what weapon?' cried the reporter.

'A weapon, lightning-like in its effect, and of which we have not the secret!'

'And who has struck the blow?' asked Pencroft.

'The avenging power of the island,' replied Harding; 'he who brought you here, Ayrton, whose influence has once more manifested itself, who does for us all that which we cannot do for ourselves, and who, his will accomplished, conceals himself from us.'

'Let us make search for him, then!' exclaimed Pencroft.

'And we will not return to Granite House until we have found our benefactor,' said Herbert.

'Yes,' said the engineer, 'we will do all that it is humanly possible to do, but I repeat we shall not find him until he himself permits us.'

'Shall we stay at the corral?' asked Pencroft.

'We shall stay here,' answered Harding. 'Provisions are abundant, and we are here in the very centre of the circle we have to explore. Besides, if necessary, the cart will take us rapidly to Granite House.'

'Good!' answered the sailor. 'Only I have a remark to make.'

'What is it?'

'Here is the fine season getting on, and we must not forget that we have a voyage to make.'

'A voyage?' said Gideon Spilett.

'Yes, to Tabor Island,' answered Pencroft. 'It is necessary to carry a notice there, to point out the position of our island and say that Ayrton is here, in case the Scotch yacht should come to take him off. Who knows if it is not already too late?'

'But, Pencroft,' asked Ayrton, 'how do you intend to make this voyage?'

'In the "Bonadventure".'

'The "Bonadventure"!' exclaimed Ayrton. 'She no longer exists.'

'My "Bonadventure" exists no longer!' shouted Pencroft, bounding from his seat.

'No,' answered Ayrton. 'The convicts discovered her in her little harbour only eight days ago, they put to sea in her, and –'

'And?' said Pencroft, his heart beating.

'And not having Bob Harvey to steer her, they ran on the rocks, and the vessel went to pieces.'

'Oh, the villains, the cut-throats, the infamous scoundrels!' exclaimed Pencroft.

'Pencroft,' said Herbert, taking the sailor's hand, 'we will build another "Bonadventure" – a larger one. We have all the ironwork – all the rigging of the brig at our disposal.'

'But do you know,' returned Pencroft, 'that it will take at least five or six months to build a vessel of from thirty to forty tons?'

'We can take our time,' said the reporter, 'and we must give up the voyage to Tabor Island for this year.'

'Oh, my "Bonadventure"! My poor "Bonadventure"!' cried Pencroft, almost broken-hearted at the destruction of the vessel of which he was so proud.

The loss of the 'Bonadventure' was certainly a thing to be lamented by the colonists, and it was agreed that this loss should be repaired as soon as possible. This settled, they now occupied themselves with bringing their researches to bear on the most secret parts of the island.

The exploration was commenced at daybreak on the 19th of February, and lasted an entire week. But though they searched the entire island, no one was found, nor any trace of the mysterious being. However, they did discover, much to their discomfort, that the volcano beneath Mount Franklin had become active and distinct rumblings were heard as they searched among the mountain's caves and tunnels. Harding remained silent and pensive for the rest of the journey after this discovery.

CHAPTER 26

THREE years had passed away since the escape of the prisoners from Richmond, and how often during those three years had they spoken of their country, always present in their thoughts!

They had no doubt that the civil war was at an end, and to them it appeared impossible that the just cause of the North had not triumphed. But what had been the incidents of this terrible war? How much blood had it not cost? How many of their friends must have fallen in the struggle? They often spoke of these things, without as yet being able to foresee the day when they would be permitted once more to see their country. To return thither, were it but for a few days, to renew the social link with the inhabited world, to establish a communications between their native land and their island, then to pass the longest, perhaps the best, portion of their existence in this colony, founded by them, and which would then be dependent on their country, was this a dream impossible to realise?

There were only two ways of accomplishing it – either a ship must appear off Lincoln Island, or the colonists must themselves build a vessel strong enough to sail to the nearest land.

'Unless,' said Pencroft, 'our good genius himself provides us with the means of returning to our country.'

And, really, had any one told Pencroft and Neb that a ship of 300 tons was waiting for them in Shark Gulf or at Port Balloon, they would not even have made a gesture of surprise. In their state of mind nothing appeared improbable.

But Cyrus Harding, less confident, advised them to confine themselves to fact, and more especially so with regard to the building of a vessel – a really urgent work, since it was for the purpose of depositing, as soon as possible, at Tabor Island a document indicating Ayrton's new residence.

As the 'Bonadventure' no longer existed, six months at least would be required for the construction of a new vessel. Now winter was approaching, and the voyage could not be made before the following spring.

'We have time to get everything ready for the fine season,' remarked the engineer, who was consulting with Pencroft about these matters. 'I think, therefore, my friend, that since we have to rebuild our vessel it will be best to give her larger dimensions. The arrival of the Scotch yacht at Tabor Island is very uncertain. It may even be that, having arrived several months ago, she has again sailed after having vainly searched for some trace of Ayrton. Will it not then be best to build a ship which, if necessary, could take us either to the Polynesian Archipelago or to New Zealand? What do you think?'

'I think, captain,' answered the sailor; 'I think that you are as capable of building a large vessel as a small one. Neither the wood nor the tools are wanting. It is only a question of time.'

'And how many months would be required to build a vessel of from 250 to 300 tons?' asked Harding.

'Seven or eight months at least,' replied Pencroft. 'But it must not be forgotten that winter is drawing near, and that in severe frost wood is difficult to work. We must calculate on several weeks' delay, and if our vessel is ready by next November we may think ourselves very lucky.'

'Well,' replied Cyrus Harding, 'that will be exactly the most favourable time for undertaking a voyage of any importance, either to Tabor Island or to a more distant land.'

As a matter of course Ayrton shared the common lot in every respect, and there was no longer any talk of his going to live at the corral. Nevertheless he was still sad and reserved, and joined more in the work than in the pleasures of his companions. But he was a valuable workman at need – strong, skilful, ingenious, intelligent. He was esteemed and loved by all, and he could not be ignorant of it.

In the meanwhile the corral was not abandoned. Every other day one of the settlers, driving the cart, or mounted on an onager, went to look after the flock of musmons and goats, and bring back the supply of milk required by Neb. These excursions at the same time afforded opportunities for hunting. Therefore Herbert and Gideon Spilett, with Top in front, traversed more often than their companions the road to the corral, and with the capital guns which they carried, capybaras, agouties, kangaroos, and wild pigs for large game, ducks, tetras, grouse, jacamars, and snipe for small, were never wanting in the house. The produce of the warren, of the oyster-bed, several turtles which were taken, excellent salmon which came up the Mercy, vegetables from the plateau, wild fruit from the forest, were riches upon riches, and Neb, the head cook, could scarcely by himself store them away.

The telegraphic wire between the corral and Granite House had of course been repaired, and it was worked whenever one or other of the settlers was at the corral and found it necessary to spend the night there. Besides, the island was safe now, and no attacks were to be feared, at any rate from men.

So passed the winter months, June, July, and August. They were very severe, and the average observations of the thermometer did not give more than eight degrees of Fahrenheit. It was therefore lower in temperature than the preceding winter. But then, what splendid fires blazed continually on the hearths of Granite House, the smoke marking the granite wall with long zebra-like streaks! Fuel was not spared, as it grew naturally a few steps from them. Besides, the chips of the wood destined for the construction of the ship enabled them to economise the coal, which required more trouble to transport.

But an event, the consequences of which might be serious, occurred in the first days of the returning spring.

On the 7th of September, Cyrus Harding, having observed the crater, saw smoke curling round the summit of the mountain, its first vapours rising in the air.

The colonists, warned by the engineer, left their work and gazed in silence at the summit of Mount Franklin.

The volcano had awoke, and the vapour had penetrated the mineral layer heaped up at the bottom of the crater. But would the subterranean fires provoke any violent eruption? This was an event which could not be foreseen. However, even while admitting the possibility of an eruption, it was not probable that the whole of Lincoln Island would suffer from it. The flow of volcanic matter is not always disastrous, and the island had already undergone this trial, as was shown by the streams of lava hardened on the northern slopes of the mountain. Besides, from the shape of the crater – the opening broken in the upper edge – the matter would be thrown to the side opposite the fertile regions of the island.

However, the past did not necessarily answer for the future. Often, at the summit of volcanoes, the old craters close and new ones open. This has occurred in the two hemispheres – at Etna, Popocatepetl, at Orizaba – and on the eve of an eruption there is everything to be feared. In fact, an earthquake – a phenomenon which often accompanies volcanic eruptions – is enough to change the interior arrangement of a mountain, and to open new outlets for the burning lava.

Cyrus Harding explained these things to his companions, and, without exaggerating the state of things, he told them all the pros and cons. After all they could not prevent it. It did not appear likely that Granite House would be threatened unless the ground was shaken by an earthquake. But the corral would be in great danger should a new crater open in the southern side of Mount Franklin.

From that day the smoke never disappeared from the top of the mountain, and it could even be perceived that it increased in height and thickness, without any flame mingling in its heavy volumes. The phenomenon was still concentrated in the lower part of the central crater.

However, with the fine days work had been continued. The building of the vessel was hastened as much as possible, and, by means of the waterfall on the shore, Cyrus Harding managed to establish an hydraulic saw-mill, which rapidly cut up the trunks of trees into planks and joists. The mechanism of this apparatus was as simple as those used in the rustic saw-mills of Norway. A first horizontal movement to move the piece of wood, a second vertical movement to move the saw – this was all that was wanted; and the engineer succeeded by means of a wheel, two cylinders, and pulleys properly arranged. Towards the end of the month of September the skeleton of the vessel, which was to be rigged as a schooner, lay in the dockyard. The ribs were almost entirely completed, and, all the timbers having been sustained by a provisional band, the shape of the vessel could already be seen. This schooner, sharp in the bows, very slender in the after-part, would evidently be suitable for a long voyage, if wanted; but laying the planking would still take a considerable time. Very fortunately the ironwork of the pirate brig had been saved after the explosion. From the planks and injured ribs Pencroft and Ayrton had extracted the bolts and a large quantity of copper nails. It was so much work saved for the smiths, but the carpenters had much to do.

Ship-building was interrupted for a week for the harvest, the haymaking, and the gathering in of the different crops on the plateau. This work finished, every moment was devoted to finishing the schooner. When night came the workmen were really quite exhausted. So as not to lose any time they had changed the hours for their meals; they dined at twelve o'clock, and only had their supper when daylight failed them. They then ascended Granite House, when they were always ready to go to bed.

Sometimes, however, when the conversation bore on some interesting subject the hour for sleep was delayed for a time. The colonists then spoke of the future, and talked willingly of the changes which a voyage in the schooner to inhabited lands would make in their situation. But always, in the midst of these plans, prevailed the thoughts of a subsequent return to Lincoln Island. Never would they abandon this colony, founded with so much labour and with such success, and to which a communication with America would afford a fresh impetus. Pencroft and Neb especially hoped to end their days there.

'Herbert,' said the sailor, 'you will never abandon Lincoln Island?'

'Never, Pencroft, and especially if you make up your mind to stay there.'

'That was made up long ago, my boy,' answered Pencroft. 'I shall expect you. You will bring me your wife and children, and I shall make jolly little chaps of your youngsters!'

'That's agreed,' replied Herbert, laughing and blushing at the same time.

'And you, Captain Hardling,' resumed Pencroft enthusiastically, 'you will be still the governor of the island! Ah! how many inhabitants could it support? Ten thousand at least!'

They talked in this way, allowing Pencroft to run on, and at last the reporter actually started a newspaper – the *New Lincoln Herald!*

So is man's heart. The desire to perform a work which will endure, which will survive him, is the origin of his superiority over all other living creatures here below. It is this which has established his dominion, and this it is which justifies it, over all the world.

After that, who knows if Jup and Top had not themselves their little dream of the future.

Ayrton silently said to himself that he would like to see Lord Glenarvan again and show himself to all restored.

One evening, on the 15th of October, the conversation was prolonged later than usual. It was nine o'clock. Already, long badly-concealed yawns gave warning of the hour of rest, and Pencroft was proceeding towards his bed, when the electric bell, placed in the dining-room, suddenly rang.

All were there, Cyrus Harding, Gideon Spilett, Herbert, Ayrton, Pencroft, Neb. Therefore none of the colonists were at the corral.

Cyrus Harding rose. His companions stared at each other, scarcely believing their ears.

'What does that mean?' cried Neb. 'Was it the devil who rang it?' No one answered.

'The weather is stormy,' observed Herbert. 'Might not its influence of electricity – '

Herbert did not finish his phrase. The engineer, towards whom all eyes were turned, shook his head negatively.

'We must wait,' said Gideon Spilett. 'If it is a signal, whoever it may be who has made it, he will renew it.'

'But who do you think it is?' cried Neb.

'Who?' answered Pencroft, 'but he – '

The sailor's sentence was cut short by a new tinkle of the bell.

Harding went to the apparatus, and sent this question to the corral: –

'What do you want?'

A few moments later the needle, moving on the alphabeticdial, gave this reply to the tenants of Granite House: –

'Come to the corral immediately.'

'At last!' exclaimed Harding.

Yes! At last! The mystery was about to be unveiled. The colonists' fatigue had disappeared before the tremendous interest which was about to urge them to the corral, and all wish for rest had ceased. Without having uttered a word, in a few moments they had left Granite House, and were standing on the beach. Jup and Top alone were left behind. They could do without them.

The night was black. The new moon had disappeared at the same time as the sun. As Herbert had observed great stormy clouds formed a lowering and heavy vault, preventing any star rays. A few lightning flashes, reflections from a distant storm, illuminated the horizon.

It was possible that a few hours later the thunder would roll over the island itself. The night was very threatening.

But however deep the darkness was, it would not prevent them from finding the familiar road to the corral.

They ascended the left bank of the Mercy, reached the plateau, passed the bridge over Creek Glycerine, and advanced through the forest.

They walked at a good pace, a prey to the liveliest emotions. There was no doubt but that they were now going to learn the long-searched-for answer to the enigma, the name of that mysterious being, so deeply concerned in their life, so generous in his influence, so powerful in his action. Must not this stranger have indeed mingled with their existence, have known the smallest details, have heard all that was said in Granite House, to have been able always to act in the very nick of time?

Every one, wrapped up in his own reflections, pressed forward. Under the arch of trees the darkness was such that the edge of the road even could not be seen. Not a sound in the forest. Both animals and birds, influenced by the heaviness of the atmosphere, remained motionless and silent. Not a breath disturbed the leaves. The footsteps of the colonists alone resounded on the hardened ground.

During the first quarter of an hour the silence was only interrupted by this remark from Pencroft:–

'We ought to have brought a torch.'

And by this reply from the engineer:–

'We shall find one at the corral.'

Harding and his companions had left Granite House at twelve minutes past nine. At forty-seven minutes past nine they had traversed three out of the five miles which separated the mouth of the Mercy from the corral.

At that moment sheets of lightning spread over the island and illumined the dark trees. The flashes dazzled and almost blinded them. Evidently the storm would not be long in bursting forth.

The flashes gradually became brighter and more rapid. Distant thunder growled in the sky. The atmosphere was stifling.

The colonists proceeded as if they were urged onwards by some irresistible force.

At ten o'clock a vivid flash showed them the palisade, and as they reached the gate the storm burst forth with tremendous fury.

In a minute the corral was crossed, and Harding stood before the hut.

Probably the house was occupied by the stranger, since it was from thence that the telegram had been sent. However no light shone through the window.

The engineer knocked at the door.

No answer.

Cyrus Harding opened the door, and the settlers entered the room, which was perfectly dark. A light was struck by Neb, and in a few moments the lantern was lighted and the light thrown into every corner of the room.

There was no one there. Everything was in the state in which it had been left.

'Have we been deceived by an illusion?' murmured Cyrus Harding.

No! that was not possible! The telegram had clearly said –

'Come to the corral immediately.'

They approached the table specially devoted to the use of the wire. Everything was in order – the pile and the box containing it, as well as all the apparatus.

'Who came here the last time?' asked the engineer.

'I did, captain,' answered Ayrton.

'And that was –'

'Four days ago.'

'Ah! a note!' cried Herbert, pointing to a paper lying on the table.

On this paper were written these words in English:–

'Follow the new wire.'

'Forward!' cried Harding, who understood that the despatch had not been sent from the corral, but from the mysterious retreat, communicating directly with Granite House by means of a supplementary wire joined to the old one.

Neb took the lighted lantern, and all left the corral. The storm then burst forth with tremendous violence. The interval between each lightning-flash and each thunder-clap diminished rapidly. The summit of the volcano, with its plume of vapour, could be seen by occasional flashes.

There was no telegraphic communication in any part of the corral between the house and the palisade; but the engineer, running straight to the first post, saw by the light of a flash a new wire hanging from the isolater to the ground.

'There it is!' said he.

This wire lay along the ground, and was surrounded with an isolating substance like a submarine cable, so as to assure the free transmission of the current. It appeared to pass through the wood and the southern spurs of the mountain, and consequently it ran towards the west.

'Follow it!' said Cyrus Harding.

And the settlers immediately pressed forward, guided by the wire.

The thunder continued to roar with such violence that not a word could be heard. However, there was no occasion for speaking, but to get forward as fast as possible.

Cyrus Harding and his companions then climbed the spur rising between the corral valley and that of Falls River, which they crossed at its narrowest part. The wire, sometimes stretched over the lower branches of the trees, sometimes lying on the ground, guided them surely. The engineer had supposed that the wire would perhaps stop at the bottom of the valley, and that the stranger's retreat would be there.

Nothing of the sort. They were obliged to ascend the south-western spur, and re-descend on that arid plateau terminated by the strangely-wild basalt cliff. From time to time one of the colonists stooped down and felt for the wire with his hands; but there was now no doubt that the wire was running directly towards the sea There, to a certainty, in the depths of those rocks, was the dwelling so long sought for in vain.

The sky was literally on fire. Flash succeeded flash. Several struck the summit of the volcano in the midst of the thick smoke. It appeared there as if the mountain was vomiting flame. At a few minutes to eleven the colonists arrived on the high cliff overlooking the ocean to the west. The wind had risen. The surf roared 500 feet below.

Harding calculated that they had gone a mile and a half from the corral.

At this point the wire entered among the rocks, following the steep side of a narrow ravine. The settlers followed it at the risk of occasioning a fall of the slightly-balanced rocks, and being dashed into the sea. The descent was extremely perilous, but they did not think of the danger; they were no longer masters of themselves, and an irresistible attraction drew them towards this mysterious place as the magnet draws iron.

Thus they almost unconsciously descended this ravine, which even in broad daylight would have been considered impracticable.

The stones rollled and sparkled like fiery balls when they crossed through the gleams of light. Harding was first - Ayrton last. On they went, step by step. Now they slid over the slippery rock; then they struggled to their feet and scrambled on.

At last the wire touched the rocks on the beach The colonists had reached the bottom of the basalt cliff.

There appeared a narrow ridge, running horizontally and parallel with the sea. The settlers followed the wire along it. They had not gone a hundred paces when the ridge by a moderate incline sloped down to the level of the sea.

The engineer seized the wire and found that it disappeared beneath the waves.

His companions were stupefied.

A cry of disappointment, almost a cry of despair, escaped them! Must they then plunge beneath the water and seek there for some submarine cavern? In their excited state they would not have hesitated to do it.

The engineer stopped them.

He led his companions to a hollow in the rocks, and there –

'We must wait,' said he. 'The tide is high. At low water the way will be open.'

'But what can make you think –' asked Pencroft.

'He would not have called us if the means had been wanting to enable us to reach him!'

Cyrus Harding spoke in a tone of such thorough conviction that no objection was raised. His remark, besides, was logical. It was quite possible that an opening, practicable at low water, though hidden now by the high tide, opened at the foot of the cliff.

There was some time to wait. The colonists remained silently crouching in a deep hollow. Rain now began to fall in torrents. The thunder was re-echoed among the rocks with a grand sonorousness.

The colonists' emotion was great. A thousand strange and extraordinary ideas crossed their brains, and they expected some grand and superhuman apparition, which alone could come up to the notion they had formed of the mysterious genius of the island.

At midnight, Harding, carrying the lantern, descended to the beach to reconnoitre.

The engineer was not mistaken. The beginning of an immense excavation could be seen under the water. There the wire, bending at a right angle, entered the yawning gulf.

Cyrus Harding returned to his companions, and said simply –

'In an hour the opening will be practicable.'

'It is there, then?' said Pencroft.

'Did you doubt it?' returned Harding.

'But this cavern must be filled with water to a certain height,' observed Herbert.

'Either the cavern will be completely dry,' replied Harding, 'and in that case we can traverse it on foot, or it will not be dry, and some means of transport will be put at our disposal.'

An hour passed. All climbed down through the rain to the level of the sea. There was now eight feet of the opening above the water. It was like the arch of a bridge, under which rushed the foaming water.

Leaning forward, the engineer saw a black object floating on the water. He drew it towards him. It was a boat moored to some interior projection of the cave. This boat was iron-plated. Two oars lay at the bottom.

'Jump in!' said Harding.

In a moment the settlers were in the boat. Neb and Ayrton took the oars, Pencroft the rudder. Cyrus Harding in the bows, with the lantern, lighted the way.

The elliptical roof, under which the boat at first past, suddenly rose; but the darkness was too deep, and the light of the lantern too slight, for either the extent, length, height, or depth of the cave to be ascertained. Solemn silence reigned in this basaltic cavern. Not a sound could penetrate into it, even the thunder peals could not pierce its thick sides.

Such immense caves exist in various parts of the world, natural crypts dating from the geological epoch of the globe. Some are filled by the sea; others contain entire lakes in their sides. Such is Fingal's Cave, in the island of Staffa, one of the Hebrides; such are the caves of Morgat, in the bay of Douarucuez, in Brittany, the caves of Bonifacior, in Corsica, those of Lyse-Fjord, in Norway; such are the immense Mammoth caverns in Kentucky, 500 feet in height, and more than twenty miles in length! In many parts of the globe, nature has excavated these caverns, and preserved them for the admiration of man.

Did the cavern which the settlers were now exploring extend to the centre of the island? For a quarter of an hour the boat had been advancing, making *détours*, indicated to Pencroft by the engineer in short sentences, when all at once –

'More to the right!' he commanded.

The boat, altering its course, came up alongside the right wall. The engineer wished to see if the wire still ran along the side.

The wire was there fastened to the rock.

'Forward!' said Harding.

And the two oars plunging into the dark waters, urged the boat onwards.

On they went for another quarter of an hour, and a distance of half-a-mile must have been cleared from the mouth of the cave, when Harding's voice was again heard.

'Stop!' said he.

The boat stopped, and the colonists perceived a bright light illuminating the vast cavern, so deeply excavated in the bowels of the island, of which nothing had ever led them to suspect the existence.

At a height of a hundred feet rose the vaulted roof, supported on basalt shafts. Irregular arches, strange mouldings, appeared on the columns erected by nature in thousands from the first epochs of the formation of the globe. The basalt pillars, fitted one into the other, measured from forty to fifty feet in height, and the water, calm in spite of the tumult outside, washing their base. The brilliant focus of light, pointed out by the engineer, touched every point of rock, and flooded the walls with light.

By reflection the water reproduced the brilliant sparkles, so that the boat appeared to be floating between two glittering zones.

They could not be mistaken in the nature of the irradiation thrown from the centre light, whose clear rays broke all the angles, all the projections of the cavern. This light proceeded from an electric source, and its white colour betrayed its origin. It was the sun of this cave, and it filled it entirely.

At a sign from Cyrus Harding the oars again plunged into the water, causing a regular shower of gems, and the boat was urged forward towards the light, which was now not more than half a cable's length distant.

At this place the breadth of the sheet of water measured nearly 350 feet, and beyond the dazzling centre could be seen an enormous basaltic wall, blocking up any issue on that side. The cavern widened here considerably, the sea forming a little lake. But the roof, the side walls, the end cliff, all the prisms, all the peaks, were flooded with the electric fluid, so that the brilliancy belonged to them, and as if the light issued from them.

In the centre of the lake a long cigar-shaped object floated on the surface of the water, silent, motionless. The brilliancy which issued from it escaped from its sides as from two kilns heated to a white heat. This apparatus, similar in shape to an enormous whale, was about 250 feet long, and rose about ten or twelve above the water.

The boat slowly approached it. Cyrus Harding stood up in the bows. He gazed, a prey to violent excitement Then, all at once, seizing the reporter's arm: –

'It is he! It can only be he!' he cried 'he! –'

Then, falling back on the seat, he murmured a name which Gideon Spilett alone could hear.

The reporter evidently knew this name, for it had a wonderful effect upon him, and he answered in a hoarse voice, –

'He! an outlawed man!'

'He!' said Harding.

At the engineer's command the boat approached this singular floating apparatus. The boat touched the left side, from which escaped a ray of light through a thick glass.

Harding and his companions mounted on the platform. An open hatchway was there. All darted down the opening.

At the bottom of the ladder was a deck, lighted by electricity. At the end of this deck was a door, which Harding opened.

A richly-ornamented room, quickly traversed by the colonists, was joined to a library, over which a luminous ceiling shed a flood of light.

At the end of the library a large door, also shut, was opened by the engineer.

An immense saloon – a sort of museum, in which were heaped up, with all the treasures of the mineral world, works of art, marvels of industry – appeared before the eyes of the colonists, who almost thought themselves suddenly transported into a land of enchantment.

Stretched on a rich sofa they saw a man, who did not appear to notice their presence.

Then Harding raised his voice, and to the extreme surprise of his companions, he uttered these words, –

'Captain Nemo, you asked for us! We are here.'

CHAPTER 27

At these words the reclining figure rose, and the electric light fell upon his countenance; a magnificent head, the forehead high, the glance commanding, beard white, hair abundant and falling over the shoulders.

His hand rested upon the cushion of the divan from which he had just risen. He appeared perfectly calm. It was evident that his strength had been gradually undermined by illness, but his voice seemed yet powerful, as he said in English, and in a tone which evinced extreme surprise, –

'Sir, I have no name.'

'Nevertheless, I know you!' replied Cyrus Harding.

Captain Nemo fixed his penetrating gaze upon the engineer, as though he were about to annihilate him.

Then, falling back amid the pillows of the divan, – 'After all, what matters now?' he murmured; 'I am dying!'

Cyrus Harding drew near the captain, and Gideon Spilett took his hand – it was of a feverish heat. Ayrton, Pencroft, Herbert, and Neb, stood respectfully apart in an angle of the magnificent saloon, whose atmosphere was saturated with the electric fluid.

Meanwhile Captain Nemo withdrew his hand, and motioned

the engineer and the reporter to be seated.

All regarded him with profound emotion. Before them they beheld that being whom they had styled the 'genius of the island', the powerful protector whose intervention, in so many circumstances, had been so efficacious, the benefactor to whom they owed such a debt of gratitude! Their eyes beheld a man only, and a man at the point of death, where Pencroft and Neb had expected to find an almost supernatural being!

But how happened it that Cyrus Harding had recognised Captain Nemo? Why had the latter so suddenly risen on hearing this name uttered, a name which he had believed known to none? –

The captain had resumed his position on the divan and leaning on his arm, he regarded the engineer, seated near him.

'You know the name I formerly bore, sir?' he asked.

'I do,' answered Cyrus Harding, 'and also that of this wonderful submarine vessel – '

'The "Nautilus"?' said the captain, with a faint smile.

'The "Nautilus"!'

'But do you – do you know who I am?'

'I do.'

'It is nevertheless many years since I have held any communication with the inhabited world; three long years have I passed in the depths of the sea, the only place where I have found liberty! Who then can have betrayed my secret?'

'A man who was bound to you by no tie, Captain Nemo, and who, consequently, cannot be accused of treachery.'

'The Frenchman who was cast on board my vessel by chance sixteen years since?'

'The same.'

'He and his two companions did not then perish in the Maëlstrom, in the midst of which the "Nautilus" was struggling.'

'They escaped, and a book has appeared under the title of "Twenty Thousand Leagues under the Sea", which contains your history.'

'The history of a few months only of my life!' interrupted the captain impetuously.

'It is true, ' answered Cyrus Harding, 'but a few months of that strange life have sufficed to make you known – '

'As a great criminal, doubtless!' said Captain Nemo, a haughty smile curling his lips. 'Yes, a rebel, perhaps an outlaw against humanity!'

The engineer was silent.

'Well, sir?'

'It is not for me to judge you, Captain Nemo,' answered Cyrus Harding, 'at any rate as regards your past life. I am, with the rest of the world, ignorant of the motives which induced you to adopt this strange mode of existence, and I cannot judge of effects without knowing their causes; but what I *do* know is, that a beneficent hand has constantly protected us since our arrival on Lincoln Island, that we all owe our lives to a good, generous, and powerful being, and that this being so powerful, good, and generous, Captain Nemo, is yourself!'

'It is I,' answered the captain simply.

The engineer and reporter rose. Their companions had drawn near, and the gratitude with which their hearts were charged was about to express itself in their gestures and words.

Captain Nemo stopped them by a sign, and in a voice which betrayed more emotion than he doubtless intended to show.

'Wait till you have heard all,' he said.

And the captain, in a few concise sentences, ran over the events of his life.

His narrative was short, yet he was obliged to summon up his whole remaining energy to arrive at the end. He was evidently contending against extreme weakness. Several times Cyrus Harding entreated him to repose for a while, but he shook his head as a man to whom the morrow may never come, and when the reporter offered his assistance, –

'It is useless,' he said; 'my hours are numbered.'

Captain Nemo was an Indian, the Prince Dakkar, son of a rajah of the then independent territory of Bundelkund. His father sent him, when ten years of age, to Europe, in order that he might receive an education in all respects complete, and in the hopes that by his talents and knowledge he might one day take a leading part in raising his long degraded and heathen country to a level with the nations of Europe.

From the age of ten years to that of thirty Prince Dakkar, endowed by Nature with her richest gifts of intellect, accumulated knowledge of every kind, and in science, literature, and art his researches were extensive and profound.

He travelled over the whole of Europe. His rank and fortune caused him to be everywhere sought after; but the pleasures of the world had for him no attractions. Though young and possessed of every personal advantage, he was ever grave – sombre even – devoured by an unquenchable thirst for knowledge and cherishing in the recesses of his heart the hope that he might become a great and powerful ruler of a free and enlightened people.

Still, for long the love of science triumphed over all other feelings. He became an artist deeply impressed by the marvels of art, a philosopher to whom no one of the higher sciences was unknown, a statesman versed in the policy of European courts. To the eyes of those who observed him superficially he might have passed for one of those cosmopolitans, curious of knowledge, but disdaining action; one of those opulent travellers, haughty and cynical, who move incessantly from placed to place, and are of no country.

This artist, this philosopher, this man was, however, still cherishing the hope instilled into him from his earliest days.

Prince Dakkar returned to Bundelkund in the year 1849. He married a noble Indian lady, who was imbued with an ambition not less ardent than that by which he was inspired. Two children were born to them, whom they tenderly loved. But domestic happiness did not prevent him from seeking to carry out the object at which he aimed. He waited an opportunity. At length, as he vainly fancied, it presented itself.

Instigated by princes equally ambitious and less sagacious and more unscrupulous than he was, the people of India were persuaded that they might successfully rise against their English rulers, who had brought them out of a state of anarchy and constant warfare and misery, and had established peace and prosperity in their country. Their ignorance and gross superstition made them the facile tools of their designing chiefs.

In 1857 the great sepoy revolt broke out. Prince Dakkar, under the belief that he should thereby have the opportunity of attaining the object of his long-cherished ambition, was easily drawn into it. He forthwith devoted his talents and wealth to the service of this cause. He aided it in person; he fought in the front ranks; he risked his life equally with the humblest of the wretched and misguided fanatics; he was ten times wounded in twenty engagements, seeking death but finding it not, when at length the sanguinary rebels were utterly defeated, and the atrocious mutiny was brought to an end.

Never before had the British power in India been exposed to such danger, and if, as they had hoped, the sepoys had received assistance from without, the influence and supremacy in Asia of the United Kingdom would have been a thing of the past.

The name of Prince Dakkar was at that time well known. He had fought openly and without concealment. A price was set upon his head, but he managed to escape from his pursuers.

Civilisation never recedes; the law of necessity ever forces it onwards. The sepoys were vanquished, and the land of the rajahs of old fell again under the rule of England.

Prince Dakkar, unable to find that death he courted, returned to the mountain fastnesses of Bundelkund. There, alone in the world, overcome by disappointment at the destruction of all his vain hopes, a prey to profound disgust for all human beings, filled with hatred of the civilised world, he realised the wreck of his fortune, assembled some score of his most faithful companions, and one day disappeared, leaving no trace behind.

Where, then, did he seek that liberty denied him upon the inhabited earth? Under the waves, in the depths of the ocean, where none could follow.

The warrior became the man of science. Upon a deserted island of the Pacific he established his dockyard, and there a submarine vessel was constructed from his designs. By methods which will at some future day be revealed he had rendered subservient the illimitable forces of electricity, which, extracted from inexhaustible sources, was employed for all the requirements of his floating equipage, as a moving, lighting, and heating agent. The sea with its countless treasures, its myriads of fish, its numberless wrecks, its enormous mammalia, and not only all that nature supplied, but also all that man had lost in its depths sufficed for every want of the prince and his crew – and thus was his most ardent desire accomplished, never again to hold communication with the earth. He named his submarine vessel the 'Nautilus,' called himself simply Captain Nemo, and disappeared beneath the seas.

During many years this strange being visited every ocean, from pole to pole. Outcast of the inhabited earth, in these unknown worlds he gathered incalculable treasures. The millions lost in the Bay of Vigo, in 1702, by the galleons of Spain, furnished him with a mine of inexhaustible riches, which he devoted, always anonymously, in favour of those nations who fought for the independence of their country.[1]

For long, however, he had held no communication with his fellow-creatures, when, during the night of the 6th of November, 1866, three men were cast on board his vessel. They were a French professor, his servant, and a Canadian fisherman. These three men had been hurled overboard by a collision which had taken place between the 'Nautilus' and the United States' frigate 'Abraham Lincoln', which had chased her.

Captain Nemo learnt from this professor that the 'Nautilus', taken now for a gigantic mammal of the whale species, now for a submarine vessel carrying a crew of pirates, was sought for in every sea.

He might have returned these three men to the ocean, from whence chance had brought them in contact with his mysterious existence. Instead of doing this, he kept them prisoners, and during seven months they were enabled to behold all the wonders of a voyage of twenty thousand leagues under the sea.

One day, the 22nd of June, 1867, these three men, who knew nothing of the past history of Captain Nemo, succeeded in escaping in one of the 'Nautilus's' boats. But as at this time the 'Nautilus' was drawn into the vortex of the Maëlstrom, off the coast of Norway, the captain naturally believed that the fugitives, engulfed in that frightful whirlpool, found their death at the bottom of the abyss. He was ignorant that the Frenchman and his two companions had been miraculously cast on shore, that the fisherman of the Loffoden Islands had rendered them assistance, and that the professor, on his return to France, had published

1This refers to the insurrection of the Candiotes, who were, in fact, largely assisted by Captain Nemo.

that work in which seven months of the strange and eventful navigation of the 'Nautilus' were narrated, and exposed to the curiosity of the public.

For a long time after this, Captain Nemo continued to live thus, traversing every sea. But one by one his companions died, and found their last-resting place in their cemetery of coral, in the bed of the Pacific. At last Captain Nemo remained, the solitary survivor of all those who had taken refuge with him in the depths of the ocean.

He was now sixty years of age. Although alone, he succeeded in navigating the 'Nautilus' towards one of those submarine caverns which had sometimes served him as a harbour.

One of these ports was hollowed beneath Lincoln Island, and at this moment furnished an asylum to the 'Nautilus'.

The captain had now remained there six years, navigating the ocean no longer, but awaiting death, and that moment when he should rejoin his former companions, when by chance he observed the descent of the balloon which carried the prisoners of the Confederates. Clad in his diving-dress, he was walking beneath the water at a few cables' length from the shore of the island, when the engineer had been thrown into the sea. Moved by a feeling of compassion, the captain saved Cyrus Harding.

His first impulse was to fly from the vicinity of the five castaways; but his harbour of refuge was closed, for in consequence of an elevation of the basalt, produced by the influence of volcanic action, he could no longer pass through the entrance of the vault. Though there was sufficient depth of water to allow a light craft to pass the bar, there was not enough for the 'Nautilus', whose draught of water was considerable.

Captain Nemo was compelled, therefore, to remain. He observed these men thrown without resources upon a desert island but had no wish to be himself discovered by them. By degrees he became interested in their efforts when he saw them honest, energetic, and bound to each other by the ties of friendship. As if despite his wishes, he penetrated all the secrets of their existence. By means of the diving dress he could easily reach the well in the interior of Granite House, and climbing by the projections of rock to its upper orifice, he heard the colonists, as they recounted the past, and studied the present and future. He learnt from them the tremendous conflict of America with America itself, for the abolition of slavery. Yes, these men were worthy to reconcile Captain Nemo with that humanity which they represented so nobly in the island.

Captain Nemo had saved Cyrus Harding. It was he also who had brought back the dog to the Chimneys, who rescued Top from the waters of the lake, who caused to fall at Flotsam Point the case containing so many things useful to the colonists, who conveyed the canoe back into the stream of the Mercy, who cast the cord from the top of Granite House at the time of the attack by the baboons, who made known the presence of Ayrton upon Tabor Island, by means of the document enclosed in the bottle, who caused the explosion of the brig by the shock of a torpedo placed at the bottom of the canal, who saved Herbert from a certain death by bringing the sulphate of quinine; and finally, it was he who had killed the convicts with the electric balls, of which he possessed the secret, and which he employed in the chase of submarine creatures. Thus were explained so many apparently supernatural occurrences, and which all proved the generosity and power of the captain.

Nevertheless, this noble misanthrope longed to benefit his *protégés* still further. There yet remained much useful advice to give them, and, his heart being softened by the approach of death, he invited as we are aware, the colonists of Granite House to visit the 'Nautilus', by means of a wire which connected it with the corral. Possibly he would not have done this had he been aware that Cyrus Harding was sufficiently acquainted with his history to address him by the name of Nemo.

The captain concluded the narrative of his life. Cyrus Harding then spoke; he recalled all the incidents which had exercised so beneficent an influence upon the colony, and in the names of his companions and himself thanked the generous being to whom they owed so much.

But Captain Nemo paid little attention; his mind appeared to be absorbed by one idea, and without taking the proffered hand of the engineer, –

'Now, sir,' said he, 'now that you know my history, your judgement!'

In saying this, the captain evidently alluded to an important incident witnessed by the three strangers thrown on board his vessel, and which the French professor had related in his work, causing a profound and terrible sensation. Some days previous to the flight of the professor and his two companions, the 'Nautilus', being chased by a frigate in the north of the Atlantic had hurled herself as a ram upon this frigate, and sunk her without mercy.

Cyrus Harding understood the captain's allusion, and was silent.

'It was an enemy's frigate,' exclaimed Captain Nemo, transformed for an instant into the Prince Dakkar, 'an enemy's frigate! It was she who attacked me – I was in a narrow and shallow bay – the frigate barred my way – and I sank her!'

A few moments of silence ensued; then the captain demanded, –
'What think you of my life, gentlemen?'

Cyrus Harding extended his hand to the ci-devant prince and replied gravely, 'Sir, your error was in supposing that the past can be resuscitated, and in contending against inevitable progress.

It is one of those errors which some admire, others blame; which God alone can judge. He who is mistaken in an action which he sincerely believes to be right may be an enemy, but retains our esteem. Your error is one that we may admire, and your name has nothing to fear from the judgement of history, which does not condemn heroic folly, but its results.'

The old man's breast swelled with emotion, and raising his hand to heaven, –

'Was I wrong, or in the right?' he murmured.

Cyrus Harding replied, 'All great actions return to God, from whom they are derived. Captain Nemo, we, whom you have succoured, shall ever mourn your loss.'

Herbert, who had drawn near the captain, fell on his knees and kissed his hand.

A tear glistened in the eyes of the dying man. 'My child,' he said, 'may God bless you!'

CHAPTER 28

DAY had returned. No ray of light penetrated into the profundity of the cavern. It being high-water, the entrance was closed by the sea. But the artificial light, which escaped in long streams from the skylights of the 'Nautilus', was as vivid as before, and the sheet of water shone around the floating vessel.

An extreme exhaustion now overcame Captain Nemo, who had fallen back upon the divan. It was useless to contemplate removing him to Granite House, for he had expressed his wish to remain in the midst of those marvels of the 'Nautilus' which millions could not have purchased, and to await there for that death which was swiftly approaching.

During a long interval of prostration, which rendered him almost unconscious, Cyrus Harding and Gideon Spilett attentively observed the condition of the dying man. It was apparent that his strength was gradually diminishing. That frame, once so robust, was now but the fragile tenement of a departing soul. All of life was concentrated in the heart and head.

The engineer and reporter consulted in whispers. Was it possible to render any aid to the dying man? Might his life, if not saved, be prolonged for some days? He himself had said that no remedy could avail, and he awaited with tranquillity that death which had for him no terrors.

'We can do nothing,' said Gideon Spilett.

'But of what is he dying?' asked Pencroft.

'Life is simply fading out,' replied the reporter.

'Nevertheless,' said the sailor, 'if we moved him into the open air, and the light of the sun, he might perhaps recover.'

'No, Pencroft,' answered the engineer, 'it is useless to attempt it. Besides, Captain Nemo would never consent to leave his vessel. He has lived for a dozen years on board the "Nautilus", and on board the "Nautilus" he desires to die.'

Without doubt Captain Nemo heard Cyrus Harding's reply, for he raised himself slightly, and in a voice more feeble, but always intelligible, –

'You are right, sir,' he said. 'I shall die here – it is my wish; and therefore I have a request to make of you.'

Cyrus Harding and his companions had drawn near the divan, and now arranged the cushions in such a manner as to better support the dying man.

They saw his eyes wander over all the marvels of this saloon, lighted by the electric rays which fell from the arabesques of the luminous ceiling. He surveyed, one after the other, the pictures hanging from the splendid tapestries of the partitions, the *chef-d'ouvres* of the Italian, Flemish, French, and Spanish masters; the statues of marble and bronze on their pedestals; the magnificent organ, leaning against the after-partition; the aquarium, in which bloomed the most wonderful productions of the sea – marine plants, zoophytes, chaplets of pearls of inestimable value; and, finally, his eyes rested on this device, inscribed over the pediment of the museum – the motto of the 'Nautilus' –

'Mobilis in mobile.'

His glance seemed to rest fondly for the last time on these masterpieces of art and of nature, to which he had limited his horizon during a sojourn of so many years in the abysses of the seas.

Cyrus Harding respected the captain's silence, and waited till he should speak.

After some minutes, during which, doubtless, he passed in review his whole life, Captain Nemo turned to the colonists and said, –

'You consider yourselves, gentlemen, under some obligations to me?'

'Captain, believe us that we would give our lives to prolong yours.'

'Promise, then,' continued Captain Nemo, 'to carry out my last wishes, and I shall be repaid for all I have done for you.'

'We promise,' said Cyrus Harding.

And by this promise he bound both himself and his companions.

'Gentlemen,' resumed the captain, 'tomorrow I shall be dead.'

Herbert was about to utter an exclamation, but a sign from the captain arrested him.

'Tomorrow I shall die, and I desire no other tomb than the "Nautilus". It is my grave! All my friends repose in the depths of the ocean; their resting-place shall be mine.'

These words were received with profound silence.

'Pay attention to my wishes,' he continued. 'The "Nautilus" is imprisoned in this grotto, the entrance of which is blocked up; but although egress is impossible, the vessel may at least sink in the abyss, and there bury my remains.'

The colonists listened reverently to the words of the dying man.

'Tomorrow, after my death, Mr Harding,' continued the captain, 'yourself and companions will leave the "Nautilus", for all the treasures it contains must perish with me. One token alone will remain with you of Prince Dakkar, with whose history you are now acquainted. That coffer yonder contains diamonds of the value of many millions, most of them mementoes of the time when, husband and father, I thought happiness possible for me, and a collection of pearls gathered by my friends and myself in the depths of the ocean. Of this treasure at a future day you may make good use. In the hands of such men as yourself and your comrades, Captain Harding, money will never be a source of danger. From on high I shall still participate in your enterprises, and I fear not but that they will prosper.'

After a few moments' repose, necessitated by his extreme weakness, Captain Nemo continued, –

'Tomorrow you will take the coffer, you will leave the saloon, of which you will close the door; then you will ascend on the deck of the "Nautilus", and you will lower the main hatch so as entirely to close the vessel.'

'It shall be done, captain,' answered Cyrus Harding.

'Good. You will then embark in the canoe which brought you hither; but, before leaving the "Nautilus", go to the stern and there open two large stop-cocks which you will find upon the water-line. The water will penetrate in to the reservoirs, and the "Nautilus" will gradually sink beneath the water, to repose at the bottom of the abyss.'

And, comprehending a gesture of Cyrus Harding, the captain added, –

'Fear nothing! You will but bury a corpse!'

Neither Cyrus Harding nor his companions ventured to offer any observation to Captain Nemo. He had expressed his last wishes, and they had nothing to do but to conform to them.

'I have your promise, gentlemen?' added Captain Nemo.

'You have, captain,' replied the engineer.

The captain thanked the colonists by a sign, and requested them to leave him for some hours. Gideon Spilett wished to remain near him, in the event of a crisis coming on, but the dying man refused, saying, 'I shall live until tomorrow, sir.'

All left the saloon, passed through the library and the dining-room and arrived forward, in the machine-room, where the electrical apparatus was established, which supplied not only heat and light, but the mechanical power of the 'Nautilus'.

The 'Nautilus' was a masterpiece, containing masterpieces within itself, and the engineer was struck with astonishment.

The colonists mounted the platform, which rose seven or eight feet above the water. There they beheld a thick glass lenticular covering, which protected a kind of large eye, from which flashed forth light. Behind this eye was apparently a cabin containing the wheels of the rudder, and in which was stationed the helmsman, when he navigated the 'Nautilus' over the bed of the ocean, which the electric rays would evidently light up to a considerable distance.

Cyrus Harding and his companions remained for a time silent, for they were vividly impressed by what they had just seen, and heard, and their hearts were deeply touched by the thought that he whose arm had so often aided them, the protector whom they had known but a few hours, was at the point of death.

Whatever might be the judgement pronounced by posterity upon the events of this, so to speak, extra-human existence, the character of Prince Dakkar would ever remain as one of those whose memory time can never efface.

'What a man!' said Pencroft. 'Is it possible that he can have lived at the bottom of the sea? And it seems to me that perhaps he has not found peace there any more than elsewhere!'

'The "Nautilus",' observed Ayrton, 'might have enabled us to leave Lincoln Island and reach some inhabited country.'

'Good Heavens!' exclaimed Pencroft, 'I for one would never risk myself in such a craft. To sail on the seas, good; but under the seas, never!'

'I believe, Pencroft,' answered the reporter, 'that the navigation of a submarine vessel such as the "Nautilus" ought to be very easy, and that we should soon become accustomed to it. There would be no storms, no lee-shore to fear. At some feet beneath the surface the waters of the ocean are as calm as those of a lake.

'That may be,' replied the sailor, 'but I prefer a gale of wind on board a well-found craft. A vessel is built to sail on the sea, and not beneath it.'

'My friends,' said the engineer, 'it is useless, at any rate as regards the "Nautilus", to discuss the question of submarine vessels. The "Nautilus" is not ours, and we have not the right to dispose of it. Moreover, we could in no case avail ourselves of it. Independently of the fact that it would be impossible to get it out of this cavern, whose entrance is now closed by the uprising of the basaltic rocks, Captain Nemo's wish is that it shall be buried with him. His wish is our law, and we will fulfil it.'

After a somewhat prolonged conversation, Cyrus Harding and his companions again descended to the interior of the 'Nautilus'. There they took some refreshment, and returned to the saloon.

Captain Nemo had somewhat rallied from the prostration which had overcome him, and his eyes shone with their wonted fire. A faint smile even curled his lips.

The colonists drew around him.

'Gentlemen,' said the captain, 'you are brave and honest men. You have devoted yourselves to the common weal. Often have I observed your conduct. I have esteemed you – I esteem you still! Your hand, Mr Harding!'

Cyrus Harding gave his hand to the captain, who clasped it affectionately.

'It is well!' he murmured.

He resumed, –

'But enough of myself. I have to speak concerning yourselves, and this Lincoln Island, upon which you have taken refuge. You desire to leave it?'

'To return, captain!' answered Pencroft quickly.

'To return, Pencroft,' said the captain, with a smile. 'I know, it is true, your love for this island. You have helped to make it what it now is, and it seems to you a paradise!'

'Our project, captain,' interposed Cyrus Harding, 'is to annex it to the United States, and to establish for our shipping a port so fortunately situated in this part of the Pacific.'

'Your thoughts are with your country, gentlemen.' continued the captain; 'your toils are for her prosperity and glory. You are right. One's native land! – there should one live! there die! And I! I die far from all I loved!'

'You have some last wish to transmit,' said the engineer with emotion, 'some souvenir to send to those friends you have left in the mountains of India?'

'No, Captain Harding; no friends remain to me! I am the last of my race, and to all whom I have known I have long been as are the dead. – But to return to yourselves. Solitude, isosolation, are painful things, and beyond human endurance I die of having thought it possible to live alone! You should, therefore, dare all in the attempt to leave Lincoln Island, and see once more the land of your birth. I am aware that those wretches have destroyed the vessel you had built.'

'We propose to construct a vessel,' said Gideon Spilett, 'sufficiently large to convey us to the nearest land; but if we should succeed, sooner or later we shall return to Lincoln Island. We are attached to it by too many recollections ever to forget it.'

'It is here that we have known Captain Nemo,' said Cyrus Harding.

'It is here only that we can make our home!' added Herbert.

'And here shall I sleep the sleep of eternity, if – ' replied the captain.

'He paused for a moment, and, instead of completing the sentence, said simply, –

'Mr Harding, I wish to speak with you – alone!'

The engineer's companions, respecting the wish of the dying man, retired.

Cyrus Harding remained but a few minutes alone with Captain Nemo, and soon recalled his companions; but he said nothing to them of the private matters which the dying man had confided to him.

Gideon Spilett now watched the captain with extreme care. It was evident that he was no longer sustained by his moral energy, which had lost the power of reaction against his physical weakness.

The day closed without change. The colonists did not quit the 'Nautilus' for a moment. Night arrived, although it was impossible to distinguish it from day in the cavern.

Captain Nemo suffered no pain, but he was visibly sinking. His noble features, paled by the approach of death, were perfectly calm. Inaudible words escaped at intervals from his lips, bearing upon various incidents of his chequered career. Life was evidently ebbing slowly, and his extremities were already cold.

Once or twice more he spoke to the colonists who stood around him, and smiled on them with that last smile which continues after death.

At length, shortly after midnight, Captain Nemo by a supreme effort succeeded in folding his arms across his breast, as if wishing in that attitude to compose himself for death.

By one o'clock his glance alone showed signs of life. A dying light gleamed in those eyes once so brilliant. Then, murmuring the words, 'God and my country!' he quietly expired.

Cyrus Harding, bending low, closed the eyes of him who had once been the Prince Dakkar, and was now not even Captain Nemo.

Herbert and Pencroft sobbed aloud. Tears fell from Ayrton's eyes. Neb was on his knees by the reporter's side, motionless as a statue.

Then Cyrus Harding, extending his hand over the forehead of the dead, said solemnly, –

'May his soul be with God! Let us pray!'

Some hours later the colonists fulfilled the promise made to the captain by carrying out his dying wishes.

Cyrus Harding and his companions quitted the 'Nautilus', taking with them the only memento left them by their benefactor, that coffer which contained wealth amounting to millions.

The marvellous saloon, still flooded with light, had been carefully closed. The iron door leading on deck was then securely fastened in such a manner as to prevent even a drop of water penetrating to the interior of the 'Nautilus'.

The colonists then descended into the canoe, which was moored to the side of the submarine vessel.

The canoe was now brought round to the stern. There, at the water-line, were two large stop-cocks, communicating with the reservoirs employed in the submersion of the vessel.

The stop-cocks were opened, the reservoirs filled, and the 'Nautilus', slowly sinking, disappeared beneath the surface of the lake.

But the colonists were yet able to follow its descent through the waves. The powerful light it gave forth lighted up the translucent water, while the cavern became gradually obscure. At length this vast effusion of electric light faded away, and soon after the 'Nautilus', now the tomb of Captain Nemo, reposed in its ocean bed.

CHAPTER 29

At break of day the colonists regained in silence the entrance of the cavern, to which they gave the name of 'Dakkar Grotto', in memory of Captain Nemo. It was now low-water, and they passed without difficulty under the arcade, washed on the right by the sea.

The canoe was left here, carefully protected from the waves. As an excess of precaution, Pencroft, Neb, and Ayrton drew it up on a little beach which bordered one of the sides of the grotto, in a spot where it could run no risk of harm.

The storm had ceased during the night. The last low mutterings of the thunder died away in the west. Rain fell no longer, but the sky was yet obscured by clouds. On the whole, this month of October, the first of the southern spring, was not ushered in by satisfactory tokens, and the wind had a tendency to shift from one point of the compass to another, which rendered it impossible to count upon settled weather.

Cyrus Harding and his companions, on leaving Dakkar Grotto, had taken the road to the corral. On their way Neb and Herbert were careful to preserve the wire which had been laid down by the captain between the corral and the grotto, and which might at a future time be of service.

The colonists spoke but little on the road. The various incidents of the night of the 15th October had left a profound impression on their minds. The unknown being whose influence had so effectually protected them, the man whom their imagination had endowed with supernatural powers, Captain Nemo, was no more. His 'Nautilus' and he were buried in the depths of the abyss. To each one of them their existence seemed even more isolated than before. They had been customed to count upon the intervention of that power which existed no longer, and Gideon Spilett, and even Cyrus Harding, could not escape this impression. Thus they maintained a profound silence during their journey to the corral.

Towards nine in the morning the colonists arrived at Granite House.

It had been agreed that the construction of the vessel should be actively pushed forward, and Cyrus Harding more than ever devoted his time and labour to this object. It was impossible to divine what future lay before them. Evidently the advantage to the colonists would be great of having at their disposal a substantial vessel, capable of keeping the sea even in heavy weather, and large enough to attempt, in case of need, a voyage of some duration.

Even if, when their vessel should be completed, the colonists should not resolve to leave Lincoln Island as yet, in order to gain either one of the Polynesian archipelagos of the Pacific or the shores of New Zealand, they might at least, sooner or later, proceed to Tabor Island, to leave there the notice relating to Ayrton. This was a precaution rendered indispensable by the possibility of the Scotch yacht reappearing in those seas, and it was of the highest importance that nothing should be neglected on this point.

The works were then resumed. Cyrus Harding, Pencroft, and Ayrton, assisted by Neb, Gideon Spilett, and Herbert, except when unavoidably called off by other necessary occupations, worked without cessation. It was important that the new vessel should be ready in five months – that is to say, by the beginning of March – if they wished to visit Tabor Island before the equinoctial gales rendered the voyage impracticable. Therefore the carpenters lost not a moment. Moreover, it was unnecessary to manufacture rigging, that of the 'Speedy' having been saved entire, so that the hull only of the vessel needed to be constructed.

The end of the year 1868 found them occupied by these important labours, to the exclusion of almost all others. At the expiration of two months and a half the ribs had been set up and the first planks adjusted. It was already evident that the plans made by Cyrus Harding were admirable, and that the vessel would behave well at sea.

Pencroft brought to the task a devouring energy, and scrupled not to grumble when one or the other abandoned the carpenter's axe for the gun of the hunter. It was nevertheless necessary to keep up the stores of Granite House, in view of the approaching winter. But this did not satisfy Pencroft. The brave honest sailor was not content when the workmen were not at the dockyard. When this happened he grumbled vigorously, and by way of venting his feelings, did the work of six men.

The weather was very unfavourable during the whole of the summer season. For some days the heat was overpowering, and the atmosphere, saturated with electricity, was only cleared by violent storms. It was rarely that the distant growling of the thunder could not be heard, like a low but incessant murmur, such as is produced in the equatorial regions of the globe.

The 1st of January, 1869, was signalised by a storm of extreme violence, and the thunder burst several times over the island. Large trees were struck by the electric fluid and shattered, and among others one of those gigantic micocouliers which shaded the poultry-yard at the southern extremity of the lake. Had this meteor any relation to the phenomena going on in the bowels of the earth? Was there any connection between the commotion of the atmosphere and that of the interior of the earth? Cyrus Harding was inclined to think that such was the case, for the development of these storms was attended by the renewal of volcanic symptoms.

It was on the 3rd of January that Herbert, having ascended at daybreak to the plateau of Prospect Heights to harness one of the onagers, perceived an enormous hat-shaped cloud rolling from the summit of the volcano.

Herbert immediately apprised the colonists, who at once joined him in watching the summit of Mount Franklin.

'Ah!' exclaimed Pencroft, 'those are not vapours this time! It seems to me that the giant is not content with breathing; he must smoke!'

This figure of speech employed by the sailor exactly expressed the changes going on at the mouth of the volcano. Already for three months had the crater emitted vapours more or less dense, but which were as yet produced only by an internal ebullition of mineral substances. But now the vapours were replaced by a thick smoke, rising in the form of a greyish column, more than three hundred feet in width at its base, and which spread like an immense mushroom to a height of from seven to eight hundred feet above the summit of the mountain.

'The fire is in the chimney,' observed Gideon Spilett.

'And we can't put it out!' replied Herbert.

'The volcano ought to be swept,' observed Neb, who spoke as if perfectly serious.

'Well said, Neb!' cried Pencroft, with a shout of laughter; 'and you'll undertake the job, no doubt?'

Cyrus Harding attentively observed the dense smoke emitted

by Mount Franklin, and even listened, as if expecting to hear some distant muttering. Then, turning towards his companions from whom he had gone somewhat apart, he said –

'The truth is, my friends, we must not conceal from ourselves that an important change is going forward. The volcanic substances are no longer in a state of ebullition; they have caught fire, and we are undoubtedly menaced by an approaching eruption.

'Well, captain,' said Pencroft, 'we shall witness the eruption; and if it is a good one, we'll applaud it. I don't see that we need concern ourselves further about the matter.'

'It may be so,' replied Cyrus Harding, 'for the ancient track of the lava is still open; and thanks to this, the crater has hitherto overflowed towards the north. And yet –'

'And yet, as we can derive no advantage from an eruption, it might be better it should not take place,' said the reporter.

'Who knows?' answered the sailor. 'Perhaps there may be some valuable substance in this volcano, which it will spout forth, and which we may turn to good account!'

Cyrus Harding shook his head with the air of a man who augured no good from the phenomenon whose development had been so sudden. He did not regard so lightly as Pencroft the results of an eruption. If the lava, in consequence of the position of the crater, did not directly menace the wooded and cultivated parts of the island, other complications might present themselves. In fact, eruptions are not unfrequently accompanied by earthquakes; and an island of the nature of Lincoln Island, formed of substances so varied, basalt on one side, granite on the other, lava on the north, rich soil on the south, substances which consequently could not be firmly attached to each other, would be exposed to the risk of disintegration. Although, therefore, the spreading of the volcanic matter might not constitute a serious danger, any movement of the terrestrial structure which should shake the island might entail the gravest consequences.

'It seems to me,' said Ayrton, who had reclined so as to place his ear to the ground, 'it seems to me that I can hear a dull, rumbling sound, like that of a waggon loaded with bars of iron.'

The colonists listened with the greatest attention, and were convinced that Ayrton was not mistaken. The rumbling was mingled with a subterranean roar, which formed a sort of *rinforzando!* and died slowly away, as if some violent storm had passed through the profundities of the globe. But no explosion, properly so termed, could be heard. It might therefore be concluded that the vapours and smoke found a free passage through the central shaft; and that the safety-valve being sufficiently large, no convulsion would be produced, no explosion was to be apprehended.

'Well, then!' said Pencroft, 'are we not going back to work? Let Mount Franklin smoke, groan, bellow, or spout forth fire and flame as much as it pleases, that is no reason why we should be idle! Come, Ayrton, Neb, Herbert, Captain Harding, Mr Spilett, everyone of us must turn to at our work today! We are going to place the keelson, and a dozen pair of hands would not be too many. Before two months I want our new "Bonadventure" – for we shall keep the old name, shall we not? – to float on the waters of Port Balloon! Therefore there is not an hour to lose!'

All the colonists, their services thus requisitioned by Pencroft, descended to the dockyard, and proceeded to place the keelson, a thick mass of wood which forms the lower portion of a ship and unites firmly the timbers of the hull. It was an arduous undertaking, in which all took part.

They continued their labours during the whole of this day, the 3rd of January, without thinking further of the volcano, which could not, besides, be seen from the shore of Granite House. But once or twice, large shadows veiling the sun, which described its diurnal arc through an extremely clear sky, indicated that a thick cloud of smoke passed between its disc and the island. The wind, blowing on the shore, carried all these vapours to the westward. Cyrus Harding and Gideon Spilett remarked these sombre appearances, and from time to time discussed the evident progress of the volcanic phenomena, but their work went on without interruption. It was, besides, of the first importance, from every point of view, that the vessel should be finished with the least possible delay. In presence of the eventualities which might arise, the safety of the colonists would be to a great extent secured by their ship. Who could tell that it might not prove some day their only refuge?

In the evening, after supper, Cyrus Harding, Gideon Spilett and Herbert, again ascended the plateau of Prospect Heights. It was already dark, and the obscurity would permit them to ascertain if flames or incandescent matter thrown up by the volcano were mingled with the vapour and smoke accumulated at the mouth of the crater.

'The crater is on fire!' said Herbert, who, more active than his companions, first reached the plateau.

Mount Franklin, distant about six miles, now appeared like a gigantic torch, around the summit of which turned fuliginous flames. So much smoke, and possibly scoriae and cinders were mingled with them, that their light gleamed but faintly amid the gloom of the night. But a kind of lurid brilliancy spread over the island, against which stood out confusedly the wooded masses of the heights. Immense whirlwinds of vapour obscured the sky, through which glimmered a few stars.

'The change is rapid!' said the engineer.

'That is not surprising,' answered the reporter. 'The re-awakening of the volcano already dates back some time. You may remember, Cyrus, that the first vapours appeared about the time we searched the sides of the mountain to discover Captain Nemo's retreat. It was, if I mistake not, about the 15th of October.

'Yes,' replied Herbert, 'two months and a half ago!'

'The subterranean fires have therefore been smouldering for ten weeks,' resumed Gideon Spilett, 'and it is not to be wondered at that they now break out with such violence!'

'Do not you feel a certain vibration of the soil?' asked Cyrus Harding.

'Yes,' replied Gideon Spilett, 'but there is a great difference between that and an earthquake.'

'I do not affirm that we are menaced with an earthquake,' answered Cyrus Harding, 'may God preserve us from that! No; these vibrations are due to the effervescence of the central fire. The crust of the earth is simply the shell of a boiler, and you know that such a shell, under the pressure of steam, vibrates like a sonorous plate. It is this effect which is being produced at this moment.'

'What magnificent flames!' exclaimed Herbert.

At this instant a kind of bouquet of flames shot forth from the crater, the brilliancy of which was visible even through the vapours. Thousands of luminous sheets and barbed tongues of fire were cast in various directions. Some, extending beyond the dome of smoke dissipated it, leaving behind an incandescent powder. This was accompanied by successive explosions, resembling the discharge of a battery of mitrailleuses.

Cyrus Harding, the reporter, and Herbert, after spending an hour on the plateau of Prospect Heights, again descended to the beach, and returned to Granite House. The engineer was thoughtful and preoccupied, so much so, indeed, that Gideon Spilett inquired if he apprehended any immediate danger, of which the eruption might directly or indirectly be the cause.

'Yes, and no,' answered Cyrus Harding.

'Nevertheless,' continued the reporter, 'would not the greatest misfortune which could happen to us be an earthquake which would overturn the island? Now, I do not suppose that this is to be feared, since the vapours and lava have found a free outlet.'

'True,' replied Cyrus Harding, 'and I do not fear an earthquake in the sense in which the term is commonly applied to convulsions of the soil provoked by the expansion of subterranean gasses. But other causes may produce great disasters.'

'How so, my dear Cyrus?'

'I am not certain. I must consider. I must visit the mountain. In a few days I shall learn more on this point.'

Gideon Spilett said no more, and soon, in spite of the explosions of the volcano, whose intensity increased, and which were repeated by the echoes of the island, the inhabitants of Granite House were sleeping soundly.

Three days passed by – the 4th, 5th and 6th of January. The

construction of the vessel was dilligently continued, and without offering further explanations the engineer pushed forward the work with all his energy. Mount Franklin was now hooded by a sombre cloud of sinister aspect, and, amid the flames, vomited forth incandescent rocks, some of which fell back into the crater itself. This caused Pencroft, who would only look at the matter in the light of a joke, to exclaim, –

'Ah! the giant is playing at cup and ball; he is a conjuror.'

In fact, the substances thrown up fell back again into the abyss, and it did not seem that the lava, though swollen by the internal pressure, had yet risen to the orifice of the crater. At any rate, the opening on the north-east, which was partly visible, poured out no torrent upon the northern slope of the mountain.

Nevertheless, however pressing was the construction of the vessel, other duties demanded the presence of the colonists on various portions of the island. Before everything, it was necessary to go to the corral, where the flocks of musmons and goats were enclosed, and replenish the provision of forage for those animals. It was accordingly arranged that Ayrton should proceed thither next day, the 7th of January; and as he was sufficient for the task, to which he was accustomed, Pencroft and the rest were somewhat surprised on hearing the engineer say to Ayrton, –

'As you are going tomorrow to the corral I will accompany you.'

'But, Captain Harding,' exclaimed the sailor, 'our working days will not be many, and if you go also we shall be two pair of hands short!'

'We shall return tomorrow,' replied Cyrus Harding,' but it is necessary that I should go to the corral. I must learn how the eruption is progressing.'

'The eruption! always the eruption!' answered Pencroft, with an air of discontent. 'An important thing truly, this eruption! I trouble myself very little about it.'

Whatever might be the sailor's opinion, the expedition projected by the engineer was settled for the next day.. Herbert wished to accompany Cyrus Harding, but he would not vex Pencroft by his absence.

The next day, at dawn, Cyrus Harding and Ayrton, mounting the cart drawn by two onagers, took the road to the corral and set off at a round trot.

Above the forest were passing large clouds, to which the crater of Mount Franklin incessantly added fuliginous matter. These clouds, which rolled heavily in the air, were evidently composed of heterogeneous substances. It was not alone from the volcano that they derived their strange opacity and weight. Scoriae, in a state of dust, like powdered pumice-stone, and greyish ashes as small as the finest feculae, were held in suspension in the midst of their thick folds. These ashes are so fine that they have been observed in the air for whole months. After the eruption of 1783 in Iceland for upwards of a year the atmosphere was thus charged with volcanic dust through which the rays of the sun were only with difficulty discernible.

But more often this pulverised matter falls, and this happened on the present occasion. Cyrus Harding and Ayrton had scarcely reached the corral when a sort of black snow like fine gunpowder fell, and instantly changed the appearance of the soil. Trees, meadows, all disappeared beneath a covering several inches in depth. But, very fortunately, the wind blew from the north-east, and the greater part of the cloud dissolved itself over the sea.

'This is very singular, Captain Harding,' said Ayrton.

'It is very serious,' replied the engineer. 'This powdered pumice-stone, all this mineral dust, proves how grave is the convulsion going forward in the lower depths of the volcano.'

'But can nothing be done?'

'Nothing, except to note the progress of the phenomenon. Do you, therefore, Ayrton, occupy yourself with the necessary work at the corral. In the meantime I will ascend just beyond the source of Red Creek and examine the condition of the mountain upon its northern aspect. Then –'

'Well, Captain Harding?'

'Then we will pay a visit to Dakkar Grotto. I wish to inspect it. At any rate I will come back for you in two hours.'

Ayrton then proceeded to enter the corral, and while waiting the engineer's return, busied himself with the musmons and goats, which seemed to feel a certain uneasiness in presence of these first signs of an eruption.

Meanwhile Cyrus Harding ascended the crest of the eastern spur, passed Red Creek, and arrived at the spot where he and his companions had discovered a sulphureous spring at the time of their first exploration.

How changed was everything! Instead of a single column of smoke he counted thirteen, forced through the soil as if violently propelled by some piston. It was evident that the crust of the earth was subjected in this part of the globe to a frightful pressure. The atmosphere was saturated with gases and carbonic acid, mingled with aqueous vapours. Cyrus Harding felt the volcanic tufa with which the plain was strewn and which were but pulverised cinders hardened into solid blocks by time, tremble beneath him, but he could discover no traces of fresh lava.

The engineer became more assured of this when he observed all the northern part of Mount Franklin. Pillars of smoke and flame escaped from the crater; a hail of scoriae fell on the ground; but no current of lava burst from the mouth of the volcano, which proved that the volcanic matter had not yet attained the level of the superior orifice of the central shaft.

'But I would prefer that it were so,' said Cyrus Harding to himself. 'At any rate, I should then know that the lava had followed its accustomed track. Who can say that it may not take a new course? But the danger does not consist in that! Captain Nemo foresaw it clearly! No, the danger does not lie there!'

Cyrus Harding advanced towards the enormous causeway whose prolongation enclosed the narrow Shark Gulf. He could now sufficiently examine on this side the ancient channels of the lava. There was no doubt in his mind that the most recent eruption had occurred at a far-distant epoch.

He then returned by the same way, listening attentively to the subterranean mutterings which rolled like long-continued thunder, interrupted by deafening explosions. At nine in the morning he reached the corral.

Ayrton awaited him.

'The animals are cared for, Captain Harding,' said Ayrton.

'Good, Ayrton.'

'They seem uneasy, Captain Harding.'

'Yes, instinct speaks through them, and instinct is never deceived.'

'Are you ready?'

'Take a lamp, Ayrton,' answered the engineer; 'we will start at once.'

Ayrton did as desired. The onagers, unharnessed, roamed in the corral. The gate was secured on the outside, and Cyrus Harding, preceding Ayrton, took the narrow path which led westward to the shore.

The soil they walked upon was choked with the pulverised matter fallen from the cloud. No quadruped appeared in the woods. Even the birds had fled. Sometimes a passing breeze raised the covering of ashes, and the two colonists, enveloped in a whirlwind of dust, lost sight of each other. They were then careful to cover their eyes and mouths with handkerchiefs, for they ran the risk of being blinded and suffocated.

It was impossible for Cyrus Harding and Ayrton, with these impediments, to make rapid progress. Moreover, the atmosphere was close, as if the oxygen had been partly burnt up, and had become unfit for respiration. At every hundred paces they were obliged to stop to take breath. It was therefore past ten o'clock when the engineer and his companion reached the crest of the enormous mass of rocks of basalt and porphyry which composed the north-west coast of the island.

Ayrton and Cyrus Harding commenced the descent of this abrupt declivity, following almost step for step the difficult path which, during that stormy night, had led them to Dakkar Grotto. In open day the descent was less perilous, and, besides, the bed of ashes which covered the polished surface of the rock enabled them to make their footing more secure.

The ridge at the end of the shore, about forty feet in height, was soon reached. Cyrus Harding recollected that this elevation gradually sloped towards the level of the sea. Although the tide was at present low, no beach could be seen, and the waves, thickened by the volcanic dust, beat upon the basaltic rocks.

Cyrus Harding and Ayrton found without difficulty the entrance to Dakkar Grotto, and paused for a moment at the last rock before it.

'The iron boat should be there,' said the engineer.

'It is here, Captain Harding,' replied Ayrton, drawing towards him the fragile craft, which was protected by the arch of the vault.

'On board, Ayrton!'

The two colonists stepped into the boat. A slight undulation of the waves carried it farther under the low arch of the crypt, and there Ayrton, with the aid of flint and steel, lighted the lamp. He then took the oars, and the lamp having been placed in the bow of the boat, so that its rays fell before them, Cyrus Harding took the helm and steered through the shades of the grotto.

The 'Nautilus' was there no longer to illuminate the cavern with its electric light. Possibly it might not yet be extinguished, but no ray escaped from the depths of the abyss in which reposed all that was mortal of Captain Nemo.

The light afforded by the lamp, although feeble, nevertheless enabled the engineer to advance slowly, following the wall of the cavern. A deathlike silence reigned under the vaulted roof, or at least in the anterior portion, for soon Cyrus Harding distinctly heard the rumbling which proceeded from the bowels of the mountain.

'That comes from the volcano,' he said.

Besides these sounds, the presence of chemical combinations was soon betrayed by their powerful odour, and the engineer and his companion were almost suffocated by sulphureous vapours.

'This is what Captain Nemo feared,' murmured Cyrus Harding, changing countenance. 'We must go to the end, notwithstanding.'

'Forward!' replied Ayrton, bending to his oars and directing the boat towards the head of the cavern.

Twenty-five minutes after entering the mouth of the grotto the boat reached the extreme end.

Cyrus Harding then, standing up, cast the light of the lamp upon the walls of the cavern which separated it from the central shaft of the volcano. What was the thickness of this wall? It might be ten feet or a hundred feet – it was impossible to say. But the subterranean sounds were too perceptible to allow of the supposition that it was of any great thickness.

The engineer, after having explored the wall at a certain height horizontally, fastened the lamp to the end of an oar, and again surveyed the basaltic wall at a greater elevation.

There, through scarcely visible clefts and joinings, escaped a pungent vapour, which infected the atmosphere of the cavern. The wall was broken by large cracks, some of which extended to within two or three feet of the water's edge.

Cyrus Harding thought for a brief space. Then he said in a low voice –

'Yes! the captain was right! The danger lies there, and a terrible danger!'

Ayrton said not a word, but, upon a sign from Cyrus Harding resumed the oars, and half an hour later the engineer and he reached the entrance of Dakkar Grotto.

CHAPTER 30

THE next day, the 8th of January, after a day and night passed at the corral, where they left all in order, Cyrus Harding and Ayrton arrived at Granite House.

The engineer immediately called his companions together, and informed them of the imminent danger which threatened Lincoln Island, and from which no human power could deliver them.

'My friends,' he said, and his voice betrayed the depth of his emotion, 'our island is not among those which will endure while this earth endures. It is doomed to more or less speedy destruction, the cause of which it bears within itself, and from which nothing can save it.'

The colonists looked at each other, then at the engineer. They did not clearly comprehend him.

'Explain yourself, Cyrus!' said Gideon Spilett.

'I will do so,' replied Cyrus Harding, 'or rather I will simply afford you the explanation which, during our few minutes of private conversation, was given me by Captain Nemo.'

'Captain Nemo!' exclaimed the colonists.

'Yes, and it was the last service he desired to render us before his death!'

'The last service!' exclaimed Pencroft, 'the last service! You will see that though he is dead he will render us others yet!'

'But what did the captain say?' inquired the reporter.

'I will tell you, my friends,' said the engineer. 'Lincoln Island does not resemble the other islands of the Pacific, and a fact of which Captain Nemo has made me cognisant must sooner or later bring about the subversion of its foundation.'

'Nonsense! Lincoln Island, it can't be!' cried Pencroft, who in spite of the respect he felt for Cyrus Harding, could not prevent a gesture of incredulity.

'Listen, Pencroft,' resumed the engineer, 'I will tell you what Captain Nemo communicated to me, and which I myself confirmed yesterday, during the exploration of Dakkar Grotto. This cavern stretches under the island as far as the volcano, and is only separated from its central shaft by the wall which terminates it. Now, this wall is seamed with fissures and clefts which already allow the sulphureous gases generated in the interior of the volcano to escape.'

'Well?' said Pencroft, his brow suddenly contracting.

'Well, then, I saw that these fissures widen under the internal pressure from within, that the wall of basalt is gradually giving way, and that after a longer or shorter period it will afford a passage to the waters of the lake which fill the cavern.'

'Good!' replied Pencroft, with an attempt at pleasantry. 'The sea will extinguish the volcano, and there will be an end of the matter!'

'Not so!' said Cyrus Harding, 'should a day arrive when the sea, rushing through the wall of the cavern, penetrates by the central shaft into the interior of the island to the boiling lava, Lincoln Island will that day be blown into the air – just as would happen to the island of Sicily were the Mediterranean to precipitate itself into Mount Etna.'

The colonists made no answer to these significant words of the engineer. They now understood the danger by which they were menaced.

It may be added that Cyrus Harding had in no way exaggerated the danger to be apprehended. Many persons have formed an idea that it would be possible to extinguish volcanoes, which are almost always situated on the shores of a sea or lake, by opening a passage for the admission of the water. But they are not aware that this would be to incur the risk of blowing up a portion of the globe, like a boiler whose steam is suddenly expanded by intense heat. The water, rushing into a cavity whose temperature might be estimated at thousands of degrees, would be converted into steam with a sudden energy which no enclosure could resist.

It was not therefore doubtful that the island, menaced by a frightful and approaching convulsion, would endure only so long as the wall of Dakkar Grotto itself should endure. It was not even a question of months, nor of weeks; but of days, it might be of hours.

The first sentiment which the colonists felt was that of profound sorrow. They thought not so much of the peril which menaced themselves personally, but of the destruction of the island which had sheltered them, which they had cultivated, which they loved so well, and had hoped to render so flourishing.

So much effort ineffectually expanded, so much labour lost.

Pencroft could not prevent a large tear from rolling down his cheek, nor did he attempt to conceal it.

Some further conversation now took place. The chances yet in favour of the colonists were discussed; but finally it was agreed that there was not an hour to be lost, that the building and fitting of the vessel should be pushed forward with their utmost energy, and that this was the sole chance of safety for the inhabitants of Lincoln Island.

All hands, therefore, set to work on the vessel. What could it now avail to sow, to reap, to hunt, to increase the stores of Granite House? The contents of the storehouse and outbuildings contained more than sufficient to provide the ship for a voyage, however long might be its duration. But it was imperative that the ship should be ready to receive them before the inevitable catastrophe should arrive.

Their labours were now carried on with feverish ardour. By the 23rd of January the vessel was half-decked over. Up to this time no change had taken place in the summit of the volcano. Vapour and smoke mingled with flames and incandescent stones were thrown up from the crater. But during the night of the 23rd, in consequence of the lava attaining the level of the first stratum of the volcano, the hat-shaped cone which formed over the latter disappeared. A frightful sound was heard. The colonists at first thought the island was rent asunder, and rushed out of Granite House.

This occurred about two o'clock in the morning.

The sky appeared on fire. The superior cone, a mass of rock a thousand feet in height, and weighing thousands of millions of pounds, had been thrown down upon the island, making it tremble to its foundation. Fortunately, this cone inclined to the north, and had fallen upon the plain of sand and tufa stretching between the volcano and the sea. The aperture of the crater being thus enlarged projected towards the sky a glare so intense that by the simple effect of reflection the atmosphere appeared red-hot. At the same time a torrent of lava, bursting from the new summit, poured out in long cascades, like water escaping from a vase too full, and a thousand tongues of fire over the sides of the volcano.

'The corral! the corral!' exclaimed Ayrton.

It was, in fact, towards the corral that the lava was rushing, as the new crater faced the east, and consequently the fertile portions of the island, the springs of Red Creek and Jacamar Wood, were menaced with instant destruction.

At Ayrton's cry the colonists rushed to the onagers' stables. The cart was at once harnessed. All were possessed by the same thought – to hasten to the corral and set at liberty the animals it enclosed.

Before three in the morning they arrived at the corral. The cries of the terrified musmons and goats indicated the alarm which possessed them. Already a torrent of burning matter and liquefied minerals fell from the side of the mountain upon the meadows as far as the side of the palisade. The gate was burst open by Ayrton, and the animals, bewildered with terror, fled in all directions.

An hour afterwards the boiling lava filled the corral, converting into vapour the water of the little rivulet which ran through it, burning up the house like dry grass, and leaving not even a post of the palisade to mark the spot where the corral once stood.

To contend against this disaster would have been folly – nay, madness. In presence of Nature's grand convulsions man is powerless.

It was now daylight – the 24th of January. Cyrus Harding and his companions, before returning to Granite House, desired to ascertain the probable direction this inundation of lava was about to take. The soil sloped gradually from Mount Franklin to the east coast, and it was to be feared that, in spite of the thick Jacamar Wood, the torrent would reach the plateau of Prospect Heights.

'The lake will cover us,' said Gideon Spilett.

'I hope so!' was Cyrus Harding's only reply.

The colonists were desirous of reaching the plain upon which the superior cone of Mount Franklin had fallen, but the lava arrested their progress. It had followed, on one side, the valley of Red Creek, and on the other that of Falls River, evaporating those watercourses in its passage. There was no possibility of crossing the torrent of lava; on the contrary, the colonists were obliged to retreat before it. The volcano, without its crown, was no longer recognisable, terminated as it was by a sort of flat table which replaced the ancient crater. From two openings in its southern and eastern sides an uncreasing flow of lava poured forth, thus forming two distinct streams. Above the new crater a cloud of smoke and ashes, mingled with those of the atmosphere, massed over the island. Loud peals of thunder broke, and could scarcely be distinguished from the rumblings of the mountain, whose mouth vomited forth ignited rocks, which, hurled to more than a thousand feet, burst in the air like shells, Flashes of lightning rivalled in intensity the volcano's eruption.

Towards seven in the morning the position was no longer tenable by the colonists, who accordingly took shelter in the borders of Jacamar Wood. Not only did the projectiles begin to rain around them, but the lava, overflowing the bed of Red Creek, threatened to cut off the road to the corral. The nearest rows of trees caught fire, and their sap, suddenly transformed into vapour, caused them to explode with loud reports, whilst others, less moist, remained unhurt in the midst of the inundation.

The colonists had again taken the road to the corral. They proceeded but slowly, frequently looking back; but, in consequence of the inclination of the soil, the lava gained rapidly in the east, and as its lower waves became solidified others at boiling heat covered them immediately.

Meanwhile, the principal stream of Red Creek valley became more and more menacing. All this portion of the forest was on fire, and enormous wreaths of smoke rolled over the trees, whose trunks were already consumed by the lava.

The colonists halted near the lake, about half a mile from the mouth of Red Creek. A question of life or death was now to be decided.

Cyrus Harding, accustomed to the consideration of important crises, and aware that he was addressing men capable of hearing the truth, whatever it might be, then said, –

'Either the lake will arrest the progress of the lava, and a part of the island will be preserved from utter destruction, or the stream will overrun the forests of the Far West, and not a tree or plant will remain on the surface of the soil. We shall have no prospect but that of starvation upon these barren rocks – a death which will probably be anticipated by the explosion of the island.'

'In that case,' replied Pencroft, folding his arms and stamping his foot, 'what's the use of working any longer on the vessel!'

'Pencroft,' answered Cyrus Harding, 'we must do our duty to the last!'

At this instant the river of lava, after having broken a passage reached the borders of the lake. At this point there was an elevation of the soil which, had it been greater, might have sufficed to arrest the torrent.

'To work!' cried Cyrus Harding.

The engineer's thought was at once understood. It might be possible to dam, as it were the torrent, and thus compel it to pour itself into the lake.

The colonists hastened to the dockyard. They returned with shovels, picks, axes, and by means of banking the earth with the aid of fallen trees they succeeded in a few hours in raising an embankment three feet high and some hundreds of paces in length. It seemed to them, when they had finished, as if they had scarcely been working more than a few minutes.

It was not a moment too soon. The liquefied substances soon after reached the bottom of the barrier. The stream of lava swelled like a river about to overflow its banks, and threatened to demolish the sole obstacle which could prevent it from overrunning the whole Far West. But the dam held firm, and after a moment of terrible suspense the torrent precipitated itself into

Grant Lake from a height of twenty feet.

The colonists, without moving or uttering a word, breathlessly regarded this strife of the two elements.

What a spectacle was this conflict between water and fire! What pen could describe the marvellous horror of this scene – what pencil could depict it? The water hissed as it evaporated by contact with the boiling lava. The vapour whirled in the air to an immeasurable height, as if the valves of an immense boiler had been suddenly opened. But, however considerable might be the volume of water contained in the lake, it must eventually be absorbed, because it was not replenished, whilst the stream of lava, fed from an inexhaustible source, rolled on without ceasing new waves of incandescent matter.

The first waves of lava which fell in the lake immediately solidified, and accumulated so as speedily to emerge from it. Upon their surface fell other waves, which in their turn became stone, but a step nearer the centre of the lake. In this manner was formed a pier which threatened to gradually fill up the lake, which could not overflow, the water displaced by the lava being evaporated. The hissing of the water rent the air with a deafening sound, and the vapour, blown by the wind, fell in rain upon the sea. The pier became longer and longer, and the blocks of lava piled themselves one on another. Where formerly stretched the calm waters of the lake, now appeared an enormous mass of smoking rocks, as if an upheaving of the soil had formed immense shoals. Imagine the waters of the lake aroused by a hurricane, then suddenly solidified by an intense frost, and some conception may be formed of the aspect of the lake three hours after the irruption of this irresistible torrent of lava.

This time water would be vanquished by fire.

Nevertheless it was a fortunate circumstance for the colonists that the effusion of lava should have been in the direction of Lake Grant. They had before them some days' respite. The plateau of Prospect Heights, Granite House, and the dockyard were for the moment preserved. And these few days it was necessary to employ them in planking, carefully caulking the vessel, and launching her. The colonists would then take refuge on board the vessel, content to rig her after she should be afloat on the waters. With the danger of an explosion which threatened to destroy the island there could be no security on shore. The walls of Granite House, once so sure a retreat, might at any moment fall in upon them.

During the six following days, from the 25th to the 30th of January, the colonists accomplished as much of the construction of their vessel as twenty men could have done. They hardly allowed themselves a moment's repose, and the glare of the flames which shot from the crater enabled them to work night and day. The flow of lava continued, but perhaps less abundantly.

This was fortunate, for Lake Grant was almost entirely choked up, and if more lava should accumulate it would inevitably spread over the plateau of Prospect Heights, and thence upon the beach.

But if the island was thus partially protected on this side, it was not so with the western part.

In fact, the second stream of lava, which had followed the valley of Falls River, a valley of great extent, the land on both sides of the creek being flat, met with no obstacle. The burning liquid had then spread through the forest of the Far West. At this period of the year, when the trees were dried up by a tropical heat, the forest caught fire instantaneously, in such a manner that the conflagration extended itself both by the trunks of the trees and by their higher branches, whose interlacement favoured its progress. It even appeared that the current of flame spread more rapidly among the summits of the trees than the current of lava at their bases.

Thus it happened that the wild animals, jaguars, wild boars, capybaras, koulas, and game of every kind, mad with terror, had fled to the banks of the Mercy and to the Tadorn Marsh, beyond the road to Port Balloon. But the colonists were too much occupied with their task to pay any attention to even the most formidable of these animals. They had abandoned Granite House, and would not even take shelter at the Chimneys, but encamped under a tent, near the mouth of the Mercy.

Each day Cyrus Harding and Gideon Spilett ascended the plateau of Prospect Heights. Sometimes Herbert accompanied them, but never Pencroft, who could not bear to look upon the prospect of the island now so utterly devastated.

It was, in truth, a heart-reading spectacle. All the wooded part of the island was now completely bare. One single clump of green trees raised their heads at the extremity of Serpentine Peninsula. Here and there were a few grotesque blackened and branchless stumps. The site of the devastated forest was even more barren than Tadorn Marsh. The irruption of the lava had been complete. Where formerly sprang up that charming verdure, the soil was now nothing but a savage mass of volcanic tufa. In the valleys of the Falls and Mercy rivers no drop of water now flowed towards the sea, and should Lake Grant be entirely dried up, the colonists would have no means of quenching their thirst. But, fortunately, the lava had spared the southern corner of the lake, containing all that remained of the drinkable water of the island. Towards the north-west stood out the rugged and well-defined outlines of the sides of the volcano, like a gigantic claw hovering over the island. What a sad and fearful sight, and how painful to the colonists, who, from a fertile domain covered with forests, irrigated by watercourses, and enriched by the produce of their toils, found themselves, as it were, transported to a desolate rock, upon which, but for their reserves of provisions, they could not even gather the means of subsistence!

'It is enough to break one's heart!' said Gideon Spilett one day.

'Yes, Spilett,' answered the engineer. 'May God grant us the time to complete this vessel, now our sole refuge!'

'Do not you think, Cyrus, that the violence of the eruption has somewhat lessened? The volcano still vomits forth lava, but somewhat less abundantly, if I mistake not.'

'It matters little,' answered Cyrus Harding. 'The fire is still burning in the interior of the mountain, and the sea may break in at any moment. We are in the condition of passengers whose ship is devoured by a conflagration which they cannot extinguish, and who know that sooner or later the flames must reach the powder-magazine. To work, Spilett, to work, and let us not lose an hour!'

During the eight days more, that is to say until the 7th of February, the lava continued to flow, but the erruption was confined within the previous limits. Cyrus Harding feared above all lest the liquefied matter should overflow the shore, for in that event the dockyard could not escape. Moreover, about this time the colonists felt in the frame of the island vibrations which alarmed them to the highest degree.

'It was the 20th of February. Yet another month must elapse before the vessel would be ready for sea. Would the island hold together till then? The intention of Pencroft and Cyrus Harding was to launch the vessel as soon as the hull should be complete. The deck, the upper-works, the interior woodwork, and the rigging, might be finished afterwards, but the essential point was that the colonists should have an assured refuge away from the island. Perhaps it might be even better to conduct the vessel to Port Balloon, that is to say, as far as possible from the centre of eruption, for at the mouth of the Mercy, between the islet and the wall of granite, it would run the risk of being crushed in the event of any convulsion. All the exertions of the voyagers were therefore concentrated upon the completion of the hull.

Thus the 3rd of March arrived, and they might calculate upon launching the vessel in ten days.

Hope revived in the hearts of the colonists, who had, in this fourth year of their sojourn on Lincoln Island, suffered so many trials. Even Pencroft lost in some measure the sombre taciturnity occasioned by the devastation and ruin of his domain. His hopes, it was true were concentrated upon his vessel.

'We shall finish it,' he said to the engineer, 'we shall finish it, captain; and it is time, for the season is advancing and the equinox will soon be here. Well, if necessary, we must put in to Tabor Island to spend the winter. But think of Tabor Island after

Lincoln Island. Ah, how unfortunate! Who could have believed it possible?'

'Let us get on,' was the engineer's invariable reply.

And they worked away without losing a moment.

'Master,' asked Neb, a few days later, 'do you think all this could have happened if Captain Nemo had been still alive?'

'Certainly, Neb,' answered Cyrus Harding.

'I, for one, don't believe it!' whispered Pencroft to Neb.

'Nor I!' answered Neb seriously.

During the first week of March appearances again became menacing. Thousands of threads like glass, formed of fluid lava, fell like rain upon the island. The crater was again boiling with lava which overflowed the back of the volcano. The torrent flowed along the surface of the hardened tufa, and destroyed the few meagre skeletons of trees which had withstood the first eruption. The stream flowing this time towards the south-west shore of Lake Grant, stretched beyond Creek Glycerine, and invaded the plateau of Prospect Heights. This last blow to the work of the colonists was terrible. The mill, the buildings of the inner court, the stables, were all destroyed. The affrighted poultry fled in all directions. Top and Jup showed signs of the greatest alarm, as if their instinct warned them of an impending catastrophe. A large number of the animals of the island had perished in the first eruption. Those which survived found no refuge but Tadorn Marsh, save a few to which the plateau of Prospect Heights afforded an asylum. But even this last retreat was now closed to them, and the lava-torrent, flowing over the edge of the granite wall, began to pour down upon the beach its cataracts of fire. The sublime horror of this spectacle passed all description. During the night it could only be compared to a Niagara of molten fluid, with its incandescent vapours above and its boiling masses below.

The colonists were driven to their last entrenchment, and although the upper seams of the vessel were not yet caulked, they decided to launch her at once.

Pencroft and Ayrton therefore set about the necessary preparations for the launch, which was to take place the morning of the next day, the 9th of March.

But, during the night of the 8th an enormous column of vapour escaping from the crater rose with frightful explosions to a height of more than three thousand feet. The wall of Dakkar Grotto had evidently given way under the pressure of the gases, and the sea, rushing through the central shaft into the igneous gulf, was at once converted into vapour. But the crater could not afford a sufficient outlet for this vapour. An explosion, which might have been heard at a distance of a hundred miles, shook the air. Fragments of mountains fell into the Pacific, and, in a few minutes, the ocean rolled over the spot where Lincoln Island once stood.

CHAPTER 31

An isolated rock, thirty feet in length, twenty in breadth, scarcely ten from the water's edge, such was the only solid point which the waves of the Pacific had not engulfed.

It was all that remained of the structure of Granite House!

The wall had fallen headlong and been then shattered to fragments, and a few of the rocks of the large room were piled one above another to form this point. All around had disappeared in the abyss; the inferior cone of Mount Franklin, rent asunder by the explosion; the lava jaws of Shark Gulf, the plateau of Prospect Heights, Safety Islet, the granite rocks of Port Balloon, the basalts of Dakkar Grotto, the long Serpentine Peninsula, so distant nevertheless from the centre of the eruption. All that could now be seen of Lincoln Island was the narrow rock which now served as a refuge to the six colonists and their dog Top.

The animals had also perished in the catastrophe; the birds, as well as those representing the fauna of the island – all either crushed or drowned, and the unfortunate Jup himself had, alas! found his death in some crevice of the soil.

If Cyrus Harding, Gideon Spilett, Herbert, Pencroft, Neb, and Ayrton had survived, it was because, assembled under their tent, they had been hurled into the sea at the instant when the fragments of the island rained down on every side.

When they reached the surface they could only perceive, at half a cable's length, this mass of rocks, towards which they swam and on which they found footing.

On this barren rock they had now existed for nine days. A few provisions taken from the magazine of Granite House before the catastrophe, a little fresh water from the rain which had fallen, in a hollow of the rock, was all that the unfortunate colonists possessed. Their last hope, the vessel, had been shattered to pieces. They had no means of quitting the reef; no fire, nor any means of obtaining it. It seemed that they must inevitably perish.

This day, the 18th of March, there remained only provisions for two days, although they limited their consumption to the bare necessaries of life. All their science and intelligence could avail them nothing in their present position. They were in the hand of God.

Cyrus Harding was calm, Gideon Spilett more nervous, and

Pencroft, a prey to sullen anger, walked to and fro on the rock. Herbert did not for a moment quit the engineer's side as if demanding from him that assistance he had no power to give. Neb and Ayrton were resigned to their fate.

'Ah, what a misfortune! What a misfortune!' often repeated Pencroft. 'If we had but a walnut-shell to take us to Tabor Island! But we have nothing, nothing!'

'Captain Nemo did right to die,' said Neb.

During the five ensuing days Cyrus Harding and his unfortunate companions husbanded their provisions with the most extreme care, eating only what would prevent them from succumbing to starvation. Their weakness was extreme. Herbert and Neb began to show symptoms of delirium.

Under these circumstances was it possible for them to retain even the shadow of a hope? No! what was their sole remaining chance? That a vessel should appear in sight off the rock? But they knew only too well from experience that no ships ever visited this part of the Pacific. Could they calculate that, by a truly providential coincidence, the Scotch yacht would arrive precisely at this time in search of Ayrton at Tabor Island? It was scarcely probable; and, besides, supposing she should come there, as the colonists had not been able to deposit a notice pointing out Ayrton's change of abode, the commander of the yacht, after having explored Tabor Island without result, would again set sail and return to lower latitudes.

No! no hope of being saved could be retained, and a horrible death, death from hunger and thirst, awaited them upon this rock.

Already they were stretched on the rock, inanimate, and no longer conscious of what passed around them. Ayrton alone, by a supreme effort, from time to time raised his head, and cast a despairing glance over the desert ocean.

But on the morning of the 24th of March Ayrton's arms were extended towards a point in the horizon; he raised himself, at first on his knees, then upright, and his hand seemed to make a signal.

A sail was in sight off the rock. She was evidently not without an object. The reef was the mark for which she was making in a direct line, under all steam, and the unfortunate colonists might have made her out some hours before if they had had the strength to watch the horizon.

'The "Duncan"!' murmured Ayrton – and fell back without sign of life.

*

When Cyrus Harding and his companions recovered consciousness, thanks to the attention lavished upon them, they found themselves in the cabin of a steamer, without being able to comprehend how they had escaped death.

A word from Ayrton explained everything.

'The "Duncan"!' he murmured.

'The "Duncan"!' exclaimed Cyrus Harding. And raising his hand to Heaven, he said, 'Oh! Almighty God! mercifully hast Thou preserved us!'

It was, in fact, the 'Duncan', Lord Glenarvon's yacht, now commanded by Robert, son of Captain Grant, who had been despatched to Tabor Island to find Ayrton, and bring him back to his native land after twelve years of expiation.

The colonists were not only saved, but already on the way to their native country.

'Captain Grant,' asked Cyrus Harding, 'who can have suggested to you the idea, after having left Tabor Island, where you did not find Ayrton, of coming a hundred miles farther north-east?'

'Captain Harding,' replied Robert Grant, 'it was in order to find, not only Ayrton, but yourself and your companions.'

'My companions and myself?'

'Doubtless, at Lincoln Island.'

'At Lincoln Island!' exclaimed in a breath Gideon Spilett, Herbert, Neb, and Pencroft, in the highest degree astonished.

'How could you be aware of the existence of Lincoln Island?' inquired Cyrus Harding, 'it is not even named in the charts.'

'I knew of it from a document left by you on Tabor Island,' answered Robert Grant.

'A document?' cried Gideon Spilett.

'Without doubt, and here it is,' answered Robert Grant, producing a paper which indicated the longitude and latitude of Lincoln Island, 'the present residence of Ayrton and five American colonists.'

'It is Captain Nemo!' cried Cyrus Harding, after having read the notice, and recognised that the handwriting was similar to that of the paper found at the corral. 'Ah!' said Pencroft, 'it was then he who took our 'Bonadventure' and hazarded himself alone to go to Tabor Island!'

'In order to leave this notice,' added Herbert.

'I was then right in saying,' exclaimed the sailor, 'that even after his death the captain would render us a last service.'

'My friends,' said Cyrus Harding, in a voice of the profoundest emotion, 'may the God of mercy have had pity on the soul of Captain Nemo, our benefactor!'

The colonists uncovered themselves at these last words of Cyrus Harding, and murmured the name of Captain Nemo.

Then Ayrton, approaching the engineer, said simply, 'Where should this coffer be deposited?'

It was the coffer which Ayrton had saved at the risk of his life, at the very instant that the island had been engulfed, and which he now faithfully handed to the engineer.

'Ayrton! Ayrton!' said Cyrus Harding, deeply touched. Then addressing Robert Grant, 'Sir,' he added, 'you left behind you a criminal; you find in his place a man who has become honest by penitence, and whose hand I am proud to clasp in mine.'

Robert Grant was now made acquainted with the strange history of Captain Nemo and the colonists of Lincoln Island. Then, observations being taken of what remained of this shoal, which must henceforward figure on the charts of the Pacific, the order was given to make all sail.

A few weeks afterwards the colonists landed in America, and found their country once more at peace after the terrible conflict in which right and justice had triumphed.

Of the treasures contained in the coffer left by Captain Nemo to the colonists of Lincoln Island, the larger portion was employed in the purchase of a vast territory in the State of Iowa. One pearl alone, the finest, was reserved from the treasure and sent to Lady Glenarvon in the name of the castaways restored to their country by the 'Duncan'.

There, upon this domain, the colonists invited to labour, that is to say, to wealth and happiness, all those to whom they had hoped to offer the hospitality of Lincoln Island. There was founded a vast colony to which they gave the name of that island sunk beneath the waters of the Pacific. A river was there called the Mercy, a mountain took the name of Mount Franklin, a small lake was named Lake Grant, and the forests became the forests of the Far West. It might have been an island on terra firma.

There, under the intelligent hands of the engineer and his companions, everything prospered. Not one of the former colonists of Lincoln Island was absent, for they had sworn to live always together. Neb was with his master; Ayrton was there ready to sacrifice himself for all; Pencroft was more a farmer than he had even been a sailor; Herbert, who completed his studies under the superintendence of Cyrus Harding; and Gideon Spilett, who founded the *New Lincoln Herald*, the best-informed journal in the world.

There Cyrus Harding and his companions received at intervals visits from Lord and Lady Glenarvon, Captain John Mangles and his wife, the sister of Robert Grant, Robert Grant himself, Major McNab, and all those who had taken part in the history, both of Captain Grant and Captain Nemo.

There, to conclude, all were happy, united in the present as they had been in the past; but never could they forget that island upon which they had arrived poor and friendless, that island which, during four years, had supplied all their wants, and of which there remained but a fragment of granite washed by the waves of the Pacific, the tomb of him who had borne the name of Captain Nemo.

NEL BESTSELLERS

T006 778	ASSIGNMENT IN ETERNITY	Robert Heinlein 25p
T007 294	HAVE SPACESUIT – WILL TRAVEL	Robert Heinlein 30p
T009 696	GLORY ROAD	Robert Heinlein 40p
T011 844	DUNE	Frank Herbert 75p
T012 298	DUNE MESSIAH	Frank Herbert 40p
W002 814	THE WORLDS OF FRANK HERBERT	Frank Herbert 30p
W002 911	SANTAROGA BARRIER	Frank Herbert 30p
W003 001	DRAGON IN THE SEA	Frank Herbert 30p

War

W002 921	WOLF PACK	William Hardy 30p
W002 484	THE FLEET THAT HAD TO DIE	Richard Hough 25p
W002 805	HUNTING OF FORCE Z	Richard Hough 30p
W002 632	THE BASTARD BRIGADE	Peter Leslie 25p
T006 999	KILLER CORPS	Peter Leslie 25p
T011 755	TRAWLERS GO TO WAR	Lund and Ludlam 40p
W005 051	GOERING	Manvell & Freankel 52½p
W005 065	HIMMLER	Manvell & Freankel 52½p
W002 423	STRIKE FROM THE SKY	Alexander McKee 30p
W002 831	NIGHT	Francis Pollini 40p
T010 074	THE GREEN BERET	Hilary St. George Saunders 40p
T010 066	THE RED BERET	Hilary St. George Saunders 40p

Western

T010 619	EDGE – THE LONER	George Gilman 25p
T010 600	EDGE – TEN THOUSAND DOLLARS AMERICAN	George Gilman 25p
T010 929	EDGE – APACHE DEATH	George Gilman 25p

General

T011 763	SEX MANNERS FOR MEN	Robert Chartham 30p
W002 531	SEX MANNERS FOR ADVANCED LOVERS	Robert Chartham 25p
W002 835	SEX AND THE OVER FORTIES	Robert Chartham 25p
T010 732	THE SENSUOUS COUPLE	Dr. C. 25p
P002 367	AN ABZ OF LOVE	Inge and Sten Hegeler 60p
P011 402	A HAPPIER SEX LIFE	Dr. Sha Kokken 70p
W002 584	SEX MANNERS FOR SINGLE GIRLS	Georges Valensin 25p
W002 592	THE FRENCH ART OF SEX MANNERS	Georges Valensin 25p
W002 726	THE POWER TO LOVE	E. W. Hirsch M. D. 47½p

Mad

S003 491	LIKE MAD	30p
S003 494	MAD IN ORBIT	30p
S003 520	THE BEDSIDE MAD	30p
S003 521	THE VOODOO MAD	30p
S003 657	MAD FOR BETTER OR VERSE	30p
S003 716	THE SELF MADE MAD	30p

— — — — — — — — — — —

NEL P.O. BOX 11, FALMOUTH, CORNWALL

Please send cheque or postal order. Allow 6p per book to cover postage and packing.

Name...

Address ....

....

Title ....
(SEPTEMBER)